Sweet Memory

LJ EVANS

SWEET MEMORY

THE PAINTED DAISIES
BOOK 1

LJ EVANS

May all your moments be Sweet HEAs.
♡ LJ

That's What She Said Publishing, Inc.

Published by THAT'S WHAT SHE SAID PUBLISHING

www.ljevansbooks.com

Cover Design: © Emily Wittig

Cover Images: © Unsplash | weston m, Deposit Photos | VadimVasenin and Dekues, iStock| Punnarong, and Adobe | npstockphoto

Content & Line Editor: Evans Editing

Copy Editor: Jenn Lockwood Editing Services

Proofing: Karen Hrdlicka

Sensitivity Editor: Hong Kobzeff

Library of Congress Cataloging in process.

Paperback ISBN: 979-8-88643-910-6

eBook ISBN: 979-8-88643-908-3

Printed in the United States

022723a

https://spoti.fi/3y21AZk

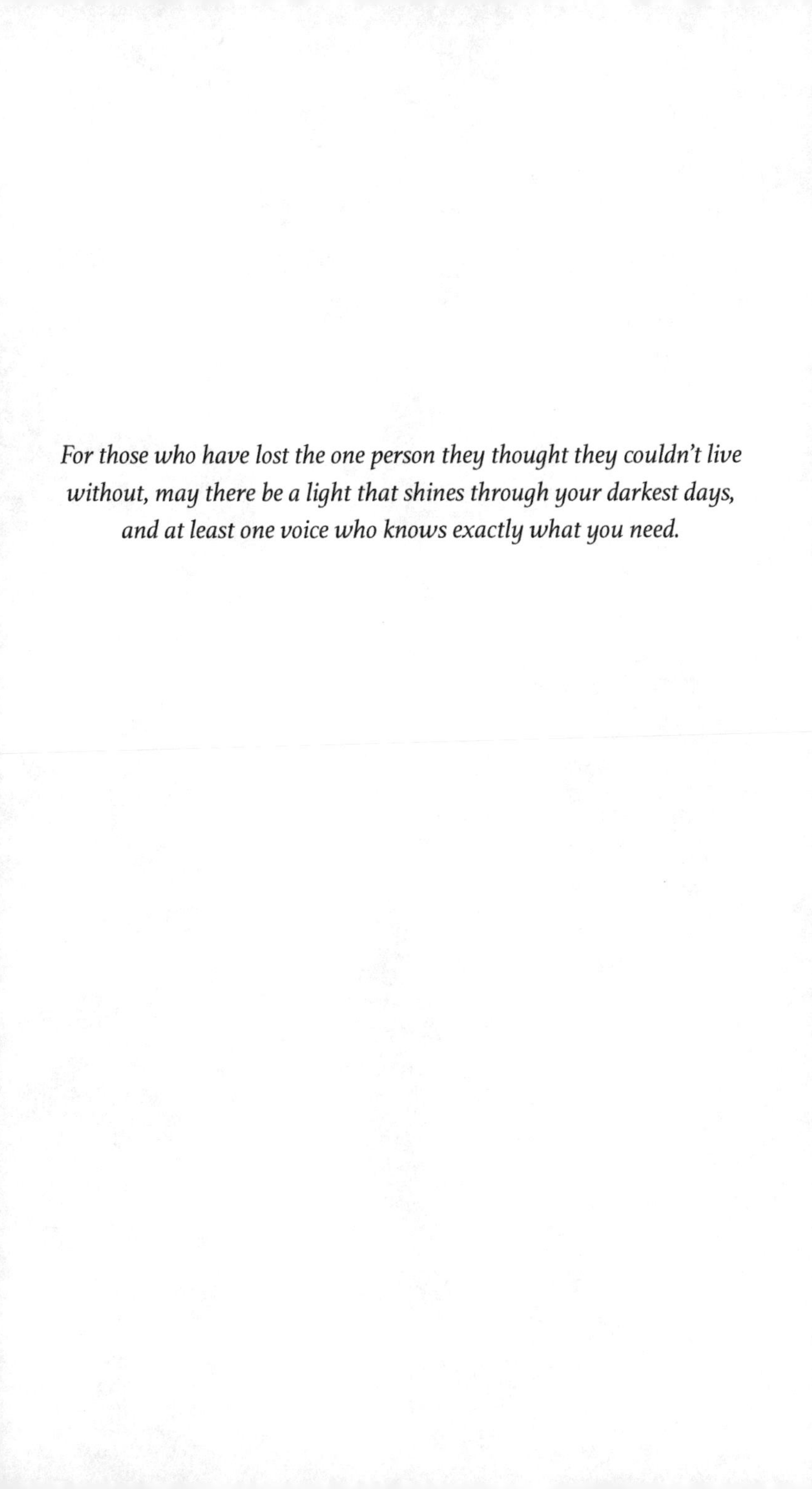

For those who have lost the one person they thought they couldn't live without, may there be a light that shines through your darkest days, and at least one voice who knows exactly what you need.

PROLOGUE

SAVING GRACE
Performed by The Cranberries

TWENTY-THREE MONTHS BEFORE

LANDRY: This photo showed up at the farmhouse this morning. I'd prefer to keep it between the two of us until we've assessed the real threat level.

****image of a blond-haired, teen guy and a black-haired, teen girl on stage with their arms around each other while singing with the rest of the band in the background. All the faces are scraped off and the words, I will make sure you're never happy, are written atop it.****

GARNER: The fewer people who know, the better chance of us keeping it from the press, but I'd advise at least telling them.

LANDRY: We're leaving Grand Orchard in a couple of days, and Paisley will never see Jonas again, so hopefully it won't matter.

GARNER: This could be about more than the two of them. It could be about the band.

LANDRY: That's why I'm sending it to you.

GARNER: The attendees at the promo event were limited. I'll go through the list and see if I can come up with a possible suspect.

TWENTY-TWO MONTHS BEFORE

PAISLEY: Is it strange that I miss Grand Orchard when we only left five minutes ago?

JONAS: Is it strange that I feel like meeting you was just a dream?

PAISLEY: If it was, then we had the same one.

TWENTY-ONE MONTHS BEFORE

TREVOR: Hey, you know that kid Jonas got into the beef with?

MARCO: Yeah.

TREVOR: He got arrested. Breaking and entering. Stole some art and computers from the girl's place. The one he and Jonas were fighting over. He tore her room up pretty good. I think he wanted to find out where her parents took her.

MARCO: Okay. Keep an eye on it for me.

TREVOR: Going to tell Jonas?

MARCO: No. He blames himself enough already. If the asshole is going to jail, there's no reason to upset him.

TWENTY MONTHS BEFORE

JONAS: CONGRATS on The Red Guitar going platinum!

PAISLEY: I sort of can't believe it. Landry is already practicing her award speech.

JONAS: You ALL should be practicing. It's absolutely going to be nominated.

*PAISLEY: ***Laughing GIF*** No way am I talking at the Grammys. I can barely get my butt onstage to perform. At least once I get out there, I have the music to lose myself in. Can you imagine all those eyes waiting for me to talk? ***Shivers GIF*** ***Puke emoji****

JONAS: Say it with me: "Paisley Kim is a FUCKING GENIUS ROCK STAR!"

*PAISLEY: ***Embarrassed emoji*** I gotta go. The band wants to celebrate.*

JONAS: Do me a favor?

PAISLEY: Yeah?

JONAS: HAVE FUN!

PAISLEY: Fun? What is this fun you speak of?

JONAS: I'm serious, Paise. You've earned this. Enjoy!

SEVENTEEN MONTHS BEFORE

JONAS: Remember months ago when I told you the album would win a Grammy? I hate to say I told you so, but I TOLD YOU SO!

PAISLEY: We saw Brady and got to thank him in person for producing our album. It wouldn't have won any awards if it wasn't for the two of you.

*JONAS: ***Embarrassed emoji*** I didn't do anything. I can't believe any of you even listened to me.*

PAISLEY: You have a natural talent, Jonas. It's not just about the lyrics or the notes. You see how it can be put together.

JONAS: Puhlease. You're the natural talent. There would be no lyrics or notes without you.

PAISLEY: How are your classes going?

JONAS: I see what you did, changing the subject. But I'll allow it. I hate high school. I don't fit in here. But then, I never fit back in Austin either. At least there I had Mel. The night classes at Wilson-Jacobs are the best part of my days now.

PAISLEY: I'm in awe of you. I barely got my G.E.D. with Landry's help. I can't imagine juggling high school and college.

JONAS: I hate to be the one to break it to you, but I don't think you'll ever need to worry about going to college.

FIFTEEN MONTHS BEFORE

JONAS: How was the show?

PAISLEY: It was really emotional being in Korea. Mom and Dad were here, and we got to visit with family we'd never met before. Then, our parents pissed Landry off because they asked when we were going to be done with the "band thing" and everything went to hell.

JONAS: Landry is scary when she's mad.

PAISLEY: I never want to be on her bad side.

*JONAS: ***Same GIF****

PAISLEY: Wait, what are you doing texting me? Wasn't prom tonight?

JONAS: I told you I wasn't going.

PAISLEY: I was sort of hoping you'd change your mind so I could live vicariously through you.

JONAS: If you were here, I would have asked you to come.

PAISLEY: If I wasn't on tour, I would have said yes. I would have danced with you under a disco ball and maybe had my first kiss.

JONAS: ...

PAISLEY: I can't believe I just said that. I wish there was a delete button.

JONAS: I would have kissed you. I would have kissed you, and the teachers would have had to tap us on our shoulders and tell us to separate because it would have gone from G to R in about two seconds flat.

FOURTEEN MONTHS BEFORE

LANDRY: Where are you?

PAISLEY: Don't panic. I'm on the roof.

LANDRY: You can't do shit like that.

PAISLEY: You all went out clubbing. What was I supposed to do, sit on my hands in the hotel suite watching Sesame Street?

LANDRY: I'm coming up.

PAISLEY: I don't need an escort, Lan. I'm not twelve. I'm older than you were when we first signed with Lost Heart Records.

LANDRY: You're right. But my eighteen was really different than yours.

PAISLEY: I can't even believe you said that.

Minutes tick by.

LANDRY: It's been fifteen minutes. Where the hell are you?!

PAISLEY: I'm in my room. I need some space.

LANDRY: Paise. I'm sorry.

PAISLEY: I'll talk to you tomorrow.

TWELVE MONTHS BEFORE

PAISLEY: How was Austin?

JONAS: I had to leave early.

PAISLEY: Why?

JONAS: It's embarrassing.

PAISLEY: Embarrassing is having your entire band treat you like you need to be tucked into bed every night. Nothing you say could be more embarrassing than that.

JONAS: I almost lost it at the taqueria. Artie's brother was saying shit about Maliyah.

PAISLEY: What does he have against your foster mom?

JONAS: Nothing. It was an excuse to take a jab at me.

PAISLEY: Are you hurt?!

JONAS: No, she dragged me out of there before I took a swing.

PAISLEY: I'm sorry.

JONAS: Back to therapy I go.

PAISLEY: Honestly, therapy is a good thing. I'm finally seeing someone. My parents don't know. They'd hate it.

JONAS: Why?

PAISLEY: They just don't believe in it. Like with my dyslexia, they thought I just had to try harder, you know?

JONAS: I'm the one who's sorry now.

PAISLEY: Don't be. I've always had Lan. She fought for me like Maliyah fights for you. She's a good sister, even when I'm upset with her.

FOUR MONTHS BEFORE

PAISLEY: It's official! We'll be in Grand Orchard to record our third album in July!

JONAS: Chills. I just got chills at the thought of seeing you again.

PAISLEY: My heart hurts it's so excited. Is that lame?

JONAS: If it is, then we'll be lame together.

THREE MONTHS BEFORE

TREVOR: Artie was released from prison.

MARCO: It's been nearly two years. That's a century in the life of a teenager. Hopefully, he's learned his lesson and moved on.

TREVOR: Still not going to tell Jonas?

MARCO: No. He's over the moon with graduation and The Painted Daisies coming back into town. I'm not going to ruin any of it for him.

TREVOR: He can handle it.

MARCO: I don't want him to have to handle it.

THIRTEEN DAYS BEFORE

JONAS: TOMORROW!!!!

PAISLEY: Less than twenty-four hours until I get to see you!

JONAS: I'm nervous.

PAISLEY: Me too.

JONAS: We're friends, right? That won't ever change?

PAISLEY: That won't ever change.

THIRTEEN DAYS BEFORE

Article in THE EXHIBITOR:

It's official! The Painted Daisies are headed back to Brady O'Neil's studio in Grand Orchard, New York.

****Image of the outside of La Musica de Ensueños Studios ****

What the world wants to know is how the band can top the Grammy award-winning songs of The Red Guitar *even with the help of the legendary country singer and the little-known Jonas Riccoli who were credited with making the band's sophomore album such a success.*

****Image of Jonas and Paisley on stage singing together with huge smiles on their faces.****

Stay tuned folks. I'm off to see for myself.

CHAPTER ONE

Paisley

CRYING UNDERWATER
Performed by Dami Im

TWELVE DAYS BEFORE

Paisley's emotions roller-coastered back and forth from high to low as she watched the apple orchards on the outskirts of Grand Orchard come into view. Frenzied excitement spread through her, the anticipation twisting in her chest until it physically hurt. She was going to see Jonas again! For the first time in two years! Just as quickly as the happiness came, it was swallowed by doubts that turned her stomach. What if it wasn't the same? What if the easy banter they'd found in texts and an occasional phone call disappeared in person? What if she wasn't what he expected?

Paisley's finger pressed automatically into the raised, star-shaped birthmark by her eye as a tap, tap, tap of metal against metal drew her gaze from the view outside the Escalade to her sister. Landry had her hands in prayer mode with the rings on her two middle fingers beating out a rhythm. Tall, thin, and willowy with a sharply pointed chin, enormous eyes, and black hair cascading past her shoulders, Landry had an almost fairy-like vibe.

"What's going on in that head of yours?" Landry asked, the huskiness of her tone a complete contrast to her fragile appearance.

Early in their career, a critic had said Landry's voice was better suited to life as a phone-sex operator instead of a singer. The intended cruelty of those words had turned Paisley's stomach even when they hadn't been directed at her. But not Landry. It had motivated her to prove him wrong. When they'd won their Grammy last year, her sister had sent the man a picture of her holding it with a middle finger extended.

"Nothing's going on. I'm fine," Paisley responded. Whereas Landry's voice was deep and husky, Paisley's was light and feathery—barely a whisper.

"Try not to get your hopes up, Paise. It's easy to pretend to be nice and calm and have your shit together in a fifty-word text." Landry's comment snagged at Paisley's doubts and irritation flared deep inside her.

Instead of getting into another one of their ever-increasing number of fights, Paisley bit her lip and pushed harder into her birthmark. She wasn't sure if Landry really didn't like Jonas, or if she just didn't want Paisley to have a life outside the band.

Landry hadn't objected when three-quarters of the songs they were set to record had come from her texts with Jonas. The lyrics put Paisley's heart on display in a very uncomfortable way. They'd exposed her underbelly to her sister and the band. What would happen when the world got them?

Paisley's chest squeezed tighter, a prick of ice spreading

through her veins as panic started to bloom, but her sister's next words replaced the ice with fire.

"You deserve someone better than a boy who was arrested for assault."

"He was never charged!" Paisley exclaimed, crossing her arms over her chest and trying futilely to stop herself from pushing into her birthmark again.

"He has anger issues, Paise. Someone like that will never change, and I don't want to see you lying on the ground because of his shitty past," Landry said.

"Oh my God, you act like he assaulted someone for simply looking at him wrong. He got in a fight with an asshole gang member who was beating his friend. You should be applauding him for standing up for someone he cared about."

"He didn't have to resort to violence," Landry said, a hardness in her voice that made Paisley's stomach twist again.

Before this year, she and Landry had rarely been on opposing sides of an argument. Mostly because Paisley knew her sister was always right, whereas she was the girl who'd barely gotten her G.E.D. But her sister was wrong about Jonas. Nothing Landry could say would convince Paisley otherwise.

"Look. I didn't want to show you this before, but you really leave me no choice," Landry pulled her phone out and handed it over.

It took a minute for Paisley to figure out what it was, and when she did, she inhaled sharply. The picture was one she treasured. It was the entire band with her and Jonas front and center on the stage in the Wilson-Jacobs Theater after they'd finished recording *The Red Guitar* album two years ago. They'd put on a little show as a thank-you to the people of Grand Orchard, and she'd called Jonas up on stage to sing the song he'd been instrumental in helping her shape.

Normally, when she was on stage, she felt like she was going to puke, at least until the music and lyrics centered her. But when Jonas had joined her, wrapping an arm around her shoulder, she'd felt a steadiness she'd never felt before. Not even when Landry held her hands and pressed her cool metal rings into her skin to ground her.

But this version of the picture was all wrong. Where each of the band members' faces should have been, huge gouge marks existed, and scrawled over their bodies in red ink were the words, "I will make sure you're never happy."

"What is this?" Paisley asked as she shot a glance toward the front seat and their two bodyguards.

"An example of what his life can do to you."

Paisley's heart thumped fiercely in her chest, as the ice returned. Her voice was barely audible as she asked, "All of our faces are scratched out. All of us. How can you be sure this is about Jonas?"

"We haven't received another one like it since we left Grand Orchard. His past came calling and briefly caught us in the crossfire. He's bad news, Paise."

The cold was spreading threw her, turning her body to stone. Jonas would be devastated if he knew about this. He'd take the blame and swallow it whole. He'd stay away...

God, she didn't want that. She'd been waiting for two years for them to be together. She couldn't tell him, could she? But how could she not?

You're so stupid. I thought you were supposed to be smart. What happened to you? Is that mark from where they sucked your brains out?

The taunts circled through her head, making a new wave of doubt fly through her. As the chants repeated in an unbreakable circle, her finger pressed deeper and deeper into the star birthmark.

Her cell phone vibrated, and even before she picked it up, she knew who it was.

*JONAS: Are you here? ***Excited GIF****

Her heart convulsed, joy at the thought of seeing him rippling over the fear and panic. She couldn't tell him. It would ruin everything. But there was also no way she could see him tonight like they'd originally planned because he'd take one look at her and know something was up. Just like he'd known when she'd called him from a roof top in Syndey.

Before she could respond, Paisley's phone went wild with a string of texts in the band's group chat.

FEE: Did Ramona get lost? I swear you should've been here by now.

ADRIA: Don't mind her, she's hangry and missing you.

LANDRY: We were only apart for a couple of days, Fee.

Paisley and Landry were the last of the band to arrive after spending the weekend with their parents at their cousin's wedding. It had been a nightmare, renewing their parents' desire to see her and Landry settled with good Korean boys who had steady, reliable jobs, and intensifying the divide between Landry and their parents.

LEYA: She's got a whole girl's night planned. Pedicures and facials and romcom movies.

FEE: It was supposed to be a surprise, Ley'.

Even panicked and scared by what her sister had shown her, Paisley couldn't hold back the small smirk she sent Landry's way at the text exchange with their friends.

NIKKI: If you're not here soon, the food will get cold.

"How much longer?" Landry asked their two bodyguards.

"Ten minutes tops," Ramona answered from the driver's seat while Dylan scanned the orchards as they flew by. These two muscled and honed guards were their personal detail. After the band's popularity had exploded while on tour, they'd had to double their security. Now, none of them went anywhere without a bodyguard in tow.

JONAS: It was the GIF, right? It was totally over the top, and you're now questioning the wisdom of seeing me again.

She swallowed hard. The ugly image on Landry's phone spun in front of her eyes again. She didn't know how she could see him and not tell him, and if she told him, he'd pull away because he wouldn't risk her in order to be with her.

PAISLEY: The GIF is exactly how I'm feeling. If anything, it proved just how perfectly in sync we are. I can't wait to see you. Unfortunately, Fee has a whole thing planned for tonight that I didn't know about and can't get out of.

JONAS: Dang. Okay. Well, we've waited two years, so I guess twelve hours is nothing.

PAISLEY: A mere blip.

The toss and turn of her stomach continued, disappointment spreading through her. She wanted to see him. Almost desperately needed to. As if she wouldn't be able to breathe much longer if he wasn't there. No picture was worth not being with him.

She turned to her sister and said quietly with a certainty she rarely felt and even less frequently showed, "He works at the studio, Lan, but even if he didn't, I'd see him. He doesn't deserve to have his past held over his head any more than you deserve to have your bisexuality held against you, or I should have my dyslexia held against me."

Landry grimaced. "That's not even remotely the same. That's part of our DNA. His issues are about his choices."

Jonas's childhood had impacted him almost as much as their chemical makeup. It was why he reacted the way he did, but the set of her chin let Paisley know she wasn't going to change Landry's mind. Not today. Maybe never.

"Did you tell the others about it?" Paisley asked.

Landry shook her head. "No. It seemed unnecessary."

Paisley didn't agree, but she wouldn't argue with Landry anymore today. The one about Jonas was enough to make her chest hurt and her stomach feel like it had turned into a briar patch with the thorns darting into her intestines.

They were silent as they drove the last few miles to the mansion the townspeople of Grand Orchard affectionately called *The Farmhouse*. It was a sprawling, early-twentieth-century Victorian tucked between the apple orchards and the mountains with a wraparound porch and more rooms than you could count.

The best part of the property was the pond, aptly named Swan River for the bevy of birds that called the tules and cattails home. The smooth waters had cast a spell over Paisley the last time they were there, easing her anxiety more than the swing set in their childhood backyard ever had.

Ramona hung a left onto a long gravel drive in the middle of the apple trees and eventually the house with its white planks and black shutters came into view. Paisley's eyes immediately landed on the porch swing where she and Jonas had once sat arguing about bands and music and lyrics. Her heart jumped at the memories as well as the thought of seeing him again, a rhythm beating inside her that she needed to capture on her keys. A song called, "Anticipation."

When the car came to a stop in the drive, Fiadh was waiting for them on the top step. She'd added a layer of lilac to her dark-red curls recently, which made them shimmer as they danced about, as wild and fiery as she was. The sunlight glinted off her diamond-studded nose ring as a large smile spread across her face.

They were barely out of the car before Fee had scurried across the circular drive to wrap them in a hug, bouncing the three of them around like a pogo stick.

"God, I missed you," she said, the pale dusting of freckles on her face shimmering in the sunset.

"Fee, I can't breathe." Landry's grouse was half-hearted, and Fiadh just laughed, squeezing even harder before letting them go.

They moved from the porch into the house, and Paisley's pulse spiraled again as more memories flooded her. The darkly stained walnut staircase was where she and Jonas had sat discussing the track order for *The Red Guitar*, and the antique, claw-footed, floral couch was where he'd tickled her until she couldn't breathe as they argued about Pink Floyd. The fake British accent he'd used to critique it had made her laugh until her sides hurt. It hit her hard in the chest with a longing she could barely contain.

"I tried to get them to wait to eat, but Leya and Nikki feigned starvation." Fiadh said as she led them down the hallway into the renovated kitchen. It was a deep contrast to the old charm of the rest of the house. Modern and chic, it had stainless-steel appliances, marbled countertops, and gray, distressed cabinets.

"Damn it, get your hands off my fries, Leya!" Fee groused, pouncing on the table and ripping the bag from Leya's hands.

Leya rolled her eyes and threw a fry in Fiadh's direction. Fee just laughed, brushing it away as Nikki, Leya, and Adria took turns hugging Paisley and Landry. When they were all tangled together like this, it was hard to tell them apart in the sea of black hair and long legs.

Their first album cover had played up their similarities. They'd worn white leather jackets with their backs to the camera. Only Paisley, who was a good eight inches shorter than the rest of them, and Fiadh, with her deep-red hair, had stood out. The rest could only be told apart by the daisies emblazoned on their jackets. It had been their manager's idea to emphasize the band's name by having each of them choose a different daisy type to represent them. Now, the flowers were painted onto their instruments, mic stands, and clothes in a way that made them almost synonymous with their real names.

"Please tell me there's a veggie burger in that mix somewhere," Landry said, flinging her purse with her Golden Butterfly daisy embroidered on it over a chair back at the large oak table.

Leya dug through the bags and handed a wrapped burger to Landry.

"You're lucky Nikki remembered," Leya said, one artfully shaped brow raising above her twinkling brown eyes, full lips, and cleft chin. "No one is used to you inheriting my vegan ways."

"Have I told you lately that I like you best," Landry said, pulling Nikki to her and kissing her cheek.

"Get off," Nikki said, pushing her away. She hadn't straightened her hair today, and the dark coils sprung about her perfectly oval face while her dark-brown eyes sparkled with the same humor as Leya's.

Paisley sat down, grabbing a burger and fries from the middle. She'd put her phone face-down on the table, and it buzzed, vibrating against the wood. Even with no sound, she knew it was another message from Jonas, and her fingers itched to read it, but Landry's frown stopped her from picking it up.

Adria chuckled at Landry's glower. "You have to let our little girl grow up, Lan. Dating is just the first step."

Her comment made Paisley want to scream, both in joy and frustration. Maybe it was because she'd never made it to five feet tall that had them treating her like a little kid, as if her tiny size had halted her growth and held her in some weird, childlike limbo. But she also appreciated Adria trying to defend her, so she sent her a soft smile.

Adria winked in return, the signature wink the world swooned over making her bright-blue eyes sparkle. Her nearly perfect features, along with her model-like figure, had helped her win multiple beauty contests in her younger years.

"I'm a tiny bit jealous of Little Bit," Fiadh announced. "It's been too long since I hooked up with anyone."

"No one is getting hooked up. We're here to record another Grammy-award-winning album. That has to be the priority," Landry said, shooting them all a glare but settling the longest on her.

Paisley twirled a French fry between her fingers, the barbed thorns that had appeared in her stomach digging farther into the lining because, as unhappy as it would make Landry, she knew she'd be spending time with Jonas. As much as she could. She'd waited almost two years to see him. Twenty-two months. Nearly seven hundred days. She wasn't going to ignore him and the way he made her feel no matter what Landry said or the picture she'd shown her. She couldn't ignore him even if she wanted to. Her heart and body were already beating out a song of expectation, one that wouldn't stop until it peaked at a breath-taking crescendo.

CHAPTER TWO

Jonas

IS THIS LOVE
Performed by Whitesnake

ELEVEN DAYS BEFORE

Jonas's fingers banged viciously on his knees bouncing under the kitchen table. The slightly nauseated feeling in his stomach had nothing to do with the way his four-year-old nephew was shoveling in chorizo quiche and dribbling it on the apron he wore over his tee-ball outfit. Normally, Jonas and Chevelle would be competing to see who could eat the fastest, but today, the waves of expectation churning through him made it impossible to think of eating at all.

"So, recording starts with The Painted Daisies today, right?" Cassidy asked, drawing his eyes to his sister-in-law as she stirred something sweet-smelling on the stove. Blonde-haired with light-brown eyes and pale skin, Cassidy was a fabulous chef and restauranteur.

Jonas rolled his eyes at her question but didn't respond. He didn't need to. She knew exactly what was happening today, and it wasn't because of the texts he'd been exchanging with Paisley Kim for almost two years or the fact that he'd been working at Brady's studio for the same amount of time. It was because his foster brother—Cassidy's husband—had been working for days on the additional coverage needed for the band's protection while in town.

Marco walked into the room just as Cassidy placed a plate in front of Jonas. It was a crepe with pieces of strawberries arranged to make a smiley face. There were chocolate chips for eyes and a dish of chocolate sauce off to the side. It was the breakfast she normally made Chevelle to cheer him up after he lost a game.

Marco chuckled, and Jonas rolled his eyes again before saying, "You're all ridiculous."

But really, his heart and eyes stung because it was sweet. It reminded him of how lucky he was to have so many people in his corner these days. If someone had asked eight-year-old him if he'd ever have this kind of family, he would have replied with a pained and emphatic, "No."

"Mama, I want smiley cakes!" Chevelle whined as soon as he saw Jonas's crepe.

Cassidy ruffled his hair and kissed the top of his head. "You need protein to help you hit another home run today. So, eat your eggs!"

While Chevelle pouted, Cassidy went back to the stove, and Marco joined her, sliding his arms around her waist and kissing her neck. It was a sickening display of ooey-gooey love that happened on an almost hourly basis between them.

Jonas passed the plate of crepes to Chevelle, whose eyes

grew wide before his tiny face broke out into a huge smile. He was the cutest dang kid Jonas had ever met. Not that he'd been around a lot of kids before he'd moved to Grand Orchard with Marco, but still.

Jonas put a finger to his lips and winked at Chevelle, who shot a look in his parents' direction before diving in. Jonas watched as Marco rested his chin on Cassidy's shoulder and settled his hands on her stomach protruding from her dress. To Jonas, she looked like she was going to burst any day. It had been sort of mind-boggling and awe-inspiring to see how her body had changed over the last nine months.

But then, women in general tended to confound him, which only set his knee bouncing at a more furious pace as his thoughts returned to the one woman he was both excited and nervous to see again. The woman who'd been haunting his dreams and messages for two years. The woman who'd taken a broken and beat-up heart and slowly mended it with her friendship.

Marco let go of Cassidy and sat down at the table, eyeing Jonas and then his son, who was now covered in chocolate. Marco's lips twitched, but he didn't scold either of them. He was an even bigger sucker for the kid than Jonas was. Chevelle might not have been Marco's son by blood, but they were undeniably a family.

Jonas's knee hit the underside of the table as it bounced, making all the dishes clatter and bang. Three sets of eyes turned to take him in. Marco's were full of concern, the teasing all but forgotten.

"What's wrong?" his brother asked as his dark brows drew together, making him look more grim-faced Aztec than normal.

Cassidy shot Jonas a soft smile, coming to stand beside Marco and resting her hand on his shoulder. Marco's tan arm skated around her waist, drawing her closer, almost as if he didn't even realize he'd done it. Jonas's heart banged harder, wondering if what he felt for Paisley was anything close to what these two shared.

"Our Jonas is in love," Cassidy teased.

Marco's frown grew. Jonas wasn't sure what he felt could be considered love, especially when he'd never even kissed Paisley. But he was drawn to her and admired her not only for her beauty and her music but also for the strength she showed every time she stepped onstage. Only a handful of people knew how hard it was for her to do just that.

"Jo-Jo—" Marco started, but he stopped when he saw Jonas grimace at the nickname.

Marco rarely used it anymore. It made him feel like a child when he was anything but. He was going to be nineteen in a few weeks, which wasn't necessarily a full-grown adult, but he wasn't a fucking kid either. He wasn't sure he'd ever really been one.

"I know. I know. She's a fu—flipping rock star," Jonas said. "And I'm not in love. We're friends, and I'm excited to see her."

"You're excited to see Maliyah when she comes into town. I don't think it's quite the same," Cassidy continued to tease.

Marco chuckled, and Jonas fought another eye roll. Comparing his foster mom to Paisley was as ridiculous as the smiley-faced crepes. Unable to take their knowing looks and his nervous anticipation any longer, he pushed away from the table.

"I'm going to *La Musica.* I don't know how late I'll be, but I'll text you." He ruffled Chevelle's brown hair as he walked past. "Have a good game, buddy. Remember to have fun and not keep score."

Then, he left, ignoring Marco's worried look while attempting to calm the knots churning in his stomach.

♫ ♫ ♫

To keep his mind occupied and his nerves in check while he waited for Paisley to arrive with the rest of the band, Jonas went to work wiring the mics in the studio's live room. He couldn't deny he'd been disappointed when she'd changed their plans the night before. He'd thought they'd have a couple of hours alone before having to face everyone. But now, their reunion would be during their first rehearsal. A rehearsal they certainly didn't need, but Brady had insisted on. He wanted to hear all the songs together before they started laying down the individual tracks.

The wiring wasn't complicated, but it was intense as the band was known not only for their unique lyrics and rhythms but the variety of instruments they played. Paisley was almost exclusively on the keyboard, but she could—and did—play guitar on occasion. Her sister, Landry, was the opposite. She played guitar most of the time and drifted to the keys to back up Paisley. Adria was their drummer. Nikki played a range of guitars, fiddle, and ukulele, but spent most of the time on bass guitar. Leya was known for a whole host of instruments from India, but she predominately used the baby sitar. And then there was Fiadh, who was probably the most musically gifted of them all with the largest range, including the piano, guitar, banjo, accordion, tin whistle, Irish flute, Uilleann pipes, and the Celtic harp. She changed instruments with almost every song, sometimes within the songs themselves.

Jonas purposefully left Paisley's keyboard for last, but it still didn't lessen the shock when he finally stood behind it, eyeing the soft-pink Sweet Memory daisy painted on it. His insides flopped and clenched as he rested a palm on the flower, remembering like it was yesterday the way his hand had felt pressed against Paisley's for a single moment years ago.

Before he'd come to Grand Orchard, he'd thought he'd been in love with his friend Mel. She'd been stunning and vivacious.

Powerful and smart. The kind of dynamic personality you knew was going to end up going places. It had radiated from her, and he'd been caught in her bright, shiny rays from the day they'd met at age nine.

But after Jonas had left Texas, it had been his attraction to Paisley that had shown him how wrong he'd been. There was no way he could have loved Mel in a romantic sort of way if he'd been drawn to Paisley only days later.

Something about Paisley's quiet energy and soft voice pulled at pieces deep inside him. Every time they talked, it was as if he found a little more of himself. Add in the jolts of energy that drifted through him whenever they'd touched, and he knew he'd never really loved Mel.

There'd been plenty of times over the last two years where Jonas had wondered if he'd imagined everything he'd felt with Paisley. Maybe when he saw her again, all of those feelings would no longer exist, but he didn't think so. He thought they'd be a flame that would be hard to put out.

The door of the live room bounced open, hitting the padded wall, and Jonas's hand slipped from the keyboard, heart going from zero to sixty in a mere nanosecond. But it was only Paisley's sister, Landry, who entered. Her dark eyes glared at him, and the knots in his stomach returned. She'd never liked the bond she'd seen growing between Paisley and him, and while part of him understood it, most of him just resented it.

Landry flicked her long hair over a shoulder, glanced toward the studio's front door where the other members of the band were filtering in, and then stepped close enough to talk without the others hearing.

"If I had my way, you wouldn't be anywhere near my sister. Instead, I'll make this perfectly clear. Hurt her, and I'll end you," Landry hissed.

Jonas's eyes went wide, and his fists clenched, nails biting into his palm as he tried to control the immediate spike of anger that flew through him.

"I have no intention of hurting her," he growled back.

Fiadh bounced into the room with her riot of curls swirling around her face like that Disney character from *Brave*. She glanced between Jonas and Landry and rolled her eyes.

"Oh my God, Lan. Please tell me you didn't say something already."

Landry ignored her, moving to the guitar Jonas had set up. She ran her hands over it, fingering the strings, adjusting and tuning it by ear.

Fiadh practically danced over to Jonas. She flung an arm around his shoulder and said, "Jonas, Jonas, Jonas. We love, love, love that you helped us create a Grammy-winning album, and we adore the way you make our serious Paisley smile, but we are very protective of our Little Bit. So, get it right the first time, okay?"

"Fee!" Landry snapped, her husky voice going down another notch before shooting Jonas another scowl.

He had to get out of the room before he did or said something he'd regret. He worked hard—with the help of a therapist and the boxing bag in Marco and Cassidy's home gym—to control his anger these days, and he couldn't let one person's dismissal of him undo it. Jonas shrugged Fiadh's arm off and stalked to the door, almost running into Nikki and Leya as they entered with to-go cups in their hands.

"Sorry," he said as he stepped around them. He felt their eyes on him as he hurried out of the studio and onto the sidewalk, hating that he'd let Landry get to him.

He leaned up against the building, fighting the well of emotions building inside him and letting the heat of the brick spread through him. He wasn't that kid from Austin anymore—neither the abandoned child nor the friend who'd been left behind. He was part of a family now. He was loved. One person's rejection didn't make him worthless, even if he had a long way to go before he was the man he wanted to be. He tilted his head back, closed his eyes, and let the warmth soothe him.

He breathed in deeply, pushing down the negative thoughts and the hollow ache of his past. He wanted to be in control when he greeted Paisley. He wanted to show her only the joy she'd brought him with a handful of texts and calls.

"Jonas?" The soft voice was barely a whisper on the wind, but it jolted him out of his thoughts and back to the sidewalk. He hadn't forgotten the glow that seemed to emanate from her like an angelic halo, but seeing her in real life, after two years of not...it hit him in the chest like an asteroid crashing to earth.

Her straight black hair was looped partially up, and a tendril had escaped, sliding over the soft arc of her cheek. Her lush, black lashes emphasized her brown eyes, making them stand out in her oval face. His gaze landed on her plush, pink lips, lingering there too long and making his body ache to have them pressed against his for the first time.

She was in tight black jeans that clung to her narrow hips, rising high on her waist where a purple crop-top revealed a tiny sliver of her stomach that called to him to touch it. Her tiny frame seemed even smaller now that he'd grown another four inches in her absence. Even in her heeled boots, she barely reached his shoulder.

She had her index finger resting on the star-shaped birthmark right below her eye, giving away her nervousness only to those who knew her best, and it was with a sharp jolt of pride that he realized he did. He knew her. Knew more about her than anyone on this planet—maybe even more than her sister.

Emotions flew through him. Happiness. Hope. Fear. He'd been holding his breath so long, his lungs felt like he'd had the wind knocked out of them, and when he tried to inhale, the air sliced through him.

Her name got caught in his throat as the reality of her being there continued to overwhelm him. Sometimes the other band members called her *Little Bit*. Her sister called her *Paise*. He'd done both, but he'd used Paisley the most because she didn't seem like someone who deserved to have their name shortened. You needed to speak all her syllables to do her justice.

Every single stunning one of them.

CHAPTER THREE

Paisley

WHAT IT FEELS LIKE
Performed by Natalie Imbruglia

Jonas had changed so much it was as if another person stood there. He'd towered over Paisley the summer they'd met, and now he was like a high-rise standing next to a single-story house. It wasn't just his height. He'd filled out in every possible way, his muscles rippling as he forced himself away from the brick wall and took a step toward her.

His dirty-blond hair was just as thick and wavy as she remembered, curling about his ears and drifting down toward the collar of his T-shirt, not quite grazing it. His face was square and strong with a slight dent in his chin that wasn't quite a cleft, and his lips had a sharply accentuated Cupid's bow at the top. But it was his vivid, green eyes that held her gaze the longest. Eyes she could easily lose herself in. Eyes that had always spoken to her, giving her all his secrets while reading hers at the same time.

The look on his face was a mirror-image of the emotions flooding through her. Hope. Excitement. Lust. She wanted to rush into his arms and kiss him. A kiss they'd never shared even though it felt like they'd shared many more intimate moments.

He knew about her bullying, and she knew his mom was in jail.

He knew she got so anxious she almost puked before walking onstage, and she knew he'd let his foster mom down by being arrested.

He knew she'd never been kissed. She knew he'd never had sex.

Intimate, personal secrets. Things you didn't share with just anyone.

And yet, they'd never even been on a date.

"Hey," he finally said, a small smile appearing on his face that turned into one so large it stopped her heart. The tray with the two coffees she held slipped and would have hit the ground if he hadn't swooped in to catch it.

It brought him close enough she could smell him—soap and mint and a hint of something smoky, like a campfire that had burned out. Their arms brushed lightly, and her body lit up. Every single vein strained, vying to be the one closest to him. A rhythm full of lyrics about dancing in the rays of sunlight hit her from nowhere as she basked in his smile.

She felt like crying tears of joy, but she fought them back in order to finally whisper out, "Hi back."

"You look..." His voice cracked. "Incredible."

Her smile grew wider.

"You two going to moon at each other all day, or are we going to make some music?" Adria's voice at the studio door brought them back to where they were, standing outside on the sidewalk.

Paisley's skin flushed, and she licked her lips, which drew Jonas's eyes to them. Was it her imagination, or did those bright-green depths turn the color of a dark forest? Jonas ran long, bronzed fingers through his thick hair, making it stick up at odd angles. She wanted to do the same, to drag her hands through the strands while his mouth found hers. While he trailed kisses down her neck and her chest and...

Jonas's eyes widened with surprise as if he'd heard her thoughts.

She blushed harder as *you're staring like an idiot* replaced the other thoughts in her brain, taunting her.

"Paise?" Adria's voice called out again.

"Coming," she said, and Jonas's eyes slid down her body.

He leaned in and whispered in a voice meant only for her, "You and me, Paisley. Alone, tonight." The low, deep growl made the flush in her cheeks burst into a fiery red, and his face broke into the widest, cockiest grin she'd ever seen on him.

He took the tray from her with one hand and reached down to hook her pinky with his. And with that simple act, it felt as if the million pieces of her that had never fit finally came together. As if she was finally whole.

They walked, fingers tied together, into the live room. Paisley felt giddy, and she had to bite her lip to keep from giggling. For the first time ever, she was there with someone who wanted her—just her.

Her happiness was short-lived as her gaze landed on Landry's face. Her sister's expression was irritated. It took Paisley's pleasure and blew it away, stomach returning to the sea of sharp, thorn-infested vines it had been the day before. As always, she was the one to capitulate, dropping Jonas's hand. But she felt the loss immediately, like a sucker punch to the gut.

As she moved away from him toward her keyboard, she risked looking back at him. His eyes had become hooded, a fleeting look of disappointment crossing his face as his eyes darted between Landry and her. While she understood her sister's worries a little better after seeing the creepy picture the day before, without telling Jonas about it, she wasn't sure he'd ever understand. He'd only see what she'd complained about in the last few months—her sister treating her like a child.

An awkward silenced filled the room, causing the rest of the band to shift uncomfortably. It was only broken by Brady O'Neil cruising in. The country-rock legend and producer was just as dynamic as Paisley remembered him. Intense but in a laid-back way that should have been contradictory and yet wasn't. His blond hair was artfully shaggy, and when his face lifted into a smile, you had no choice but to return it.

"Welcome back to *La Musica de Ensueños Studios*! We can't wait to help you create another Grammy-award-winning album." He gave them all a charming smile, one that a good portion of the world's population would have drooled over, but all it did was draw Paisley's eyes back to Jonas. To the quiet strength standing next to him.

Brady didn't wait for them to respond. Instead, he waved an iPad he was holding. "Jonas and I have listened to all the songs you've sent, and we have some ideas for amping them up. Before we lay down any of the individual instrumentals and voice tracks, I'd like to listen to everything together. This way we can work through some of the suggestions, and ensure we're clear on the message you want each song to deliver as well as the album as a whole."

And with that, they got to work, playing songs, stopping and talking about them, moving frames and chords around, and starting a list of the tracks on a huge white board. The entire time, she felt Jonas's eyes on her. A delightful heat and tension built inside her, curling through her body, bubbling over, and creating new songs in her mind. But every time she looked over at her sister and saw the scowl that was growing deeper and deeper, her heart twisted and turned.

Why did the beautiful things she felt for him have to be causing a rift between her and her sister? No matter what Landry thought, Jonas would never hurt her, and even if being with him ended up being a mistake, which she highly doubted, at least she'd have a host of wonderful, grown-up experiences to add to her limited list of them.

The thrum of anticipation she'd felt for days kicked up again, heady and all-consuming, the rhythm of it almost taking over the songs she was supposed to be playing. She had to force herself back to the music in front of her. To focus on the tracks she'd already written instead of the secret ones trying to escape.

♫ ♫ ♫

Hours later, when Brady was satisfied they had a solid handle on the changes and a place to start actually recording the next morning, they broke for the day. The band stood in the control room, making plans for the evening. Paisley's feet found their way to Jonas. She glanced up into his face, seeing again the way it seemed the same and yet different. Stronger. More mature.

"So, what's your plan for this evening?" Paisley asked, her voice barely reaching him over the clamor of the rest of the band. *Stupid*, the taunt rebounded in her head. *What's your plan? Really?*

Jonas seemed to weigh her question, dragging his eyes down her and then finding their way back up to her face. Her body responded as it had this morning, turning into a pool of heat and lust and want. She didn't care where they went, as long as they were alone so she could finally touch him as she'd been dreaming about for years.

Any reply he would have made was lost, however, as Landry said, "I think we should head back to the farmhouse and work through some more of the changes."

Fee literally rolled her eyes. "We've done more than enough for one day. What we really need is a treat, like the insanely good toffee from Sweet Lips Bakery that Nikki and I couldn't stop craving for months."

Landry's scowl increased while Leya teased, "The last thing you need is more sugar, Fee."

Fiadh flipped her off.

"Fine, we'll all go," Landry said, very clearly including Paisley in that arrangement.

When she risked looking at Jonas, his brows were furrowed.

Paisley's insides clenched. She hated this. Hated keeping secrets from Jonas and fighting her sister. Hated that the one person who'd fought for her when the bullies had come after her and when their parents tried to stop her from being part of the band was now at odds with the man who'd kept her on an even keel over the last year. The man who'd seen her not as a little girl needing shielding, but as the person she'd always wanted to be—brave and strong and resilient.

As if sensing her turmoil, Jonas grabbed her hand, twining their fingers together, and waves of emotions flew through her. A sense of rightness but also a rush of desire that had her skin erupting in goosebumps. Her eyes met his, and she saw the same desire rippling in them but also a layer of concern.

As the band headed for the door, and she went to follow, he held her back.

"What do you want to do?" he asked.

She wanted so many things. Him. Them. Bodies twined. But at the moment, she wanted peace. She wanted Landry to get a chance to know him. To understand him. For the picture Landry had tossed at her to be some weird anomaly that had nothing to do with Jonas and just some random, gross fan.

"Maybe it's better for them to see us together first?" she suggested, softly, more uncertainty filling her that she despised. Why did she always doubt herself?

But Jonas didn't question her response. He didn't even hesitate. He just nodded and pulled her toward the door, keeping her hand in his much larger one. As they stepped onto the wooden sidewalk, the July humidity hit them at the same time as a sea of flashing lights and voices.

The press had arrived in droves, and while their bodyguards attempted to hold them back, the crowd pushed forward, and Paisley's feet stalled.

"Think O'Neil can pull off another Grammy win for you?" one of the reporters called out.

"What's this album called?"

"What happened with you and Lars Ritter, Fiadh?" one of the reporters asked, saying her name wrong, Fee-uh-duh, instead of Fee-uh.

"Jesus, Mary, and Joseph," Fee snapped. "If you're going to cover our beat, at least get my fecking name right."

Only those who knew her as well as the band did would catch that Fee's Irish accent appearing proved just how upset she was—not over the guy getting her name wrong, but over the breakup with Lars that had hit her harder than she let on.

"Fee," Landry warned quietly.

The reporter was pissed Fiadh had corrected him in front of an audience, and so he tossed out nastily, "Heard Lars tossed you aside because you kissed girls better than guys."

Fee lunged, but Landry and their bodyguards filled in the space between her and the reporter before there was any contact.

"Calm down. The last thing we need is some shithead suing

us. Violence is never the answer. Never," Landry hissed, dragging their friend toward the SUVs instead of the bakery. Fiadh didn't respond. She just sent glares in both the reporter's and Landry's directions before getting in the vehicle and slamming the door.

"Who's the guy with Paisley?" another reporter asked.

Paisley's heart stopped at her name being mentioned. The cameras all seemed to suddenly be focused on her. The flashing sent every nerve ending in her body a message to run. Flee. Hide. But her body was frozen, feet turning into cement blocks. Panic filled her veins like it did right before she stepped onstage. Chest seizing. Lungs forgetting to breathe.

Landry twirled around at Paisley's name, finding Jonas and Paisley on the sidewalk with their hands joined. She took a step toward them at the same time the reporter risked inching closer.

"Stay back," their bodyguard, Dylan, told the guy. The man continued to take their picture. Flash after flash after flash. And with each shot, Paisley felt herself retreat farther inside her shell.

Jonas moved, placing his back to the cameras so he was facing Paisley and blocking the reporter's view of her. His hand holding hers tightened while the other tilted her chin up until their gaze met. "Paisley, sweetheart. Breathe."

His fingers burned through her skin, but it was the *sweetheart* that ignited her. The endearment was so tender it made her stopped heart slam back into action.

"I...I..." Her words got locked up in her chest, and her gaze traveled around him to the waiting crowd. The world grew blurry, and the sounds got louder—car engines, clicking cameras, the rustle of clothing.

Jonas's thumb ran along her cheek. "Hey, look at me."

Her eyes jolted back to his.

"I'm right here." His deep voice coasted over her. "Right here.

Which way do you want to go? Back into the studio? To the bakery? The cars? You tell me."

The warmth of his touch started to melt the ice in her veins as she forced herself to focus only on him, forgetting the people shouting her name and the cameras. There was just Jonas. The person who made her laugh and told her she was a fucking rock star. The man whose lips she'd wanted on hers for too long now—with a desperation that was almost painful.

Landry joined them, gaze flickering from their joined hands to Jonas's fingers on her chin before settling on Paisley's eyes with a glower. Paisley blushed, wondering if her sister could see just how much she wanted Jonas.

"Let's not give them a show, shall we?" Landry's voice was dry and brittle.

It made Paisley's face heat even more. She wished she could just blink it all away. Her sister. The crush of people. The town. Until there was nothing left but her and Jonas.

CHAPTER FOUR

Jonas

RUN
Performed by Taylor Swift w/ Ed Sheeran

Worry flew through him as he watched Paisley in full panic mode. Frozen and yet shriveling up inside. Every protective instinct he'd ever had flared to life. He wanted to pick her up and sprint with her to a place no one would find them, but he could only imagine the looks on everyone's faces if he did. Instead, he spoke quietly, touching her gently, trying to ground her to where they were and the fact that he wasn't leaving her. He'd almost gotten her back, pushing past the wall of ice she'd surrounded herself in, when Landry threw out her taunt, raising new alarms.

He didn't know why Landry was being such a bitch, but it was pissing him off. He snapped at her in reply, "It's not like I've got my tongue shoved down her throat."

Landry glared at him, and Paisley squeezed his fingers tighter—reassuring him or warning him. He wasn't sure which.

"We should go back to the farmhouse, Paise," Landry said.

Jonas ignored her, holding Paisley's gaze as he asked, "What do you want to do?"

It was a repeat of what he'd asked her inside, but it was the only question that mattered. He could literally feel Landry vibrating with disapproval next to him. She didn't like him showing Paisley she had options other than just doing what her sister wanted.

"W-would you like to come with us? Maybe?" Paisley asked, hesitant, eyes begging him to say yes as her blush continued to grow. God, she was so beautiful it caused him to lose his voice. All he could do was nod.

Landry huffed. "I don't think that's a good idea. They'll see him coming with us, and it'll get blown out of proportion."

Jonas clenched his jaw so he wouldn't respond to her jibe with something he'd regret later, trying not to let her nastiness prevent him from focusing on Paisley.

"Is there a problem here?"

Jonas's gaze was drawn to Marco's best friend and partner striding down the wooden sidewalk in front of the studio. Trevor worked for Garner Security along with his brother. While he was normally on Brad O'Neil's detail, he was playing double duty while the Daisies were in town by covering them along with their regular team.

Trevor's pale blond eyebrows were scrunched together as he took in the sea of reporters, the bodyguards keeping them at bay, and the SUVs waiting for the last two bandmembers. Trevor's mere size had a couple of the photographers stepping back as he closed the distance and stopped near Jonas and Paisley. His muscles rippled under the black uniform of cargo pants, T-shirt, and military boots the entire security team wore.

"Why don't you go with the band," Jonas suggested to Paisley. "I'll come and get you at seven."

"Like a date?" Paisley's voice was a mere whisper, and her huge eyes were uncertain in a way he didn't understand. This is what they'd talked about, wasn't it? Being together. Exploring their connection in real life instead of over a string of messages.

"Absolutely," he said with a confidence he wasn't sure he felt.

Landry huffed next to him, but Paisley finally smiled, and it about stole his heart right from his chest.

He let go of her hand as Trevor and Dylan guided the sisters into the waiting vehicles, and Jonas fought every instinct to run after her. When Paisley looked back over her shoulder, her face was flushed, full of hope and trust, and it fucking filled him with pride but also pain.

She had so much faith in him. What if he screwed up? He had a history of doing just that with women he cared about. His mom. Maliyah. Mel. He wanted so badly to get this right. For him and for her.

Once Paisley's vehicle took off, Jonas headed in the direction of home with Trevor tagging along with him, easily keeping pace with his long strides.

"You know what you're doing?" Trevor asked.

Jonas shrugged. "Yes... No... Maybe," he choked out a half-laugh. "I like her, Trev. I don't want to fuck it up, but...well...I'm still me."

"I didn't mean you'd screw it up, Jonas. It's just...your lives are extremes."

The fact that Trevor was simply looking out for him tugged at something deep in his chest. But even still, the words burned deep because they were true. It wasn't like he was thinking of getting married and having kids right now, but he was trying to pull their worlds closer together. He'd gotten his AA in music production and enrolled in bachelor's classes for the fall. He'd worked his tail off with Brady at the studio, learning the ins and outs. He wanted to believe there was a possibility of something more for him and Paisley, a place where they could belong, where the bond they already had could bloom into something deeper.

"I'm working on it," Jonas told him and met Trevor's gaze with a sure one.

For the first time in his life, he might have someone choosing him—choosing to stay—and he was going to do everything in his power to make sure he didn't fuck it up.

♫ ♫ ♫

Two hours later, Jonas left the apartment above Brady's parents' garage just behind his brother's house and headed for his car and his date with Paisley. His mind was on her and them and all the things they were finally going to get to say and do when a man with a camera stepped out of the hedge along the driveaway. It was the same creep who'd thrown shit at Fiadh. The man's stomach sagged over his belt and his thinning hair blew in the warm breeze.

Anger flew through him at the idea of the man following him home, but he held it in check while stating firmly, "This is private property."

"I'll pay. A thousand dollars for the story. More for pictures of the sweet little thing being not so sweet. Our readers would eat it up."

The words caused bile to hit Jonas's throat. Through gritted teeth, he said, "I'll repeat it in case you're too dense to have understood. Get. Off. This is private property."

The man was stupid enough to shove a business card in Jonas's direction, and when he didn't reach for it, the man placed his hand on Jonas's bicep and tucked it into the pocket of his button-down. Jonas's muscles tightened, body going on high alert, mind flashing to the times his mom's boyfriends had done something similar. Gotten into his space. Restrained him. Held him back.

Jonas's fist clenched, and he threw the man's arm off with enough force the man had to take a step back. And yet, the idiot still didn't get the hint. The reporter headed for the sidewalk, whistling, before turning back and saying with a wink, "I think I'll get a story out of you one way or another."

Jonas went to follow him but Marco's voice saying his name halted him. He turned to find his brother jogging over from his house, thick brows furrowed together.

"You okay?" Marco asked, chin jutting toward the guy still whistling his way down the street.

"Just your everyday asswipe being his douchebag self."

Marco assessed him. While Jonas still wanted to shove the man's head against a wall, the farther the reporter moved away, the more the tightness in his chest eased.

"I'm good, honest."

They stared at each other for a moment.

"Date?" his brother asked, staring at Jonas's dress shirt and jeans.

Jonas rubbed his hand through his hair. "Yeah."

Marco smiled at him, bumping his shoulder. "Have fun. Be good. Don't do anything I wouldn't do."

Jonas laughed, "I'm not sure you want to say that after the things I've seen you do to Cass."

Marco's grin grew. "Right. Do I need to have the protection talk?"

Jonas rolled his eyes and headed for the black Mustang he and Marco had restored together. "She's never even been kissed, Marco. I'm not going to be getting down and dirty with her anytime soon."

He almost had the door shut before Marco's reply hit him. "You're a good man, Jonas. She's lucky to have you."

The words wrenched through his chest. He wanted nothing more than for it to be true, but his reaction to the reporter was exactly what he feared. Uncontrollable fury. A need to hit. He'd worked hard to be rid of his demons, but they didn't want to let go, popping up when he least expected them to.

On the drive to the farmhouse, he turned up the music, letting Paisley's voice coming through the speakers soothe him in ways nothing else in his life ever did. The creep of a reporter might try to make them into something they weren't, Jonas couldn't stop that, but he could control his own emotions. He could be what Paisley needed.

When he got to the farmhouse, it was Fee who answered the door with a grin, calling up to Paisley that he was there. And then he got the breath knocked out of him all over again as Paisley came down the stairs looking like an angel in a short summer dress with baby-blue flowers on it. She'd left her hair down in soft curls, and it spun around her bare shoulders in a way that made him want to twine his fingers in it. He ached to pull her head back, expose all the sweet skin of her neck and chest, and devour her.

He swallowed hard as she all but danced down the stairs to stop in front of him with eyes glowing and cheeks flushing.

"You look nice," she said quietly.

"You look like a fucking dream," he said, low and guttural.

Fee laughed behind them, and Paisley blushed.

"Shall we?" he asked, offering her his arm. As soon as her hand slid into place, sparks flickered to life between them—like a lightning storm ready to crackle through the sky.

"We have an early start tomorrow morning." Landry's hard voice at the top of the stairs called down to them, and it bit at his joy.

He looked up at her sister, doing his best to keep the peace by offering her a smile as he replied, "I promise I won't keep her late."

"Ignore her. Just have fun, you two," Fee said, smile growing as she shut the door behind them with a wink.

He led Paisley over to the Mustang. When he opened the passenger door, she smiled one of her heart-stopping smiles at him and said, "I get to ride in Sheila?"

"You and that ridiculous name."

"Every muscle car needs a good name," she tossed back as she slid inside. "And you refused to come up with one."

Because the only name he could think of was too good for a car. But he kept that to himself. Jonas got behind the wheel and looked into the rearview mirror, watching as Paisley's bodyguard, Dylan, climbed into the SUV behind them.

Paisley grimaced. "After today, it was the only way she'd even consider letting me leave the house."

After Jonas had been approached by the reporter, he thought it was probably smart, even though he doubted it was the reason Landry had insisted. Disappointment and frustration wafted over him, stealing another piece of his joy.

"Why does she hate me?" he asked.

As soon as the question was out, he wished he could take it back. It shouldn't matter. If Paisley cared about him, that was all that was important. But Landry was the most influential person in her world, even more than their parents, and he knew her sister's opinion would leave a stain on them if he couldn't fix it.

Paisley flushed, looking away, finger going to her birthmark, proving the question had made her nervous. "She doesn't."

But they both knew it was a lie. "Is it because of what happened when we first met with Mel and Artie?" he pushed instead of backing off.

She sighed but wouldn't meet his gaze, and his gut churned, knowing instinctively she was keeping something from him.

"She's always been my protector. I think, like we've talked about before, she's just having a hard time accepting I'm not her kid sister anymore. She's worried..." She faded off.

"I'd never hurt you," he growled.

"I know that!" Paisley insisted.

"But she doesn't," he said. The thought made him inexplicably sad, and when Paisley didn't respond, all the insecurities he battled pushed to the forefront of his mind again.

His hands were suddenly sweaty, and he took turns wiping them off on his jeans as he drove. In truth, he was exactly what Landry saw—a boy from nowhere with a shady past and a future he was scrambling to claim. With anger issues and a violent streak. But Landry couldn't see his hopes and dreams or the progress he'd made. She couldn't know that just talking with Paisley gave him not only a sense of peace but a vision of a future where they both could have everything they'd ever wanted. Love. Success. Family. Home.

Paisley's index finger rubbed a small circle over her star, and he realized his silence—his glower—had made her nervous. More things to regret.

He pulled her hand from her face, running his thumb over the knuckles. "I'll prove to her I can be the man you deserve."

And he meant it. He'd show the entire world that Paisley Kim wasn't settling for a boy from the wrong side of the tracks, but a man who held her up and made her shine.

CHAPTER FIVE

Paisley

KISS ME

Performed by Sixpence None the Richer

Paisley's heart hammered inside her chest at his words. Sweet and bitter all at the same time. Words she knew he meant and came from years of not feeling as if he could ever be good enough. From being abandoned by a mother who'd been so high she hadn't even known he was in the back seat when she'd crashed the car and killed another driver. She hated that Landry had made him feel that way all over again.

When she looked at Jonas, all she could see was a man radiating strength and character and honesty. He looked handsome and strong in the blue-and-white-striped dress shirt and snug fitting jeans he'd worn for their date, even though it was too hot for either. The heady scent of him mingled with the leather and oil and history of the car, tapping out a story in her head that she wanted to pound out on her keyboard.

"You have nothing to prove, Jonas. Not to me. Not to Landry.

You're beautiful just as you are." She grimaced as soon as the word escaped her. *Idiot.* The voice in her head screamed. *Who calls a man beautiful?*

He shook his head. "I'm just your average Joe, Paisley. You... you're pure magic. Like the shimmer of colors along the water at sunset. Like...holding a rainbow in your hand."

Her breath caught at the sweetness of the words, wanting to add a rhythm to them so they became a song that was called "Them." If she hadn't been friends with him for so long, she might have thought they were a line to get in her pants, but she heard the sincerity in every syllable, and when she looked over at him, his eyes reflected the truth. There was so much emotion in his gaze that she had to close her eyes to stop them from overwhelming her. Hope. Desire. Gratitude. Belonging. But there was heartache there as well.

Or maybe that was in her because she knew the truth. Their time together was limited. Measured in a handful of days before she'd have to leave again. And then what would happen to them?

"It physically hurts when you say things like that," she breathed out.

"Why?"

Her throat closed. She didn't want to ruin the beginning of their night with talk of the end they both had to realize was coming. Wasn't she allowed to have these precious first moments without tainting them with reality? Couldn't she pretend, for just a few hours, that somehow an answer would come to her even when she knew, from harsh experience, that no matter how long you stared at a page, the answers wouldn't just show up?

She was saved from having to respond as they pulled up outside his sister-in-law's restaurant next to the music studio. A small group of reporters was still there, and before she and Jonas could duck inside, they were already taking pictures.

Dylan blocked them as best he could, attempting to hurry them into the café, as Paisley's blood ran cold and her feet attempted to take root in the ground. Landry was going to be furious.

She stumbled, and Jonas caught her before she fell, steadying her and twining their hands together. The sensation of his warm skin settled over her, bringing her back to where they were, grounding her like normally only Landry had been able to do, and she finally was able to walk again.

Inside, Jonas led her to a table at the back, hidden behind the enormous metal tree of life fountain that took up the middle of the restaurant. Twinkle lights glimmered and wind chimes blew from its branches, filling the space with sparkling vibrancy. The restaurant was one of her favorite places in Grand Orchard.

While they ate, the conversation turned lighter only because Jonas had a knack for making it so. They talked about her favorite parts of the tour, the classes he'd taken, and his family. He made her laugh with stories about his foster mom, the huge family she had back in Austin, and the pranks they played on one another.

"If Landry or I had ever pulled a stunt like that, we would've been grounded for life," Paisley said with a small smile.

Her childhood had not been full of laughter. While she hadn't suffered any of the abuse and poverty Jonas had before Maliyah had taken him in, the expectations of her parents had been a heavy mantle she'd failed to carry.

"What's your favorite memory of your parents?" he asked as if sensing the dark thoughts that spun through her.

"Making *kimbap* with Mom," Paisley replied immediately and easily.

Jonas frowned. "What's that?"

Paisley smiled. "Like sushi rolls but Korean. Mom would

have the ingredients lined up on the counter, and she'd play ABBA music while we spent an entire afternoon making them."

"Ah-ha. This is the real reason you like ABBA!" he teased.

She laughed but thought he might be right.

Her parents had loved her, but it seemed as if the love had been infected by their disappointment. They'd been embarrassed by her academic struggles, brushing it under the table and insisting she try harder rather than admit there was a real issue. Her failures had somehow become theirs. Not even Landry's escapades in school could keep the focus off her for long. It had only gotten worse when discussions about grades had turned into arguments over the band and Paisley dropping out of school completely.

Jonas reached across the table, taking her hand in his and squeezing it as if he'd heard where her thoughts had gone. He helped her out of the booth, and the spark of awareness dancing between them called her back from the heartache of her childhood.

"Want to take a walk?" he asked.

She nodded, and he hooked his pinky with hers, leading her out the back of the restaurant instead of the front. She knew instinctively he'd done it so she could avoid the press, and it warmed her heart in a way that Landry's protectiveness no longer did.

The sun had set, but the sky hadn't turned completely to night yet as they weaved behind the quaint red-brick shops that made up Grand Orchard's downtown. He took her through the back streets to the Wilson-Jacobs campus where old cobble paths mixed with ivy-covered buildings. The summer humidity clung to the air, and a quiet hovered over the university absent of the students who'd be there in the fall.

Dylan followed behind at a distance, giving them a degree of privacy, and when Jonas stopped at a bench partially secluded by foliage, the bodyguard stepped farther away into the trees. She and Jonas sat quietly for a moment in the semi-darkness, watching the lightning bugs dart over the grass, and breathing in the heady scent of apple trees that always seemed to surround the town.

"So, this is where you've spent your evenings while I've been gone," she said.

"Yep, and in the fall, I'll be back," he replied, pride in every syllable.

"Pretty impressive, Mr. Riccoli," she said it as a tease, but it was also true. She'd never go back to school.

"Says the Grammy-award-winning rock star," he teased back, holding her gaze.

The air suddenly felt thicker. Heavier. More intense. She wanted to kiss him. She wanted his body pressed against hers just to feel the zap of electricity that flew through them when they touched. But she was nervous to make the first move. Fee would have laughed at her and told her just to take the leap, but Paisley wasn't known for taking leaps. She was known for freezing when the action hit. She hated it. She didn't want it to be her anymore. She wanted to reach for him and this moment with both hands. To hold on to it before it disappeared like the twilight.

CHAPTER SIX

Jonas

I'LL NEVER LET YOU GO
Performed by Steelheart

Paisley looked beautiful. Soft and feminine. He ached to touch her—had been aching to touch her since she'd first arrived at the studio this morning looking exactly like the rock star she was. As they sat on the bench with only the hum of the night surrounding them, her silence spoke to him, something heavy coasting through it.

"What's wrong?" he asked.

Instead of replying, she slid closer to him on the bench until their legs were touching from hip to knee. She put a hand on his arm and glanced up into his face, and Jonas thought he might lose his mind just looking at her. Even though there was barely any light left in the sky, he still felt like she was glowing. Bright. Beautiful. Stunning.

"I'm afraid," she said, and it was even quieter than she normally was.

"Why?" His throat bobbed. He would never hurt her. Never.

"I'm afraid I'll fall completely, head-over-heels in love with you, and that you'll fall back. I'm afraid we'll discover we're the missing pieces of each other's souls." The words had a beat—a rhythm—like it was a song she'd already written.

"And that would be bad?" he asked, trying to hide the apprehension her words caused. He was already too far gone. He'd already lost his soul to her.

"I think it would be wonderful...but then..." She looked like she was going to cry, and he couldn't stand it. He wrapped his arm around her waist, and drew her even closer, tugging until her legs were over his lap and their chests were aligned.

"But then?" he asked, meeting her gaze.

"But then I'll leave, and all we'll have left is a handful of sweet memories, right?" She said it as if they were destined to be pulled apart, and it stabbed again at the dark places inside him.

He'd loved two women who'd abandoned him. His mom had done it repeatedly, never once answering the hundreds of letters he'd written to her in jail. And Mel had walked away without ever looking back. He wasn't sure what he'd do if he lost the friendship he already had with Paisley. But he also couldn't sit next to her and not attempt to turn their friendship into something more. She might only be in town for mere weeks, but there was no way he wanted the end of her time there to be the end of them.

"Just because you leave Grand Orchard doesn't mean we have to be apart forever."

"Wh-what?"

"Why do you think I'm doing all this?" He waved to the campus. "The music production and the studio time?"

"Because you love music."

He chuckled. "Well, yes. Being behind the mixing console... feels right. Like I've found what I'm supposed to do with my life. But it also means I might be able to find a place in *your* world."

Every minute he'd been in class, he'd been thinking about her. He wanted to learn everything he could about the industry and making music, not just for himself, but for Paisley. So he could somehow earn a place at her side.

She looked a little shocked, and he was glad the dark hid the red in his cheeks. It was ridiculous to have said it out loud, to assume she'd want him in her life or that there would be a place for some newbie who was just learning the ropes. Everything he'd learned with Brady in the last two years was still just a drop in the bucket compared to what he didn't know.

Before he could really register what she was doing, she leaned forward, put both her hands on his cheeks, and drew his face toward hers until their lips met, soft and easy, the barest of pressure. A mere touch that felt both too much and too little all at the same time. His chest seized for one painful moment. He'd been longing for this, aching for it for so long that it seemed impossible to actually be happening. His hands went to her hips, gripping, holding on as if to make sure it was real.

A sigh escaped her, the air coasting over him, and he groaned, sliding his tongue into her parted mouth and sweeping inside. Exploring. Touching. Tantalizing. He tangled one hand in her hair and another at her back, pushing them together in an attempt to remove every molecule of space left between them. He held on tightly as if she was a lifeline pulling him toward his future.

They sat that way, intertwined in the most beautiful way, for what felt like hours. He was hard and uncomfortable. She was panting, nipples taut against his chest through her thin dress. And then he finally remembered they were on a bench in the middle of campus with her bodyguard watching from the trees.

It was enough for him to slowly remove his lips from hers

and tip their foreheads together, allowing them to catch their breath. The zing of desire wafted between them, matching the flicker of the fireflies flitting about the grass around them.

It was a moment he'd never be able to forget.

She pulled away from him a bit more, but the smile on her face made him groan. It was sweet and happy and full of lust all at the same time.

"Don't look at me that way, sweetheart. I won't be able to stop," he grunted out.

She surprised him by laughing, a tinkle of joy that darted through the night.

"Thank you," she said.

His brows drew together. "For?"

"Making my first kiss so beautiful."

Damn. He hadn't forgotten that she'd never been kissed before. He'd even said as much to Marco earlier, but lost in the moment, he'd taken her first kiss too far. He should have stopped at a simple press of lips.

"That was probably more than it should have been," he said tenderly, hand rubbing along her arm and thrilling at the goosebumps that rose at his touch. Shivers that had nothing to do with the night air that was warm and heavy about them.

"Don't do that," she said. "Don't put it down. It was perfect. You're perfect."

"We're perfect," he replied, and he meant it in every fiber of his being.

Her smile grew.

He pulled her up from the bench, wrapped her fingers in his, and started back toward Main Street. Dylan emerged from the trees and trailed along at a distance, and Jonas tried not to be embarrassed at the thought of him watching as they'd made out on the bench.

When they got to the car, Jonas opened the door for her and

couldn't help dropping a sweet kiss on her forehead as she slid by him. This first taste he'd had of her would never be enough. Not in a million years. It only fueled his determination to do whatever it took to bring their worlds closer together.

♫ ♫ ♫

Jonas was unable to sleep, mind tossing with everything that had happened the day before and his promise to Paisley that this wouldn't be the end of them. Doubts had circled through him once he was alone in the dark of his bedroom because she'd never really replied when he'd said he was going to school to bring their lives closer. She'd just kissed the hell out of him—or started to kiss him and he'd kissed the hell out of her? He wasn't sure which. All he knew was he'd had to take a cold shower when he got home, and the scent of her had still lingered on his skin and his tongue.

Giving up on sleep in the wee hours of the morning, Jonas headed for the studio. The only good thing about being there so early was the press hadn't set up camp yet. Instead, the Garner Security team was there, putting up barricades to hold the media away from the studio. Jonas nodded to them as he unlocked the door, turned off the alarm, and stepped inside.

Yesterday, they'd recorded the rehearsal just for shits and grins. So, they could rewind and hear what had been said about the music and the changes. He replayed some of it, losing himself in Paisley's quiet voice. The only time she ever spoke with a hundred percent confidence was when she talked about music. She doubted herself everywhere else...but last night, when she'd kissed him, he'd felt it again. Her strength. Her certainty. He was stupid to let doubts in the dark of the night get to him.

He lifted his head hours later when the bell above the door

jingled, a leftover from when the studio had actually been a music store owned by Brady's wife's family. The band strolled in with Brady on their heels, and everyone was laughing at something he'd said. Jonas's gaze met Paisley's, and a blush settled over her cheeks as her eyes fell to his lips.

"Hello, lover boy," Fee said, bumping his shoulder with a fist. "Paisley was all smiles last night, so I guess you must have done something right."

Most of the band chuckled, but Landry didn't. She just wore her ever-prevalent frown as she led the way into the live room. Paisley gave him a soft smile as she followed her sister.

Jonas watched them for a moment before turning his eyes back to the mixing console. Brady joined him, running through the schedule Jonas had made for the band's time in the isolation booth. Jonas barely heard anything Brady was saying as his eyes kept drifting back to Paisley. When Brady nudged him, Jonas looked up to see a goofy smile on his boss's face.

"So...anything I need to know?" Brady asked, eyes twinkling.

Jonas shrugged, keeping his emotions tucked inside. "We went on a date."

Brady chuckled, the warm sound bringing a smile to Jonas's lips, but before either of them could say more, Fiadh's voice cut through the air, sharp and brittle. "What the feck?"

Her mouth had dropped open in shock as she stared at a piece of paper in her hand. The other band members hurried to Fee's side.

"*Dios*!" Adria's voice panicked. When she went to grab the paper, Landry halted her.

"Stop. Don't anyone else touch it!"

Jonas's heart slammed into his chest, fear flooding his veins at the alarm in their voices. He and Brady sprinted into the live room.

"What is it?" Brady demanded.

The smiles and humor that had bounced through everyone moments ago had completely disappeared. Now, everyone looked pale and shaky.

Fiadh turned the paper toward them. It was a photograph of the entire band on the sidewalk the day before with Jonas and Paisley holding hands. The image itself would have been harmless if every single one of their faces hadn't been scratched out—the cuts ugly and deep, tearing through the paper. Across the gouges, the words, *You don't deserve to be happy,* had been written in bright-red ink.

His stomach clenched and his chest tightened. When he looked at Paisley, she was frozen in fear. He strode across the room, pulling her to him. She shivered, hiding her face in his chest as if the action alone could make the note go away. His breath got caught in his lungs. What the fuck did it mean? Who'd gotten into the studio to deliver it?

Brady whipped out his phone, barking into it in a decidedly un-Brady-like way, "Marco, we have a problem."

The room was tense and silent, the fear palpable as they waited for his brother. The Garner Security offices in Grand Orchard were across the street, above the bakery, so it took less than a minute for Marco, Trevor, and a sea of security to storm into the studio.

The first thing his brother did was look Jonas over to make sure he was okay before turning to the task at hand. He bagged the note while Trevor went to check the surveillance feeds and another bodyguard was sent back to the office for a fingerprint kit.

Jonas's anger simmered. He wanted to hunt down whoever had sent the note and punch them in the face until they bled. Instead, he took his cue from his brother, attempting to claim the calm Marco had brought to the room while rubbing comforting circles on Paisley's back.

When Trevor returned, Brady demanded, "What did you find?"

Trevor's normally easy-going expression was grim. "Nothing. There's no one on any of the feeds from last night or this morning."

"Someone was in here, Trev," Jonas said, and while he'd tried to keep his tone even, the fury he felt at a creep getting this close to them bled through.

Paisley's body went stiff in his embrace, and she raised her head to shoot a look at Landry, whose expression was squinty and pissed-off. Landry's attitude did nothing but add to the roiling fury Jonas felt burning in him, not only at the fucking note but also at her continued disapproval.

Jonas closed his eyes, concentrating on his breathing and the feel of Paisley in his arms. Focusing on anything that would prevent him from blurting out something he'd regret. Something that would make things between him and Landry even worse.

CHAPTER SEVEN

Paisley

DEAR READER
Performed by Taylor Swift

TEN DAYS BEFORE

Paisley felt sick. Not only because of the grotesque image but because of the disapproval radiating from her sister. Nausea gave way to flashes of fear that thudded through her like a military cadence, strong and fierce, threatening to take over everything just like her panic attacks did before she went onstage.

They'd had some weird fan mail before, mostly fans declaring their love in fairly pornographic ways, but nothing as violent and evil as this note and the one Landry had shown her the other day. It was terrifying to think someone in the quaint, little town was capable of something this awful. Not when everyone seemed the epitome of small-town friendliness.

She breathed in the scent of Jonas, trying to let it and the warmth of his body ground her. When she looked up, her sister was staring at her, expression dark and moody.

Paisley's voice shook as she said, "You need to tell them about the other one."

Landry's eyes narrowed.

Locked as she was in Jonas's embrace, she could feel the shocked rumble as it escaped his chest. "Other one? There's been more of these?"

"Only when you're around," Landry shot back.

He growled, "Excuse me?" just as Paisley said, "Lan!" and Adria demanded to know what the fuck was going on.

"It's true," Landry tossed at Jonas. "In the two years we've been gone, we've never gotten anything like this again. Now, here we are, you've got your arms around my sister, and another picture shows her with her face gouged out."

"Someone better start explaining," Marco demanded.

"What are you even talking about, Landry?" Leya asked with a quiver in her voice.

Paisley looked up at Jonas and swallowed. Would he be upset that she hadn't told him? Would he take this to heart as something else he'd caused and decide it was best to walk away? Would it wound him? He looked so sturdy and strong, but she knew, deep inside, there still beat the heart of a scared little boy who'd been abandoned.

She squeezed his hand and fought to find her voice through the waves of panic. "When we were here last time...after you and I sang together at the theater...someone sent a note just like this," Paisley said quietly.

His eyes widened, and she felt it the moment he made it about him because his arms around her loosened. "Why didn't you tell me?"

"I just found out...Lan—"

"This is exactly what I knew was going to happen. I told you he was bad news!" Landry snarled, and it bit into Paisley. Thorns scratching and clawing again like they had before, but it also made her angry because she could feel the way Jonas trembled underneath her touch.

It was his brother who picked up Jonas's defense before she could. "This isn't about Jonas! It's not like *he's* been getting threats he hasn't told anyone about."

"All of our faces are scratched out, Lan," Paisley insisted. Landry stepped back as if she'd hit her, and Paisley looked away, doubt and frustration and fear spiraling through her.

"Where's the other note?" Marco demanded.

Landry raised her chin in defiance. "Talk to your boss. He has everything."

"You had no right to keep this from us," Nikki said, meeting Landry's gaze. And for a moment, Landry looked remorseful before the regret disappeared as quickly as it had come.

"I was protecting Paisley," Landry said, making Paisley grimace.

"You're not the only one with family to protect!" Adria exclaimed, frustration and anger shimmering through her words. "*Dios*, Landry. Leya's dad is running for Vice President of the United States. My dad has death threats from guerillas on almost a daily basis. They needed to be told about this."

Paisley hated it. The tension blooming in the room was almost as ugly as the note.

She buried her head in Jonas's chest, and he responded by wrapping his arms tighter around her.

"Everyone needs to just take a fucking breath," Jonas barked.

Her sister didn't like his command. "You don't get to tell us—"

"What the hell is going on in here?" The angry voice of their manager caused Paisley to jerk away from Jonas just as Tommy strode into the room. Jonas didn't let her get far. He put a hand on her waist, holding her close, as if he needed her comfort as much as she needed his.

Tommy's eyes were narrowed in a concern that didn't at all match his aging rock-star vibe. The first time she'd met him, she'd thought he was the lead singer of a hair band instead of a music manager. Today, just like then, his black hair was gelled into perfect spikes, and he was wearing black leather pants and a torn T-shirt over his lean but muscled frame.

His hands were planted on his hips, and he was glaring at each of them, even Paisley when he always took extra care to be gentle with her.

It was Nikki who answered him, her voice shaky as she rubbed her temples in the way she did when a migraine hit her. "We got hate mail."

Tommy stepped closer to Marco and grabbed the bag with the letter in it. His eyes grew wide, and he swallowed hard before returning it and asking, "It's just a one-off, right?"

The silence that settled in the room spoke volumes, heavier than even before.

It was Marco who broke it. "We'll have this fingerprinted, loop in the local PD, and get the information from Garner about the other note. Then, I'll send everything off to a friend I have at the FBI."

"What other note?" Tommy demanded, and Adria shot an accusing look in Landry's direction.

Guilt riddled Paisley. Her sister had done all of this to protect her, just like she always had, and now Paisley was letting everyone take it out on her without speaking up. But she didn't know what to say. She couldn't even look at Landry.

As Marco headed for the door, he shot a look in Jonas and Paisley's direction, eyes falling to the way Jonas was rubbing her back. Was he worried Jonas would react like he had back in Austin with Mel two years ago? With his fists? God, it made her sick to even think about it. She didn't want to be the reason Jonas went over the edge, not only because she didn't want him to hate himself but because if he did lose his temper, it would only prove Landry's point.

Paisley pulled farther away from him and felt the loss deep in her soul as his warmth drifted away. The icy cold that normally filled in her body during an anxiety attack swam back over her, making her limbs heavy and useless.

Marco issued one more command before he finally left. "We'll double up your detail. Two with each of you at all times until we know more."

He didn't wait to see if anyone would complain, and no one did, even though Paisley knew they were all battling a mixture of relief and resentment. It was hard enough to have one person following you around everywhere you went, let alone two or more.

Adria broke the silence, twirling her sticks as she asked Tommy sarcastically, "What's the Hollywood Player Prince doing here?"

For the first time, Paisley noticed the man standing behind Tommy, and she groaned internally. He was the last thing they needed right now. Ronan Hawk was a narcissistic director who'd filmed three of their music videos. Drama followed him everywhere as he flirted and bedded every female who'd let him.

Ronan smirked at Adria from where he stood, carelessly leaning up against a wall. He was dressed in jeans and an old Ferris Bueller T-shirt. The gray beanie partially covering his cinnamon-colored hair thrust his closely shaved beard and stormy gray eyes into prominence.

Tommy twisted one of the many gold chains around his neck, shot Ronan a look, and said, "He wants to film a documentary on the Daisies. Show you recording the album, layered with one-on-one interviews. A getting-to-know-the-band kind of thing. He's already pitched it to RMI, and they want it for their new streaming service."

"No," Adria said.

Paisley almost jumped at the sharp retort that was so unlike her friend. Whenever the band disagreed on anything, Adria was the first one to make a pros-and-cons list to help them decide what to do. A hard no was never her style, and Paisley wasn't sure if it had to do with a documentary in general or just Adria's new and unrelenting hatred that had bloomed recently for Ronan. Hatred that seemed to go well past his player ways and easy flirtations.

"Ads—" Fiadh started.

"No," Adria said, shooting a glare at Ronan. "No. No. No. We can't trust him to have our best interest at heart. He'll twist everything we say."

While Adria was vehemently upset, Ronan seemed strangely calm. This disagreement, on top of the scary note, Landry's displeasure, and Jonas's simmering anger, made Paisley's vision tunnel. It felt like their entire world was on a precipice, ready to tumble over at any moment.

"We'd have full review and edit rights," Tommy insisted. "Ronan won't put anything in it we don't want, right?" He glanced at Ronan.

The man shrugged full of cocky nonchalance. "Sure."

Paisley's stomach sank. It was hardly the way to reassure Adria.

"Jesus, Tommy. Did you need to do this today?" Landry groused, finally speaking up. It was the first time she'd said anything in several minutes when normally she would have been shouting directions and leading them back into action. It proved her sister had been more rattled by the image and the argument than she was letting on.

"Well, it's not like I knew there'd be a note from a crazed fan waiting for you," Tommy tossed back. "A documentary would be good for the band. I wouldn't have agreed if I didn't think it was a smart move. Fans eat up these kinds of exposés."

"You need to leave while we talk," Adria growled at Ronan.

He arched a brow, and Paisley wanted to shake him for antagonizing her further. "Fine by me. I'll scope out some film locations and have a list of ideas ready for you when we start."

He strolled out as if he was completely confident they'd agree. Paisley wondered what it would feel like to be that confident all the time. To know for sure that every decision you made was the right one.

As soon as he was gone, Landry said, "I think we should consider it."

Adria's face turned brittle, but she didn't comment. Paisley's chest knotted further. Being followed around by their bodyguards was one thing, but having Ronan and the cameras there purposefully trying to uncover their secrets was almost as terrifying as the creepy note. Landry and the rest of the band had done everything they could to keep Paisley's anxiety attacks and stage fright out of the media, especially when she'd been so young when she'd first joined. Everyone had thought she'd grow out of them, and while she now had techniques to get herself onto the stage, it really hadn't gotten easier.

"If we do this, my dad's team has to have veto rights with the election this close," Leya reminded them.

Leya's dad had won his senate seat right before the Daisies had begun playing gigs. The only way he'd agreed to let Leya be a part of the band was if his people reviewed everything in advance—tour schedules, official statements, interviews, everything—and that had been before he'd become the shoo-in for the vice-presidential nominee on Guy Matherton's ticket. Now, with the Daisies having blown up and the senator's career taking off, it was even more complicated.

"It would be a good opportunity for people to truly get to know us individually instead of seeing us as some weirdly interchangeable daisy image," Nikki said, sending an apologetic look in Adria's direction.

"I can't believe you're all considering this," Adria growled. "It would mean having him around for weeks."

"The true objection emerges," Fiadh said in a false whisper, and Landry snorted.

"What's that supposed to mean?" Adria asked, sliding one drumstick down the back of her tank top like a samurai sword while twirling the other in her hand.

Fiadh tangled her arm through Adria's. "It's okay not to like him. I mean, he's hit on all of us, but that doesn't mean he doesn't do good work. *The Red Guitar* won video of the year because of him."

Adria's fingers stilled on the drumstick, and Paisley felt her heart do the same thing because it meant they were doing this. Even if Paisley spoke up against it now, she and Adria would be outnumbered.

For the first time since the conversation had started, Jonas squeezed Paisley's hand as if he'd somehow sensed her response. As if he knew just how much she'd hate having Ronan digging into their truths.

Landry's voice was soft and cajoling when she turned to Adria. "Come with me and Tommy to talk to him. We'll set whatever ground rules you feel comfortable with."

Adria's added the stick in her hand to the other one already tucked in her shirt and uttered a disgruntled, "Fine."

She grabbed her bag and headed for the door.

Landry looked at Brady and said, "I'm sorry we've blown the schedule for today."

"We have plenty of time," Brady said. "I don't have anyone else coming to use the studio until September, and truth be told,

I'm not sure we'd get anything useful today. Try to regroup, and we'll start fresh tomorrow."

He gave them all an empathetic look and walked out.

"What are the rest of you going to do?" Landry asked, but her gaze landed on Paisley and Jonas.

"I'm going to go take a nap before this headache turns into a full-blown migraine," Nikki said.

"I'll go back to the farmhouse with you," Leya said. "I need to call my parents and let them know what's happening."

"Fee?" Landry asked.

"I'll stick around until Paisley is ready to leave," she said.

Landry hesitated for another second and then left with Tommy on her heels.

As soon as the room was clear, Fiadh grabbed her bag and headed for the door. "You're not staying?" Paisley asked, voice quivering.

She turned. "I know she's just trying to protect you, but your eighteen, Little Bit. You deserve your privacy and your fun." Fee's look settled on Jonas. "Don't make me regret leaving her with you."

Paisley felt Jonas stiffen next to her, but he didn't respond.

Once Fiadh had left, she turned in his arms, resting her chin on his chest and looking up at him. He was so much taller than her. Almost a foot and a half now that he'd grown even more since the last time she'd been in town.

"I'm sorry I didn't tell you about the picture, but I honestly didn't know until the day we arrived back in town," she said quietly.

He looked away for a second and then back. "She thinks this is because of me…I haven't had any interaction with Artie since I left Austin. Mel disappeared with her parents after the single scathing note she sent me when Marco told her parents what was happening. I don't see how this could be about me…"

But as he trailed off, she knew he was uncertain.

She'd spent two years getting to know him, even if she hadn't been able to see the emotions crossing his face while they'd texted as she did now. She'd still read them in each syllable he'd typed, so she knew what he was going to say before he did.

"Maybe, we should—"

She stood on her tiptoes, placed her hand behind his neck, and pulled his mouth to hers, cutting him off. It was fierce in a way she was never fierce. Certain when it was the last thing she ever felt. A kiss that refused to let him walk away from her. For several heartbeats, he didn't respond, he held himself tight and stiff, and then he groaned, and slowly devoured her. The kiss turned heated and hot. Wet and sloppy with tongues and teeth seeking a jagged relief from the harsh emotions that had filled the room.

A jangle of the bell in the studio brought them to their senses.

She ran a thumb over his mouth, wiping her lip gloss from him.

"That's why I didn't tell you. Because I knew you'd think walking away would be the best thing for me, but it's not Jonas. It can't be." His brow furrowed, deep grooves between his eyes that she knew she needed to ease. "Can I show you something?"

He didn't say no, so she pulled her phone out, and brought up her voice memos. She hesitated for a moment, embarrassment flushing her cheeks because she knew the titles were full of misspellings and reversed letters that even autocorrect couldn't pick up. Normally, no one saw either her recordings or her written notes until Landry had fixed them, but she needed him to understand what he'd done for her...to her life.

Slowly, she turned the screen to him. The first memo said, "Song for Jonas," and the second one said, "How Jonas Makes Me Feel." A third memo read, "About Jonas." It went on and on and on. It was like a diary in many ways, except she just happened to express herself through chords and lyrics.

When she looked back up at his face, there was a stunned look on it.

"You make me feel seen for the first time in my life," she told him softly. "Not as a daughter or a little sister or a teen rock star, but as Paisley."

He closed his eyes and then bent down and placed a gentle kiss on her forehead. A devotion. A promise. And her heart was suddenly lighter than it had been all morning. She was going to get to keep him. Maybe their worlds were too different, maybe when she left Grand Orchard they'd fall apart, but he was working on finding a way to blend their lives together, and she'd do the same. A way for both of them to let go of the things holding them in the shadows, so they could truly shine.

CHAPTER EIGHT

Jonas

HYSTERIA
Performed by Def Leppard

Jonas's heart was beating wildly in his chest, slamming against his rib cage in a way that threatened to break it. Her words...her kiss...Everything about Paisley left him in awe.

He hated that the band had gotten evil as fuck notes. Hated that there was even the slimmest chance that this was his past raining down on them, but he also didn't know how to walk away from her. Not after two years of yearning to be at her side and finally being there.

Her eyes were wide and full of an adoration he wasn't sure he'd earned. It filled him with determination. She wouldn't be hurt. Not on his watch. Not by her sister or some sick creep. Not if he could help it.

Noise in the control room reminded him they weren't alone. His cheeks flushed at the idea of Brady having witnessed their kiss from the studio window. It was bad enough her bodyguard had witnessed it the night before.

"Want to get out of here?" he asked.

She nodded and picked her bag up from where she'd set it by her keyboard. He looped his pinky with hers and drew her toward the back of the studio. They ducked out of the rear entrance in order to evade the media with Dylan following them once more. Jonas led her through the back streets like he had last night, but this time, they went to his apartment.

Her bodyguard remained at the foot of the stairs, and it was only when he'd unlocked the door that he thought to hesitate. He hadn't exactly expected her to be there, not today.

"It's a bit of a mess," Jonas warned her.

She smirked at him. "Typical bachelor pad, is it?"

He shrugged, rubbed his hand through his hair, and then opened the door. He stepped inside, trying to see it through her eyes. It wasn't unclean as much as cluttered. Instruments, school books, and soda cans were strewn over the floors, counters, and tables, and a pile of dirty clothes overflowed a hamper in the corner.

He let her hand go to stuff all the clothes in and shut the lid as she wandered around picking up various instruments. She held a saxophone up, eyebrows lifting. "How many of these do you know how to play?"

Jonas shot her a wry smile. "I know how to play them all, but I'm good at none of them."

Her lips curled upward more, and it eased the pressure that had settled over his heart after everything that had happened this morning.

"No keyboard," she noted with some disappointment.

"No, but I do have a guitar," he said. He disappeared into the bedroom for a moment and came back out with an old, beat-up

Art & Lutherie Roadhouse that had been his first instrument purchase.

Paisley took it from him and sat down on the couch. He joined her as she strummed, closing her eyes and tuning it by ear.

"This reminds me of Landry's first guitar," she said, meeting his gaze. "She bugged my parents for two years to get one, and then when they finally relented, she took me to all her lessons so I could learn too."

His throat tightened thinking about the sweetness of what she'd said, and maybe understanding Landry a bit more. She'd been looking out for Paisley for so long, it would be difficult to stop. To trust that she didn't need to anymore. To trust someone else to also guard her sister.

"Why didn't your parents want her to have one?" he asked.

"They thought it would be a distraction from school. Grades were important to them," Paisley said. "They judge every success by numbers. It's what makes them really good investment bankers."

"They must be really proud of you then because the Daisies numbers are off the charts. Sales. Dollars. Fans," he said it as a partial tease, to ease the hurt he'd heard beneath her words.

She stared at him for a moment and then burst out laughing. "Maybe you can tell them that when you meet them."

Then, she flushed as if she'd just realized what she'd said. But he loved the idea of someday meeting her parents. He didn't know another guy his age who thought the way he did about their future. Not even friends who'd been dating girls for a couple of years in high school. But when he was with Paisley, all he could think about was forever. It didn't matter that they were young and inexperienced. They'd found each other, and it felt like it was the only way their lives were supposed to be.

She ducked her head to the guitar, playing a few chords

"This one came to me on the ride into Grand Orchard," she said quietly and started playing and singing about anticipation and first kisses and being truly seen. It was them, but it was also something nearly everyone in the world could relate to...those heady moments of falling for someone and the intense rush of those first touches.

He watched in awe as she played and sang. She stopped every so often, going back and changing a word or a chord or the pace. Her voice was so much stronger than it had been two years ago. When she'd been on the keyboard the day before, he'd thought the same thing.

"You've gotten even better," he said quietly.

Paisley flushed.

"It isn't just your voice or the way you play," he said "You've learned so much about life."

She scoffed. "Learning is definitely not my thing."

"Learning facts in a book, that's nothing. The knowledge you have...it's deeper and truer. You have an incredible insight into the world and people."

He could tell she didn't believe him, and it was frustrating in so many ways because she was a flipping rock star. She had millions of people idolizing her, and yet all she saw were the ways she felt broken instead of the ways she sparkled—like a celestial being calling others home.

"Seriously, Paisley...You're so damn talented it's almost indescribable."

Her eyes slipped to his lips, and her fingers stalled on the strings. She leaned over the guitar and kissed him, slow and soft. Heat spread through him at the gentle kiss. A burning ache that screamed for something more. Something bigger. Something that would complete them and the song she'd started about anticipation and need.

She broke the kiss long enough to set the guitar down before moving closer to him, putting her arms around his neck, and sliding her fingers through his hair.

"You make me forget to be anxious. You make me feel like I'm enough," she whispered against his lips.

He groaned. "Paisley...God...you're not just enough. You're everything."

His mouth took possession of hers. Needy. Searching. Sucking and licking and moving with an intensity that left them both panting and breathless. Hands slowly exploring. His palm slid under the hem of her shirt, dancing along smooth skin. She mirrored every motion, fingers gliding along every curve and groove of him as if she was playing him like she did her instruments.

When she tugged at his shirt, he pulled back enough to yank it over his head and toss it aside. Her gaze turned dark, and she bit her bottom lip before hooking her fingers under her shirt, a beat-up Painted Daises tee with their original logo, and throwing it to the ground with his.

They stared at each other for a moment. Her eying the muscles he'd earned at a boxing bag, and his gaze traveling over her small, gentle curves. The thin lace bra she wore did nothing to hide how turned on she was, and he placed his hand on the valley between her small breasts, palm opened wide, feeling the banging of her heart. Then, he closed his eyes and replaced his hand with his ear.

He stayed there lost, listening to the music she was making with her body, just for him. He was there so long she finally whispered his name in confusion. "Jonas?"

"Shh. I'm listening to your heartbeat. I'm finding your rhythm so I can match it."

She made a strangled noise in her throat as if his words had hurt her, and then she was pulling him up and kissing him again. Hot and fierce like she had at the studio. As if proving to him that this, them together, was all they ever needed to face the world.

♫ ♫ ♫

After kissing and caressing until they'd both been on the brink of exploding, he'd dragged himself away from her body in order to make her lunch in his tiny kitchenette. Then, they'd spent more time talking about the album. Her songs. The ones already included and the ones she still had spiraling in her head. It was just like every text and call they'd made over the months they'd been apart, but this time, they'd kept one part of them touching at all times.

Early in the afternoon, a frantic call from Landry demanding to know where Paisley was, had made her retreat into her shell. Instead of begging her to stay like he wanted to, he was the one to force her to leave because he didn't need to give Landry one more reason to hate him. He didn't want to be the wedge that drove the sisters apart.

He walked her back to the studio and the Escalade Dylan had waiting for her, placed another tender kiss on her forehead, and promised to see her in the morning. Then, he'd spent the rest of the night wishing he hadn't. Wishing he'd just taken every single moment they had together while she was there, screw Landry and what she thought.

As he approached the studio the next morning, the sleazy reporter who'd offered him money, joined him, matching Jonas's steps.

"Larry Wolcott, *The Exhibitor*. We met the other day," the man said, chomping on a piece of gum and smacking his lips in a way that made Jonas cringe.

"Bug off," Jonas growled, but Larry wasn't put off at all.

"I think I can get you at least five grand for an exclusive," he said, and when Jonas didn't respond, he added, "At least tell me if she tastes as sweet as she looks."

Jonas's feet stalled, and he shot the man a glare, fists clenching, stomach twisting while he fought to keep control. "Leave me the fuck alone. Leave her alone. They're dealing with enough shit. They don't need you being an asshole too."

Larry's eyebrows went up. "Yeah? What kind of shit?"

Fuck. Jonas realized what he'd said too late. He turned and almost jogged the remaining steps to the studio as Larry laughed behind him. "Like I said, I'll get a story out of you yet."

Jonas ducked below the barricades, nodded to the sea of bodyguards, and let himself in much as he had the morning before. He picked up an envelope that had fallen to the floor, mind reeling from the sleazy reporter's words and his stupid response. He turned to the mixing console and brought up the schedule they hadn't used the day before because of the creepy note.

That's when his heart started banging fiercely in his chest, and he turned back to the envelope he'd dropped. His hand shook as he tore it open, seeing exactly what he'd hoped he wouldn't. The image was of Jonas and Paisley when he'd dropped her off at the Escalade the day before and kissed her on the forehead. Their faces were scratched out again. His stomach fell as he read the bright-red words: *You don't deserve to be happy.*

Fear crawled up his back, sending goosebumps over his skin. And then the fear gave way to anger. Some asshole was out there, trying to scare the band, and he'd had the audacity to take a picture right outside the studio with their bodyguards standing there. And to top it off, the jerkoff had the balls to walk up and stick it under the studio door. Where the hell had the Garner Security team been? How had he gotten that close to the studio without anyone seeing him?

He yanked out his phone and called his brother.

"There's another note."

There was a surprised beat of silence on the other end before Marco asked, "Where did you find it?"

"Inside the fucking studio again. In the picture, Paisley's bodyguard is standing right there. What the hell kind of security is this?"

As soon as he said it, he regretted it. When Marco had been in the Marines, things went down that he'd felt responsible for and had never really gotten over. It was why he'd gone into security—to make sure he'd never leave someone unprotected again. And even though it hadn't been Marco standing at the door when this jackoff had gotten in, he knew his brother would take it personally.

"I'll be there in five," Marco said and hung up.

The door swung open, and Brady walked in with the Daisies. They were all laughing, and Ronan Hawk was behind them, camera in hand, filming it all. It made Jonas's stomach flip again. His eyes beelined to Paisley, taking her in from head to toe as if to reassure himself she was okay. Reading his mood, Paisley rushed over.

"What's wrong?"

His stomach churned. He didn't want to tell her. This picture had just the two of them, and surely Landry would insist this was about him and his past, but he also knew he couldn't keep it from them. They needed to know. They needed to keep their eyes out for this asshole.

"There was another note," he said quietly, his body trembling, the rage he felt barely leashed. When his eyes met Landry's over the top of Paisley's head, she was glaring at him.

Paisley's arm went around his waist, and he hugged her tightly, wanting to reassure her but not sure how to do so. Her face rested against his chest, and he ran a hand up and down her back soothingly, just like the goddamn day before.

Marco, Trevor, and the cops showed up at the studio, repeating everything all over again. Except, this time, Ronan was there recording it all. There was a certain smugness to him that pissed Jonas off even more as the man paced the room.

"Do you really think you should be filming this?" Jonas bit out before he could stop himself. Paisley looked up from where she stood beside him while Landry's eyes narrowed even more, but it was Ronan who replied.

"It's absolutely perfect. I couldn't have scripted it better myself. It's going to make a great storyline. You know, 'The Daisies rise above stalker threats.' I'll think of better words, but you get the gist," he said.

Jonas clenched his fists, the nails biting into his palm. What the fuck? Ronan was going to take advantage of their fear? Paisley grabbed his hand, forcing him to open his fingers, sliding his palm until it rested on her chest just as it had in the apartment the day before when he'd tried to match their heartbeats. The touch, the beat of her pulsing against his hand, soothed him.

But when his eyes skittered to Landry's, her scorn was written on her face. Rubbing their connectedness in her face wasn't helping him win Landry over.

He wasn't really sure anything he did would.

One of them was going to lose, and he had the sinking feeling, it might be him.

CHAPTER NINE

Paisley

KISS YOU ANYWAY
Performed by Dami Im

NINE DAYS BEFORE

The plan had been to record one of the saddest songs on the album that day. It was about the all-consuming loneliness you can feel even when standing in the middle of a crowd. It was how Paisley had felt almost every day on their tour. The band, the crew, and the fans had all surrounded her, but she'd always felt somehow removed. Separate.

But singing about such abject loneliness seemed too hard after another morning tortured with creepy notes and images. They also couldn't afford to skip another day in the studio, so the band decided to work on one of the more upbeat tunes. It was the song Paisley and Landry had written together for Fee. It showcased her bubbling energy that was like an infectious drug.

What most people didn't know was Fiadh's smile hid the wounds her family had delivered by disowning her once they'd discovered she was bisexual. The song layered those complexities. It was light and effervescent until you really paid attention to some of the words and the darker undertone.

The band spent most of the day on that one song, each of them taking turns in the isolation booth, repeating take after take, while Brady had them try different arrangements, to accent the depth of the song. Landry was as much of a perfectionist as Brady, and between the two of them, the process was agonizingly slow.

When they finally reached an agreement, they were tired and strangely amped up, the emotions a heady combination that was similar to how Paisley felt after a concert.

"I need sustenance and maybe a drink," Fee said, flinging an arm over Adria. "Shall we go to Mickey's?"

Normally, Paisley would have been frustrated by them leaving her to go to the local bar when she couldn't join them—yet another time she'd be sent home to be tucked in like a little kid—but tonight, she didn't care. She wouldn't be alone. She'd have Jonas. Her heart skittered as her gaze met his and a slow, knowing smile lit his face. The look coiled through her, warming her belly.

"We need everyone at the farmhouse tonight," Landry insisted. "Ronan wants to start filming some of the one-on-one interviews by the pond."

Adria made a noise like a groan that matched the tight feeling in Paisley's chest.

"I can pick up pizzas and bring them out," Jonas offered, and instantly, her chest loosened again, even though she knew Landry wouldn't like it.

Before Landry had a chance to object, Paisley jumped in. "I can go with you seeing as I know what everyone likes." She turned to meet Landry's gaze, offering an olive branch. A compromise. "I'll meet you there."

Landry didn't respond. She couldn't without looking like a jerk, so she just grabbed her bag and headed out to the vehicles waiting to take them back to the farmhouse.

Dylan and Ramona came with Paisley and Jonas to the brick oven pizza place at the end of Main Street. Along the way, people talked to Jonas, smiling and asking about Marco and Cassidy and when the baby was due. It was incredibly sweet, tugging at something deep inside her. She'd never had anything like this. They'd lived in the middle of Orange, inside a gated community, where the neighbors barely acknowledged each other let alone visited along the street.

"You're happy here," she said quietly when they got in his car with the back seat smelling of garlic and basil.

He shrugged. "It took a lot of getting used to. When the college is in session, I don't get stopped every ten feet by people asking about Cass, but during the summer, the only people here are the locals, and they've known each other most of their lives."

"Do you miss Austin?"

"I miss Maliyah and her family, but no, other than that I don't."

"It's hard to believe someone here could be sending the ugly notes," she said softly.

Their eyes met for a pained moment, and he nodded.

When they got to the house, everyone was on the back deck. After being locked in isolation booths all day, Paisley appreciated the wide-open space even though the heat still hung heavy in the air as the sun started to drop toward the horizon.

Landry and Ronan were conspicuously missing.

"Where's Lan? She's not jogging in this humidity, is she?" Paisley asked, worry dripping through her. Landry was pretty much obsessed with working out. Even when they were on tour, she'd never missed a chance to go jogging or take advantage of a hotel gym.

Nikki shook her head. "No, she's down by the pond doing the first interview."

Paisley's gaze followed the tilt of Nikki's head to where someone had placed a pair of Adirondack chairs on the grass near the water's edge. Landry's hands were waving, and it was hard to tell from this distance, but it seemed like there was a smile on her face. Ronan was leaning in and laughing at something she'd said.

It hurt Paisley's heart all over again because she missed seeing her sister this way. Laughing and joking, without the frown that was always there now when she looked at Paisley. She missed the smooth harmony that had been them together.

"You okay?" Jonas asked, handing her a plate with the mushroom and olive pizza she liked without even needing to ask her what she wanted.

She nodded, swallowing back the ache over the widening gap between Landry and her, and sat down on a wicker loveseat. Jonas joined her, and the rest of the band found seats in the chairs around them. As she went to take her first bite, Paisley noted a muscled blond man standing at the corner of the house wearing mirrored glasses reflecting the pond and the sky. His blue suit was completely out of place in the heat.

"Who is that?" she asked.

Fee laughed, "That hunky Captain Avenger is Leya's new Secret Service agent."

Leya blushed. "Keep your voice down, Fiadh. And he's not *my* anything."

"He's only here because of you, I believe that makes him yours," Nikki said dryly.

"My dad's been getting a lot of hate mail from white supremacist groups now that Guy Matherton announced him as his running mate," Leya explained. "And even though it's doubtful the pictures we got are related, my parents freaked out and asked for the Secret Service to assign someone to me."

"I didn't know you could just ask the Secret Service for protection," Jonas said, eyes going wide.

"Key nominees and their families can request it," Leya said, shooting an eye toward the man on the corner. "I don't know what they think he can do that my Garner Security can't."

Paisley's stomach flipped over, and the pizza was suddenly too much for it. She put her plate down, looking out again in the direction of Landry and Ronan. Their faces were serious now, and Landry was looking straight at Paisley where she was tucked up against Jonas, his arm slung over the back of their chair. What were they saying?

Was Landry telling him about her anxiety and stage fright? No. She wouldn't do that. Landry had protected her for too long. Maybe she was simply saying she was tired of carrying around a person who always had to be fixed and had to constantly be reassured.

Stop! she shouted silently at her brain. Landry wouldn't turn on Paisley even if they disagreed about Jonas. One thing—one person—couldn't undo eighteen years of sisterhood, right?

"I think I need to get out of the heat," Paisley said, standing up and almost causing Jonas's plate to hit the ground.

She felt his worried eyes on her, just like the other Daisies, but she just kept moving toward the back door. Normally, if she bailed out of a place and Landry wasn't around, it was Fee who came after her. But tonight she knew it would be Jonas who followed her.

She sat in the spot they'd been at many times that first summer, at the bottom of the staircase, staring at the stunning art on the walls. She knew nothing about art, but Leya did, and she'd said whoever had done these was very talented. Maybe it was Brady's wife who was a well-known painter.

Jonas broke the seal on a water bottle and handed it to her before squishing his large body onto the step next to her. Their shoulders, hips, and knees were aligned. A different kind of heat than the heavy air from outside rushed through her. A fire that grew deep in her belly. A need to have him touching her anywhere and everywhere.

She drank some of the water and then set it down on the floor below them.

"Tell me what's really going on in that beautiful mind of yours because we both know it's not the weather."

She swallowed, beating back her thoughts of him and her and hands on skin, and gave him the truth of what had sent her running from the porch. "It's just everything...Lan and me being at odds. The notes. Ronan." Her stomach twisted. "I don't want to give him my secrets."

"Then don't."

Paisley laughed. "You say that like it's so easy."

"They're your secrets, Paisley, no one else's."

"The entire band is impacted by them. We have this whole stupid routine we have to do just to get me on stage," she said in a rush.

"You aren't the only famous musician with stage fright."

She sighed, tilting her head and placing it on his shoulder. Even though she knew it was true, she wished it wasn't. She wished she had Landry and Fee's confidence. She wished she was just...more."

"You're the reason they have any songs to play at all. You write them. Not Landry or Fiadh or any of them."

"I just start them," Paisley said with a shrug.

He shook his head. "You brought them into this world. They're your creations. You heard the rhythms and words in your head, so why do you let her make so many decisions about the tracks in the studio?"

Because she's smarter than me, her brain shouted, but she knew he'd disagree with it, so she tried to explain it a different way. "It's like how you and Brady see the larger picture, the entwined messages and repeated chords and beats that we can use throughout the album to unify it. I'm too entrenched in the details and the emotions of each song. They're self-contained to me. But Landry...she sees how to make the album a beautiful story. Why would I argue with her? How could I when I can't even see it until she's put it together."

He pulled her finger from where she'd been unconsciously rubbing her birthmark, twining her hand with his, and said, "She's just bringing your vision to life."

"I think you're biased. That song today, about Fee, it wouldn't have even become something we'd put on an album without Landry's feedback."

"Sure, it's like an author handing over their book to an editor who takes the raw words and helps shape them like a jeweler shining a diamond, but it doesn't mean the editor wrote the book. It wasn't their heart and soul on the page."

She didn't know what to say to his words. She often didn't. It was like he saw her in a completely different light than anyone ever had. As if she was already the more she wanted to be.

"Will you do me a favor?" he asked softly, and when she just looked at him expectantly, he continued, "Tomorrow, when they talk about changing something, I want you to close your eyes, shut them all out, and hear the song in your head the way you originally did. Think about how it felt and what it meant, and then listen to what they're saying, and if it changes what it was when you heard it in the beginning, then tell them. Make them hear what you did."

Her fingers tightened on his, and she rubbed his palm like

she often rubbed Landry's rings when she needed to be grounded to the present, to stop the spirals in her head that were screaming things she didn't want to hear.

She wanted everyone in the band to stop treating her like the eleven-year-old who'd first joined them. The child. The little girl. She wanted to be taken seriously. She craved it almost as much as she craved Jonas. But in order to do that, she had to stop letting Landry make all the decisions. She had to shove the voices in her head telling her she was stupid into the closet and try to have the faith in herself that others did.

What would Landry think if she contradicted something she suggested? Would it become just one more thing for them to argue about? Her stomach became a mess of barbed wire at the thought. Was she ready to turn the crack between them into a chasm?

Yes...No...Maybe...

CHAPTER TEN

Jonas

MISS YOU IN A HEARTBEAT
Performed by Def Leppard

EIGHT DAYS BEFORE

The air was already heavy and hot as Jonas walked into town the next morning. His head was filled with images of Paisley, as it always was, but even more so since she'd arrived in Grand Orchard. Instead of just texts and her voice, he now had a million new images of her in his head as well. Images of her with a wide smile and closed eyes as he kissed her, images of her lost in the music as she sang. But he was also filled with her sadness last night on the steps inside the farmhouse. She was a fucking genius rock star and yet she'd been so sheltered, so shoved into a corner by those around her who allowed her demons to box her in, that it was frustrating.

He knew she could shine with confidence if they held her up instead of letting her retreat under the covers. Then, he felt guilty for even thinking of it. It wasn't that he wanted to change her. Fuck, he knew what it was like to live with demons saying you were always wrong...that you screwed everything up.

But she was just so damn breathtaking. She was everything he'd thought her to be as they'd texted for two years, and yet somehow even more. And when they touched...it was like a forest fire burning through them—hot, heady, and full of emotions. It was hard to keep his hands to himself when others were around. It challenged his restraint in a new way.

When he got to the studio, the asshole Larry Wolcott was right at the front of the barrier, chewing his gum, and whistling an annoying tune. He gave Jonas a chin nod and a grin as if they were the best of friends.

"Whatchya got for me?" he asked, and Jonas flipped him the bird.

Larry laughed, snapping a picture.

Shit.

As he was debating whether to say something more, the SUVs with the Daisies arrived, and they all clambered out looking tired and shaken. Except for Landry, she looked pissed, as always. Jonas's stomach churned with concern, and he waited for Paisley to join him.

"What's wrong?" he asked as he grabbed her hands.

"There was another note. This one was waiting for us on the front porch this morning," Paisley said, her voice shaking.

His stomach turned. How the hell did this guy keep leaving things in places that should be secure?

"The picture was of all of us on the back porch yesterday when we were eating pizza. Our faces were all scratched out again..." Paisley said, a shiver going through her that he felt.

"Can we please go inside so we don't give this asshole another shot at us?" Landry said, storming by them.

Jonas walked with Paisley, blocking her from the cameras.

"Trouble in paradise, Jonas?" Larry yelled as they stepped toward the studio, the reporter having picked up the same vibe from the band as Jonas had.

Jonas hated the man. Hated that he epitomized every negative stereotype about the media. There were dozens of reporters there today and yet none of the others were being assholes. Only this one man.

Once they were inside, the band turned immediately to the music, as if they needed the distraction to keep them from thinking of the third note they'd received in as many mornings. A chill went up Jonas's spine that he couldn't quite remove, not even when Paisley's voice filled the air.

After they'd recorded her track, she came out of the booth and a discussion started between Landry and Brady about speeding the song up.

"It just feels like it needs to be faster. As if she's mad at the world for taking this from her," Landry said.

Brady tilted his head. "If it's going after 'Riding the Green,' I disagree, but if we put it after 'The Girl in the Rainbow,' then maybe."

"I think we also need to add more bass and a stronger cadence," Adria said.

Jonas's eyes settled on Paisley. Her finger had gone to her birthmark.

"How did you hear it in your head when you first created it?" Jonas asked her.

His question brought a silence to the room that immediately felt thicker. Heavier. Everyone's eyes had turned to Paisley, and he could almost feel her retreat into herself because of it.

Landry crossed her arms over her chest, but she didn't look as pissed as Jonas had expected her to be with him inserting Paisley into the conversation. "She's not mad...she's...frustrated...lonely..." Paisley's eyes flitted to Jonas and away, swallowing hard. "Aching."

She flushed, a light pink sheen coating her cheeks and traveling down her face. It was adorable, and he craved to touch it. To follow the pink all the way down her neck and farther. All thoughts he should decidedly not be having amid her friends, his boss, and half a dozen bodyguards. Instead, he let a smile fill his face so when her eyes finally met his, she could see how damn proud of her he was.

"More bass, like Adria suggested, then," Jonas said. "But keep the pace as is, right?"

Paisley swallowed, her gaze going to Landry's, and she shrugged. It was only then that Jonas noted Landry's jaw tick, and he wondered, for the first time, if he'd misjudged Paisley's sister. Maybe she was waiting, just like him, for Paisley to stand up and take her place at the helm.

Before anything more could be said, Ramona inserted herself in the middle of the group, her dark hair pulled back in a tight bun. The woman's muscles were as big as Jonas's. She was definitely not someone you would mess with in a dark alley.

"The FBI is on its way. They have questions for everyone about the pictures and whoever might be behind them."

All the pride and joy Jonas had felt for Paisley taking a little bit of a stand was wiped away with the reminder of the asshole who was out there stalking them.

"I guess we'll call it a day then. Jonas, maybe you and I can mess around with the songs we've laid out and see what we've got?" Brady said.

"We need Jonas as well," Ramona said, shooting him an unfathomable look. "He's been in every picture."

His stomach bottomed out as guilt and fear and frustration blew through him. It wasn't that he'd forgotten Landry's accusations about him and his past bouncing back on them, but it wasn't just his face in the images. He wasn't the only one scratched out with a viciousness that screamed fury.

The studio door opened, and Marco and Trevor strode in followed by Leya's new secret service agent and two other men in suits. They led the band up to Brady's office on the second floor where a long table at the back acted like a conference room whenever they needed it. The larger of the two suited men introduced himself as former FBI agent, Cruz Malone. He said he was now a consultant for the FBI on stalkers, because of his first-hand knowledge of these types of cases as well as his in-depth knowledge of the music industry.

"I'm handing out a set of questions to each of you," Malone said. "In addition to answering those, I need you to think about every single person you've ever had any kind of an altercation with. List as many details about the person and the situation as you can, and then we'll take it from there to start crossing them off as potential suspects.

"What about the white supremacists targeting my dad?" Leya asked, voice shaky as her eyes darted to the Secret Service agent.

"The Secret Service has eyes on them as we speak," Special Agent Holden Kent said. "And none of them have been in this area. With the Democratic Convention only a few days away, their activity will likely be centralized there. So, for now, as Malone said, we need to focus on the ties the stalker might have to each of you."

The band turned to the papers they'd been given and started writing. Occasionally, they'd remind each other about different situations that had occurred since they'd first started playing together. "Remember the guy who jumped the stage and kissed Landry? We were in Denver, right? He promised she'd never be anyone else's."

"God, I forgot about that," Landry said, rolling her eyes.

"We should have his information on file already," Marco said, turning to the tablet in his hands and pounding away at it.

"What about the critic you sent the finger to?" Nikki asked.

Landry's jaw ticked, and Jonas could tell she didn't like the fact that so many of the situations they brought up had something to do with her. She shot a look toward Paisley and then over to Jonas. "This all started after Jonas beat up that kid in Austin, right? Or what about his druggie mother? She killed someone, didn't she?"

Jonas stilled as a series of emotions flew through him. His fingernails bit into his palms, and his teeth clenched not only at the question but at the idea that Landry knew so much about him. His eyes went to Paisley's, and hers widened. She shook her head as if trying to tell him that she hadn't told her sister anything, but how else would she have known?

Paisley shot a look at her sister that was as near to anger as he'd ever seen on her face, and when she spoke, the single word was full of quiet rebuke. "Lan."

Landry's chin went up. "This started after he attacked that kid. He's in the pictures, Paise. All of them. Even the ones of the whole band."

The blood pounded through Jonas's ears, hating that she was right. Even as his stomach spun, he denied it. There was no way this was because of him. He'd left Austin and the crowd there two years ago. Whenever he went back to visit Maliyah, he only saw her, Maria Carmen, and her family. Mel didn't even live in Texas anymore.

But then he remembered Artie's brother confronting him last summer in Austin, and his chest tightened.

"I doubt a gang kid from Austin would really give a shit about what was happening here in Grand Orchard." It wasn't Jonas who said the words he was thinking. Instead, it was his brother's voice, defending him, easing his worries. Jonas met Marco's eyes, relief and worry intertwined.

"Still, write it down. We'll double-check he hasn't been in the area," Malone said.

Trevor cleared his throat. "He was in prison. Got out in April and never checked in with his parole officer."

The pen in Jonas's hand fell to the table as he shot Trevor and Marco a shocked look. "What? You've been keeping tabs on him? Why didn't you tell me?"

"There was no reason for you to know," Marco said, eyes turning soft.

Fuck...Everything about that awful day in Austin came back to him. The faded bruise on Mel's face from where Artie had hit her days before. The purple handprint on her arm. The fury he'd felt inside him as he'd taken a CarShare from Maria Carmen's house to Artie's brother's garage.

He'd walked into Smokey's chop shop alone and without a weapon. Artie hadn't even known he was there before Jonas had yanked him up from the tire he'd been installing, thrust him against the wall, and promised to end him if he ever touched Mel again. The actions had done nothing to ease the raw anger inside him.

When Artie had laughed and swung a punch, landing it on Jonas's jaw, he'd swung back. From seemingly nowhere, the asshole had flipped open a switchblade and sliced Jonas's bicep. Jonas hadn't even felt the pain. He'd just been consumed with a desire to bury him. He'd gotten in a lucky kick that caused the knife to go flying, and then they'd pounded the crap out of each other while Artie's brother and his friends had circled them.

If the cops hadn't shown up, Jonas doubted he would have made it out alive.

At the time, he hadn't cared.

It wasn't just Mel he'd been upset about. He'd been full of

hurt and heartache for other things. For the last notice he'd received about his mom's parole being denied. For Maliyah's heart incident he'd thought he'd caused. For finding joy in a shy musician while Mel had been on her own with a chauvinistic pig who used verbal and physical assault to wound.

In the end, he and Artie had both lost Mel because of the fight. After Marco had enlightened her parents about what was happening, they'd hauled her to California, and he'd never heard from her again.

He hadn't known Artie had been in prison. Hadn't cared, and even if he'd ducked his parole, it seemed practically impossible for the weasel to be in Grand Orchard now. But Jonas wrote down everything about the incident anyway, just like he wrote down the incident with Smokey at the taqueria and what the disgusting excuse for a human had said about Maliyah.

His pen shook in his hand when he wrote down his mom's name and the name of the man she'd killed when she'd been high as a kite. She'd left Jonas, bleeding and alone, in the back seat that day while she'd tried to ditch town, knowing she was facing prison time. It was ridiculous when he thought about her running when now she did everything in her power to not get released. She'd even had time added to her sentence for shivving another prisoner.

Every memory sliced at his hidden wounds, but he wrote them anyway. Landry wanted him to be ashamed of his past. But he wasn't. Did he regret some of his actions? Hell yes, but he also knew much of it had been outside of his control. He wasn't responsible for his mom's drug habit at eight. He wasn't the one who'd laid a hand on Mel. And he was working really hard to be a better man. To be one Paisley could look at with pride if she decided to keep him.

He swallowed hard as waves of emotions threatened. He tightened his finger on the pen and continued to write. After long moments of quiet in the room, with everyone scribbling away, Jonas finally looked over at Paisley's paper to see it was blank. He couldn't stop the smile or the chuckle that burst from his lips. "No one, Paise? Really? There's no one you've even argued with?"

"Do you count?" she came back with the quick quip, and that brought another chuckle from deep inside his chest. Paisley flushed and bent her head back to the paper, curling the corners as her bandmates looked on, trying not to laugh themselves. Even Landry looked like she was fighting a rare smile.

Malone collected the papers, and his jaw clenched at the number of names and incidences. The list was pretty damn long. The band was a diverse group, not only in race but sexual preferences, causing prejudiced jerkoffs to say shitty things. And in addition to Leya's dad's politics, Adria's family's company in Colombia had been targeted numerous times.

As the security teams and the agencies dispersed with papers in hand, Marco asked Jonas, "You going to be home for dinner?"

He didn't want to be away from Paisley. Their time together felt finite, whereas his time with his family felt unending, and yet, he also wanted to share her with them. Share them with her. He may not be proud of his real mom, but the opposite was true of the family that had made him theirs. He looked at Paisley and asked, "Would you like to come over?"

That brought the frown back to Landry's face.

Paisley either didn't see it or didn't care as she nodded.

Landry stood up, pushed herself away from the table, and said, "Well, try to keep your faces out of the goddamn cameras at least."

And then she left the room, leaving a black cloud in her wake.

CHAPTER ELEVEN

Paisley

ALL YOU'RE DREAMING OF
Performed by Liam Gallagher

It was late by the time Paisley made it back to the farmhouse. She'd spent a wonderful night with Jonas and his family. She was in awe of the way he'd interacted with his brother's stepson and the love that bloomed between the entire group as if they'd always been together.

Unable to do a voice recording while at their house without embarrassing herself, Paisley had scribbled down words and chords, a harmony inside her that felt like it wasn't finished yet. It was about love in all its forms. Brothers and sisters, mothers and fathers, lovers and friends. It needed work.

It needed something that was dangling outside her grasp. Something that had been pounding through her veins when she and Jonas had shared a heated kiss on the back porch in the shadows of the night. A kiss that had sent twirls of lust through her. She wanted their skin twined together again like it had been the day before in his apartment. No shirts. Maybe even no pants. Only fingers and mouths and bodies touching.

But instead of taking her back to his apartment, he'd walked her to the Escalade where Dylan and another bodyguard had waited to take her home.

She wondered if he was taking things slow because of her lack of experience, or if he, like everyone else in her life, thought she needed to be treated with kid gloves. She hadn't dared to ask him. Hadn't had the courage to demand more. Not yet. But definitely before she had to leave town.

When she stepped into the darkened house, she heard Landry's voice in the kitchen and traveled through to see her on the phone. It was clear she was talking with their mom because Landry had a pained look she only had when on with their parents.

She saw Paisley and a look of relief crossed her face.

"Paise just walked in, why don't you pepper her with questions instead of me."

Landry didn't even wait for their mother's response before handing over the phone and walking out of the room.

Paisley sighed, took a deep breath, and then said, "Hi, Mom."

"Who is this boy?" her mom asked, wariness in her voice, and Paisley's heart fell to her stomach.

"He's not a boy, Mom, and his name is Jonas."

"What does he do for a living?" she asked.

"He's in college, but he got his AA while in high school, so he'll likely be done early."

Her mother harrumphed, and it was as close to approval as she was going to get.

"What is his major?" she asked, and Paisley's blood pressure dropped to almost nothing because she knew her mom wouldn't like the answer.

"Music production."

"Oh, good Lord. That isn't a degree."

"The thousands of people working in the over twenty-three-billion-dollar industry would probably disagree with you." Paisley couldn't help but snip back.

Her mom was quiet for a moment and then chuckled. "Did you just throw numbers at me?" When Paisley didn't respond, she continued, "Min-Ji said you were at his family's house."

Paisley tried not to cringe at the sound of her sister's Korean name on her mother's lips. Names they rarely used outside the family, and were often used when their mother had a point to make. A scold or a lecture or just a reminder that they belonged to something other than the band.

"Yes. They had me over for dinner."

Another hmm erupted from her mother's lips before she asked, "This is serious, then? When do we get to meet him?"

Her stomach sank at even the thought of putting Jonas in the same room with her parents.

"I don't know. I'm not sure what will happen when we're done here," Paisley said, and the words felt like a shot to her heart.

"Well, don't let Min-Ji scare you off. Just because that girl can't focus on anything but the damned band doesn't mean you have to lose your life to it also." Paisley almost laughed because Landry telling their mom about Jonas had sort of backfired. While she didn't want to give her mom hope that she was going to give up her music career anytime soon, she also couldn't handle arguing with her mom about it without Landry to defend her, so she said nothing.

Mom was used to Paisley's silence, especially when there was an argument in the works about her sister, so instead of waiting for her reply, she dove into her next complaint. "When are you coming home?"

Their mother knew the date. It was circled on the calendar

at home, and they'd repeated it multiple times to her, but this was just her way of saying she didn't approve of what they were doing. Or maybe that she missed them. Or maybe both.

"In a few weeks."

"Fine. We will have dinner with the Haks. Joey just started his residency."

Paisley couldn't help the small twitch as she headed up the stairs toward Landry's room so she could give her the phone back. Joey was the man her parents wanted Landry to marry. He was on course to be an orthopedic surgeon—a career choice they certainly approved.

"We can talk about it when we get back. I'll see you soon, Mom."

"Soon, Ji-An."

The phone went dead, and she stared down at the picture of her mom on her screen, Paisley's Korean name hanging in the air like it was the "I love you" they never said but felt.

When she walked into Landry's room, it was to find her sister in her workout gear, pulling her hair back into a ponytail she looped into a loose bun.

"You're going running? Now? It's dark and late."

"It's too hot during the day," Landry said. "Ramona is coming with me. Why don't you come too?"

Paisley met her sister's eyes in the mirror. Paisley didn't like any kind of workout, and she literally despised running, but she couldn't turn it down, not when she saw it for the peace offering it was in Landry's eyes. She groaned, and said, "Okay, let me go change."

She knew she'd regret it when her body was sore and achy in the morning. But maybe it would help ease the ache in her for other things. For Jonas's kisses to turn into something more. For his body to be twined with hers in the most intimate way possible.

She shook herself out of her reverie, donned her workout gear, and followed her sister and Ramona into the darkness around the pond. The full moon was bright, and they barely needed their phones to light the way as they traveled around the quiet expanse. The swans were asleep, but a wind rustled through the tule reeds and branches, adding a quiet music to the night. The smell was strong, wet earth and grass and the ever-prevalent scent of the apple trees.

"I don't hate him," Landry said, breaking the quiet.

Paisley didn't have to ask who she meant. She said nothing.

"But I know in my heart he's the reason this is happening to us."

"You can't know that, Lan. Maybe it's just someone here in town who doesn't like us for whatever reason. Because we're Korean or because you're bi or because of any of the band's ethnicity."

"He's not good enough for you."

Paisley's heart banged more from her sister's words than from running. "Now you sound like Mom. She's planning to bring Joey to dinner when we're back."

Landry snorted. "She doesn't realize Joey is only interested in men. I don't think even his parents know he's gay."

Paisley laughed, and it felt like such a relief after the days of tension between them. It all disappeared though as the house came into view and Landry spoke again.

"Ronan has saved your interview for last. We're going to do a big bonfire next week, and he'll record you then. You should tell him about your anxiety."

Paisley's feet came to a stop, rooting to the ground as a cold took hold that was an absolute contrast to the humid air. "Wh-what?"

Landry stopped pacing in a circle with her hands on her hips. "Plenty of our fans struggle with similar anxiety issues,

Paise. This gives them a voice. A way to connect with us on an even deeper level."

God. This was about the band again. Always about the band. In so many ways, their mother was right. Was there anything Lan cared about more?

"I…I can't…" Paisley barely choked out as an array of emotions tightened around her lungs. Doubt. Hurt. Anger.

"You can, you just won't," Landry said and started walking toward the house, leaving Paisley in the darkness at the edge of the pond.

Those words were sharp and brutal. So like her parents' words when Paisley had struggled in school. *Try harder. Do better. You can, you just don't try*. Tears stung her eyes, falling down her cheeks and mixing with the sweat covering her body.

Landry had been the one to defend her when their parents had said those things. She'd been the one to research techniques to help Paisley with her reading. She'd been the one to find audiobooks and online videos that she could listen to instead of having the letters swim on the page.

Her sister had been the one to believe in her when no one else had…and now that was gone.

Paisley barely held back a sob by putting her hand over her mouth. She squeezed her eyes shut, willing the tears to stop.

"Miss Kim?" Ramona's voice was soft, encouraging her to move out of the darkness, but she wasn't sure she ever would again.

Her phone buzzed in the pocket at her thigh.

Jonas.

That single word allowed her to move her feet again. But every step hurt.

CHAPTER TWELVE

Jonas

WHAT YOU WANTED
Performed by OneRepublic

SEVEN DAYS BEFORE

Jonas was full of anger as he pounded the boxing bag in the home gym at Marco and Cassidy's place as his conversation last night with Paisley swam in his brain. He'd been unable to sleep. Furious with Landry for the words she'd said. He needed to get his anger in check because losing it with Paisley's sister would only prove Landry's point.

He'd thought he had a handle on it after he'd worked out so long his knuckles felt raw, but after he'd showered, he'd come out of his apartment to find a note on the windshield of his Mustang. The image was so dark it was almost hard to see, especially with the cuts in the paper, but he finally realized it was Landry and Paisley in workout gear near the pond at night. They'd gone running, Paisley had said. Gone running and then Landry had torn her sister to shreds, just like this image.

The words on the picture read, "It's going to be over soon. Kiss your happiness goodbye."

He slammed his way into the back door of his brother's house, startling Cassidy and Chevelle and causing Marco to look up from the table with a frown.

He handed the photo to his brother. "Fix this, Marco. Fix it before I lose my freaking mind."

He didn't wait for a response, he just left.

He hated that the stalker was still out there, watching them. Hated that even with the heightened security, the asshole had found more ways to deliver the letters.

He hated even more the puffiness around Paisley's eyes when she showed up at the studio. The entire band was subdued, as if they could feel the tension that had grown between the sisters. He didn't tell them about the note, but he knew they'd hear about it anyway. Instead, he wrapped Paisley in his arms and hugged her as if he'd never let her go.

Over the top of Paisley's head, his eyes met Landry's.

Neither of them said a word, and yet there were volumes being shared.

Swords being drawn.

It was Landry who looked away.

That tense day started several more days of the same. Landry and Paisley were at odds, he and Landry barely tolerated each other, and the more Paisley spoke up in the control room with his encouragement, the more her sister dug her heels in. The band was quiet, the laughter all but disappearing. The music was moody and intense. Brilliant, but dark in many ways.

Fee tried to lighten everything with taunts and teases, but it seemed to fall flat.

And all the while, Ronan was there capturing it all with a

raised brow as if he was getting exactly what he wanted—drama. It made Jonas want to knock him to the ground.

Every day, after they were done recording and the band left the studio, Paisley stayed with him. Sometimes they remained at the studio where she carved out more songs as if the emotions were bleeding from her. Sometimes they went to the farmhouse, sitting on the deck or walking along the pond. Sometimes, they were in his apartment, lost in just the two of them.

Their kisses became more heated. The touches were more desperate. The clothes grew fewer, but he continued to stop them from going all the way. He wasn't sure exactly why. Maybe it had to do with his old insecurities, the need to prove he was more before he claimed her. Maybe it was because he was afraid there wouldn't be anything of himself left if he had her completely, and then she drove out of town.

Every day, more letters arrived to torment them. Some were delivered by mail to the studio or Brady's home. Some were left at Cassidy's café or the other stores the Daisies frequented. Each note was a variation of the others—pictures of the band as they came and went, as well as some of just Jonas and Paisley, with their faces scratched out. The words always threatened their happiness. Even though the entire band was being careful, it was as if whoever was taking the pictures knew exactly where they were going to be at any given moment. The worst for Jonas was when the images caught him and Paisley in an intimate moment, their expressions full of emotions he was afraid to name.

"Putting this on display isn't any different than talking about your anxiety," Landry had said to Paisley. "You're actually showing something more personal, more private here."

Paisley's eyes had darted to where Ronan was recording in the corner.

"I'm not sharing it with anyone, Lan. One creep taking a picture isn't the entire world seeing it."

"It's just a matter of time before one of the dozens of reporters out front catches you," she said and stormed out.

Which only had Jonas doubling his efforts to restrain himself from touching Paisley unless they were completely alone.

♫ ♫ ♫

As the album grew closer to being done, and Paisley's days in Grand Orchard began to dwindle, he started having nightmares about her leaving. In the dreams, Landry was always pulling her sister away, and Paisley had a tormented look on her face, but she wasn't fighting back. She never stayed. It felt disloyal to think she wouldn't fight for him when he saw her struggling more to stand up to her sister. Every day, she offered more and more feedback in the studio, and every day, she held his hand as they left regardless of the glower Landry sent their way.

But it felt like there was something heavy hanging in the air over them that wasn't just the stalker. It felt like there was an ending coming. Jonas's therapist told him it was just his past trying to take over his future.

Maybe.

As he strode down Main Street toward the bakery one morning with his brain full of Paisley and music and their future, he was brought to a stop by an eerie sensation of being watched. Goosebumps traveled over him, and he slowly spun around, searching the street, but he saw no one or anything out of the ordinary. Ten minutes later, when he came out of the shop with a coffee in hand, his skin prickled all over again.

He took a sip and surreptitiously glanced over the top of the cup, noting the people out and about this early. Brady's wife and their kids were dancing along the sidewalk with large smiles and Hannah's shawl flying behind her. The manager of Cassidy's restaurant was writing the daily special on the chalkboard sign. The owner of the antique store was just unlocking the door for the day. There was no one he hadn't known since the day he arrived in Grand Orchard.

His eyes caught on a dark-haired, muscled man in a black T-shirt with tattoos down both arms as he disappeared around a corner. Jonas didn't get a look at his face, but the man could easily have been one of the many new recruits Garner has sent to town who Marco and Trevor were overseeing.

Jonas crossed the street to the studio and hesitated in front of Paisley's bodyguard, wondering if he should tell him. But what exactly would he say? "Man, I got a bad feeling?" It would be ridiculous.

As he reached for the studio door, Paisley emerged, and they both stutter-stepped, eyes meeting. A faint blush hit her cheeks as her gaze settled on his lips, and damn if it didn't instantly make him hard. They moved at the same time until they were standing toe to toe. He bent and placed a soft kiss on her lips, hand traveling to the bare skin at her waist where it had been exposed by another enticing crop top.

"It's always the quiet ones." Larry's voice behind him made Jonas jerk back.

Jonas spun around to find the reporter giving him a slimy grin. He winked, took a picture, and said, "Five grand, Jonas. Another thousand for detailed pictures. Just think, you get to tell the world that you were the one to fuck her first."

"What the hell did you say?" Jonas asked, taking a step toward the man as first disgust and then anger spiked through him. He was so tired of this asshole. So tired of everything. The creep with the pictures. Landry's animosity. The feelings of insecurity whenever he was alone in the dark.

Jonas felt Paisley step closer to him. She placed a hand on his back, as if to reassure him, but it did nothing to slow the roll of emotions growing inside him.

"Are you the one sending the pictures?" Jonas moved toward the man.

Larry's grin didn't even slip as Jonas towered over him. Instead, he said, "Bet she's wild as hell, right? I can just imagine her sweet mouth wrapped around my co—"

Jonas swung, hitting the man straight across the jaw. Larry staggered back, tripping over the edge of the sidewalk and landing on his ass with a grunt. Fury bigger than Jonas had ever felt at Artie swam through his veins as everything they'd been going through came bubbling to the surface in one awful moment.

Jonas stepped over the man, lifted him by his collar, and growled, "You ever come near her or any of the Daisies again, and I'll end you."

The man lifted the camera clutched in his hand and snapped a shot of Jonas's angry face. The man raised his brows with another gross grin. "Told you I'd get a story out of you one way or another. Thanks for the awesome headline. This is going to earn me some big cash."

Jonas ripped the camera from his hand while still holding onto Larry's shirt.

"Jonas! Don't!" Paisley's panicked voice barely registered through the rage rolling through him. He smashed the camera to the ground, and it shattered, pieces going in every direction.

"You're going to pay for that, asshole," Larry grunted, truly displeased for the first time.

The man huffed and puffed as he tried to loosen the hold Jonas had on him. A voice in the back of Jonas's head was screaming at him to stop, but his fingers itched to punch Larry's smug face again. His fist curled just as a hand as large as his own tore him away. Jonas turned his head to find Marco's brow wrinkled in concern.

"Jo-Jo, stop."

With a disgusted shove, Jonas let the reporter go.

Larry scrambled to his feet and yelled, "He owes me three grand for my camera!"

"He's always around, Marco. I want you to check him out. I want you to make sure he's not the one sending the notes," he growled.

Marco's eyes drifted to something behind Jonas, and when he turned around, the rage inside him all but disappeared into a well of shame and regret at the shocked look on Paisley's face. A knife danced through his gut. Behind her stood Landry, and her expression said everything. He'd just proven her point—he was violent and volatile.

His chest tightened and his stomach churned. He reached for Paisley, cupping her cheek just as her sister's voice filled the air. "Don't you dare touch her!"

Landry rushed forward, grabbing his wrist and yanking it away from Paisley.

Paisley didn't say anything. She didn't stop Landry. She just stared, stunned. He wondered if Paisley would finally believe her sister's words. If his nightmare was manifesting itself into a reality where she saw him as an aggressive asshole who would never be able to leave his past completely behind.

"I told you, Paisley," Landry said. Then, as if she'd suddenly realized the scene they were making, she lowered her voice. "Someone who hits will always hit. I don't trust him, and neither should you."

Her words echoed his own thoughts, dragging shards along his already tortured soul.

"I would never hurt her," Jonas growled.

"Me, then? Would you hit me because I piss you off?" Landry

surged into his space, shoving a hand into his chest, and bringing back dark memories Jonas fought daily against. But her sister's reaction seemed to jerk Paisley out of the trance she'd retreated into, and she forced her body between them, saying, "Knock it off, Landry!"

Landry's mouth dropped open. "You're going to defend him?! Still! After he just beat up some photographer."

"You didn't hear what the man was saying..." Paisley shivered. "The awful things..."

"So, it's okay to just beat up whoever says something we don't like? Fee would be in jail if we let her hit everyone who said something inappropriate to her," Landry insisted.

Out of his peripheral vision, Jonas saw Marco hand the reporter off to Trevor before making his way over to them.

"We're going to question Larry at the station, but I don't think he's our guy, Jonas. He's just a slimy reporter, looking for a story," Marco said quietly.

Jonas's insides writhed, shame and despair filling in behind the fury. He couldn't believe he'd let the man goad him into hitting him. He'd given the man exactly what he'd wanted—a story. And now, he owed the sleazebag three grand for a fucking camera. His eyes burned with tears he barely held back.

"I don't want him anywhere near us," Landry said to Marco, darting another glare in Jonas's direction. "He's going to go off the rails and hurt someone, and I refuse to let it be any of us."

"Landry!" Paisley said, worry and a hint of anger filling in the syllables of her sister's name.

"Perhaps we can take this inside?" Marco suggested grimly, glancing around the street and the handful of other reporters who were routinely on the Daisies' beat.

Landry turned on her heel and slammed her way into the studio. Marco followed, but Jonas couldn't move. All the fury he felt was now self-directed. He needed a boxing bag and an hour of beating the shit out of it, and even then, he knew he wouldn't feel better. No amount of self-flagellation could change what had happened.

Paisley touched him gently, hooking their pinkies, and the sweet touch almost unraveled him. She pulled him toward the studio as if he was the one who was fragile and easily broken when he'd always thought it was her.

They'd barely gotten in the door when he dropped his hand from hers. She turned toward him with a pained expression, and Jonas closed his eyes, unable to stand looking at it. He didn't want her to think less of him, to know he really wasn't the better man yet—maybe never would be.

"God, Paisley. I'm so sorry," he whispered, the choke of emotions making every syllable raw and pained.

A soft palm to his cheek drew his eyes back open. She reached down and grabbed his hand again, this time staring at the red knuckles that would be bruised from the hit he'd landed. She brought it up to her mouth and kissed the stinging skin.

He let out a garbled groan. Landry was right. He shouldn't be around any of them. The tears at the backs of his eyes threatened again, and he bit down on his cheek, trying to stem them.

"Jonas," Paisley said, bringing his hand to her chest, opening the fingers until his palm could feel her heartbeat underneath. "You defended me. I've never..." She shook her head. "Thank you."

"Oh my fucking God!" Landry stormed. "You're thanking him! We're going to be all over the news for this. The press is going to rip us apart. He needs to leave, Paisley. Now!"

Paisley flipped around to her sister. "No."

"No?!" Landry's eyes widened in shock. "Paisley, he's a ticking time bomb."

"You have no idea who or what he is, Landry, because you've

not taken one moment to come down from your high horse to get to know him. To understand him."

Landry's arms crossed over her chest. "I know I'm afraid of him."

Paisley laughed. It was dry and sarcastic. "Liar. You're not scared of anything."

Waves of emotions flew over Landry's face. Hurt. Fear. Anger. Loss.

"I never wanted to make you choose. I thought you'd see for yourself, Paise, but he can't stay!"

"I'm tired of you making all my decisions for me, Landry!"

"Because you make so many good ones on your own!" Landry snapped, and as soon as the words were out, Paisley's head reeled back as if she'd been slapped.

Jonas's heart was pounding, and he knew he couldn't let this happen. He couldn't be the thing that tore the sisters apart—tore the Daisies apart. It would eat at him for the rest of his life because, at the end of the day, Landry meant everything to Paisley. She was more than just a sister. She'd been Paisley's dearest friend and biggest champion. He didn't have to like Landry. He didn't have to respect the way she kept Paisley covered in cotton as if to shield her from the world, but he understood to the very bottom of his soul why she did it.

"Landry's right," he said, and Paisley flipped around to stare at him with eyes wide.

"Wh-what?"

"I should leave."

"Don't you dare!" Paisley said.

"Maybe everyone should take five minutes to calm down," Marco said.

The studio door jangled, and the rest of the Daisies filed in and immediately noticed the sisters' upset expressions and the tension in the room.

Fiadh hustled over. "What's going on now?"

Landry threw her hands up in the air. "He hit a reporter, Paisley's defending him, and I've asked him to leave."

Fee's expression would have been comical if the situation wasn't so damn heartbreaking. "Well, hell. I always miss the good stuff."

"Don't even try to make this funny, Fee," Landry growled.

"What did the reporter do that made Jonas hit him?" Adria asked, one drumstick stuck behind her back, the other flipping through her fingers.

Silence filled the room. Jonas wouldn't repeat any of it. Not ever. It was Paisley who spoke with a shiver. "He said some really disgusting stuff. About me...and Jonas."

"I'm a little jealous. I can't tell you how many times I've wanted to slug one of those assholes," Fee said.

Leya nodded in agreement before saying, "The things they've been saying about my dad lately? It makes me want to go all Lara Croft on someone. And it's only going to get worse once Dad accepts the nomination."

"Violence is never the answer!" Landry insisted. "We've worked hard to keep our image positive. To prove our haters wrong. We don't need this shit bringing us down."

The room was silent for a moment, a strained energy that could be felt in every breath.

Nikki rubbed her head, eyes turning squinty. "I'm not sure we're going to get anything done today. Maybe we should let everyone cool down and come back tomorrow?" When the silence persisted, she pressed, "I'd really like things to be calm when my mom shows up tomorrow. She's worried enough as it is."

Paisley took a deep breath, and Jonas suddenly realized she was trembling as she and Landry continued to glare at each other. It broke his heart, and he couldn't stop himself from pulling her to him. It was the complete opposite of what his mind was telling him to do. His mind was screaming to leave. To walk out of her life and let her find someone who wouldn't complicate it. Someone Landry and her band and her family would approve of. But as her face found his chest and her arms surrounded his waist, he felt the shuddery breath she exhaled and knew he couldn't walk out. Not now.

Landry's eyes met his gaze. Besides the disdain that was always there when she looked at him, there was sadness now because, for two seconds, Paisley had chosen him over her.

"I would never hurt any of you," he said quietly, talking to the room, but really the words were meant for Landry.

"I wish I could believe you," Landry replied. Then, she turned on her heel, grabbed her bag, and left the studio.

The others watched Paisley and Jonas for a minute before following her. Only Marco remained, his stance wide, arms crossed over his chest, with his brows still furrowed in concern.

"Do I need to stay?" he asked as if Jonas was going to lose his shit again at any minute, and it added another layer of sorrow and regret to the well of it already inside him. After all they'd been through, Jonas had never wanted his brother to see him lose his cool again.

Jonas shook his head. "No. I'm good. If I'm not, I'll call you."

Marco stared at him for a moment, as if assessing how much he believed Jonas's words, and it knotted his chest even tighter. "I'll head over to the station and see what we can get out of Larry."

As soon as Marco left, Jonas let go of Paisley and stepped away.

"I think you should go with them," he said, every word a tortured truth.

"No," she said vehemently.

"I'm not saying that because I want you to. I'm saying it

because you need your sister, and she needs you, and I don't want to be the thing that comes between you."

Needles pricked his heart. Repeated stabs. If he sent her away now, would Landry convince her of the truth? That he couldn't be trusted? That the boiling anger seething in his veins would always make him a risk? Would his nightmare become the reality?

Doubt flooded Paisley's face, and it pulled at the shredded pieces inside him. He didn't know if her doubt was over her, or him, or both of them, but he despised it. She'd been stepping farther and farther out of her shell, becoming more and more decisive, and he didn't want her to slip backward, thinking she didn't know what was right.

He brought her hand to his lips, much like she'd done with his minutes before, and kissed it. "Go. I need to call my therapist and burn out some anger on a boxing bag. You need to fix this with Landry."

Her eyes filled with tears she blinked back. Then, she spread her palm wide over his chest where she could feel the unsteady rhythm underneath and said, "See. Right there. That's why I'll never fear you, Jonas. You want what's best for me, even at the cost of yourself."

Then, she turned and left, and his heart shredded a bit more from her words and her departure.

CHAPTER THIRTEEN

Paisley

NOBODY'S PERFECT
Performed by Sheryl Crow & Emmylou Harris

ONE DAY BEFORE

When Landry wasn't in the house, Paisley knew she'd gone jogging at the pond. So, she found her way to the shore and sat there waiting for her sister. The swans glided smoothly over the surface, serene and elegant, and she wished she felt the way they looked. She wished the terrible twisting and turning inside her would turn into a blissful calm.

Instead, her heart hadn't stopped its furious pace since Jonas had landed the punch on the reporter's chin. She had this uneasy feeling as if they were all standing atop a cliff, and it was crumbling below their feet. It wasn't just what was happening with her and Jonas. The album was struggling. She and Landry were struggling. The band was suffering because of it all.

Landry's words at the studio weren't all that far off from the truth. Her decisions weren't usually wise.

You're so stupid. Did they suck all your brains out through that mark?

Her finger pressed into her star, deeper, deeper, deeper.

"Paisley?" Landry was out of breath, and her body was sweaty as she came around the last bend. She made her way over, dropping down on the grass next to her.

"You're wrong about him, Lan," Paisley said quietly.

"Maybe. Or maybe you are," Landry said, and it increased the doubts plaguing Paisley.

She didn't think she was wrong. The way she felt about Jonas was how she felt when she knew a song had finally come together. Like all the stars had finally aligned in the right order. Like she'd found something missing that had always belonged to her.

"I don't understand how you can be mad at him for defending me. If you'd heard what that man said..." Paisley shivered again. "You would have lost it too."

"You know how I feel about violence. I'd never hit someone."

Paisley didn't have a response, and a tense quiet settled between them.

"I don't have time for this." Landry got up. "I'm trying to pull together this documentary with Ronan, finalizing the album lineup, and trying not to piss off a creepy stalker. Be with him, don't be with him, whatever. It's obviously your call, and it seems like you've already made up your mind, but I don't have to agree to be around him. I guess it doesn't really matter anyway. We'll be out of Grand Orchard soon, and then we won't have to see him again."

Landry's last words stung the most. The thought of leaving Jonas, of ending what they'd just barely started, was almost too much to bear. Landry seemed to read her mind as she added in a softer voice, "Did you think he'd just give up his life here? To what? Follow after you like a little puppy? Would you even want him to do that?"

Paisley didn't want Jonas to walk away from the people he loved. His job with Brady. The degree he was working on. And yet, she couldn't imagine being without him. She couldn't imagine going days, weeks, or months without feeling his skin sliding against hers. Without feeling their pinkies joined together. Without knowing there was someone standing at her side who only cared about her. Not the band. Not the album or the songs. Just her.

Landry didn't say another word. She just walked away, taking any chance of peace with her and leaving Paisley in even more knots than when she'd sat down.

There was only one place Paisley would find relief now. So, instead of going inside, she went out front and had Dylan take her back to the studio. There, she sat at the keyboard and played until her fingers ached as much as her soul.

The chords and lyrics echoed with conflicting emotions. Anticipation. Expectation. Being Lost. Being Found. First Love. Lost Love. Broken relationships. Anxiety, and fear, and hope. It all poured out of her. And when she was done, she had the last two songs that she'd known were missing from the album, the last act and the big finale.

When she finally became aware of her surroundings again, hours had passed. The studio was dark except for a lamp above her keyboard. A movement in the shadows made her heart race until her eyes adjusted, and Jonas stepped forward. He sat down next to her, twining their pinkies.

They didn't say anything. Not about the reporter, or Landry, or the emotions that raged through them like fire through dry brush. Instead, their mouths met, speaking the words of the song, the rhythms dragging along their veins. Lips and teeth and tongues beat out the patterns and chords until all that was left was the fact that this...this was where they both belonged.

As always, it was Jonas who pulled away, slowing them down, and where she normally would protest, she didn't. Because maybe it was better this way. Maybe they could stay away from their finale by holding on to the bridge longer. Maybe by remaining tucked inside these chords where anticipation and hope still belonged, they could keep the reality of their future at bay.

"You need to play these for them," Jonas said. His voice was full of pride and awe.

She rested her head on his shoulder and spoke the truth that had been hiding in the recesses of her brain since she'd started making music with him at her side.

"I'm afraid if I let everyone hear them, they won't belong to me anymore—to us."

"They might have started out as ours, sweetheart, but the world...the world deserves to hear them. The world *needs* to hear them. They'll make people feel seen and understood. It's a gift you can't keep to yourself."

His words pounded through her, similar in so many ways to what Landry had been saying. But sharing her music was so much easier than announcing to the world she had stage fright and anxiety so strong it paralyzed her at times. She didn't respond. She just sat, looking at the recordings on her phone with their titles all messed up because she couldn't spell and the words shifted on the page, and for the first time in nineteen years, she didn't care.

CHAPTER FOURTEEN

Jonas

SWEET CREATURE
Performed by Harry Styles

With a heart full of sadness mixed with awe and pride, Jonas walked Paisley to her vehicle with Dylan following them. He tried again to convince her to play the songs for the band, and she didn't respond, but he wouldn't push because it had to be her choice. She had to see she could make the right decisions—both with the band's music and with him. Even if he wasn't sure he was a good choice.

Neither his talk with his therapist that afternoon nor the boxing bag he'd beat to smithereens had shed one ounce of the self-reproach burning through him. He was still angry that he'd let the stupid reporter egg him into actions he'd spent two years trying to break.

He bypassed Marco and Cassidy's house, not feeling like he deserved the solace and forgiveness he'd find there. Not wanting to face Marco after his brother had seen him at his worst once again.

Instead, he went to the apartment and placed a video call to Maliyah.

Her chestnut hair was wrapped up in a bun, and her hazel eyes sparkled in a face that was wrinkled and getting more so every day. "*Mijo*! I wasn't expecting to hear from you today."

She'd visited them for his graduation almost two months ago and had looked fine, but today she looked overly tired. Worry flew through him.

"Are you okay?" he asked.

She laughed. "Same old Jo-Jo. My heart is fine. I'm taking my meds. Nothing is wrong with me. Stop worrying so much. It will make your hair fall out."

Jonas ran a hand through his thick hair with a wry grin, knowing he'd never stop worrying about her. Just like she would never stop worrying about him.

"Now, tell me what has you calling me midweek," she demanded.

He didn't know what to say or where to begin. He wasn't really sure why he'd called her instead of going into Marco's place. Maybe he just needed to hear the voice of the person who'd believed in him first, who'd thought he could be something better—something more than his past.

Instead of answering with all of that, he shrugged, and she laughed.

"You've practically become Marco. Neither of you talks."

Marco might not talk much, but he laughed a lot these days. He actually laughed all the damn time with Cassidy and Chevelle and even Jonas. It was like falling in love with Cassidy had taken the guilt of Marco's past and lifted it. As if he and Cassidy carried the load together now instead of him carrying it alone.

When Jonas was with Paisley, he thought he might feel that same way, like together they could weather any storm. Did it mean he loved her? He wasn't sure because he had so little experience with that emotion.

"The Painted Daisies are in town," Jonas finally croaked out.

"Ahh." Maliyah's eyes lit with knowledge. "The girl you've been pining over. Has she broken your heart?"

"You're the one with the broken heart, *Tía*," Jonas groused.

She chuckled. "Don't try to change the subject, young man. What happened?"

Jonas's stomach contracted at the idea of telling her the truth. His fingers pounded out a rhythm on his knees, and then he let out a pained breath before saying, "I got angry and hit a reporter who was saying some ugly shit about her..."

Maliyah's teasing smile disappeared. "Oh, Jo-Jo."

She looked like she might cry, and it added another layer of guilt to the weight that was already upon him. When he didn't say anything else, she asked softly, "Did this frighten her? Your anger?"

Jonas ran a hand over his face, thinking about Paisley's panicked face that had turned to concern for him. "Yes and no. But her sister didn't like me to begin with because of what happened with Artie. This just proved to her that I'm a loose cannon."

Maliyah touched the screen as if she could touch him, and he had to clench his jaw tightly to hold back the tears. If there was anyone who would understand the wounds his past had left in him, it was Maliyah. She'd been a foster kid herself, abandoned and bounced around from home to home until she'd landed with her best friend's family.

"Everyone makes mistakes, *Mijo*. It's the only way we learn," Maliyah said softly.

They were words she'd said to both Marco and him in the past. Words Marco now said to Chevelle whenever the little boy was too hard on himself. But they were words that weren't easy to accept.

"I keep making the same ones," he said, frustration ringing through his voice. "And every time, it costs me something—someone—I care about. Am I any better than her?"

Maliyah was serious in a way that was rare for her. "You are not your mother!"

Every day when he was little, he'd come home from school, hoping that was the day his mom would stop repeating her same mistakes. That she wouldn't get angry and let loose her fists. That she'd give up the drugs and alcohol just because she loved him and wanted to be better for him. Every damn day, he had the same hope, until he'd ended up with a broken wrist and a concussion while she'd walked away, leaving him in a smoking car. Every day, his heart had been shattered, feeling like he was being rejected all over again.

"Don't you see," Maliyah said with love and sadness in her voice because she knew exactly where his head had gone. "By even caring about the mistakes and trying to make them right, it proves you're different from her."

Did it? He wasn't sure if simply wanting to be better than his mom would ever make him so. It was a rabbit hole he'd traveled down many times and still didn't have an answer for.

"Well," Jonas said, swallowing and trying to remove the lump from his throat. "I should get some sleep. It's going to be a long day at the studio tomorrow."

Maliyah stared at him for a long moment before saying, "I love you, *Mijo*. Remember, making mistakes doesn't mean you aren't worthy of love and happiness."

His throat closed, tears swelling again. He had to go before he broke down like a freaking child. "Love you too, *Tía*. Please take care of yourself."

"I will. I don't plan on going anywhere for a long time."

They hung up, and he fell back on the bed in his one-room apartment, glancing at the slew of instruments all over the place that he'd never mastered. More mistakes. Another bad habit in a long list of them. But he had put some of his knowledge of the instruments to use behind the mixing console. Knowing more about them had allowed him to see the way they should blend together. Another favorite saying of Maliyah's was that sometimes you couldn't see the road you were really on because it was disguised by branches and thorns. That sometimes you had to wait until the forest broke to see the path winding down before you.

Maybe that was the problem with Paisley and him. They were in the forest, the brambles clinging to them, holding them back. Maybe they just had to make it to the clearing to find their way out.

♫ ♫ ♫

The next morning, Jonas purposefully delayed arriving at the studio until he knew the band would be in the live room warming up. He didn't want to start something else with Landry, but there was also no way he could stay away. He had to be there if and when Paisley showed the band her new songs.

Instead of Jonas's eyes finding Paisley's through the glass, it was Landry's glower that hit him. She didn't want him there. His heart sank. While he understood her objection to his violence, he also would have thought she'd appreciate someone defending her sister.

Brady's voice brought him back to the control room. "So...I guess more shit went down yesterday, huh?"

Jonas nodded.

"They're all under a lot of pressure. I'm not sure anyone who isn't an artist with a huge following can ever truly understand it. The need to outdo yourself. To make sure the fans get even more than they did the last time. And that's not even throwing in this whole stalker issue. But I've been there too. The idea that there's someone out there who is coming for the people you care about..." Brady's voice choked on his emotions.

Jonas didn't say anything while Brady collected himself. He'd forgotten that Brady had once had a stalker who'd tried to murder his old public relations manager—a friend of the family—someone Brady cared about. There'd even been a shootout at an award show before it had all been over.

He didn't get a chance to respond as Paisley's quiet voice brought his eyes back to the sound room. She was nervous, touching her birthmark. "I know we were going to work on the last song today, that we've pretty much finished the lineup for the album, but..." She shot a look at Jonas through the glass before taking a deep breath and continuing. "But...I'd like to play a couple of new ones to see if you might like to add them in...maybe?"

Damn, he hated that the confidence she'd been finding was suddenly wavering. The new songs weren't just good. They were brilliant. They would weave the album into a story. She'd insisted Landry was the one that made it happen, but he knew the truth. It was all Paisley.

When an expectant silence settled over the room, Paisley looked down at her keyboard, swallowed, and started in. Her fingers were light on the keys, her voice strong and full like it only ever was when she was singing. She glowed. Fucking glowed. The other Daisies were watching her in stunned silence, and Adria's twirling sticks had gone still. But Landry... Landry's face was contorted with a mix of emotions. And suddenly, Jonas realized the truth. Landry loved her sister, needed Paisley, but she was also jealous.

Jonas's body tensed, ready to do battle. If Landry said even one negative thing about the songs, he was going to slam his way into the sound room. He'd never touch Landry. Never. But he wasn't going to just stand by and let her shatter her sister's limited confidence. Not on his watch.

CHAPTER FIFTEEN

Paisley

RUN TO YOU
Performed by Lea Michele

THAT DAY

Paisley lifted her head from the keyboard after she finished the second song and was surprised to find the recording studio completely silent. The air held a strange vibration as if the chords were still traveling through the room. A sea of eyes stared at her. Landry's face came into focus first before Jonas's gaze caught her attention through the glass. There was a mix of pride and awe in both their expressions, and it filled Paisley's chest until it almost burst.

They were good. The songs were really, really good.

She felt it all the way down into the depths of her soul. Paisley had been scribbling away on napkins, notebooks, and school papers long before Landry had formed The Painted Daisies with her friends. And even though this was the band's third album, even though they'd been playing to sold-out stadiums and the music critics had been sending accolades their way, nothing had felt like these songs. Nothing.

Paisley's gaze shot to where Jonas stood by the mixing console. Her insides leaped, and her pulse thrummed as if Adria was still pounding away on her drums. She wished it was just the two of them—her and Jonas—sitting behind her keys so he could kiss her. So he could wrap his arms around her and prove the truth of her words. That love was the only truly meaningful part of humanity's existence.

Jonas's face broke into a huge smile. He shoved a hand through his waves, and then, he put his palm to the glass, fingers wide. Her heart squeezed tight with pleasure and joy. It was as if she could feel the pressure of his hand on her chest where it had lain multiple times as he listened to the rhythm of her heartbeat. If there hadn't been an entire room between them, she would have met his palm with hers and let the emotions of the songs fill the space between them with the sense of coming home.

"Holy shit, Paise!" Landry's voice broke the quiet that had settled over all of them, drawing Paisley's eyes back to her sister. Even though she could hear the admiration in Landry's gritty tone, guilt swarmed through her at the hurt on Landry's face. Paisley had never finished any of their music on her own before. She'd never gotten all the way to playing them for the band without her sister having had a say in them.

Except...she hadn't been alone with these songs either. She just hadn't been with Landry.

"We'll have to move everything around," Landry said, tapping the rings on each of her middle fingers together in thought. She swirled to look at the handwritten track list scrawled on the whiteboard that she and Brady had been agonizing over.

Fiadh bounced over to Paisley, slinging her arm around her shoulders.

"Little Bit, love sounds good on you!" Fiadh laughed. Paisley felt her skin flush as she shot a glance at Jonas in the control room. Relief settled through her when she realized Jonas hadn't heard. Instead, he was deep in discussion with Brady.

"She's right," Leya said, eyes darting to Landry who was still assessing the album's tracklist. "These are your best songs yet. You and Landry outdid yourselves."

Landry whipped around to face them. "I had nothing to do with them. They're all Paisley."

Maybe it was just Paisley's guilty conscience that heard the quiet rebuke in her sister's tone, but she didn't think so. This was just one more thing to pile onto the tension between them.

Sensing the friction, Adria twirled her sticks and climbed out from behind her drums to tuck her arm through Landry's. Her gaze flickered to Paisley with a slight frown, but it was Nikki who actually spoke.

"Love is in the air, Lan. Get ready for a whole slew of new songs."

Nikki's tease sent Paisley's heart into overdrive, and she shot yet another glance toward the glass. Her stomach flipped because it was obvious Jonas had heard this time. His grin grew, and he winked at Paisley—a damn wink that said *I told you so*. A wink that should have annoyed her but really just made her melt inside until she was nothing more than a boiling pot of desire.

Brady strode into the room, excitement radiating from his face. "Okay, with the first song, I think we should start with just Paisley's voice. Then, after the second measure, I want Adria to come in on a gentle beat with the tom-toms. Every two measures, we'll add another instrument. Leya's sitar, followed by Fiadh's banjo, then Landry and Nikki on guitar before Paisley finally joins in on the keyboard. Do we want to try it or just start laying tracks?"

It was Fee who laughed and replied, "I think we should try it a few times together before we start recording anything."

He shrugged, "Sometimes, just going with it is better than anything you could plan."

While everyone went to grab their instruments, Paisley shot another smile in Jonas's direction. Landry stepped in front of her, breaking her view.

"Are you really just going to forget everything that happened yesterday?" Landry whispered, her disappointment pounding through each syllable.

Paisley's heart grew heavy. She hated that being with Jonas was causing this rift between them. So, instead of replying with words they'd both regret, she turned back to the music and the suggestions Brady had made.

♫ ♫ ♫

Paisley's voice was scratchy by the time she came out of the iso booth hours later. She was surprised to find their manager Tommy had been joined by their label owner, Nick Jackson. Nick hadn't shown up for a recording since their first album, and she wondered what had dragged him all the way from New York City. Whereas Tommy looked like an aging rock star, Nick looked like a banker in a perfectly pressed gray suit with short brown hair that was graying at the temples and a clean-shaven square jaw.

Tommy, Nick, and Brady were in deep discussion with Landry about the new songs and the track order. Watching her sister in action was usually impressive, but today, it only made her knotted stomach twist more, wishing she could somehow fix everything between them.

Jonas appeared at her side, offering a gentle smile along with the cup of tea he'd brought to soothe her achy vocal cords. Before he'd entered her world, all Paisley had wanted to do after a day of recording was find a quiet space where silence would be her only companion. But now, all she wanted was to lose herself in Jonas.

"You ready to get out of here for a while?" Jonas asked.

Paisley nodded, and Jonas joined their fingers. When she looked down at them, she could see how different they were in size and shape and color, and yet it felt as if they were perfect this way—with his enormous hand dwarfing hers.

"Where are you going?" Landry's voice halted them near the door.

"To Jonas's," Paisley said, not quite meeting her sister's eye.

"Nikki's stepmom is here, and Ronan and his crew will be at the farmhouse at eight for the bonfire. I need your help setting up," Landry said, the admonishment ringing through her words as she took in Paisley's fingers twisted with Jonas's.

Jonas bristled, shoulders going back, and Paisley knew he was mere moments from exploding again. She couldn't handle it right now. She was too exhausted from the hours she'd been at the keyboard and still too battered and bruised from the harsh words that had gone unforgiven between her and Landry.

"I know. We'll be there," Paisley promised.

Landry left the men, crossed the room, and lowered her voice so the others couldn't hear her.

"Maybe it would be better if Jonas didn't come," Landry said quietly. "We'd hate for him to hit one of the film crew if they accidentally said something wrong."

"Lan!" Paisley exclaimed right as Jonas growled, "Fuck you."

Landry just glared, as if his outburst proved her point.

"At least I actually *want* to make Paisley happy," Jonas said, voice dark with emotions he was trying to hold back.

Landry stepped even closer until she was almost nose-to-nose with Jonas. "What the hell are you insinuating?"

"I don't think I need to spell it out for you," Jonas snapped.

"Stop!" Paisley cried. She loved that they were both trying to protect her in their own way, but it only made the chasm between them widen further. "This isn't helping. We need to talk. All of us. But not today. Not now, when everyone's tempers are still high."

She pushed Jonas in the chest so he moved backward toward the door. She could hear the tapping of Landry's rings banging out her frustration and worry behind her, but she didn't turn around. She just headed for the exit with Jonas.

"I refuse to let you ruin your life with one wrong decision, Paisley," her sister's voice followed them.

Her grief turned to burning hurt and anger as Landry's words hit every single sore spot in her soul. She'd almost forgiven Landry for the words said in the heat of the moment the day before about her decision-making. But today, they were so much worse because Landry knew what she was saying, knew how they'd make her feel, and she'd still said them.

Paisley dropped Jonas's hand and spun around. "Wrong decision?! How could you, Lan? Just because my decision isn't the one that makes your life easier, doesn't mean it's wrong. I know what makes me happy. I know who I want at my side, and if you don't like it, then you don't have to be a part of it."

Landry's eyes widened at Paisley's passion as much as at the words. Paisley regretted them instantly, wishing she could take them back, but she wouldn't, not with Landry still shooting venomous looks in Jonas's direction.

"Paise," she said, her tone only slightly regretful. "You don't understand."

"No. *You* don't understand. Because Mom is right, you've

never cared for anything more than you've cared for this band. Stay out of my personal life! You no longer have a say in it."

Then, Paisley turned on her heel and stormed out with Jonas right behind her. As soon as the door of the studio slammed shut, the bitter remorse building inside her escaped in a quiet sob. Paisley had never struck out at Landry that way before, and it hurt. It had stung not only Landry but Paisley too. She didn't want her sister out of her life in any way, shape, or form.

Jonas caught up to her, pulling Paisley into his chest and wrapping a muscled arm around her. He kissed the top of her head.

"Paisley, I'm sorry," he said, knowing he'd pushed when she'd wanted to run. But maybe that was the problem. Maybe she'd been running and hiding for so long that no one else knew how to see her as anything but the person in the shadows.

Paisley rested her forehead against his chest, arms going around his waist as he tugged her closer, the husky male scent of him filling her senses and making her feel safe and warm. She lifted her chin, stood on her tiptoes, and pulled his face toward hers, letting their lips touch as she'd been longing to do since she'd first played their love song for the band hours earlier.

The moment their mouths touched her veins flooded with heat. This was no slow build, just a complete and utter longing that raged through her. Desire so strong she forgot everything except how good it felt to have their bodies aligned with his soul calling to hers. At first, Jonas barely returned her kiss, but when she darted a tongue along his seam, he let out a guttural groan before devouring her completely. Lips and teeth and tongue battled with hers as if trying to own her in some deeply primitive way that Paisley should have hated but only loved.

A loud cough interrupted their fiery embrace, followed by Dylan saying, "Perhaps we should take this inside, away from any potential cameras."

Paisley's eyes opened to find Jonas's filled with more regret. If their heated kiss ended up on some website—or worse, in another scary note—it would be just one more thing for him to feel sorry about.

But this hadn't been his fault. This had been all her. She gave Jonas a soft smile and said, "Sorry I attacked you in broad daylight on the street."

He didn't return the smile. Instead, his eyes darted around, as if searching for the asshole photographer, or the stalker, or both. She grabbed his hand and tugged him in the direction of his apartment. She needed to be alone with him. She needed to fill herself with the sense of belonging, of being seen, of being adored that only Jonas had ever given her. And this time, she didn't want it to end until they'd lost every single article of clothing and twined themselves together from head to toe in the closest way possible.

She wanted this. She wanted him. No...she *needed* him. Like the dark needed the sun to push away the shadows. It was time they gave in and found the crescendo that had been waiting for them for years.

CHAPTER SIXTEEN

Jonas

DREAMS
Performed by The Cranberries

Jonas's heart continued to feel shredded as he led Paisley into his apartment. But as he turned from the door to take Paisley in, he couldn't keep the hope from slowly curling through him. There was an unshakeable truth she'd sung about in her lyrics. They fit. They blended together. The jagged pieces of their souls had collided, finding a home. It was as if they'd been two lost scraps drifting in the breeze until the wind had blown them together.

She watched him as he took a step toward her. A tendril of her hair had escaped her clip and fallen in front of her eyes, hiding some of the emotions swimming there. She was completely still, shoulders back, gaze heated, but he also knew she was nervous because her index finger had landed on her birthmark.

"Paisley." Her name came out as an agonized groan, unsure

of what was the right thing to do. Push her away or pull her close.

And then, he didn't have a choice because her body collided with his. Her arms went around his neck, and she stood on her tiptoes to join their mouths together just like she had on the sidewalk. Heat traveled through him, curls of desire leaving a heady trail as it worked its way through every vein and nerve ending until his body was standing at attention, ready to surrender after the frenzied battle with passion and restraint he'd been waging for days.

He put his arms around her waist, lifted her with ease, and set her on the counter in the bite-sized kitchen. Standing between her legs, he trailed his fingers and mouth down her face, her neck, and her chest. He swooped aside the tank top she wore that barely hid the pink Sweet Memory daisy tattooed there and lavished a taut nipple with his tongue. Paisley moaned, arching into him, hands mussing with his hair before she reached for his T-shirt and tugged.

He stepped back, lifting his shirt from the back, pulling it off, and tossing it aside. Then, he lifted her tank and did the same, unhooking her bra before sliding their bodies back together and relishing in the perfect warmth of their skin gliding together.

Their mouths fused hungrily, tongues seeking their inner recesses while fingers explored. The air grew heavier, thicker, fuller. She moaned and the sound had him straining against his jeans, the pressure almost unbearable.

"Take me to your bed, Jonas," Paisley demanded, her voice deeper than he'd ever heard it before. More like her sister's than her own soft one.

He rested his forehead on her chest, eyes closed, listening to the rhythm of her heartbeat.

"No," he said quietly.

She drew his chin up, searching his face with eyes that ached. "Why?"

He couldn't voice all his reasons for stopping them. Fear of losing her. Fear of doing something she'd hate him for. Fear that her friends and sister would hate him even more. Fear that was ridiculous. He didn't know one heterosexual man his age who would have said no to Paisley's demand. They would have simply fucked her senseless. And maybe that was yet another of the many reasons he wouldn't. He refused to be just some damn guy who screwed her until she screamed.

Not that he was sure he could even make her scream. He wasn't sure he could even last long enough to give her the climax she deserved. But that wasn't the point, and he couldn't voice any of those fears, so he said the one thing that was closest to the surface. "I'm not going to make love to you just so you can spite Landry."

He regretted it as soon as he said it.

She inhaled sharply, pain hitting her eyes, and then she was pushing him away. She jumped off the counter, retrieved her clothes, and reassembled them on her body all while he watched.

When she lifted her beautiful eyes to his face, they were no longer soft. They were hard and angry, but she was still painfully quiet when she finally spoke.

"You really think I'd do that to either of us?" she demanded, hands on her hips, looking very much like some fiery sprite. "Bring her anger into this with us?"

He ran a hand through his hair, wondering how he was going to get out of this without pissing her off or leaving more wounds on her heart.

"I think, right now, you want to prove she's wrong."

Her eyes closed and opened almost as if the words had been a slap to her face. "She is. But that isn't why I want this. I want this because I never feel like I'm truly home until you're touching me. I want to know what it feels like when you're fully inside me and our bodies become one. I want to find the end of the song we've written together. There's no reason to keep stopping us."

He swallowed hard, her words echoing what he'd been thinking moments before and settling into his heart like a Band-Aid over cracks that always seemed to bleed. But he reminded himself of the harshest truth. The number one reason he refused her. He simply wasn't sure he was the man she deserved. Not yet. Maybe never. Right now, he was still a broken kid who tended to ruin everything he touched with roiling anger.

He had so much work to do before he became...something worthy. He wasn't sure he'd ever get there, but he wanted to try because Paisley Kim...she was his whole world. A shiny star in a sea of dark. She brought so much damn beauty into his life that it physically hurt, and he wanted to make sure he could give her the same thing back.

Paisley closed the distance between them, drawing his hand into hers, aligning their palms.

"Two years, Jonas. I've missed you...wanted this...for two years. And now that we're here, this close, I don't want her to be the reason we aren't together." Paisley shook her head, tears filling her eyes.

Jonas swallowed. "We barely knew each other then, sweetheart. And now...now I've got a lot of things to work on, and I think you know that as much as Landry does."

"We belong together. We're two pieces of a whole. You need me to ground you, and I need you to lift me up," Paisley said quietly, eyes begging him to admit the truth. "She shouldn't be able to take that from us."

He nodded. Unable to see the pain in her eyes without touching her, he pulled her close and held on tight. "She won't.

But you have to remember, she loves you too. She loved you first, and no matter what I said back there, she does want what's best for you."

"Only if it's what's best for her as well," Paisley said, and it sounded sad and tired, as if she couldn't fight the world one more second.

"I don't think you really believe that."

They were silent for a long moment, and Jonas tugged her toward the couch. When he got there, he pulled her onto his lap, and she rested her head on his chest. They sat that way for a long time, just listening to each other's heartbeats as the sun slanted across the sky and the room grew dim.

After what felt like days, she finally broke the quiet, asking, "Do you remember the very first argument we had about ABBA?"

He laughed softly. "I still think they're shit, but if Brady's daughter heard me say that, she'd skewer me alive."

"Normally, when someone challenges me, I can't breathe. I can't talk. I freeze. It's like I'm a deer caught in the headlights. But with you...all the thoughts inside of me pour out easily. Freely. That first time we argued, you just stared at me as if my words were awe-inspiring, revolutionary. It was like you could actually see me. The real me. The one who's afraid to be onstage and has anxiety attacks, and sometimes can't even speak when someone asks her a question."

Jonas hated her anxiety almost as much as he hated the way she doubted her opinions were valid. She had so much to say, so much talent to share, and yet she'd always hidden it behind Landry because she'd been afraid to step out of the shadows. She deserved more than the sliver of light the band shined her way. Landry was pissed that Paisley was starting to see that. It challenged the status quo. And when that happened, there were always arguments. Adjustments. He had to believe they'd get through it though, because they loved each other.

Pounding on the door caused Jonas's eyes to fly in that direction, cutting him off from saying anything more. He dragged himself up, threw on his T-shirt, and opened it.

Trevor stood there, frowning.

"Hey," Jonas said, his brow furrowing as concern flew through him.

"Dylan went back with Landry, so I grabbed a car to take you to the farmhouse for the bonfire," Trevor said.

Jonas looked back at Paisley waiting on the couch. "We gotta go, Paise."

She flicked her eyes to the darkened windows and jumped up. "Crud. How late is it?"

"You still have time," Trevor answered.

"But Landry needed help setting up," she said, regret filling her tone because even still angry and upset with her sister, she hated letting Landry down.

Jonas followed Paisley as she all but ran down the steps after Trevor. Once they were loaded into the SUV and headed out of town, Paisley ran a hand through her long hair, as if trying to straighten it, before pushing into her birthmark with her fingertip. He could almost feel the nervousness crawling through her veins as if it was its own entity. This was more than just concern about Landry. She was worried because she was supposed to talk with Ronan again tonight, and she hadn't decided whether to tell him about her anxiety and stage fright or not.

Paisley's phone started to blow up just as Trevor's did the same thing in the front. Ping after ping.

"What is it?" Jonas asked.

"Oh my God," Paisley said, color draining from her face as she flicked through the messages.

He pulled her close, pulse quickening. "What's wrong?"

"Adria's sister was kidnapped!"

Jonas's eyes met Trevor's in the rearview mirror, dread curling through him.

"Her dad received a ransom note, and the detail has taken Adria to some undisclosed location because he's worried that whoever did this will come for her too."

Goosebumps littered his skin as Paisley turned to him with panic written on her face and her hands trembling.

"Leya's gone to D.C. early for the convention, and Fiadh has something to tell us about Nick's label." Her eyes filled with tears. "What on earth happened after we left this afternoon?"

Jonas's stomach spasmed. In a ridiculous series of blows the band was teetering and Paisley right along with it. He struggled to quell his nerves, to find a sense of calm so he could be the stable ground beneath her feet. He tugged her into his chest and wrapped his arms around her.

When they pulled up in front of the farmhouse, there was a van there. Ronan had brought in a film crew for the bonfire, and they were unloading equipment in the near darkness with only the porchlight illuminating the drive. He lifted his chin in their direction as Paisley and Jonas slid out of the back of the SUV.

Ronan sauntered over to them with an unnecessary beanie covering his hair. Jonas's stomach tightened, hating his arrogant assuredness. Hating that this man would have no qualms asking Paisley questions that would upset her even more—all for the sake of his damn film.

"Hey, no one answered when I knocked. Wasn't sure what was up. I kind of expected everyone to be here primping," Ronan said, gray eyes twinkling and lips twitching as if he'd said something hilarious.

"Only Landry and Nikki are here at the moment," Paisley said, finger pushing into her star. "There's a lot going on."

Ronan frowned, waiting for her to explain, but she didn't. She turned and ran for the front door instead.

"We'll just head over to the pond and get things set up," Ronan called after her, his brows bent in confusion.

Jonas jogged after Paisley, and if he hadn't been right behind her, he wouldn't have seen her stiffen or seen the shiver that went through her.

"What?" he asked, and when she didn't move, when she continued to stare at the door as if it was a ghost, he moved around to see what had caused her to go numb.

There was a picture taped well below the handle, as if someone had been ducking out of the camera's view while sticking it there. It was of Jonas and Paisley from that afternoon as they'd left the studio and locked lips in the middle of the street. The image had words scrawled on top of it. Words that were running in deep red and turned Jonas's stomach.

You'll die before I let you be happy.

The red dripped into the two deep grooves carved into Jonas's and Paisley's faces.

Emotions swam through him so fast it was hard to capture them. Fear. Panic. Anger. Disgust. And then back to fear. Regardless of everything else going on with the band tonight, this...this seemed to be about them.

CHAPTER SEVENTEEN

Paisley

GONE AWAY
Performed by The Offspring

The blood dripping from the image of Jonas and her made her stomach lurch.

Whoever was doing this had been there on the street today. Watching them. Filming them. Why hadn't their security seen them? Why was this happening at all?

Landry!

Paisley grabbed the handle above the picture and thrust open the door. "Landry! Nikki!" she called into the quiet of the house.

There were a few lights on, a lamp in the downstairs living room and the can lights in the kitchen, but other than that, the house was still and shadowy.

"Landry!" Paisley cried again, scrambling for the stairs with Jonas and Trevor right behind her. She threw open the door of her sister's room with her pulse hammering. It was empty, but the outfit she'd had on earlier was tossed on the bed, which meant she'd been there.

Knowing Landry, she'd gone for a run around the pond. It was late and dark, but that hadn't stopped her the other night. Paisley turned to leave and saw Trevor throwing open other doors, calling for Landry and Nikki.

She heard Nikki's voice, groggy and startled. Paisley raced down the hall just as Nikki sat up in bed wearing nothing but a camisole and underwear. There was a glazed expression on her face that she often had when fighting her migraines.

"Have you seen Landry?" Trevor demanded.

Nikki shook her head, wincing.

They all ran down the stairs, searching the other rooms.

Later, Paisley would doubt what had sent her out the back door. It was as if she heard Landry calling her but from far away, like through a crowd that was loud and clamoring.

She flipped on the porch lights, stepped out onto the wooden slats, and rushed to the edge, searching the darkness. There. Down by the pond, a soft light like a phone glowed. Thank God.

"Landry!" Paisley called in relief.

She flew down the stairs and out toward the water. As Paisley drew closer, fear started to drift back in. The phone was on the ground, and a dark mound lay beside it.

"Landry..." Paisley called softly this time as her skin broke out in goosebumps, even though the night was hot and humid.

"Lan," Paisley called.

She was near enough now to know it was actually Landry on the ground. The bright-yellow sneakers she'd had made to match the Golden Butterfly daisy the world associated with her were glowing in the darkness. But Landry wasn't moving. She just lay there.

Paisley's vision blurred, ice filled her veins, and she had to force herself past it in order reach down and touch Landry's shoulder. "Lan..."

Her sister sagged, and that's when Paisley saw it. The blood. The gaping wound at Landry's neck. The unfocused, staring eyes. She screamed. She screamed Landry's name. She screamed at the horror. She screamed and screamed and screamed.

Strong arms wrapped around her waist, and she fought against them before Jonas's deep voice spoke near her ear, "I got you, Paise. I got you."

Trevor appeared, stepping around them and grabbing Landry's wrist, checking for a pulse before blocking Paisley's view of her sister. But even with Trevor's muscled torso in front of her, all she could see was Landry's face and the dark, gruesome cut on her neck.

Paisley's voice was hoarse. Was she still screaming? The screams turned into violent sobs as she pushed her face into Jonas's chest.

"God, Paise. Jesus... Trevor, what the hell?" Jonas's voice broke with raw emotions.

Trevor put his arms around them both, hugging them tightly as if he could somehow take away what they'd seen. Make it better. Fix it. Fix her sister.

She dragged herself away from them both, somehow fighting off their muscled arms. She fell to the ground, hands pushed to her stomach as she knelt at her sister's side. "Landry... Don't leave, Landry. I'm sorry. I'm so sorry. I love you. I love you! Do you hear me? God. Please don't die."

CHAPTER EIGHTEEN

Jonas

EVERYBODY HURTS
Performed by The Corrs

Jonas's chest was on fire, agony ripping through him at Paisley's pained cries. Her tortured words. He wrapped his arms around her, lifting her from where she'd collapsed next to her sister.

Paisley kicked out. "Let me go."

"Paise, come away. You can't. You don't want to see this. Come away." His voice was crammed with tears. For her. For Landry. For all of them.

"Make her live, Trevor! Make her live. Get the ambulance. The doctors. Make her live!" she screamed at Trevor standing in front of her sister's body, blocking them from the gruesome sight. But it was too late. It was burned into his irises.

Jonas carried Paisley away, taking her back toward the house.

At the top of the porch steps, Nikki waited, hand to her mouth, horror in her eyes.

"No... No!" Nikki said, shaking her head, fear and sorrow echoed in her words. It made Paisley's tight body crumple into violent sobs in his arms.

Jonas grabbed Nikki's hand, pulling her into the house with them.

He set Paisley down on the couch in the front room, and Nikki collapsed next to her, hugging Paisley to her chest like Jonas wanted to do.

Ronan stood there with his crew behind him, cameras rolling, as sirens ripped through in the air.

"What is it?" Ronan asked, looking at Jonas with the most serious expression on his face he'd ever seen on the man.

Jonas shook his head. He had no words to describe what he'd seen, especially not on camera.

"Turn the fucking cameras off," Jonas said.

Ronan bristled. "We're here—"

Jonas reached over to the man holding the camera next to Ronan and placed a hand over the lens. "Turn the fucking cameras off before I toss them all in the pond."

Jonas's voice was laced with both threats and promises. Ones he would absolutely follow through on just as he had with Larry the day before. The cameraman looked to Ronan, and Ronan nodded. The camera light went out, and Jonas turned back to Paisley and Nikki.

He fell at Paisley's feet, grabbed her hand, and put it on his cheek. "Paisley. I got you. I'm here."

Paisley's eyes lifted from Nikki's chest. They were red-rimmed and tortured. Her voice almost disappeared as she whispered the words, "That picture on the door... Is this our fault? Did that happen... Did he think she was me?"

Jonas's heart clogged his throat, making it hard to breathe. He didn't know what to say. He didn't know the right answer. Thoughts of the blood dripping from the photograph and the image of Landry's neck sliced open caused his stomach to lurch, threatening to let loose everything he'd eaten at lunch.

The house filled with police and the Daisies' security team. Marco strode through the room as if he owned it, the other security detail making room for their leader. His face was impassive until he saw Jonas, and then relief filled it, dark eyes meeting his. "Thank God, you're okay."

But his words caused Paisley to convulse, and a wounded cry ripped from her because her sister wasn't okay. Her sister was dead.

Marco looked regretful, rubbed a hand through his hair, and then tilted his head at Jonas toward the kitchen.

Jonas looked at Paisley and Nikki huddled on the couch, tears pouring down their faces. "I'll be right back, Paisley. I'll be right in the kitchen."

He didn't know what else to say. He didn't know how else to help, except to let her know he was there. That he wasn't going anywhere.

When they got to the kitchen, Marco wrapped Jonas in a hug that was tight and hard, as if he was afraid to let him go, and Jonas hugged him back equally as hard. He needed his brother's strength to wash off on him so he could be strong for Paisley.

"Jo-Jo," Marco said.

"Where the fuck was her security?" Jonas said into his shoulder.

"Ramona's dead too," Marco said quietly. "Trevor found her."

Fuck.

"I'm going out there to help with the investigation. You going to be okay in here?" Marco asked.

Jonas nodded even though he wasn't sure it was true.

Marco squeezed him one more time and then left out the back. Jonas turned around, heading for Paisley, as the front door burst open, and Fiadh rushed in. Tommy and Nick were at her side with some man in a suit Jonas had never seen before.

Fiadh's wide eyes met Jonas's.

"Tell me...just..." Her voice trailed off as she saw Paisley and Nikki wrapped together, weeping.

Fiadh's throat bobbed as she whispered, "Lan..."

Jonas swallowed hard, and the words came out like a croak. "She's...she's dead."

Tears filled Fiadh's eyes, and then they were pouring down her face as she joined the other two women on the couch, locking them in a fierce embrace.

"Fuck," the man in the suit said, flicking his hand over his jacket as if brushing off lint. He looked at Nick and said with a blandness that seemed completely out of place, given the situation, "I guess that discount I asked for is going to be back on the table."

Nick blanched but ignored the man. Instead, he turned to Ronan and the crew. "I think it's best if you leave."

"We don't want anyone going anywhere," a police officer said from behind them. "Everyone who was on the property needs to stay put until we have a chance to debrief them."

In the officer's hand was the picture that had been on the door—the picture of Paisley and Jonas with their faces scratched out in blood.

Despair sliced its way through Jonas's heart. Was Paisley right? Had Landry been killed because of them?

♫ ♫ ♫

The minutes ticked by, each one an eternity, while the agents, officers, and crime techs scoured the property and the scene by the pond. Hours went by before Jonas saw the black body bag being wheeled toward the coroner's car. He blocked the windows as best he could, refusing to let Paisley have even one more awful image to add to her nightmares.

With Leya and Adria miles away, the three remaining Daisies huddled together on the couch in grief. Paisley's tears hadn't stopped and every sob, every hiccup, tore a new hole in Jonas's soul. But every time he tried to join her on the couch, she burrowed further into her friends' arms, and he felt the vice grip on his heart tighten another notch.

She blamed him. She blamed them. The pictures were of them.

Fuck.

Was this really Artie?

Was this really because, once upon a time, he'd tried to be the hero? Had it turned him into a villain instead?

Jonas wasn't even sure Paisley had registered Fee telling her that Nick had sold Lost Heart Records to the asshole in the suit who'd arrived with them. Asher Riggs stood, cold and aloof, talking on his phone as if he didn't give a damn as the band's entire world crumbled.

An officer approached Nikki, said some Professor was there to see her, and asked if she wanted him to send the man away. Nikki turned a wide-eyed gaze toward the open front door and the sea of officials who'd been pouring in and around the property. She hesitated before pulling herself from the couch and joining the man on the porch. As Jonas watched from his sentry at the window, the two had a hushed conversation. The man, who looked like some Indiana Jones throwback with a bow tie, turned panicked eyes toward the door and pushed up his glasses with a long finger. When Nikki went to turn away, he grabbed her arm, saying something else as he passed her a small package she tried to refuse, but he practically shoved it into her hands.

Nikki looked like she would have thrown it at the man if the arrival of two more people hadn't stopped her.

"Mom!" Nikki cried, rushing down the steps to all but fall into the arms of a tall woman with brown hair drawn back in a tight bun. The older man with her had a buzz cut and a frame that screamed military. Neither of them looked anything like Nikki.

"What's happened?" the man's voice boomed through the open doorway.

The question rebounded through the living room, and it turned Paisley's cries frantic again. Jonas's heart almost imploded at the sound, and as he stepped toward her, she pushed away from Fee to throw up on the thick rug.

Everyone stood there dazed for a moment, and it was Nikki's mom who suggested someone get an EMT to give her a tranquilizer. Jonas could only watch as the needle sunk into her skin, and she drooped into Fiadh's arms.

The silence that followed her tortured cries was almost worse.

It was broken only by Tommy's voice and the anguished words he spoke into the phone as he placed the call no one ever wanted to make to Paisley's parents.

Through it all, the anger in Jonas grew, stewing, festering until it felt like it was going to consume him. He knew better than to take the emotions out on a human being, but he didn't have a punching bag in sight, and when the man with Nikki strode through the house toward the kitchen and the back door, Jonas followed.

"Jerome Barry, I'm a friend of Nikki's family. What happened here?" the man demanded of Marco and the crowd of muscled men who'd been chartered with protecting the band.

Nausea washed through Jonas at the sight of all of them. They'd been useless. Unable to stop one shitty excuse of a human from taking revenge. Jonas didn't wait for his brother to answer the man. Instead, he shouldered his way through the group and slammed Marco in the chest.

"You were supposed to protect them!" Jonas growled.

Marco just took it. He stood silent, arms across his chest, stance wide. It didn't ease Jonas's anger when he saw regret and pain flash over Marco's face. It only redirected the fury at himself because he knew how much this was costing Marco too. How it was bringing Marco's past back to haunt him. More women he hadn't protected. But Jonas didn't let that ease the fury he felt inside. He needed the anger. Otherwise, he'd crumble just like Paisley.

Jonas spun around, meeting each of the men's gazes, and they all looked away with faces full of regret and sadness, just like Marco. "You all fucking failed."

"Let's take a walk, Jo-Jo." It was Trevor who said it and not Marco, because his brother was still swimming in his own tortured memories. Jonas wanted to feel like an ass for making Marco feel worse, but he couldn't. Not with his own emotions so raw.

Trevor took his arm, tugging at him.

Jonas swung, fist landing on Trevor's chin and making him stagger back. He waited for the return volley, but it never came. Trevor just ran a hand over his chin and held his ground. "Make you feel better? Need to take another swing?" Trevor turned his cheek the other way.

"Fuck you," Jonas said and stormed past him. He headed around the side of the house to the front where there was a pile of SUVs in the driveway. He didn't have his car, but he had to get the hell out of there. Away from the blood and the darkness and the regret and the sorrow. He started to jog, heading down the drive toward the main road. The jog became a run, and the run became a frenzied sprint as he let the pain soar through him.

He'd lost her.

He'd lost her at the same time she'd lost her sister. It wasn't just the shock or the grief. She wouldn't be able to get past the fact that this was because of them. Because of him. Every time she looked at him, all she'd be able to see was her sister's dead body. She'd never forgive either of them for bringing this to Landry's door, for filling their last days with anger and sharp words. You could forgive one mistake. Maybe two. But that was it. After that, you cut your losses and ran.

So that was what he did.

When Marco pulled up alongside him in his Escalade, he didn't demand Jonas get in. He just slowly trailed him, watching over him. It filled Jonas with more rage because someone had failed in their job watching the band. Jonas had never deserved anyone's protection, but the Daisies had. Landry hadn't deserved what had happened to her.

The long slit with blood oozing from her throat came back to him. It was burned into his eyes...his memories. It would never let him go.

♫ ♫ ♫

After a tortured night of tossing and turning, Jonas was staring into his empty fridge when the door of his apartment opened. His eyes glanced toward it, hope filtering in for all of two seconds. Hope that it was Paisley. He'd texted her over and over again, asking her to tell him when she woke, asking if he could be there for her.

Silence had been his only answer.

It was Marco who appeared around the door, carrying a tray that he set on the counter and waved at. "Cassidy... Feeding people is her way of helping. You might not feel like eating, but it's there."

Jonas opened the domed lid and saw, with relief, that it

wasn't smiley-face crepes. He might not have been able to resist the urge to toss the tray against the wall if it had been. Instead, it was biscuits and gravy with eggs. Hearty and homemade. Food Cassidy knew he loved. He ran a fork through it, but the thought of putting it in his stomach made it turn violently. He threw the fork down.

"What happened? Have they found the guy?" Jonas asked.

Marco's jaw clenched. "No. There are a lot of theories floating around between all the fucking agencies involved. Everyone has their own version."

Jonas stood opposite his brother, arms crossed over his chest. "What's yours?"

"Honestly, Jo-Jo. I'm not sure. They all look so much alike when you see them from the back, and there are reasons someone could have been coming for almost all of them. The Colombian group who kidnapped Adria's sister said they were coming for her last night, and the white supremacists targeting Leya's dad have threatened his family. Then, there's..."

Marco trailed off.

"Just say it. There's me and Paisley."

Marco shifted uncomfortably. "We don't think the guy who did this is the same one who's been writing the notes."

Jonas scoffed. "Did you see the blood on the photograph?"

"It wasn't Landry's," Marco said, trying to reassure him. When Jonas didn't say anything, he went on. "The notes have been erratic. Frantic. Full of hate. If it had been the same person who'd written the notes who killed her, it would have been messy. I'm not sure they would have taken out the bodyguard too. What happened to Landry and Ramona...it took skill. Someone trained. Someone who could make the kill in less than thirty seconds."

"So, you're saying it's two different people?" Jonas frowned.

"I'm saying we don't know jack shit."

"You should fucking fire everyone."

"Including myself?" Marco said. He shook his head and leaned against the wall as if the weight of it had hit him all over. "Garner will likely fire most of the team who was on duty. His company...it's going to take a huge hit for this."

"Fucking deserved."

Marco closed his eyes. "I know."

Jonas felt like an ass all over again. Marco was taking this especially hard, but it was really difficult not to blame the people who'd been responsible for the band's safety. That included his brother. Jonas eased over, leaned against the wall next to him, and bumped his shoulder.

"You weren't on duty," he said quietly.

Marco looked up at him. "But I hired and trained a good portion of those men and women."

"Didn't you tell me once that if someone really wanted to kill you, there'd be no way of stopping them? They'd find a way."

"You trying to make me feel better, Jo-Jo? You should hate me right now."

"I could never hate you," Jonas said. "I hate the son of a bitch who did this. I hate that it might have been because of me..."

"It wasn't Artie," Marco said.

"How do you know?"

"Just my gut."

They stood there in silence, somehow comforting each other by just being there.

"How's Paisley?" Marco asked.

The pain sliced through him from heart to gut. "I don't know. She won't return my calls or texts."

Marco stared at him. "Try not to take it personally. She's grieving. She probably doesn't even know how to answer you."

Jonas's jaw clenched, fighting the tears that swelled.

"Give her time," Marco said.

But Jonas knew, because he knew Paisley. He saw into her soul when they were together, just like she saw into his. She wouldn't come back to him. They'd lost before they'd ever really begun.

♫ ♫ ♫

Unable to sit in a quiet apartment while Marco returned to the farmhouse and the investigation, Jonas made his way downtown toward the studio. He needed to do something. Anything. Even if it was listening to recordings that may never see the light of day now. Songs the world needed but had been caught in the worst kind of nightmare.

As his feet hit the sidewalk outside *La Musica*, Larry approached, and Jonas's entire body tightened. He wasn't sure he'd be able to keep his fists to himself if the man said even the tiniest of things wrong.

"I'm not in the mood for your shit today, Larry."

The reporter nodded with a solemn expression. "I just wanted to say how sorry I was to hear about Landry. All of us on their beat are pretty shaken up."

His condolence did nothing to ease the turmoil inside Jonas. The self-hatred. The desperate longing to have Paisley in his arms. The grief. He didn't respond. Instead, he turned away, but Larry's words stopped him again.

"Some of us have been trying to talk to the police or their detail, but no one will let us anywhere near them. Everyone thinks we're just trying to get the scoop."

Jonas just gave him a knowing glare, and the man had the decency to look chagrinned. "I get it. But we have some important information. The guys and me," his hand drifted out to the dozens of reporters who'd reemerged from the woodwork like cockroaches. "We've been swapping stories, and I heard that there were some South American guerilla types asking around at the café yesterday for information about where the Daisies were staying."

Jonas's breath left his body.

Could there be a chance that this hadn't been about him?

Had this more to do with Adria and the men who'd taken her sister?

"Have you seen them again?"

Larry shook his head. "I didn't see them at all. That was Mindy. But I did seem some big ass motherfucker slinking into the shadows. Has to be at least six-seven, if not taller. Always in black from head to toe."

"That could be any of their detail," Jonas scoffed.

"Not this one. I'd have remembered seeing him. He doesn't fit."

Jonas turned away from the door of the studio, jogging back the way he'd come.

Paisley may not want to see him. He may never get back what he'd already lost with her, but maybe he could still find a way to bring her some peace. If this information helped catch the asshole who'd killed her sister, he could at least give her that.

CHAPTER NINETEEN

Paisley

BIGGER THAN THE WHOLE SKY
Performed by Taylor Swift

When Paisley woke from the drug-induced sleep the medic had put her in, everything was hazy. Her head hurt, her eyes were swollen shut, and she felt like someone had hit her with a bat. It took mere seconds for her to register why.

Landry!

A sob escaped her chest but no tears came.

She stumbled to her feet, listening to the quiet. The house was completely silent, much as it had been when they'd arrived last night. Her skin broke out in goosebumps thinking of the note...thinking of Landry's unseeing eyes...the blood.

Her stomach heaved, she raced to the bathroom, but nothing but acid and bile came out. She headed out of the room, unsure of what she'd find, but needing anything besides the nightmare in her head.

At the bottom of the stairs, she saw a familiar set of luggage. Her parents. She flew down the hall toward the kitchen and the soft murmur of voices.

But it wasn't her mom and dad, it was Ronan with his back to her. His shoulders were moving up and down as if in silent sobs. There was a computer in front of him with a video playing. Paisley's hand went to her mouth. It was Landry. There was a knowing smile on her face that spoke of hidden secrets.

"Tell me about the band. Why did you decide to start it?" Ronan's voice asked off camera.

"Paisley," Landry said confidently.

Paisley's heart flipped over, sinking down into the pit of thorns that lived permanently in her stomach now, but she couldn't help easing forward on quiet feet until she was right behind him, able to see her sister better.

"She was only what… eleven?" Ronan asked again.

"My sister had more talent in her at ten years old than most artists have in their entire life. Right now, I have the privilege of helping her shape the music she makes, but someday, she's going to step out from behind everyone and stun the world with what she can do."

The sob she'd held back finally escaped, jerking Ronan's eyes from the screen to Paisley. His were red-rimmed and bloodshot as if he'd been crying for a long time as well.

"Shit, I'm sorry." He went to shut it off, but Paisley stilled his hands, hypnotized by her sister as pain and anger and awe filled her in equal measures.

"What's stopping her?" Ronan's voice on the video asked.

And Paisley thought knew what Landry had wanted to say. She'd wanted to tell Ronan about her anxiety. But instead, her sister's words surprised her. "Me. Jonas. The whole band." Landry's expression turned sad, eyes turning toward something. Ronan shifted so the camera pointed to the rest of the band sitting on the back porch with Jonas and Paisley wrapped together.

It was the moment Paisley had thought they'd been talking about her. And she'd been right. But it was nothing like she'd imagined.

"I'm afraid she'll use Jonas like she uses me," Landry said softly, her deep voice throaty and emotional in a way Paisley had rarely heard it.

"What do you mean?" Ronan prompted.

"I'm afraid she'll use all of us as an excuse to hide. To never show the world what she really is."

"What's that?"

"A legend. A legacy."

Another tortured cry broke free from Paisley. Ronan closed the screen, standing up and placing a hand on her shoulder.

"I'm so sorry, Paisley."

"Sh-she was the legacy. N-none of this would have happened without her drive and determination." Her voice was hoarse and rough from screaming and crying and begging the universe to give her sister back to her.

Ronan shook his head slightly. "None of it would have happened without your music. That's what she was saying. She was..." He looked away in thought and then turned back. "She was building the mountain so you could stand on top and shout to the world from its heights."

Paisley shook her head violently. Guilt and horror and pain inching their way through every single part of her. "I'll never be able to do this without her. She was the strength keeping me going."

"She didn't believe that."

"She saw wrong."

Paisley left the room. Shame and regret shuffled through her like a knife. She'd been blaming Landry for everything. Pushing her away. Acting like the stupid child she'd been begging them not to treat her as. Running away from the one person who'd always looked out for her. Who'd started an entire band just for her. To give her a mountain so she could sing to the world.

Tears flew unchecked.

As she reached the foot of the stairs, the front door opened to reveal her father. He had on a white button-down and khaki pants that were the most wrinkled she'd ever seen on him. His black hair was mussed and his brown eyes were red in a face that was pale and tired.

"Ji-An," he croaked, opening his arms, and she went to him, burying her head in his chest. Slow silent tears dripping down her face. She felt his own drop on her arm and her neck. They stood there, just holding each other.

♫ ♫ ♫

Her parents had chartered a private plane, flown through the night, and arrived at the farmhouse, looking battered and bruised. But it was her mother's rage that caught Paisley off guard. The I-told-you-sos unspoken in the air because their mom had always said the band would lead to nothing good. The anger was layered over the top of the grief as she packed Landry's things and refused to let Paisley help.

When Paisley checked her phone, she had a dozen or more texts from Jonas and as many calls. She wanted him with an ache that was physical. She wanted to have him at her side, filling in the gaps and holes, holding her up, and making her a better person. But at the same time, having him there would only serve to remind her of where she'd been, what she'd been doing, and the anger she'd sent her sister's way all while Landry had been dying. Would only serve to remind her that maybe he was the reason for all of this... Paisley couldn't...she didn't know how to look him in the eye and not see her own regrets. Her own loss.

To hear Landry's voice saying Paisley would use him to hide behind.

So, she did the only thing she could. She did nothing.

The loss of him added more pain on top of the jagged agony she was already feeling, but she just wasn't strong enough to face him. She wasn't brave enough. She was exactly what her sister had said—a shadow who'd always stood behind a fierce light who'd led the way. And now that light was gone.

The band seemed to be crumbling apart even while a handful of them were still together. The remaining Daisies packed in silence, the farmhouse whispering their footsteps and movements, but no words were spoken. Fiadh, Nikki, and Nikki's stepmom packed Adria's and Leya's rooms, sending their things off to them while Paisley drifted. Lost. Alone. But feeling like it was deserved.

Tommy and Nick held a press conference with the new owner of Lost Heart Records conspicuously absent. The fact that their label had been sold only added to the feeling that had haunted Paisley for days—the ground had fallen out beneath them. Fiadh was livid, almost purple in color, as she ranted about Asher Riggs and what a despicable human being he was, but Paisley thought she was using the anger to hold back her grief.

The only time Fee wasn't ranting was when she was hugging Paisley, as if the act itself would somehow shore them both up. But the more she did it, the more Paisley felt like she was going to vomit. Eventually, she just moved away every time Fiadh reached for her, and she saw that it cut into her friend. Just like she knew in not responding to Jonas, it was cutting him. But she was helpless to change her actions.

Helpless. Hopeless.

Angry.

Full of shame.

The next day, as Paisley walked up the stairs to the private jet set to take them back to California, she felt eyes on her, but when she turned and looked out at the small airport, there was no one there. She wondered if it was Jonas. She hoped it was, because otherwise...otherwise, it meant the killer was still there, eyeing what he hadn't finished. The mistake he'd made.

Her stomach turned. A silent fury building that she shoved behind a wall. Feeling nothing was better than feeling too much. She joined the others on the plane with the silence of the farmhouse following them back to California.

♫ ♫ ♫

The coroner in New York held Landry's body in autopsy for days, which delayed her funeral. It made everything feel unreal to Paisley, as if she'd wake up and it would all have just been a stupid dream, one that Landry would laugh off. The only thing that seemed real was her sister's absence—the quiet in the house without her—but even that could just mean she was off at Fee's apartment, where she'd spent a lot of time whenever they were home.

Paisley's dad was withdrawn and grim. Her mom cried silent, slow tears multiple times a day, and Paisley retreated to her sister's room, seeking refuge in the place they'd always come together. She spent days and nights on the yellow-and-orange floral cushioned window seat where they'd learned to play guitar together. Where they'd huddled over songs and lyrics. Where they'd screamed and danced once they'd seen the Grammy nominations for *The Red Guitar*.

Every day she got texts from Jonas, every day she tried to answer, and every day it brought back the bloody note with their faces scratched out and the image of her sister on the ground with a gash in her throat. It made her hands shake and her stomach turn until she wanted to throw the phone. So, instead of answering, she simply deleted the messages as if she could pretend they weren't there. As if none of it was happening.

She'd lost so much more than her sister. She'd also lost the band, who'd scattered in all directions, and the man she'd thought completed her. A body and mind could only take so much, and it was as if hers had shut down, going into some sort of protection mode, retreating behind a wall. After those first awful hours at the farmhouse, when she'd vomited with tears and Ronan's video had broken her open, she hadn't cried a drop because she wasn't really feeling at all. What remained was an empty shell of a person with a void on the inside.

Fiadh was in and out of their house, offering to do whatever her parents needed, and Paisley felt guilt try to stab at the void. When Fee came up to Landry's room and sat at her feet, Paisley took it out on her.

"You're not Landry. You can't replace her."

Fee's face turned stricken, looking away. "No one could ever be Lan."

It pricked at Paisley's numbness again, so she just turned away and looked out the window to the backyard and the silent swing set she and Landry had once played on together. She said nothing, and eventually Fee left.

Silence was better than talking. It allowed her to bury herself in a sweet cocoon of nothing.

But her silence, the silence of the entire band, was driving the press and the fans wild. Everyone wanted answers to what had happened. But with the investigation still on-going and the non-disclosure agreements everyone had signed, nothing was forthcoming. In addition, Ronan had been granted exclusive rights to anything and everything that happened to the band during their time in Grand Orchard, and he'd been clear that anyone who talked needed to do so through him, but he also wasn't pushing them. He'd withdrawn as well.

So, Paisley stayed where she was, lost in her sister's room.

Fee retreated to her apartment alone.

Leya joined her parents on the campaign trail, face pale whenever she appeared on screen.

Adria went with her shaken family, searching for a sister who still hadn't been found even after a ransom was paid.

Nikki returned home with her widowed stepmom, even more quiet and reserved than ever before.

Somewhere deep inside Paisley, below the emotionless shell, she knew Landry would hate what was happening. She'd hate that they'd drifted apart instead of coming together, but Landry had been wrong in that video to Ronan. She'd been the force behind everything, and now it was gone.

CHAPTER TWENTY

Paisley

SLIPPED AWAY
Performed by Avril Lavigne

When the coroner finally released Landry's body, the cause of death was clear but nothing else. There were no clues. Not a single fiber. Not a single fingerprint. Not a single witness. Just a pile of leaves and bird feathers from the pond. It was like a phantom had snuck up behind Landry and then disappeared into thin air. It didn't matter what the coroner's report said though, because Paisley had convinced herself she knew the truth. Landry had died because Paisley had let herself fall for a boy with a troubled past.

She wanted to hate Jonas, but really, she just hated herself. For walking away that day instead of going with Landry back to the house. If she'd been there, then she would have died and not her sister.

With her body returned to Orange County, the funeral

finally moved forward. Paisley's parents tried to keep the details of the service private, but it was practically impossible with the press watching every step. Add in the vice-presidential nominee attending alongside his distraught daughter, and it became a circus. The number of fans who showed up at the cemetery caused traffic jams and pushed the police, FBI, Secret Service, and the Daisies' new detail, Reinard Security, to their limits.

Like every day since returning from New York, Paisley watched the people and the world move around from inside a bubble that dimmed everything around her. Sights, sounds, colors were all muted, as if watching a black-and-white movie. She couldn't cry, not even at the graveside when her mother clutched her hand with tears streaming down a face that had aged more in mere weeks than it had in years. It should have moved Paisley, but instead, she remained safe behind the shield she'd erected.

Only two things made her wall waver.

The first was seeing Jonas and Brady arrive in dark-gray suits with tortured, red-rimmed eyes. Paisley felt something twist and groan deep down inside her at Jonas's obvious grief, before she pulled the bubble tighter, ensuring she could shut him out like she'd shut out everyone else.

Then, when the other Daisies twined their bodies together and sobbed as Landry's coffin was lowered into the ground, it wasn't grief but a flicker of almost jealousy that coursed through her. They had each other, and she was by herself, holding her parents' hands, separated from them. Different. Alone. Cold.

Like she'd always been.

The fans at the cemetery gates were in hysterics. The news showed them beating their chests and throwing themselves on the ground while Golden Butterfly daisies piled thick along the cemetery walls, and all Paisley could think was how ridiculous their tears were when they hadn't really known her sister. They'd known a watery reflection of the truly amazing human being she'd been.

After the burial, the band and their families retreated to the Kims' home. The private, gated community kept the rabid followers and media at bay, but their new detail and the Secret Service still swarmed the house as if it was going to be invaded by an army.

As people came and went, Paisley stood motionless, staring out the window in the formal living room that normally went unused. Her parents saved it for when they were entertaining important clients—new firms wanting their investment company to choose them or millionaires they were courting. The space was crowded today with people, and yet, it was still quiet. The talk hushed. The pale blues and yellows of the room should have been warm and friendly, but to Paisley, it felt stiff and cold. Just another room, another place she'd never felt she could be herself.

There'd only been one place she'd ever felt like the real Paisley.

Her eyes shot across the room to the archway where Jonas stood with Brady in the kitchen. Jonas looked haggard—sad and broken. It was how Paisley should have felt, wretched, but she was glad she felt nothing.

"Little Bit," Adria said, wrapping Paisley in a hug and turning her to face the band who'd gathered around her. Paisley felt a tug at her bubble, a flicker of warmth and grief before she slammed virtual hands up against her wall to keep it from cracking.

Paisley knew she should have been comforting her friend as much as Adria was trying to comfort her. The Rojas family was still looking for her kidnapped sister, and Paisley couldn't imagine the strain they were all under. Adria's eyes were puffy and red, and yet she still looked beautiful—magazine-cover ready. The black dress she wore clung to her curves and showed off her warm skin.

"We want you and Fee to come and stay with one of us," Adria said.

Paisley's eyes drifted from Fiadh's face to Nikki's and then Leya's. They'd all traded their rock-band apparel for black dresses, making them look nothing like The Painted Daisies the world knew.

It was Fee who looked away first with pain and loneliness etched across her face, and a bolt of shame shot past Paisley's barrier. She'd been so lost in her own grief she'd forgotten how alone in the world Fee was. Fiadh had come by the house almost every day, helping her mom with the funeral arrangements, but Paisley had just drifted by her, unable to connect, unable to reach out.

"Fee should go," Paisley croaked out, wanting Fiadh to have the support she'd been unable to offer. "But I can't leave my parents right now."

It wasn't true. While her parents were furious and grieving, they hardly seemed to notice Paisley. It hadn't upset her. It had been a relief. She wanted them to mourn in their own way without encroaching on hers. The real reason she was saying no was that if she left the house, she'd have to leave Landry's room, and it was the only place she could still feel her sister's presence.

"If you stay, I stay," Fee said firmly, eyes watery.

Before anyone could object, Tommy walked into the room and joined them, smelling of stale alcohol. He tugged at the chains on his neck and then stuck his hand in a back pocket. "I know this is the last thing you want to think about right now, but we need to make plans to finish the album and reschedule dates for the tour."

None of them responded, and the air thickened with tension. He looked down, throat bobbing, and when he looked back up, his eyes were tortured and pained. “Look. I don’t want to talk about it either, but Asher Riggs is threatening to sue us for breach of contract if we don’t meet our commitments.”

“What the hell?” Fiadh growled.

“He expects us to just climb back behind our instruments when our leader—the reason we had the band at all—is gone?” Nikki demanded, voice cracking.

“He says he’ll give us six months. But after that, he expects us back at it, or we’ll have to repay him every penny he’s spent.”

“It was Nick who spent the money, not him,” Adria insisted through clenched teeth.

“But he’s bought the label, profit and all, and he’s not a man to just sit back and swallow losses. He’d already had concerns about the amount of money Nick poured into you before this... and now that it’s going to dry up...” he trailed off.

“Hate to be crass, but our record sales have gone through the roof. Everyone’s out there buying her songs...buying her...” Leya faded off into a silent sob.

Fiadh gasped, clutched her chest, and broke into an anguished cry.

Paisley’s bubble cracked like a windshield hit with a rock, the spidery webs splintering across it as their cries surrounded her. If it broke completely, she didn’t know what she’d do, so she forced herself away from Fee and ran. She threw open the back door and scrambled to the rear of the manicured garden where a large oak tree shaded a swing set her dad had built when she and Landry were little.

It was a place Paisley had run to many times in her life when she felt like things were unmanageable. Here, she could control the speed of the swing when she couldn’t control anything else. It had always been Landry who’d come and found her and talked her out of her anxiety-locked state. But Paisley would never have that again. Never have a sister who grounded her and defended her.

For some reason, it didn't surprise her when it was Jonas who came for her now.

He hadn't stopped texting her every day. He'd begged her to talk to him. To forgive him. But how could she when she couldn't even forgive herself? She'd let Landry die with anger resting between them. She'd run off with Jonas, and her sister had been murdered because of it.

As Jonas crossed the grass, she saw the toll this had taken on him. He had deep-purple shadows under his lashes, almost as if he'd been punched in the face. His color was sallow, his normally glowing bronze skin faded and pale. But it was his eyes that stabbed at her heart, sending more splinters through her icy shield until, finally, ragged and raw pain made it through, hitting her in the chest. The need to scream and cry and rant and rail simmered right below the surface for the first time since that awful night.

She resented it—every wave of emotion. She wanted the shell of nothingness back, and she hated that he'd thrown the last stone to destroy it with just a look. He sat down on Landry's swing, and that caused a whole new range of emotions she couldn't push back. Desperation. Longing. Sorrow. It welled up into her throat, a lump forming she couldn't push away.

"Paisley..." His voice was gritty with tears.

"Please don't," she said. The words were quiet and choked.

He tugged at the chain of her swing, jerking it to a halt, bringing her toward him, and tangling their legs. Awareness drifted through her, the heat he always brought to her body pushing against her cold, frozen state even more. She didn't think she'd be able to hold it together if his warmth leaked through her barrier too.

"Goddamn it," he growled. "This isn't your fault. This isn't my fault. We can get through this but only together. We're better together, Paise. Apart...apart we're just jagged, broken pieces. Together...together we're everything."

She felt the first tear hit her cheek, and it filled her with rage because she didn't want to cry or feel or explain to him that she couldn't do any of it right now. So, she was cruel when she shouldn't be.

"Better? Really, Jonas? Don't you get it? We destroyed everything. There is no together."

His eyes shuttered, grief flowing over his features, and she fought every instinct to comfort him, to wrap her arms around him and allow them to lose themselves in each other. Instead, she forced her body away from his. She stood, breathing hard, trying to hold back the tears that now threatened.

"She was right, Jonas. There is no way our worlds will ever work."

Then, she walked away with every single fiber in her being clamoring to run back to him. To crawl into his lap and forget everything but him so she didn't have to be Paisley without Landry. So she could just be Paisley who belonged to Jonas. But that wasn't a possibility. Not now. Not ever.

She bit her cheeks, nails biting into her palms as she fought against the flood threatening to release itself. She bypassed the kitchen and family room, climbing the back stairs and going into Landry's room as she had every day. She could still smell her sister there. Hear her voice. See her smiling and dancing and laughing. So full of life and determination and strength.

Paisley grabbed Landry's guitar and clambered onto the window seat that looked over the backyard. Jonas wasn't on the swings anymore. Her heart flipped, and her stomach sagged. He'd left. Just like she'd told him to.

She leaned her head against the paned glass, the coolness

calming her somehow. Just like Landry had always calmed her. When her anxiety spiked the worst, it was Landry who'd always saved her. She'd tug at Paisley's hair, surround her hands with her own, and push her metal rings into Paisley's skin. The rings they'd buried her with today.

The pressure grew inside her chest and throat, swelling, swelling, swelling. She rubbed a finger over the new anxiety ring her doctor had prescribed, fighting the tide, trying to push it all back down. The beads on the ring slid back and forth, somehow soothing her and reminding her of Landry all at the same time.

"Your funeral was today," Paisley said, talking to Landry as she'd been doing in secret for days. "It was unbearable, and every time I tried to grab your hand to help me through it, I was torn apart all over again because it was you we were burying."

The silence of the room echoed back.

Not even a ghost of her sister remained. She'd heard one tormented call that night in Grand Orchard—a voice that had said her name in the dark before it had vanished. She'd heard nothing since then, but she could hope. She plucked a chord on the guitar, wishing the sound was Landry's voice answering.

"Jonas has been trying, Lan. He's tried so hard to be there, to stand beside me. And all I can think is that if I hadn't been off with him... If I hadn't been so determined to prove you wrong, to cast you off, to shine on my own, I would've been at your side. You wouldn't have died. That asshole would have found me instead of you."

The well broke over, a sob erupting from deep within her.

"You got what you wanted, Lan. Jonas and I are not together anymore. I can't look at him without seeing all my mistakes. Somehow, I know this wouldn't make you happy. You wouldn't want to tear *me* apart just to tear *us* apart. But it's happened anyway."

Paisley fingered the strings more and then slid her hand

down to the Golden Butterfly daisy etched and painted into the rich wood as tears tumbled from her face onto the smooth surface. The more Paisley tried to brush them away, the stronger they came, her loss of Landry mingling with her loss of Jonas.

She tried to force the pain back, turning her thoughts from the two people who'd meant everything and were now gone. Forcing herself to think of the band and Tommy's words.

"Asher and RMI won't wait, Lan. He only cares about money, but the rest of us...we don't know how to do this without you. You'd be making a list, and placing calls, and pushing us all back together, but none of us know how to be you. Not even Fee..."

Another violent sob erupted from her chest. Paisley plucked the strings again. She could play the guitar, but it wasn't her favorite. The piano was where her soul really belonged. Except, these days, the words and the notes that were always rattling around in her brain were quiet—silent—as if even the music was mourning.

"I don't know if we can be The Painted Daisies without you." She sniffled. "I miss you. I wish I knew what to do. I wish..."

Paisley looked down at the guitar case and saw a piece of paper tucked into the inside back pocket. It must have come loose after all the times Paisley had batted the case around over the last few days. She grabbed it, opened it, and read. Sobs wracked her body, making it difficult to get through, but somehow, it felt like Landry was finally talking to her. Finally whispering her thoughts so Paisley would know what action to take.

Little Bit,

You stormed out with Jonas today, and I wanted to run after you. I wanted to apologize. I wanted to take back the words I'd said in anger.

I was wrong.

I was jealous.

But I was also afraid.

Not just of losing you to him. But of losing my control over the band. Like you said, it's the only thing I ever wanted for myself. It's the only thing I'm good at—leading this mixture of souls. You...you're good at a million and one different things, even when you think you're good at nothing.

Today, when you took the lead on your new songs, when you told us that we needed to add them to the lineup for the album, I saw exactly what I'd somehow forgotten until Ronan reminded me of it again recently...I saw that the band could survive my loss but not yours. You are the core of it. You're the words and the lyrics, but you also have the best voice and the most heart. We could replace any of us easily and readily, but we couldn't replace you.

That's why I lashed out at you.

I wasn't afraid of just no longer being needed by my sister but of no longer being needed by any of you.

Knowing me and how much I hate showing my weaknesses to anyone, I probably won't show you this. But I'll pretend that you've seen it. Just like I'll pretend I've actually issued the apology I owe you and Jonas both.

If, for some reason, you do read it, can you promise me three things?

Promise me you'll never stop making music.

Promise me you'll never stop giving your heart to people.

Promise me you'll see yourself as the leader you truly are.

The Painted Daisies aren't Landry, Fee, Nikki, Adria, or Leya. The Painted Daisies are Paisley Kim. The rest of us are just backup.

It feels better to have just written this. I wish I had the courage to give it to you. Maybe I will. Maybe if I hold on to it long enough, it will be easy to just pass it over.

Whether I do or don't—whether you know it or not—I'm going to do my best to help you keep those three promises. I'm going to do everything in my power to make sure you see yourself as the beautiful, strong, heart-filled leader you are.

Forever your sister,

Lan

CHAPTER TWENTY-ONE

ASHES OF EDEN
Performed by Breaking Benjamin

TWO WEEKS AFTER

JONAS: I know you said there isn't an us anymore, so why does it feel like there is? Why does it feel like the entity that was us together is floating in limbo, waiting to be reclaimed? I'm here. If and when you're ever ready. I'm here.

ONE MONTH AFTER

JONAS: I'm a full-time student now. It feels strange to be on the campus where you never attended school, but everywhere I turn, I think of you. I've been trying to keep up with you through the news, but things on the Daisies are hard to find. You've all gone underground. I see glimpses of Leya on the campaign trail with her family, but no one else. I miss you.

FOUR MONTHS AFTER

JONAS: Merry Christmas, Paisley. You probably hate those words. You've probably been scowling at everyone who has said them today, making you look especially like Landry. I can't imagine how hard this first holiday without her is for you. I just wanted you to know that, somewhere in the world, there's someone wishing you a moment of peace. A moment where the heavy burden is lifted off your shoulders.

FIVE MONTHS AFTER

JONAS: Music in Waves was supposed to release this month. Instead, the songs sit here on tracks at the studio that I can't help but listen to over and over again. Words the world still needs. Will you ever finish them? Are you still making music? I'd bet anything that your writing is now painful and raw. I bet it would speak to people's souls. I wish I could hear it so it would speak to mine.

NINE MONTHS AFTER

JONAS: Everybody thinks I've moved on... But how do you move on when you gave your heart to someone, and they never gave it back? Somehow, I have to find a place in this world without you. I have to find reasons to be happy. To be fulfilled. But every time I try to convince myself I'm going to do just that, I remember how we felt together, and I know I'll never be whole again without you.

TWELVE MONTHS AFTER

JONAS: I promised myself I wouldn't text again...but today must be hard for you. I'm full of my own regrets as memories of that day wash over me. I wish what I've been wishing for a year—that I could comfort you somehow. That I could hug you one more time.

EIGHTEEN MONTHS AFTER

JONAS: I heard today that the band is coming back to finish the album—or at least some sort of album, because you're changing it. I am so fucking happy you haven't given up on the one thing you were born to do. But I'm also so fucking angry that I haven't heard from you. My therapist tells me to express it, not just by laying my fists on the boxing bag, but in words. So there. I said it. I'm fucking angry with you. For not letting me be there. For giving up. For building a wall I couldn't climb.

JONAS: I'm sorry. I shouldn't have sent that. But I'm just so fucking sad for both of us.

NINETEEN MONTHS AFTER

PAISLEY: ...

CHAPTER TWENTY-TWO

Paisley

ROAD TO EDEN
Performed by The Corrs

NINETEEN MONTHS AFTER

As Paisley approached the lounge in the private terminal, she watched the other Daisies through the glass without them knowing she'd arrived yet. Her heart stampeded, jumping from one emotion to the next at the sight of them. Joy. Despair. Determination. Fear.

She pushed the fear aside. She had to. Otherwise, everything she'd planned would be for naught. She placed her hand over her heart, trying to gather courage from the tattoo there, wishing she could feel Landry's cool fingers around hers. Instead, she rubbed the beads on her anxiety ring, fighting the waves of panic that threatened to take hold. She couldn't afford to give into it anymore.

As she watched, Fiadh laughed, and at first it made Paisley's heart leap, but then she noticed how brittle the edges seemed, as if Fee's laugh might turn into tears at any moment. Out of all the Daisies, Fiadh was the one she worried about most because she'd refused to go with the others, staying with Paisley in California but really being alone in the world. Paisley had failed Fee after the funeral. She'd been unable to fill the gaping hole Landry had left behind in their friend's life anymore than she'd been able to fill the hole her sister had left in her family's.

For months after they'd buried her sister, Paisley had let herself get lost in writing songs. Landry's letter had lit a burning ember in her to do something—anything—to keep the band together. The problem was, all she knew how to do was create the music, bringing it to actual life had been Landry's job. So, she spent her days on the part she could achieve. That had all changed when she'd walked into Fee's apartment and found her and Tommy deathly still on opposite sides of the couch with two empty bottles of vodka between them. The fear that she'd lost Fee too had been the push Paisley needed. She became determined not to let Landry down again, and if she'd let Fiadh slip away—let the band slip away—that was exactly what it would have been.

That same night, Paisley had reached out to Asher directly, without Tommy knowing, and had negotiated extra time by hinting at the songs she'd been working on. Asher had acted like she was asking him to give her the moon, but then he'd reluctantly agreed.

"I'll give you six more months, but I'm taking ten percent of the band's advance back, and if you don't have a solid plan by then, I'll take it all."

And he'd hung up.

His arrogance and cold-hearted brutality had fueled her even more. She'd gone to her sister's room and sifted through all the songs she'd written, finding the best of them. Then, she'd dragged Fee to the house and pulled the rest of the band together on a video call. She'd played a few songs for them, saving "The Legacy" for last. She'd barely made it through the song, grief and tears leaking into her voice and making the song choppy, but they'd understood what she was trying to do. They'd heard the core of it. After she'd stopped playing, they'd all sat on the line, crying together. A cathartic wash of emotions after months of silence between them.

Fee had hugged Paisley tightly and said, "It's fecking beautiful."

Nikki, Adria, and Leya had all chimed in over the screen.

"Landry would be so proud of you," Leya had said quietly.

"Can't you feel her? She's here, kicking our asses because it's taken us so long to pull it together," Adria had said.

"Kicking our asses because we've let Asher Riggs dictate our next step instead of us setting our own terms," Nikki had said, and Paisley had felt Fee stiffen at Asher's name.

But they'd all agreed they needed to finish the album and the tour. For Landry...and for themselves. But that was all any of them could commit to at the moment. The one album. The one tour.

Paisley's eyes journeyed back to the terminal lounge as Leya plopped down into a chair next to Nikki and said, "Tell us about your sailing adventure."

Nikki had practically disappeared for nine months with her stepmom on a sailboat that had once belonged to Nikki's dad.

"After the second month of beautiful oceans and islands in the Mediterranean, I was ready to be done, but Mom loved every minute of it, so it was worth it," Nikki said with a small shrug.

"Poor you! Blue oceans and sunshine for months," Fee teased.

"There were a couple of scary storms in there," Nikki said with a shrug. Those last few months before Landry, Nikki had been wound tight, migraines hitting right and left, but she'd never shared with any of them what was going on. She'd been an enigma, keeping her thoughts close to her chest, and it didn't seem like that had changed.

"Where was your favorite place?" Adria asked. She had one of her drumsticks tucked behind her back, samurai style, and it tugged Paisley's memories. All the times they'd been together just this way.

"San Fiore," Nikki said but then grimaced, as if she wished she hadn't said it.

"I've never even heard of it," Leya said. "And that's saying something because I think Dad has met with every foreign government on the planet since he's been in office."

"It's like Monaco but an island. Lots of wealth and celebrities hiding out there. The locals...they were just...it's hard to describe. It was like happiness bubbled from the entire place." Her face was wistful and yearning, as if she longed to go back, and Adria picked up on it.

"Maybe we should all take a trip there together for a week after the album is complete and before we have to be in Boston," Adria said. "We could use the downtime together."

Paisley's heart was heavy for Adria and her family. The grief she felt over Landry and the unknowns surrounding her murder was hard enough. She couldn't imagine not knowing if her sister was alive or dead for years. And yet, you'd never know the turmoil Adria was going through by looking at her. She appeared like she always did, as if she was ready to step onto a runway.

Nikki didn't respond, turning quiet and thoughtful, retreating into silence as she always did.

Fiadh slouched down in the chair so she could rest her head on Leya's shoulder. "How's the White House?"

Leya rolled her eyes. "I wouldn't know. We don't live there, thank goodness. When I am there, it's almost impossible to even breathe without someone eyeballing me. I don't know how Guy and his family do it."

"So, you're there a lot? Anything going on between you and Lincoln Matherton?" Adria asked with a sly smile.

Leya swung her foot, kicking Adria in the shin playfully. "No!"

"All I'm saying is that, at the inauguration, he about drowned you with his stares."

"He's not my type," Leya said with a shrug. "Besides, you know I've already got an agreement with Krish."

Fee grimaced. "Love can't be *arranged*, Ley."

"Speaking of love," Nikki said quietly. "Anyone else worried about what will happen with Jonas and Paisley now that we're going back to Grand Orchard?"

The band turned silent, but just hearing Jonas's name flipped Paisley's stomach all over again, like it did every time she thought of him. God...she missed him. Every single day. It was like she'd had two parts of her torn out when Landry had died. Two parts she'd never get back. She'd told him to go, and he had...

That wasn't completely fair. He'd tried to be there, texting and calling. He'd tried to keep her from falling just like, once upon a time, she'd hoped he would. But every time he texted her, the visual of Landry by the pond would hit her, and the guilt would carve its way into her heart, pushing away her sweet memories and leaving her with the bitter knowledge that she'd chosen Jonas, and it had killed her sister. So, she never replied, even when it ate at her soul a little more each time not to.

Paisley's phone lit up with a text from her mom, drawing her eyes from the band.

MOM: Don't go.

It was the same thing her mom had been saying...yelling... screaming for days. More remorse filled Paisley. She'd taken the brunt of her parents' anguish for the first time in her life, making her feel the loss of Landry even more. Her sister had always been the one to stand between them, taking the heat. Paisley had nearly crumbled every time either of her parents had threatened—or begged—her to forget this foolish idea, reminding her the price they'd already paid for the band was too high.

PAISLEY: I have to.

MOM: It's just money.

PAISLEY: This isn't about the money.

And it wasn't, really. She had to do this for Landry—for all of them—but she couldn't say that to her mother. When her mom didn't respond, Paisley's heart ached even more. It was unfair to put her parents through this. It wasn't just the fact she was going back to the exact place they'd lost Landry that made her feel regretful. It was the secrets she was keeping, the plans whirling in her brain. If they knew those, they would have handcuffed her to the bed.

"Ms. Kim? Everything okay?" her bodyguard asked.

She'd forgotten Zane was standing beside her. Tall with lean muscles, dark hair, and blue eyes, Zane looked like a famous Olympic swimmer instead of personal security. He'd joined Reinard shortly after Landry's death and had requested to be on her detail. He'd said it was because he knew what grieving a sibling was like, and eventually, he'd shared with her that he'd lost a sister.

"I'm good, thanks, Zane. Just...seeing them together again...

it's beautiful and sad all at the same time." Her eyes pricked with tears as she said it, but Landry wouldn't have cried. Landry would have stormed into the waiting room full of confidence. Paisley pressed her finger harder into the beads on her ring until pain bit at her.

"You really sure you want to go back into the spotlight?" he asked cautiously.

She looked up at him to find his brows furrowed in concern, and regret tugged at her insides for what she had planned before she pushed it away. Landry never doubted herself, but then, Landry hadn't made a decision that had cost someone their life. Paisley had one chance to fix it…one…because who knew what would happen when the band walked away at the end of the tour.

"One hundred percent," she finally responded and then turned, walking into the lounge in Landry's heels with Landry's guitar slung over her shoulder, hoping her sister was with her.

"Little Bit!" Fiadh said, bounding over to her and surrounding her in a warm hug.

The others joined them, twining themselves into a mess of arms and legs that brought more tears to Paisley's eyes. It had been so long since they'd been together in person. Too long. God, Landry would have hated it.

"You're looking good," Nikki said, snapping a finger gently into Paisley's muscled bicep. "I see you've been working out with Jerome!"

"Who's Jerome?" Fee asked with a frown.

"You know, Jerome. My dad's ex-Green Beret buddy. You met him when he came with my mom to Grand Orchard…" Nikki's voice faded away, but it was enough for Fiadh to get the idea.

Paisley forced back the memories that threatened to overtake her, swallowed hard, and then answered. "I did meet with him. He gave me a couple of lessons, but then Zane came on board and took over."

Leya slid in next to her to give Paisley another side hug. "You look even more like her now."

Paisley's heart squeezed tight, but she funneled every single ounce of her inner-Landry she could find. Bold. Beautiful. Strong. Confident. She had to be her sister. She had to step into the role Landry had wanted for her, not only for the band but so *he* could see it. A silent dare for him to come after her.

CHAPTER TWENTY-THREE

Jonas

LOSE YOU TO LOVE ME
Performed by Selena Gomez

Alice tapped Jonas on his bicep with a pencil, bringing his eyes back to the drawing in front of them on the table and away from the music drifting up the staircase from the live room below. When he didn't look at her, she poked at him until he lifted his chin to meet her gaze. Her gray eyes were full of concern as she pushed the pencil behind the line of hooped earrings filling her lobe. She'd shaved the sides of her black hair recently, leaving only a set of fuchsia-colored spikes on top.

She was dressed like Jonas, in Chucks, worn jeans, and a T-shirt. Except, where his shirt was from Brady's last album, hers said *Black Authors Do It Better*. Alice's girlfriend was a well-known young-adult fantasy author who was about ready to give birth to their first baby, just as the Daisies tour was scheduled to start. It was why Jonas was in the room, planning the tour with Alice and her right-hand woman, Zia.

"You sure you really want to do this?" Alice asked Jonas quietly as Zia stepped off-screen in the middle of their video conference. Alice's eyebrows were drawn together, worry leaking into her voice.

His stomach clenched, but he gritted his teeth and responded, "I can handle it."

"You couldn't even be in the control room when they showed up, so what makes you think you're going to be okay practically living with them on tour for over a year?"

It was a valid question. One Jonas had asked himself a dozen times in the last four weeks since Alice and Tommy had asked him to help Zia manage the tour in Alice's absence. The answer was convoluted, tied into warring pieces of him.

But it would have been stupid to turn down the opportunity they were giving him. It was an honor they thought he could do this at twenty years old, even if he wouldn't be doing it alone. Even if he and Zia were splitting the role as Alice's hands and feet on the ground. There was no way he could let his feelings for Paisley derail his future any more than they already had.

"It'll be different, Alice. What they're doing in there...the music..." Jonas shot a look to the door and the notes still bouncing up from the first floor. "We did that together."

Pain shot through him. Pain he thought would have lessened by now but was still as sharp as the day, months ago, when Paisley had pulled herself away from him on a swing set in her backyard and basically told him they could never be.

"This"—he waved at the papers in front of them—"is just me and Zia making sure everyone follows your schedule and your plan. I'll hardly have to talk to the band."

Alice rolled her eyes. "You'll be talking to the band. Believe me. Do you know how often I have to pull Brady away from Tristan's arms and drag him onto the stage before the fans tear the place apart?"

The thought of having to pull Paisley from anyone's arms made him want to lose his lunch. Not that he'd had lunch—or breakfast. He'd been unable to even think about eating knowing The Painted Daisies were going to be in the studio today. It had brought back unwelcome memories, and he'd ducked out of the house before Cassidy had the chance to feed him smiley-face crepes like she had the last time the Daisies had been here.

"It's fine, Alice. I got this. What happened between Paisley and me...that's in the past. It was obvious from the get-go it was never meant to be." His heart screamed at him for lying, but his brain pushed the truth back into the deep recesses that he only let himself see in the middle of the night when he was by himself in a darkened room.

Alice rose from the table, closed the door to Brady's office so the sound of the music became even more muffled, and then sat back down with him. "Well, we've got a few weeks for you to build up your protective shield. If you change your mind between now and then, I won't hold it against you. Tommy won't either."

Zia bounced back onto the screen, just in time to hear Alice's final words. She pushed her curly, mahogany-colored hair away from her warm, brown face. "Wait, are we talking about Jonas's lingering love for Paisley?" Zia asked.

He grimaced and shot Alice a look of betrayal, hating that everyone could still see the truth so clearly. Alice gave him a small, consolatory smile. "She had to know, Jonas. If things get tense between you and Paisley, it's going to be Zia's job to smooth it over."

"Nothing is going to happen," Jonas said, and in his mind, he meant every word, as long as he ignored the shrieking of his soul. He couldn't afford to have his heart pulverized once more, especially when he was still trying to staunch the bleeding from the last time.

♫ ♫ ♫

Two hours later, the studio was silent as Jonas rose from the table and stretched. He'd finished all the lists, ordered the necessary equipment, and was finally ready to head home. While he hadn't purposefully been waiting for the music to stop, he was glad it had. It meant there was less of a chance of running into her—into any of them.

Jonas stuffed his laptop into his backpack, shouldered it, and headed down the stairs.

His feet froze on the last step when Paisley came into view. His heart slammed to a halt before jumping back into gear at a pace that felt like drums running through him.

Fuck.

The only Daisy to be in the news since Landry's death had been Leya while she'd been on the campaign trail and then at the inauguration where her father was sworn in as Vice President. The rest of the Daisies had barely been seen. A random shot here and there, but none of Paisley. It was as if she'd disappeared right along with her sister.

Now, she looked older, muscled and toned in a way she'd never been, but otherwise entirely the same.

Her long hair was swept up on top of her head, thin curls escaping here and there and trailing down her back. She was in a strapless, leather bustier that laced down the back with strings dangling over a tantalizing strip of skin that showed above her dark jeans. Her legs looked longer and shapelier than ever before, the spiked ankle boots she wore adding to her tiny height.

Every single vein in his body came to life, including those

flowing to his dick, and he had to physically restrain himself from sliding up behind her and circling the pale skin at her waist with his hands. A pained grunt left his body, and the garbled sound drew her eyes. She turned to face him, and he about lost his mind all over again.

The structured top pushed her small breasts up, putting them on display in a way Paisley never would have done before. It showed off the pink daisy tattoo above her heart that was no longer a single flower. Instead, there were vines and thorns twining it with a Golden Butterfly daisy in a way that said there'd never be an escape. One would always belong with the other.

When his eyes finally met hers, he saw a flash of pain in them before she hid it. Her shoulders went back, her chin rose, and she became someone else. She became Landry.

"Jonas," she said. Her voice reached him across the distance with ease. Still quiet, but no longer a whisper.

He gave her a curt nod, unable to speak with the flood of emotions choking him. His jaw clenched as he fought for control. He couldn't afford to let his body rule. If he did, he'd be as lost as he'd been before. He inhaled deeply and took the last step onto the studio floor. She watched him as he crossed the room, taking the path around the chairs that would allow him to stay as far away from her as possible. He couldn't risk being pulled into the gravity that was Paisley Kim.

"You leaving?" he asked, thanking God his voice didn't sound broken or pained. Instead, it sounded as curt as his nod had been, projecting an emotionless void that hid the way his soul felt like it was shattering.

"Waiting for the okay from my detail," she answered.

The door opened, and a man Jonas didn't know entered. Garner Security had been replaced by a new company and had been damn lucky the Kims hadn't sued them. Of course, if they'd sued Garner, they would have had to sue the Grand Orchard PD, FBI, and the Secret Service as well because every one of those organizations had been involved with the band that summer.

"We're ready, Ms. Kim," the man said, eyeballing Jonas as if he might be a threat.

Paisley picked up her bag and moved toward the exit. It brought her close enough to Jonas that he could smell her—a floral scent layered with a sugary sweetness.

As the bodyguard held the door for Paisley, his eyes trailed after her, and there was something about the man's look that made Jonas's stomach churn. It spoke to a relationship that was much more than just his role on her detail. Fury and possessiveness he had no right to swarmed through Jonas's veins.

If she'd moved on, if she'd lost herself in someone else for a while, it was fair. He'd done the same, hadn't he? *But it had never felt right*, his heart screamed.

He locked up and turned, colliding with Paisley, who'd stopped unexpectedly just outside the door. He had to steady them both by putting a hand on her waist, and it seared through him—a burn that would leave a scar like every other damn time they'd touched. Her gaze met his, locking them together, and even with the shield he'd erected, he was afraid she'd read every thought and emotion running through him just like she'd done in the past. Slowly and painfully, Jonas withdrew his hand before stepping back and running into the door. Paisley didn't move farther away. She remained in his space.

"You don't have to stay out of the control room because of me," she spoke firmly. A statement. No question.

"I'm not," he insisted, running his hand through his hair—a movement she tracked with her eyes. "I'm not in the studio a lot these days."

Ever since Landry had died, he'd struggled at the board,

unable to "see" what needed to be done with the music. A flash of regret crossed her face, as if reading his thoughts again, but then it was gone.

She turned and, without another word, headed for the SUV and passenger door the bodyguard held open for her. She didn't glance his way again. She just got in and drove off. It felt like every other time she'd left him, as if his veins and limbs were being pulled apart.

Keeping his distance—not feeling anything—was going to be a million and a half times harder than he'd imagined.

And he'd already been afraid it would fucking break him.

CHAPTER TWENTY-FOUR

Paisley

NOTHING MISSING
Performed by Natalie Imbruglia

Paisley's heart was beating so fast she thought she might pass out. Seeing Jonas again had been just as hard as she'd thought it would be. The last time she'd been in Grand Orchard, her excitement and anticipation had fueled a new song, but today, the music in her head spoke of regret and longing. Of brutal heartache. She had no one to blame but herself for every crack and groove she'd carved into both of their hearts.

She couldn't change it. But did he have to look so beautiful? So strong and handsome? So perfect? It was as if he'd added yet another inch of muscle to his stature. His shoulders were impossibly wider, and his face had aged more. He was only twenty, but the emotions he'd experienced in his short life had left their mark. She'd left her mark.

God, she hated being just another woman who'd abandoned him.

She stared out the window, deep in thought, heart thudding out a beat that only Jonas had ever caused, as Zane drove her to their hotel on the outskirts of town. She missed the farmhouse even as the thought of it made her stomach turn. A strange dichotomy. Sweet memories torn apart by brutal ones. She was determined to visit it while she was here, but not yet. She wasn't ready.

She wasn't sure she'd ever be ready in time, because they weren't going to be there for long. They just had to get through four songs, and then they'd be leaving Grand Orchard behind. Her heart sank, another layer of loss settling over her. In the back of her brain, she'd always known she'd be coming back to finish what they'd started, but what would happen after? Would she ever be back? Would she ever record another song at *La Musica* again?

Being in the studio today—where every corner only served to remind her of Jonas, of their kisses, of his awe and pride in her, of his faith in her—had shredded her nerves almost as much as hearing her sister's voice on the tracks they'd laid last time. Paisley had stupidly expected to see Jonas there, standing behind the mixing console, beaming at her as he always had. She'd ached to know his thoughts on "The Legacy."

But it had only been Brady at the soundboard. When he hadn't mentioned Jonas, she'd been afraid to ask. Afraid she'd hear that he'd moved on just like she'd told him to do with her silence as much as her words.

She was afraid when she should have been relieved. She didn't need to drag him into this with her. She didn't need to risk him in order to make this right.

She shifted in her seat, a heavy weight settling on her, winding up her nerves.

She felt unsettled, expectant in a completely different way than the last time she'd been here. This was all dread and determination hiding the fear and panic.

Her finger pressed into the beads on her ring so fiercely she was sure they'd leave a permanent mark.

"We working out?" Zane asked, pulling her eyes to him as they drove into the parking lot of the chain hotel on the edge of town. His brow seemed to have been permanently bent in concern ever since leaving California.

She'd had other things she'd planned to do this evening, but the idea of burning away some of her emotions was suddenly much more important. She needed to regain a teeny bit of the shield she'd surrounded herself in when Landry first died. The one Jonas was so good at ripping apart without ever even trying. His mere presence called to her, made her long to rest her head on his chest and feel the weight of his arms at her waist as they forgot the world, and their pasts, and the pain she'd caused him. Was that even possible?

No. She couldn't even let herself think it. It wouldn't be fair to him or her. She couldn't afford to get lost in a sea of Jonas again, not when there was a chance that it could all go to hell once more.

"That would be great," she said.

He walked her to her door, cleared the room even though Jim had been standing outside it the entire time they'd been downtown, and then stepped back into the hall.

"I'll be back in ten. Let Jim know if you need anything before then," Zane said.

She nodded and was already shedding Landry's spiked boots as the door shut. She traded her jeans for exercise gear, forcing her mind to think only about the routine she'd go through with Zane.

When he'd first started with her, she'd just begun taking

lessons with Nikki's dad's friend. The ex-Green Beret had been teaching her not only self-defense but how to be the attacker if needed. But once getting to Jerome's without her parents knowing had grown complicated, Zane had offered to take over her training, and she'd gratefully accepted.

The hours they'd spent together in the gym each week meant that Zane, while not quite a friend, was something more than just a member of her detail. Sometimes, late at night, when she lay in her bed, looking out at the swing set, plotting her next steps, she wondered if she should tell Zane. But then, she knew, as her bodyguard, he'd never let her take the risks she had planned. As it was, he hated it when she went to the same coffee shop every morning at the same time. He begged her to switch it up, repeatedly stating how a routine was the worst thing she could do. She ignored him, hoping his words were right. That *he'd* find her this way.

Zane knocked and announced himself. As soon as she opened the door, he ran his gaze over her, as if checking to make sure she was okay, before leading her to the hotel's exercise room. They spent an hour in the gym, working out on the treadmill and then using the mats for some sparring. She'd always thought Zane was a large man, but after seeing him and Jonas in the same room, he suddenly seemed smaller.

Thoughts of Jonas distracted her, and she missed her punch.

He grabbed her before she could fall to the mat, his hand landing in almost the same spot Jonas's had outside the studio. Jonas's touch had felt like he was branding her while Zane's just felt clammy from their workout. She jerked back, and Zane's brows creased.

He'd never once made her feel uncomfortable in all the months they'd been working out together. If anything, he'd been overly respectful, always telling her before he was going to touch her so she'd be prepared. And yet, today, there was something in his look she couldn't place and twisted inside her. Something personal.

"What's wrong?" he asked.

She wiped her brow with the back of her hand. "I'm more tired than I thought I'd be. The studio always drains me. I should probably just get some food and try to sleep."

He stared for a moment, then went to the wall, picked up her towel, and handed her a water. She thanked him, and they left the room, heading for the elevator.

Her phone rang, and she grimaced, looking at her mother's face on the screen.

"Hi, Mom."

"You promised to check in every day," her mother scolded.

"I was going to. You just beat me to it," Paisley said. It was the truth. She hadn't forgotten. She'd just been putting it off.

Silence settled between them for a moment. "I hate this," her mother said.

"It'll be over before you know it."

"And then what? Will you keep doing this? Album after album? Causing your father and me to worry, seeing us once in a blue moon?"

"I don't know, Mom. None of us do." Everything she was doing there was for her sister, but her mom would only argue more if she said that.

"We never should have agreed to let her start the damn band," her mom said, bitterness and regret in her voice.

"We can't change the past," Paisley said as Landry's vacant stare filled her mind, followed by the hurt in Jonas's eyes. She hated that she'd caused both. Hated that, even now, she selfishly longed to be with him when it would only cause him more heartache.

"I gotta go. The band is waiting for me to get dinner," Paisley lied. They were all doing their own thing tonight, which was how they'd been for months now—siloed souls instead of a cohesive unit. Landry had thought Paisley could lead them, and while she'd brought them physically together, she hadn't brought them together in their hearts and souls. She didn't know how to.

She hung up with her mom with I love yous in the air they both meant but didn't say. The weight on her shoulders felt heavier than ever.

"You're having dinner out? I thought you said you were ordering in?" Zane asked, wiping the sweat from his forehead, brows still bent together, as if everything about her was suddenly confusing and worrisome.

He'd caught her lie, and it made her cheeks flush even more than they already were from the workout. "I just needed to get off the phone. I don't plan on going anywhere."

He didn't respond, but his jaw tightened.

When they got to her room, he cleared it again, but his feet stalled at the door, shooting her a funny look, as if waiting for her to say something else.

"Thank you for working out with me. I'm sorry my mind was all over the place," she said quietly.

He gave her a curt nod. "It must be stressful being back here. It would put anyone out of sorts."

For some reason, his response irked her, but when she didn't respond, he opened the door.

"Goodnight, Ms. Kim."

"Goodnight, Zane."

As soon as she was alone, her mind went to the next step in her plan. Her gut twisted. A weird eagerness tangled with trepidation inside her chest.

She showered quickly, ordered food from room service, and then opened an app on her phone. Then, she did something she hadn't done since Landry died. She posted images on all her social media accounts. Pictures of the band arriving at the studio, a video of them performing with the sound turned off, and pictures of her at Sweet Lips Bakery this morning. She was smiling at the camera in all of them, but it was her fake smile, one that didn't reach her eyes, but she hoped no one else would notice. She hoped it would appear as if the band was happy again. Happy enough to taunt and tease someone who didn't want them to be.

Then, she locked her phone, shut off the light, and tried to sleep.

It didn't come. She was tormented all night with green eyes and large hands, with memories of kisses that had heated her and made her feel whole. She finally gave up in the wee hours, reaching for her bag and pulling out the note from Landry. It was now wrinkled and curled on the edges from months of her handling it. It had broken the silence of her music after Landry's death, and it was fueling her now because she wanted to be worthy of Landry's belief in her.

She folded it away, carefully putting it back, and then got ready for the day. She dressed in jeans, one of Landry's old halter tops with a deep V and ribbed lines down the front, and thigh-high leather boots. She pulled her hair halfway up in a clip on the top of her head with the rest hanging straight down her back. Her gaze faltered on her eyes in the mirror. They looked so much like her sister's. Her fingers danced over the yellow daisy twined with her pink one on her chest.

"I'm trying, Lan. I know you'd hate some of what I'm doing, but I'm doing my best with the band. I'm trying to finish what you started," she whispered.

She waited for the response that never came, grabbed the leather jacket with her daisy on the back, and left her room. Zane was already at her door with Jim, and he greeted her with a lift of his chin and a quiet, "Good morning," before leading her out of the hotel and driving her downtown. Once parked, she headed for Sweet Lips for coffee, and he followed.

The day was barely breaking, and the early twilight cast long shadows on the sidewalks. Only a handful of people were out, mostly owners of the shops getting ready for the day. The silence of Main Street felt oddly foreboding this morning, as if there was something waiting for her around the corner. God, she hoped so.

The smell of baked goods hung in the air as she entered the bakery. It was a little earlier than her normal time, but her past routine and the images of her at Sweet Lips she'd posted should clue *him* in to where she'd be.

The dark-haired owner, Belle, looked up as the door chimed, and she smiled at Paisley.

"Do you want anything?" Paisley asked Zane as his eyes cleared the room, and he took up a stance at the door.

He gave her a strange look, as if she'd never asked the question before when she almost always did. Then, he slowly shook his head. "No, thank you. I'm good, Ms. Kim."

After placing her order, Paisley took another picture of herself with a forced smile, making sure to get the bakery sign in the image. When she glanced back at the door, Zane's eyes were narrowed, and he shifted, turning away to look out at the street. She fought the remorse she felt at making his job harder.

"Here you go," Belle said, handing Paisley her drink.

"Thank you so much," Paisley said and started to walk away, but Belle's quiet voice halted her.

"Oh, wait, I forgot. Hold on."

She went over to the register, ducked down, and then came back with an envelope in her hand with Paisley's name typed on it.

"Sorry, someone left this late last night for you. I wasn't sure if I should...but it had your name...some fan, I'm sure." Belle was flustered handing the envelope over, clearly regretting that she'd given it to Paisley instead of tossing it.

Paisley's heart pounded, and her stomach clenched. Hope. Fear. Regret. She had to restrain herself from snatching it from Belle's hands and doing a victory dance.

"It's fine. It happens more than you think," Paisley said, slowly pulling the envelope from her grasp. It didn't happen. It didn't happen at all. All her mail was delivered to her security team. They went through it and only passed on things she needed to see. To her knowledge, there'd been nothing out of the ordinary. Nothing but fan mail and official Painted Daisies business.

Paisley shot a glance at Zane, but he was still eyeing the street instead of the empty shop. She tucked the letter into her bag quickly and then joined him at the door. Her fingers itched to open it, but she didn't want to risk him seeing it.

They crossed the street in silence to where a trio of bodyguards stood in front of *La Musica de Ensueños*. They let Zane in first, and once he'd ensured the studio was empty, he allowed her inside. The control room and live room beyond it were both quiet.

"I'll be at the door if you need me," Zane said.

She nodded but wasn't really listening. Her heart and mind were full of the letter.

She made her way into the live room and sat at her keyboard. She darted a look toward the glass separating the two rooms. When she didn't see Zane, she pulled the envelope out with a trembling hand and put it on top of the tablet she'd left there the day before. She stared at her typed name for a long moment before slowly tearing it open. Her heart seized, and her breathing stopped as hope and fear mixed inside her.

There were two pictures. One was of her and Jonas on the street at the moment when he'd slid his hand around her waist to balance her as they'd collided. The other was the one of her at Sweet Lips that she'd posted on her social media accounts the night before. Both images had the faces scratched out just like two years ago. The words read: *Don't go down this road again. It will only end in misery.*

It was awful. Terrifying.

Memories of the note with blood dripping from it hanging on the door of the farmhouse made her tremble.

But as terrifying as it was, it was also exhilarating.

Movement forward after months of nothing.

This time, she'd be ready for him.

CHAPTER TWENTY-FIVE

Jonas

IN MY DREAMS
Performed by Dokken

EIGHTY-FIVE WEEKS AFTER

Jonas had promised Brady he'd listen and give his thoughts on the prior day's session before the band arrived. He thought Brady might be testing him. While Jonas couldn't sit at the console and watch them record the songs he'd basically written with Paisley, he also had to get used to hearing and being around them if he was going to work on their tour.

Jonas barely registered the bodyguards at the door of the studio. The Garner men were always there, and while the detail had been increased with The Painted Daisies' new company merging in with Marco's men, it still wasn't unusual to have a group there this early. Marco and Trevor had been grim and unhappy about Reinard Security overseeing everything they did, but then, the last time the Daisies had been in town, someone had died, and that wasn't something anyone could forget.

Jonas was at the mixing console, pushing dials and levers before he realized he wasn't alone in the studio. Paisley was at the keyboard in the live room. She looked pale, and her hand shook as she put a piece of paper back in an envelope.

He couldn't help it. His mind went immediately to the creepy notes they'd received last time the band was in Grand Orchard.

Before he could even register what he was doing, he'd slammed his way into the room. It startled her, causing her hands to go flying, hitting the tablet off the keyboard and sending it flying.

"Shit," she said, putting a hand to her chest. "Don't scare me like that."

Jonas joined her, picking up the tablet.

"What was that?" he asked.

"What was what?" she said, her face shutting down. Calm. Impassive. The way he wanted to feel, but instead, his heart was hammering so loud he was afraid she could hear it.

Their hands touched as he passed her the tablet, electricity zapping through him and filling his head with images of her fingers pushing through his hair and their bodies aligned. He shoved the visual away as fast as it had come. It wasn't going to happen.

"What were you reading?" he asked.

She gazed at him, eyes narrowing. "Nothing that concerns you."

"You seemed upset," he persisted.

"I wasn't. Don't read anything more into it than it was, Jonas. It was just some notes I've been making for a new song," she lied, eyes flicking upward and to the left. Heat curled through him, not from the lie, but from his name on her lips.

It was just his damn name, for God's sake, but she'd been the only one to ever say it quite that way...as if she accented the syllables differently. As if it meant something more coming from her.

But he'd never be more to her. Never.

He forced himself to move, walking back toward the door.

"Did you listen to it?" Her voice halted him. His chest grew heavy at the tiny bit of hope and insecurity he heard there. He hadn't seen either emotion in the new, controlled Paisley yesterday. Even now, she hid it quickly, but in some twisted way, he liked that it was still there. That the Paisley he'd known and fallen for was still inside her somewhere.

"Not yet," he said, meeting her gaze.

She looked down at the tablet gripped tightly in her hand. "It's just..." she trailed off. Then, her shoulders went back, and her chin came up, and she wasn't his Paisley anymore. She was channeling her best Landry imitation. "Never mind."

He warred with himself. He wanted to run, to get as far away from her as he could, but he was perverse enough to also want to stay right there. To hear what she thought about the song. To know what was worrying her.

"I told Brady I'd listen to it this morning. Do you want to listen with me?"

He should bonk his head against the glass window because the last thing he needed was to be around her for longer than necessary.

She eyed him for a moment.

"No. I trust you," she said with a surety that had never been hers.

It pissed him off. That she was different. That she said she trusted him when, clearly, she hadn't. He scoffed, the sound loud in the silence.

Her eyes narrowed again. "I do."

"Paisley, if you'd trusted me, I wouldn't have spent the last nineteen months sending unanswered texts and wondering what the hell I could have done differently."

They stared, his heart pounding, her breath unsteady, her knuckles white as she squeezed the tablet even harder. She didn't say anything else. She had no response. Why should she? She'd had none for months.

It stabbed at all his scars and wounds. He hated that she could still affect him this way. He turned on his heel and went back to the soundboard. He put on the headphones and hit play on the track from the day before.

And fuck. If seeing her and briefly touching her had hurt, the song was like being sliced open from neck to gut. It was one of the songs Paisley had created that summer. The song that spoke of anticipation and love and hope. The hope they'd felt before it had collapsed around them like fall leaves crumbling underfoot. Even though it tore at him, he also realized it was just as good as he'd remembered it. Really good. Like, award-winning good. The emotion bled from all their voices. Fiadh's harp echoed Leya's flute. Nikki was now playing lead guitar, and they had some guy named Finn playing bass in the background.

Jonas didn't have anything to add. The song was perfect.

He skipped back to the track before it.

As Paisley's voice traveled through his head, he stilled. The pain was raw and ragged, but it wasn't her voice that had him frozen. It was Landry's. They'd faded it into the track on purpose, a whisper like Paisley's used to be, a ghost answering from the grave.

He was shaking when it ended. Tears threatened to fall, and he barely held them back by closing his lids. When he opened his eyes again, Paisley was watching him, leaning against the doorframe of the live room.

"I wish it was real," she said. Her expression echoed the emotions in the song, agony that she hid by doing what he'd done, shutting her lids and holding back the tears. She shook her head. "Stupid. I'll never hear her voice again, but every day, I wake up hoping I will."

He wanted to go to her. He wanted to wrap her in his arms and give her whatever comfort he could. It was the same damn feeling he'd had ever since that awful night. But the day of the funeral, she'd been clear she didn't want it—not from him.

The door of the studio opened, and the rest of the band came in. Adria was in the lead. Her blue eyes widened, darting between Jonas and Paisley. They weren't standing anywhere near each other. There was nothing intimate in their stance. And yet, the moment had been filled with intimacy.

"Everything okay here?" Adria asked Paisley.

Paisley nodded. "Of course. Jonas was just listening to 'The Legacy' for the first time."

"Ah," Adria said. "That's enough to do anyone in."

Nikki threw her bag on the couch and glanced over. "Rips your heart out, right?"

Jonas gathered himself together. He wanted to run out the door and not look back. He wanted to be far away from all of them and the bittersweet memories they brought, but he also knew he had to get used to being in their presence.

"My heart has officially been broken for the day," he responded, and he forced his voice to be filled with humor rather than pain.

Fiadh looked between Paisley and him, her deep-red curls still hidden in a lilac sheen that danced around her. "Now our nickname as the heartbreak queens will be justified."

Leya snorted. "It was only you, Landry, and Adria who were ever called that."

Jonas tried not to notice it, but Paisley flinched ever so

slightly at her sister's name. He wondered if it was always like that. If every time she thought about Landry, she felt like her soul was being cut open. It was how he felt about Paisley. Every time she was mentioned, it was like someone tearing a scab off his heart. It might bleed a little less each time, but it still did.

Feet on the staircase drew their eyes. Brady was coming down holding his four-year-old daughter, who looked so similar to him it was spooky. She had a palm on her dad's cheek. Brady's grin was big as he looked down at her as if there was nothing better than her in the entire world.

Brady took in the band, and he gave them a small shrug. "Sorry, I'm going to have her with me for a while today. Tristan has a deadline, and my parents have class. Hope that's okay?"

"Are you kidding? Aria is one of my favorite people," Fiadh said, sticking her hands out for the little girl, who easily fell into Fee's arms. Fiadh swung her around, and Aria giggled.

The band made their way into the live room with Aria tagging along.

Brady joined Jonas at the mixing console. "So?" he asked.

Jonas couldn't meet his eyes for fear the feelings he was still trying to rein in after listening to the song—after being with Paisley—would show. "The songs are incredible, Brady. I don't have anything to add. The way Landry's voice faded..." he choked and had to stop talking.

Brady's hand landed on his shoulder. "They're pretty amazing songs, but then you already know that. Paisley said you wrote two of them with her. She's giving you song credits."

Jonas swept a hand through his hair, brushing it off his face. He needed a damn haircut—like always. "She wrote those last time...that summer. I didn't do enough for song credits."

Even though he could feel Brady's gaze boring into him, he didn't look up.

"Want to stay and work here today?" Brady asked.

No, his mind screamed. *No fucking way. Get out. Retreat.*

But his body didn't agree. His head was already nodding, and his hands were already reaching for the headset. It was going to be a long-ass day.

CHAPTER TWENTY-SIX

Paisley

IN YOUR SHOES
Performed by Sarah McLachlan

By the end of the afternoon, they'd recorded the last two songs and finalized the track order. *The Legacy* album was everything Paisley knew Landry would have wanted it to be. Powerful chords. Catchy lyrics. Angst and drama that would wriggle their way into people's hearts. For a moment, she let herself relish the satisfaction of having done it. She'd brought them together, and they'd recorded four new songs, and they'd done it without Landry when, two years ago, they would have all thought it was impossible.

Not only had they finished it, but they'd finished it early. They still had a couple of days left in Grand Orchard. Tomorrow, they'd use the time to meet with Alice to discuss the stage and theatrics for the tour. While they didn't have any choreographed dancing as part of their show, they did have a visual plan for each song and a finale that would include a special video, bubbles, and fireworks.

As much as Paisley wanted to get the hell out of the town that was just a sea of painful memories, she still had a few more things to do while there, a few more things to accomplish before she said goodbye.

She turned to take in everyone in the studio and said loudly, "We're celebrating tonight at Mickey's."

A chorus of *hell yeses* and *we'll be theres* went through the small collection of humans.

"You're not twenty-one for two more months, Little Bit," Leya said with squinty eyes.

Paisley shrugged. "Mick said it would be fine as long as anyone underage didn't try to order a drink."

She couldn't help it. Her eyes were drawn to the back of Jonas's head. He was talking with one of their roadies as they packed their instruments.

Fee slid her arm through hers and glanced the same way. "He coming too?" she asked quietly.

Paisley shrugged again. "Don't know. Don't care."

But her cheeks flushed as she said it, a tell she couldn't stop.

"Liar," Fee whispered.

Paisley extracted herself from Fiadh, grabbed her bag, and headed for the door. "I'm going to the hotel to change. Who's coming?"

Leya, Adria, and Nikki said they were heading over to Sweet Lips first, but Fee joined her. Once they'd climbed into the SUV, Fiadh turned to her with a frown. "You still have feelings for him. Why are you denying it?"

For the first time in a long time, Paisley's finger found its way to her star. Another tell she'd worked hard to banish over the last year. It frustrated her that she'd done it when she saw Fee's eyes follow the movement. She dropped her hand, finding the anxiety beads instead.

"Doesn't matter what I feel, Fee. Jonas and I...our stars will never align."

It hurt to say it, just like it hurt to ignore him. Just like it hurt to be around him. Some days, she wondered if she'd ever go a day without feeling some kind of soul-crushing agony. Her stupid decisions had cost her everything, and it was too late to change them.

♫ ♫ ♫

Paisley's chest was a mix of joy and sorrow as she walked into Mickey's later that night. Landry would have been a buzz of energy celebrating another album in the bag. For Paisley, it was terrifying to think there might not be a fourth one. She couldn't imagine not making music, but she also wouldn't want to join another band. It was the Daisies or nothing. If they went their separate ways after this, it would mean Paisley had failed Landry again. That she hadn't been able to hold them together. That she wasn't the leader her sister had imagined.

She pushed aside her darker thoughts because she truly wanted to revel in the success tonight. She needed this not only for her friends and herself but so that, somewhere out there, a man would take a picture and send her a note saying she didn't deserve to be happy.

As if sensing the opportunity for danger that lingered in the dim bar, Zane objected as soon as they walked in. "I'm not sure this is a good idea. It's shadowy and dark. It'll be crowded. There are too many things that can go wrong."

His jaw clenched as his gaze took in the distressed-wood siding that matched the floors and the scuffed burgundy leather booths before returning to her.

She was in a white halter dress with bright-red daisies on it, as if the original incantation of their band's logo had found her again. It was a dress the old Paisley would never have worn, but she'd been drawn to it in the store anyway. It was tight from top to bottom, landing well above her knee. She'd partnered it with a pair of red stilettos she'd pilfered from Landry's closet, like so many of the clothes she wore these days. She was lucky that, for a tall woman, her sister's feet had been small.

Zane didn't seem to approve of her outfit any more than he did the bar.

"The band and I need this, Zane," she said. "A small celebration after the hell we've been through. But I know parties bring back bad memories for you." His sixteen-year-old sister had lost her life at a party when she'd snuck out of the house one night and a bitter, uninvited teenager had shown up, taking out a dozen kids with a gun. Zane had only been fourteen at the time. "Don't feel like you have to stay tonight. There'll be plenty of security here."

"I'm not leaving you," he grunted.

He rarely left her, only disappearing on Sundays for church and then coming right back. In California, she'd been grateful for his constant attention. But here, with *him* out there and her trying to lure him in, it was better if Zane left.

"Then, wait outside. At least it won't weigh on you this way."

She walked away, dismissing him like she never had before and feeling guilty about it immediately. But she had to be free of him for a few hours. Even better if she could find someone to dance with. To touch her. To give a fake smile to so that *he* thought she was truly happy.

Her thoughts immediately went to Jonas. They'd never danced together in public. They'd had their bodies twined, dancing to their own rhythms, but not on a dance floor for everyone to see. She swept aside the thoughts of him. She couldn't risk tangling herself with him again, for so many reasons, not the least of which being that, tonight, she needed to appear as if she didn't have a care in the world, and with Jonas, she would care too much.

Four hours later, with Mickey's packed from door to stage, she felt like she might actually have a real smile on her face as she watched their crew, Brady's staff from the studio, Reinard's men, and some of the locals partying loudly and voraciously. They all seemed happy—God, what was that emotion? It had been absent from her life for so long she wasn't sure she remembered what it truly felt like.

She turned her eyes to where Brady and his wife were wound together, like they had been for hours, moving in perfect harmony. It was almost sickening how much they loved each other. A bitter pain shot through her, making her smile drop. Once upon a time, it had felt like there was a chance for her to have that kind of love.

Adria bumped her shoulder, drawing Paisley's eyes from the happy couple.

"What's he doing here?" Adria asked.

Paisley's heart leaped, mind going to the one person she'd just been thinking about—Jonas. Her stomach fell when she saw not Jonas, but Asher Riggs instead. He was leaning against the bar talking with Tommy. The man was the epitome of arrogant billionaires everywhere. She wasn't sure she'd ever seen the man smile. Right now, his brows were drawn together, and there was a glare on his face he was directing toward the dance floor.

Paisley's eyes drifted in the same direction and saw Fee swaying with Leya and Nikki in a dress shorter and sexier than Paisley's. Their bodies moved sensually and languidly to the beat. It wasn't a Daisies song, but it was still moody and alternative like theirs.

"I better go see what he wants," Paisley said. As she moved

around the room, Adria stuck to her heels. When they reached the two men, Paisley put on her best fake smile and said, "We're glad you're here to celebrate finishing the album with us."

Asher dragged his eyes from their dancing bandmates to Adria and Paisley. "It's about damn time."

Paisley felt Adria stiffen next to her, but Paisley wouldn't let him bait her.

"It has been a long time coming," she admitted. "Have you had a chance to listen to it?"

"No," Asher said, his face stone-like. God, the man wasn't human.

"I think you'll see it's right on brand. The fans are going to eat it up like snack cakes," Tommy interjected, and Paisley winced when his words came out slurred. After the incident when Paisley had found Fee and Tommy incoherent in her friend's apartment, Fiadh had slowed down. Now, she rarely indulged, but Tommy seemed permanently drunk.

Asher's eyes narrowed in on Tommy, taking in the drink in his hand and his half-masted eyes. Her stomach churned at Asher's obvious distaste. He ignored Tommy, directing his attention to Paisley. "The Palace Theater in Albany has offered me a last-minute opening in their schedule. You'll use it as a trial run for the show."

She tried not to bristle at his command in the way Fee would, but it was hard not to.

"When is it?" she asked.

"Next Saturday."

Adria scoffed. "Do you have any idea what it takes to get ready for a show like this? You really want us to throw in another stop before everything has even come together?"

Asher turned cold eyes in her direction.

"You get up onstage, shake your pretty little asses, and sing. What else is there?"

"Shake our pretty—" It was Fee who growled out the response from behind Paisley, and it took all her strength to hold her friend back as she lunged for Asher.

Asher looked down at Fee with disdain.

"Have you been drinking too? Is this"—Asher swept a hand toward Tommy and then all the Daisies who were now standing together—"how you want the world to perceive you? Just another rock band that's slid off the rails into drugs and alcohol?"

It took all four of them to push Fiadh away from him.

"We had one drink, asshole," Fee growled. "One drink. To celebrate. But you wouldn't know how to celebrate if it bit you in your stuck-up derriere."

"Get her out of here," Paisley said, looking to her bandmates.

Adria, Leya, and Nikki dragged Fiadh back toward a booth in the corner.

Paisley turned to Asher with a grimace. "She's not normally like this. You...you bring out the worst in her."

His jaw ticked. He tugged at the sleeves of his jacket, and then he said slowly, as if he was carefully controlling each word, "It's mutual. I apologize if I overstepped."

Paisley eyes widened as the shock of his apology rolled through her, and maybe that was why she ended up throwing out the peace offering. "Look. We're meeting with our tour manager tomorrow. Why don't you come and see what it's going to take for us to get ready, and then you can decide if it's really worth putting on a show that might be less than what we want it to be."

He assessed Paisley for a long moment. "Fine."

Then, he turned on his heel and left, striding through the bar as if he expected everyone to part like the Red Sea. And they did because his entire aura screamed power and confidence.

Paisley glanced at Tommy. "Maybe you should go back to the hotel."

"What? Why?" His pupils were dilated, and Paisley suddenly wondered if he'd done more than one too many shots.

"Come on, Tommy. I'll walk you out," she said, sliding her arm through his. They made their way through the crowd toward the kitchen and the back door where their detail had parked their cars.

As they exited, the cool air hit them along with the scent of the apple blossoms.

She'd only taken two steps with Tommy before Zane appeared. He slipped an arm around Tommy's other shoulder, and the two of them headed toward one of the black SUVs. Paisley opened the back door, and between her and Zane, they got Tommy inside. She shut the door and leaned against it, trying to get ahold of her emotions.

"Let me see who can drive him to the hotel without leaving us short here," Zane said and stepped around the car to talk into his mic.

Paisley rubbed her thumb over the beads on her ring as the weight of everything settled over her shoulders. As if it wasn't enough she had a tour to arrange and a murderer to catch, now there was Asher's demands, Tommy's drunkenness, and Fee's uncontrollable hatred to deal with too. *How did you do it all?* she silently asked her sister.

"Paisley?" the deep voice had her jerking her head up and looking into the darkness as Jonas's body emerged from the alleyway. "Are you—"

Tommy shoved the door of the SUV open, causing Paisley to fly forward. She had half a second to realize she was going to hit the ground and fling her arms forward, but the expected pain of landing on the asphalt never reached her. Instead, she was wrapped in strong arms that pulled her to a chest she'd ached to be held against for almost two years.

"Jesus," Jonas groused.

Awareness and belonging flew through Paisley. Comfort. It was so beautiful and so painful it brought a wave of tears to her eyes.

Tommy's head peeked around the Escalade's door. "What's going on? Why the hell am I in the car?"

Zane stepped back around the SUV, eyes narrowing as he saw Jonas with his arms around Paisley.

"You're drunk, Tommy. Go back to the hotel and sleep it off," Paisley repeated what she'd said inside. Her voice shook with anger at Tommy and from the way her skin burned everywhere her body touched Jonas's. A sudden fear hit her. Fear that she might not be able to step away from him now that Jonas had her tucked up against him.

"What? No." Tommy started to climb out. "Not with Asher-fucking-Riggs here."

Paisley pulled herself slowly from Jonas's arms, and it felt like tearing a scab open. Sharp. Bitter. Painful. Her hands shook as she shoved one against Tommy's chest.

"You've already screwed things up enough tonight. Don't make it worse."

Tommy's brows drew together, and he dragged a hand over his face. "Shit. I'm sorry. What did I say?"

"Just go sleep it off," she snapped.

Tommy looked at her with surprise. He wasn't used to quiet and anxious Paisley calling the shots, but she didn't have a choice anymore. Without Landry, this was who she had to be.

Tommy fell back into the vehicle, and Zane shut the door before turning to look at Jonas, who was standing a few feet away now. Zane's expression was strange, a mixture of anger and caution, as if it had been Jonas who'd almost had her face-planting in the parking lot instead of Tommy.

She put a hand on Zane's arm, and his eyes jerked down to her. "Can you stay with Tommy until the driver gets here? Please don't let him get out of the car."

He looked like he was going to protest, but she didn't wait for his response. She just headed back toward the bar with her heart racing and the heavy weight of responsibility pushing her down.

Jonas slid in beside her, matching her step with an easy gait. At the back door, he stopped her with a gentle hand to her elbow.

"Hey. Are you really okay?"

Paisley closed her eyes as the smooth cadence of his voice swept over her. Concern. Caring. She didn't deserve it after the way she'd treated him—the way she and Landry had both treated him—but God, did she still ache for it.

When she opened her eyes again, they got caught in the depths of vivid green ones.

"Sometimes...sometimes I hate that I have to be this person. But then I remember it's my fault she's gone..." Her voice cracked, and she barely held back the sudden rush of tears.

"It isn't your fault." Jonas's response was instantaneous, full of heartache and emotion.

It was ridiculous how easily her secrets slipped out around him. Truths she didn't want anyone to know. Things she held deep inside her. It had always been this way whenever they'd been together, but it couldn't be this way again. She had to fight it. She had to push him away because there was a chance, when this was all over, she wouldn't be here either, and the last thing she wanted to do was add one more scar to Jonas's already wounded heart.

She pushed Jonas's hand away and entered the kitchen. She

tossed her words back over her shoulder, not waiting for his reply, "I'm fine. Everything's fine. Thanks for catching me."

Then, she slid through the kitchen and back into the bar to try and paste another fake smile on her face in order to lure out a murderer.

CHAPTER TWENTY-SEVEN

Jonas

LOVER'S EYES
Performed by Mumford & Sons

Just like two days before, Jonas's leg was bouncing a mile a minute, and the pen in his hand had joined the beat, tapping on his jean-clad leg at the table in Brady's office. The room was past capacity with extra chairs shoved in so they could discuss the plans for the tour with everyone involved. In addition to the band and Alice, there were also the crew leads from each department all the way from security to lights and sound.

Zia was on a monitor hanging from the wall, and below the screen sat Asher Riggs in a suit that didn't match the laid-back jeans and band T-shirts most of the crew wore. He looked like he did every time Jonas had set eyes on the man—like an asshole who thought he was a king.

But the person who drew his eyes, as always, was Paisley Kim. She sat at the head of the table, stage plans sprawled out in front of her with Leya on one side and Adria on the other. Leya covered Paisley's hands with hers, and Jonas almost flinched from the desire to do the same thing. Leya's voice was full of concern as she asked the question everyone in the room was thinking. "I love the idea of the tribute video, Paisley. But are you sure? You'll have to see it every time we perform."

Paisley didn't even hesitate. "I wouldn't have asked for it if I wasn't sure." Her eyes met her bandmates. "Are you sure *you* can handle it?"

"I'm not," Nikki's voice was softer than normal. "But that doesn't mean it isn't the right thing to do. I'm just saying I might be a fucking mess after every single concert."

"Lan would have done it for any of us." Fee's voice was choked, and for the first time, Jonas saw an expression on Asher Riggs' face. It was a flash of pain, a tortured ripple, before it was hidden again. Asher's voice, when he spoke, was devoid of the emotions Jonas had seen. Instead, it was flat and commanding.

"So, we're set, then. I'll confirm with the Palace."

"We won't have the pyrotechnics until Boston," Jonas spoke up, reconfirming the limitations of putting on a show at the last minute. Alice wasn't happy either. He could tell by the tightness that lined her jaw and shoulders.

Asher rose from his seat and headed for the door, turning at the last minute. "One last thing. Ronan Hawk and his crew will be there. They need some additional footage for the documentary, and they never got their one-on-one interview with Paisley."

If he hadn't been sitting so close to the band, Jonas wouldn't have heard Adria's muttered, "*Dios*," or Paisley's sharply inhaled breath.

Asher didn't wait for a response. He just walked out.

The silence he left behind stayed until Alice and Zia eventually filled it, handing out assignments to the crew leads, who took off one by one with jobs in hand. Soon, it was just the band, Alice, and Jonas left.

Leya's Secret Service agent popped his head into the room and said, "Ms. Singh, your father needs a word."

Leya looked around and asked the band, "We okay?"

They all murmured quiet yeses before Leya headed toward the door. "He could have just called me," Leya tossed at the agent.

"He did. Is your phone off?"

"Shit," she said, digging it out of her bag as they left the room.

Alice gathered together all the papers and her laptop before saying, "I'm going to place a few calls and make sure there's no way to get the pyro folks on board by next week."

Fiadh, Nikki, and Adria left the room, talking about the toffee at Sweet Lips and hitting the shops on Main Street. Jonas watched as Paisley slowly gathered her things. The others hadn't even seemed to notice that she hadn't joined them.

He wanted to say something, but he wasn't sure what. Last night, when he'd seen her leaning against the Escalade behind Mickey's, she'd looked as if the weight of the world was on her shoulders. He'd wanted to comfort her even before she'd almost hit the ground and he'd wrapped his hands around her.

He hated that, after everything, after nearly two years of silence, he still felt fiercely protective of her. As if he was the only one who could stand by her side when it was ridiculously clear she had a whole host of people keeping her safe.

She glanced up at him, fidgeting as if she too wanted to say something, but then just grabbed her bag and headed for the door. Her purse hit the doorjamb, slipping from her grasp and sending the contents flying.

He was at her side in a flash, helping her reassemble everything, but his entire being froze when his hand settled on a note—a fucking letter with an image printed on it. It was an image of him and Paisley behind the bar when he'd grabbed her elbow last night. Their faces were scratched out. His stomach lurched as fear, anger, and frustration welled in him.

"What the hell?" he growled, eyes darting up to meet Paisley's.

She saw what he was holding and paled. She jerked it from his hands, shoving it into an envelope where he thought he saw another letter.

He reached for her bag and the letters, but she drew back.

"Paisley." His voice showed every bit of the shock and anger he was feeling. "Have you been receiving more goddamn notes?"

Her chin went up. "It's none of your business."

"The fuck it isn't. That was my face scratched out. Have you been getting these the whole time? For two years? What is your team doing about it?" No one had said anything. Not one thing. Marco and Trevor may no longer have been in the loop because Garner Security had been replaced by Reinard, but the security business was a small world. He would have thought they'd have heard something.

"No. They just started again," Paisley said.

His heart sank to the bottom of his chest. "Since you've been here? Are they all with me?"

She hesitated.

Shit.

Every tortured thought he'd had from nineteen months ago slammed back into him. Was this because of him? Or was this just some fanatic fan of Paisley's who didn't want to see her with anyone?

He stood, reached for his phone to call Marco, and Paisley shot out a hand and grabbed it from him.

"You can't tell anyone."

He stared at her in shock.

"Excuse me?"

"If anyone finds out, they'll make it harder for him to get to me," she said.

"That's exactly the point."

A surge of pain flew over her face that she brushed off. "I want him to come, Jonas. I need him to."

Jonas's pulse hammered through his veins. She wanted to die...fuck. She read his silent thoughts as she always had and shook her head.

"It's not that. I don't want him to actually succeed. I just want it to end. I want him to come for me so I can show him that I'm ready for him."

"What in the hell does that mean?"

He took a step toward her, and she backed up, hitting the wall. He closed the distance again, caging her with his arms on either side of her head, that primal need to protect her raising its ugly head.

"I know what I'm doing. I was trained," she said with her chin held high.

"Trained in what?"

"Self-defense. How to protect myself. How to kill someone if I need to," she said, eyes blazing.

His mouth tightened as he stared at a Paisley he didn't know. She'd always been braver than she thought, but this Paisley... This was a warrior. Someone ready to swing a sword.

"So, you're willing to risk your life for a chance that you can what...get even? A life for a life?" he hissed, pain scuttling through him at the thought of her coming face-to-face with her sister's killer on her own.

"I don't *want* to kill him. But I will if I have to," she said.

He couldn't even believe the words that had come out of her mouth. He'd left her on her own for almost two years, as she'd wished, and she'd gone off the deep end. There'd been no one there to pull her back. Or maybe she just hadn't let anyone else see this side of her. The avenging angel.

"Give me my phone," he demanded.

She shook her head and stuffed it down her shirt. "Not until you promise not to tell anyone."

"No deal, sweetheart. I'm not going to let you get yourself killed."

"I can defend myself."

"Can you?" he said, and he hated himself, but he was desperate to prove to her how foolish she was being, so he grabbed both her wrists and flipped her around so her face was up against the wall and her arms were twisted behind her. His body leaned in tight, pushing against every inch of her. His mouth moved close to her ear. "I just disarmed you in two seconds, and I'm not really trained. The asshole who murdered Landry...he was a professional, Paisley. Someone who fucking kills for a living."

"You have two seconds to let go of me."

He laughed. It was cold and bitter and full of fear because he had to prove to her that she was dreaming if she thought she could defend herself against someone determined to end her.

He switched his hold so he had both her wrists in one hand and grabbed her neck with his other. "Paisley. Show me how you'd get away. Right now. If I was him, what would you do?"

"I don't want to hurt you, Jonas, but I will." Her breath was uneven but not panicked. He was the one panicking.

"Hurt me, Paisley? You've already ripped my heart out repeatedly, and now you're going to finish me off by letting a professional killer into your life. Welcoming him."

He barely had time to register she was moving when a heel crashed down onto his foot. He groaned as pain ratcheted through him, and it loosened his hold ever so slightly. She lifted herself up on her toes and slammed her head back into his face.

It hit his chin, causing more pain to fly through him. If she'd been a hair taller or he was a hair shorter, she would have smashed his nose.

"Goddamn," he hissed.

She took the opportunity to elbow him in the gut with an unexpected force, and she slipped out from his hold. But she'd only gone two steps before his long legs allowed him to catch her. He wrapped an arm around her waist and pushed her up against the wall again as his eyes watered and his foot ached.

She raised a knee and would have jammed it into his balls if he hadn't shifted to the side just in time.

"What the hell is going on?" Trevor's voice traveled down the hallway, stilling them both.

Paisley glared at Jonas and whispered, "If you tell him, I'll hate you forever."

"You already hate me," Jonas growled back.

That took all the steam out of her. She went limp in his hold, leaning against the wall as if he'd just punched her in the gut when it had been the other way around.

"God...do you really think that? That I hate you?" her voice croaked, and suddenly, tears were flying down her face.

Trevor was on top of them now, yanking at the hold Jonas had on Paisley. "Have you lost your ever-loving mind, Jonas?"

"Not me. I have every last brain cell accounted for. I can't speak the same for her," Jonas said as he stepped back. It wounded her. He saw it. The old taunts of her being stupid. The poor decisions that Landry threw at her. And he hated himself immediately. He ran a hand up over the hair flopping in front of his eyes, pushing it back. His body was sore from the places she'd hit him with strength and purpose, knowing what she was doing. But she hadn't been able to escape him—someone who didn't want to hurt her. If he'd been anyone else... If he'd been the killer...

His stomach heaved.

Fuck. Fuck. Fuck.

Trevor's narrowed eyes took him in and then darted back to Paisley. "Are you okay, Ms. Kim?"

Paisley let out a shaky breath and closed her eyes briefly before opening them again, staring right into Jonas's eyes. Like always, she read every emotion, including his worry, and all it did was tighten her jaw. "I'm fine. It was a misunderstanding."

"Tell him, Paisley. Tell him, or by God..."

"You'll what? Slam me against the wall and hold me captive? Oh, wait. You've already done that."

Jonas stepped toward her again, but Trevor's open hand on his chest prevented him from getting close.

"Someone better start talking now, or I'm calling Marco, Reinard, and Fiadh. And I'm not sure who you should be scared of the most, but Fiadh terrifies the shit out of me when she's mad."

He'd been trying to lighten the mood, but it didn't work. Jonas just glared at Paisley, waiting for her to open her mouth and spill the truth, hoping that if she wouldn't listen to him, she'd listen to one of the gazillion people around her slated with her protection. If she didn't...he'd have to become a stalker himself. He'd have to follow her to the ends of the earth and back.

CHAPTER TWENTY-EIGHT

Paisley

FLESH AND BLOOD
Performed by Sarah McLachlan

Jonas was furious. It was coming off him in a steady stream as he glared at Paisley with daggers. In another lifetime, before Landry had died, it would have had her quivering in fear and regret. But she had one chance to get this right. One chance to lead the asshole to her. She couldn't afford for anyone to screw it up. Not Jonas. Not Trevor, or Zane, or any of the other million bodyguards who hovered around them daily.

She'd been surprised to find the second note on the treadmill in the hotel gym after Zane had cleared the room this morning. The fact that whoever had taken the photograph had been close enough last night to get a clear shot of Jonas and her at the back door of Mickey's had been surprising. But then, he'd been a ghost two years ago as well—unseen by their security. It seemed that changing companies hadn't made a difference. This guy knew how to blend into the night.

Her body had shivered when she'd opened it to reveal their scratched-out faces and the words *He can't have you* scribbled on top. But then her eyes had been drawn to the way she and Jonas had been leaning together. Bodies speaking, as if they knew something their brains did not. Even though the stalker had scratched out their faces, in Paisley's mind, she could still see the concern and caring in Jonas's eyes when he'd looked at her.

Every nerve ending in her body had been on high alert last night in a very different way than it was now in the hallway. Last night, it had been full of aching longing. Desire that had curled through her just like it always had whenever Jonas had touched her. Just like it had when he'd caged her against the wall two minutes ago. She shouldn't have been turned on by it. She should have been angry and terrified, but deep inside her, she knew Jonas would never really hurt her, and she wanted him tucked up tight against her. Wanted the anger and frustration and years of longing to escape them as their bodies slammed together.

It was humiliating. Aggravating.

But it also caused a little seed of doubt to form in her head, because what would've happened if it had been the stalker who'd been there? She'd barely escaped a man who hadn't wanted to hurt her, and Jonas had easily recaptured her. Sure, she would have fought harder if it had been the killer. She would have used more of the things Zane had taught her, but still...Jonas hadn't broken a sweat, had barely been out of breath while they'd struggled.

"Seriously, somebody needs to start talking," Trevor repeated.

"Tell him," Jonas growled.

Paisley shook her head.

"She's gotten new letters," Jonas said, jaw tight, lips turned down, brows drawn together.

A choked grunt of frustration escaped Paisley as she shot him a glare.

Trevor's eyes turned wide. "What?"

"They're in an envelope." Jonas turned to search the ground and found the envelope Paisley had dropped during their altercation. He picked it up and handed it over to Trevor.

"Do not open that. You're not part of my team. You have no right," Paisley said, reaching for the envelope that Trevor easily kept away from her.

The movement caused Jonas's phone that she'd tucked into her bra to slide out and hit the ground with the movement. Jonas reached down and picked it up, tucking it into his pocket as Paisley stomped and glowered at both of them.

Trevor didn't even bat an eyelash. He just pulled out both letters.

"Jesus," Trevor said, rubbing his forehead. He glanced at Paisley with concern. "You didn't show these to anyone? They could have dusted them for prints and checked the cameras where they were delivered. We might have caught the guy by now."

"Like you did two years ago?" Paisley threw back, and Trevor visibly flinched. It was cruel, and Paisley hated being cruel, just like she hated so many things about the person she'd become since Landry had died. But then, there'd been things she'd hated about herself before too. A trade-off had been made. One bad trait for another.

"This is serious. Why the hell wouldn't you show these to anyone?" Trevor demanded.

"She has some fucking wild-ass notion of using herself as bait," Jonas grumbled.

Trevor's jaw dropped.

Paisley crossed her arms over her chest and looked away. She swallowed hard as more tears gathered in her eyes. "It's not just that..."

The words slipped out before she could stop them, and she felt both men staring at her. She swallowed, gathered her thoughts, lifted her chin, and met their gaze. "I can't trust anyone... How can I..." She shook her head. "How can I...when..."

"None of us protected Landry," Trevor said gently.

She wiped at the tears but didn't look away.

"Do you think it's someone close to you?" Trevor asked, darting a look both ways down the hall.

"It's me," Jonas's tortured words slipped out of his mouth, and Trevor gave him a confused look. Jonas shook his head. "No. I mean, I'm not the one sending them. Fuck, Trev. Really? It's just... I mean, I'm in them again. Paisley said the notes didn't start back up until she'd arrived in town and had been seen with me."

Her heart sank with his words. She wasn't sure if it was Jonas. She'd posted her smiling face all over social media as well. It could simply mean the stalker didn't want Paisley to be happy with anyone. She said as much to them, but Trevor shook his head.

"No, look. It says, '*He* can't have you.' This isn't just someone wanting you to be miserable. I get your hesitancy to tell anyone, but we need people to know. We need your detail on alert," Trevor said.

"No."

"Paisley, you can't do this on your own," Jonas said, equally as frustrated.

He was probably right. Paisley hated that she couldn't. She hated that all she'd done was lure the stalker into sending more notes. She wanted him to show up. She wanted to see him in person so she could slam her heel into his nuts and hit him with one teeny-tiny fraction of the pain he'd given her by taking Landry away.

"Look. We can probably work out a compromise, keeping the people who know about the notes down to a minimum. I'd suggest the FBI and the head of your security team. If you let me, I'll ask to come onboard as Jonas's protection. I promise you that I want what you want. I want this to be over. I want the guy who did this to pay," Trevor said, his voice deep and sincere.

The old taunts suddenly filled her mind. *Did they suck all your brains out through that mark?* She was an idiot to think she could do this on her own. That she'd be able to lure a killer out and catch him all the while keeping it a secret from her team, the band, and the world. Jonas's reaction... Trevor's reaction... They were justified. She could have lost her life this way. Her chest squeezed tight as she thought of the daily, pained calls with her mom, the white hair and wrinkles that had found their way into her mother's ageless image. What if she'd caused them to lose her too?

Stupid.

She was stupid.

Her entire body sagged.

"Fine. But I don't want the band to know. I don't want anyone but the three of us and the bare minimum."

"I don't agree with the band not knowing," Jonas said. His stance was wide, arms crossed. He looked like his brother. Like someone you could trust with your life. She suddenly wanted that so badly it hurt almost as much as her memories of Landry. She wanted to be able to trust someone with her thoughts and feelings, and her body and heart just as she had once before. Not just someone. She wanted to trust *Jonas* with everything.

But she couldn't. Could she?

He would never take her back after the way she'd ghosted him for two years.

Trevor held up the envelope with the letters. "I'm going to take these."

She nodded.

He started to step away and then shot a concerned look in Jonas's direction. "Do I need to wait for you to walk away?"

Jonas shook his head. "No, I'm good." Trevor looked doubtful. "I won't touch her again, Trev. I promise."

Trevor shot another look at Paisley and then left, taking the stairs two at a time.

Paisley turned to Jonas and exhaled a shaky breath she hadn't known she was holding. "I'm..." her voice trailed away. Sorry wasn't enough, not only for what had just happened in the hallway but for the hurt she'd caused him repeatedly.

"No, I'm the one who's sorry. That was uncalled for." He shot a look at the wall where he'd had her pinned with his old regrets of not being able to control himself written on his face. She hated herself one more time for pushing him past his limits.

"You should tell the other Daisies," Jonas said.

"We're barely holding ourselves together now. I can't lay this at their feet. It's obvious this is about us."

"Me," Jonas frowned.

"If it was about you, you'd be getting the notes and not me."

"Maybe I shouldn't go on the tour with you," Jonas said quietly. "If it's us being together that he hates so much, we should take me out of the equation."

"If it's us together, then that's what I want to show him. I want him out of the shadows, Jonas," Paisley said, believing every word.

"I'm not letting you use yourself as bait."

"Not just me."

"What do you mean?" Jonas's gaze turned hooded.

Even as the idea hit her, it snagged at her heart that he might not want to be anywhere near her. Not even for this. Not even to help catch her sister's killer. She couldn't blame him because all she'd ever done was add grief to his life.

"I mean..." She took a shaky breath. "If you're willing... maybe we could hang out some, while we're here and then in Albany. Let him see us together."

His jaw ticked. "I'm not sure that's such a good idea."

"I promise. After we've caught him, I won't take any more of your time. You won't have to be near me again. Just..." Her voice broke in a way she hated. "Please."

He searched her face with his emotions tucked away behind an impassive mask. It was sad to see him so guarded when, before, she'd been able to read him easily.

Finally, he gave a curt nod, and relief flooded her. Relief because they might actually find who did this to her sister. Relief that they might actually be able to put this behind them once and for all. Relief because her soul had missed him for two years and was crying out to be next to him again, and even a brief taste would be better than nothing.

They stood there in the hallway for a long moment, and she wondered if he was thinking of their past as much as she was, if he ached as she did from every single part of her body that had briefly touched his when he'd caged her. All she knew was that she wasn't ready to see him walk away yet, and it had nothing to do with the stalker watching them.

"So..." she breathed out, finger finding her ring and worrying the beads. "Want to go to lunch? At The Golden Heart?"

She almost laughed because it was ridiculous to go from screaming and fighting and pushing him away, to pulling him close and asking him to lunch as if nothing had happened. *Stupid.*

He dragged a hand over his face, hiding in a different way.

The more seconds that slipped past with no response, the more her heart cracked. She couldn't blame him for not wanting this.

"It's okay...never mind." She started to walk away, but his tortured, strangled voice halted her.

"Let's go."

He turned on his heel and led the way to the hidden door at the opposite end of the hallway, the one that joined Brady's studio to his sister's café.

Jonas's back was tight, and tension radiated from him as she followed him down the stairs and over to a booth in the corner hidden by the giant tree of life springing from the fountain. The room filled her with nostalgia. It wasn't just Cassidy's amazing food she missed. It was the cherished memories and the way being at the café felt like being in Jonas's home with people he considered family.

Her phone buzzed against her leg. She pulled it out and read the message.

FEE: Where are you? Zane looks panicked because he can't find you. Expect to get your phone pinged any second.

Paisley grimaced, feeling bad that she'd made Zane worry—feeling worse that he'd soon know the secrets she'd been keeping from him. He'd helped her train, helped her learn to defend herself, and she'd used that knowledge to lead her enemy to her. She wasn't sure how he was going to react to that knowledge, because he took pride in his job, handling it with a seriousness that bordered on overbearing. She'd appreciated it before because she'd needed to feel safe, needed the knowledge he was willing to hand out, and it had made her parents feel safe to have a familiar face there every day.

PAISLEY: I'm grabbing lunch at the café.

FEE: Oh. Okay. Want company?

Fiadh was going to freak out when she saw Paisley spending time with Jonas again, and she wasn't sure if it would be with an "I told you so" in the air or frustration that she was bringing the drama back into their world.

PAISLEY: I'm good. Go shopping with Adria and Leya. Have fun.

The door of the café swung open, and Zane entered. His eyes scanned the restaurant until they landed on her with Jonas. His eyes narrowed, and he stalked across the café to their table.

FEE: We'll let you know when we head back. Please keep us posted about your whereabouts though.

PAISLEY: Will do.

"Ms. Kim," Zane said. "We were worried."

"Sorry," Paisley said. "Got distracted."

Zane's eyes shot to Jonas, and Paisley wished she could be distracted in the way Zane thought she meant. A lips-and-skin-and-hands-tangled kind of distraction. Things that would likely never happen again because, even if she wanted it, she didn't think Jonas could forgive her.

Zane's squint took Jonas in one more time before he said, "I'll be by the door."

And he turned on his heel and left them.

Willow, a woman with bright-red hair, who'd been at the café for as long as Paisley could remember, greeted them, sliding menus onto the table.

"Hey, Paisley, good to see you again. How are you?" Willow asked, and you could hear the true concern in her voice. It was the same one she heard in every person she'd encountered in Grand Orchard since arriving. It was like everyone took it personally that she'd lost her sister here. That murder had invaded their small community, and yet... someone there had been responsible.

"I'm good. I've sure missed Cassidy's food though. I'd like the soy chorizo quiche, a s'more cookie, and an iced tea, please," Paisley told her.

Willow nodded. "And for you, sir?"

She flashed Jonas a wink, and Paisley's heart stopped at the pure flirtatiousness of it. Sudden images of the two of them together filled her mind, making her breath catch. Willow was at least six years older than Jonas, but six years didn't always mean much these days. Jonas was mature in a way that most men his age weren't.

"Lasagna and a Coke, please. How come you're waiting tables?" he asked.

"Can't trust Laney to not drop a plate in Paisley's lap. And you know she's still drooling over you," Willow teased. "I'll be back with your drinks."

She sauntered away, and Paisley turned to look at Jonas again, trying to be objective. It was impossible because all she could see was the man she'd fallen for. A dirty-blond-haired, chiseled Adonis who wore the weight of abandonment on him like it was a penance he had to pay. A man who saw people's inner souls in a way not many could. A man who'd given her every part of him before she'd stomped on it and walked away.

CHAPTER TWENTY-NINE

Jonas

IT'S NOT OVER
Performed by Daughtry

Jonas watched as Willow headed back toward the kitchen, because if he didn't, he knew he'd stare at Paisley until it got uncomfortable. His heart was thudding loudly in his chest, and his body throbbed, not only from where she'd slammed him with her foot, head, and elbow, but from the plea that had been in her voice when she'd basically begged to spend time with him—for all the goddamn wrong reasons.

It was a mistake. He knew it. And yet, he was sitting across from her with an ache in his belly he couldn't heal. When would he learn? He was a fucking hopeless idiot when it came to women he cared about. He couldn't seem to let them go no matter how many times they hurt him.

"Are you two dating?" Paisley's words drew his eyes to her.

"What?" Jonas asked.

"You and Willow? Or you and Laney?" Paisley's eyes darted

away after asking it, as if the question had been difficult for her even when it seemed impossible to think she cared about who he dated. She ran a finger over her ring. It was her new tell. Instead of placing her index finger on her birthmark, now she worried the little beads.

Jonas swallowed hard, forcing his gaze away and landing on Laney. She was dark-haired and blue-eyed, pretty, but she wasn't the one he'd dated. He searched for Ashley, but it didn't look like she was working this afternoon. Blonde, smart, and almost done with her bachelor's in social service at Wilson-Jacobs, Ashley and he had hooked up several times. She was three years older than him, but they'd had a couple of classes together last year. She'd been getting over a boyfriend at the same time he'd been getting over Paisley, and one night, they'd moved from studying to drinks, which had slipped into a heated kiss. He'd been too old to lose his virginity, but Ashley hadn't cared. She'd let him explore and showed him all the things she'd wished her boyfriend had done when they'd had sex. It had been good. Pleasant. Fulfilling, but not satisfying.

Maybe because neither of them had brought emotion to the act. They hadn't been looking for something permanent or even semi-permanent. They'd been seeking release. A temporary reprieve from the jagged wounds they'd both felt after losing someone who'd been important to them.

He'd taken so long to answer that Paisley jumped to her own conclusions.

"Wow. So, which one was it?" she asked, a forced tease to her tone.

"Neither of them," he said finally.

"But there was someone?" she pushed.

For some reason, the layers of unasked questions beneath that single one pissed him off. Maybe because he wanted her to be angry and jealous, and what he heard most was the tease.

Maybe because he wanted her to have asked him to lunch because she missed him instead of needing him to lure a fucking stalker from the shadows.

"Is this really what you want to talk about, Paise? Me screwing someone else to try and burn your memory out of me?" He hadn't truly intended to be cruel, but the way she jerked back from the table showed his words had hit home anyway.

"You're right. It's none of my business," she said, face shuttering, and instead of allowing him to remain angry, it made him feel like a jerk. He brushed the long strands of his bangs back. He really needed to get it cut.

"Ashley. Her name was Ashley," he found himself saying even though she'd just admitted she had no right to know. Paisley met his gaze, the tension between them building, the air crackling with the emotions and unsaid words. "But it didn't work."

Paisley's brows drew together in confusion.

"Nothing can burn your memory out of me," he said quietly, immediately kicking himself and wishing he could take it back.

She looked away but didn't respond. Her chest was heaving slightly. He wanted to slide around the booth, take her hand in his, and show her what he'd learn at Ashley's side. Make her gasp and moan because, almost two years ago, he might not have been certain he could give her the pleasure she deserved, but now, he knew he could. And the thought of Paisley Kim crying out his name as he touched and licked and plunged into her...it was enough to make him hard and uncomfortable in the middle of the café.

He was thankful the table hid his groin when Willow set down their drinks and then hurried off to another customer.

"So, you're working with Alice now?" Paisley asked, changing the direction of the conversation.

"It started because of a class I was taking. I had to interview someone in the industry who worked backstage, and then I started helping out here and there. When she realized the Daisies' tour was going to be in the middle of her paternity leave, she asked if I'd help Zia be her feet on the ground."

"Which do you like better? The time at the soundboard or the tour stuff?" she asked, as if she really cared, as if they hadn't spent months in silence at her request.

Every word they spoke was like some weird twist of pain and joy. Each question took him a long time to answer because he overanalyzed each word, wondering how much of himself he was revealing to her again.

"I don't have an answer for you yet. This will be my first time actually being on tour. Everything else I've done has just been behind the scenes from here. But, the mixing console..." He stopped, getting ahold of his emotions before continuing. "It hasn't been the same."

Paisley looked away and then back. "I'm sorry...for so many things...but if I took music away from you..." She shook her head, throat bobbing, and as always, her emotions became his. The heartache. The sorrow. God, he should hate it, but instead, it felt like he was finally sliding home after months away. When he didn't say anything, she continued, "At first, after Landry died...I lost the music too. I thought I'd never get it back, and it hurt so goddamn much. But then...I found a letter she wrote, and after that, it all came rushing back. It was the only thing that kept me going. I wrote hundreds of songs...most of them crappy and painful—but true." She took a sharp breath, as if she hadn't meant to say any of it and was surprised by the outpouring. "Anyway...if you lost music because of me...I can't apologize enough."

When their eyes met, instead of the shuttered, emotionless

shield they'd both been wearing for two days, there was pain. Loneliness. Regret.

"What was in Landry's letter?" Jonas asked as his heart sped up.

She didn't answer right away as one of the other waitresses dropped off their food. They both played with the dishes, and Jonas could tell she was nervous, because her hand shook as she held the fork.

"She wrote it the day she...after you and I left the studio and before she..." She shook her head, tears filling her eyes. She looked down and took a slow, deep breath before continuing. "She felt awful, for everything she'd said about you. About us. She said she was jealous and that she was afraid she'd lose it all when the band realized they didn't need her if they had me. But look what happened when she was gone. We fell apart."

It was really hard to stay mad at a dead person, someone who'd been murdered—potentially because of you—but he had been for years. Landry had seemed so...strong and confident and determined, as if she'd never admit to any mistake. So, it was surprising to find out she'd apologized.

"It doesn't look like you've fallen apart to me," Jonas told her, and Paisley lifted tear-filled eyes to his and smiled softly.

"Thanks...but it's all just a mirage, you know. We're all here, ticking the boxes, finishing what we started, but there's still something missing. No matter how much I want to be, I'm not Landry. I can't lead like she did," she said in a whispery volume that was more the Paisley he'd known before. The Paisley who thought she was invisible and stupid and not enough. It ripped at the scab on his heart and made it bleed some more—for her and him and for her dead sister.

"You're right. You're not Landry," Jonas said, and her shocked eyes lifted to his, wounded by the words, and he rushed to finish his thought to ease the pain of them. "But you don't need to be. I told you then, and it's the same now. You're the heart of the Daisies, Paisley. Landry was right. You're the one they'd never survive losing. Those songs you've added... 'The Legacy'... Landry couldn't have done that. It was you. You made it happen."

Paisley's jaw shifted as she continued to fight her emotions. "Thanks for saying that."

They drifted into silence. Jonas was reliving that summer, the beautiful moments that had happened before hell had hit them, aching for something he'd lost...they'd lost. They ate, but neither one of them really did full justice to the food. When they went to leave, Willow wouldn't let them pay because Jonas never paid when he ate at Cassidy's place, and he and Paisley made their way out onto the sidewalk.

They both glanced around, suddenly remembering the fanatic that was out there somewhere with a camera and a grudge. Nobody on the street looked out of place. No one seemed to be paying them any mind. It was the same as it had been almost two years ago. How could so much have changed and yet nothing?

Because Jonas felt exactly like he had then. There was a wild need to protect her mixed in with the knowledge that if he didn't have Paisley in his life, he'd never be the man he was supposed to be. And he hadn't been. He'd been some alternate-universe version of himself for nineteen months. What had Paisley said? They'd all been ticking the boxes? That had been him. Going through the motions. Finishing what he'd started. Hoping that somewhere along the way his life would right itself again.

CHAPTER THIRTY

Paisley

FOR WHAT IT'S WORTH
Performed by Liam Gallagher

Paisley's emotions zigzagged back and forth. It was hard to keep up and left her feeling tired and raw as she stepped out into the sunshine with Jonas on her heels.

Zane was there immediately. "Do you need the car, Ms. Kim?"

She hesitated, looking back at Jonas. She wasn't ready to leave him yet, not only because of the stalker but because his presence was sliding into the empty spaces and filling in holes she thought she'd feel for the rest of her life.

There was something she wanted to do while she was here, but she hadn't had the courage yet. But maybe...maybe with Jonas at her side, she could do it.

She swallowed hard and looked up into green eyes that still seemed cautious, asking, "Can I ask you to do me another favor?"

He ran his hand through the long strands falling over his face. It might have been even longer than when she'd been there last time. She itched to touch it again, her fingers recalling the softness of it, sending heat curling through her.

When he didn't reply, she continued. "I need... I need to do something at the pond."

She swallowed as his eyes widened.

"You really want to go back there?" he asked, brows scrunching.

"Yes. But I need to make one stop first," she said.

He looked up at the sky, as if trying to find a way out, and she suddenly knew she couldn't do this without him. She'd never have the courage.

"Please." It was the second time she'd all but begged him that day. It was definitely not something Landry would do. This was all old-Paisley. She didn't know if she hated or loved that Jonas brought it out in her.

He gave her a curt nod, and relief filled her, showing in the smile that hit her face. He stared at her lips for a long moment, the air between them heavy and electric again.

She dragged her eyes away from him and turned to Zane. "Can we stop by the hotel? And then we need to go to Swan River Pond."

Zane didn't like it. His jaw ticked, but it wasn't his place to object, and he knew it. So, he just requested for one of the cars to pick them up, opened the door for her and Jonas, and then climbed into the passenger seat.

Jonas waited in the Escalade while she ran up to her room at the hotel with Zane on her tail.

"I have to object," Zane said as he stood in the doorway, watching her retrieve the bag she'd brought with her from California for just this purpose.

"Because of where we're going, or because of Jonas?" she asked.

"Because you're purposefully aggravating a stalker."

She stilled completely, bringing her eyes from the bag's contents up to his face. He was glowering and unhappy. She held her breath for a moment before letting it out.

"You heard."

"Of course! I was the first call Reinard made. I'm lucky to still have a job."

It was bitter and sharp in a way Zane had never been with her. He'd been all patience and gentleness, and Paisley's chest grew heavy with remorse because she was the reason for it.

"I'm sorry. I...I just need answers. I need to finish this. You know what happened to your sister. You saw her killer brought to justice and put behind bars. Me? God, my family lives with the knowledge every day that he's still out there." There was grief in every syllable. Grief she couldn't hide.

His jaw softened. "You should have come to me."

"I couldn't risk you telling me no."

He assessed her for a moment.

"So, all of this, Grand Orchard, the party last night, the social media posts...Jonas..." His jaw clenched. "It's just a scheme to draw him out?"

Her heart flipped. Yes. No. That's the way it had started. But what if...what if she could make amends with Jonas? Was there any possible way he could forgive her enough to become a part of her world again? What if she didn't have to have two pieces of her soul missing but only one? She closed her eyes against the flood of tears at the thought—painful, happy, remorseful tears that left a tiny taste of hope at the bottom. But she couldn't say those things to Zane. She could barely even dare to think them.

"Yes," she said.

When she opened her eyes, he was still staring at her.

He turned and left the room, and she followed.

Jonas eyed the bag as she got back into the SUV, but he didn't say anything. They rode to the farmhouse in silence. It was a path they'd ridden many times together, and yet, today, it felt like the day she'd ridden in the limousine to her sister's funeral, as if she was going to have to say goodbye when she wasn't ready.

The long driveway and the farmhouse surrounded by orchards appeared exactly the same, but her heart hammering fiercely in her chest as they stopped in front of it was completely different. The last time she and Jonas had arrived there together, there'd been a bloody note on the door, and her sister was dead. Tears filled her eyes before she even got out of the car, but she forced herself to move forward.

Jonas was at her side in a flash, and when he reached out and twined their pinkies together, it caused the dam to break. She didn't brush the tears away. She let them come. Just like she'd let them come while playing "The Legacy" for the band and the hallway with Trevor and Jonas. Holding them back, refusing to feel, hadn't helped her heal or forget.

When Jonas started toward the front steps, she pulled him back and shook her head.

Instead, she led him around the side of the house and out toward the pond.

It was a bright, sunny day, and the pond sparkled, the glare off the water almost too intense. A pair of swans floated by with a serenity Paisley had always ached to have but never accomplished. The scent of tules and grass filled her senses.

The air wasn't muggy as it had been that night. In fact, there was a chill to it today that sent shivers up her spine. Jonas noticed it, a worried gaze searching her face for a sign that she was ready to retreat.

She squeezed his pinky one last time before dropping it, feet traveling to the spot where she'd found Landry. There was no sign of the trauma that had occurred there. Nothing to show that her sister had taken her last breath, fighting an unseen attacker.

She sobbed, and Jonas's hand touched her back, a gentle consolation.

God, she could have had this for two years if she'd let him in.

It didn't help the tears. She could barely see when she dropped to her knees and opened the bag. He knelt beside her.

"What do you need?" His voice was full of the tears she was crying.

She pulled out a tiny potted plant, a trowel, and a baggie.

There were just a few golden flowers on the deep-green leaves at the moment, but when the plant grew, it would be full of them. The little plant would flourish here—at least, that was what the lady at the gardening store had said.

She dug into the ground with the trowel with shaking fingers, and when it was harder than she expected, Jonas took it from her and made the hole for her.

She opened the baggie and poured out a handful of Landry's guitar picks—the ones she'd liked best, not only from The Daisies but from other artists she'd loved. Ones she'd collected years before they'd ever started the band. Then, she pulled the plant from its pot, set it gently into the ground, and used her hands to replace the dirt around it.

Jonas helped in silence, and when she looked up at him, his face was tear-stained as well. She wondered who they were for—her sister or her or him or all of them?

"Grow, little plant," she whispered. "Grow and remind the world there was once a daisy named Landry who was as stubborn and beautiful as you."

She ran her hand softly over the leaves, as if she was running it over her sister's hair. Then, she stood and brushed herself off, looking up at Jonas who'd risen with her.

"Thank you," she said.

He pulled her into him, chin resting on the top of her head, and they both cried. She could feel the way his chest jerked with the silent tears, the unsteady pace of his heart and his breath, and it only added to the furious flow that traveled down her cheeks.

She wasn't sure how long they stood there, but something between them shifted.

The walls they'd both assembled were cracking, even if they hadn't come tumbling down.

And hope soared through her heart.

CHAPTER THIRTY-ONE

Jonas

BETTER DAYS
Performed by Breaking Benjamin

Her body was wracked with silent sobs, ones that matched his.

He wished he'd been able to hold her this way for two years. To give comfort simply by standing next to her. And that was when the anger filtered back in. Anger at her for pulling away when they'd needed each other most.

He slowly withdrew, doing his best to hide the anger she didn't need at this moment—not after trying to celebrate a little piece of her sister's life in the place she'd died.

Paisley looked up at him with a tumultuous smile. "Thank you. Again."

He nodded, picking up the empty bag and trowel in order to give himself time to collect his emotions.

They turned, and her bodyguard, Zane, was there watching them with a hooded gaze. The man had been clearly unhappy about coming to the farmhouse, and he definitely didn't like Jonas. Maybe her bodyguard's clear disapproval was because he was unused to seeing her with anyone, and Jonas's body reacted with a fierce pleasure at the thought.

Paisley started toward the side of the house leading to the drive, and he and Zane followed her. At the last second, she turned back, glancing toward the little flower they'd planted at the shore, waving, as if saying goodbye to a person. His entire insides clenched at the simple act.

In the car, she gave the driver the address for the O'Neils' place and the apartment he had over their garage. Then, she turned to him with wide eyes, asking, "Wait. Do you still live there?"

His lips twitched. "Yes."

She smiled as if relieved this piece of him was the same.

When they pulled into the driveway, she slid out of the car with him, glancing up at the windows of his apartment and swallowing. The last time she'd been there had been the night her sister died.

"Are you coming with us the day after tomorrow when we leave?" she asked, fingering her ring. "Or are you coming closer to the concert?"

"I'm coming with you."

Paisley shifted on her feet, rubbing a palm on her jeans and then fiddling with the ring again.

"Maybe we can have lunch again tomorrow?" she asked.

Like everything she'd asked all day long, he was a mix of yeses and nos. His walls were crumbling, but if he couldn't be around her for a few hours now without falling apart, he'd never last months on tour. It would be easier if they could be friends. If they could somehow manage to slip back into the easy camaraderie they'd had years before kisses and trauma had removed it.

He shrugged, responding with a quiet, "Sure."

Her face burst into a huge smile, like a rainbow coming out as the storm dissipated and stunning him with its beauty.

He was fucked. So screwed. Because he'd never want just friendship with Paisley Kim. He'd want all of her. He'd want to own every little piece of her heart and soul the way she had always owned his.

But then he remembered her real reason for wanting to spend time with him was because of the killer. He clenched his teeth, turned, and dragged himself away.

"I'll text you the location," she said softly.

His feet stalled. Text. A fucking text. One he'd waited to receive for nineteen months.

He didn't respond. He couldn't. He just waved a hand in the air and headed for the apartment. He felt eyes on him the whole way. Hers. Her bodyguard's. Maybe even ones he didn't know that had his gut clenching for a different reason.

♫ ♫ ♫

In a failed attempt to forget everything that had happened that day and to try and resurrect the shield Paisley had batted aside in a few hours, Jonas spent the rest of the afternoon sending emails and making arrangements for Albany.

He skipped dinner with his family because he wasn't sure he could look at Marco and not spill everything. The letters. Paisley. The hope he hated feeling.

But after he'd also skipped out on their workout, it wasn't surprising when Marco showed up at the door, knocking and letting himself in. His face was grim, and Jonas wondered if Trevor had actually told him the truth about the notes.

"Want to tell me what the hell is really going on?" Marco asked, leaning up against the counter, arms crossed.

Jonas pushed his laptop aside and stood, stretching his arms, delaying his response.

"What do you mean?"

"Trevor tells me he's joining Reinard."

"I heard something about that," Jonas hedged, going into the kitchen and grabbing two water bottles. He offered one to Marco, but his brother just shook his head.

"Jonas, I'm not stupid. What's going on?"

"Don't know anything about their detail, Marco. I'm just a hired hand. I know the Albany stop has them scrambling. Maybe they're short-handed?"

Marco scoffed. "You and Trevor need to get your fucking stories straight."

Jonas's eyes widened. "Why? What did Trev say?"

"He was tired of sitting around twiddling his thumbs in Grand Orchard and needed to feel like he was back in the action again."

Jonas hated not telling him, but if Marco knew what was going on, he'd leave Cassidy, Chevelle, and Skylar to tag along, to try and put right the things he felt had gone down on his watch. He didn't want his brother anywhere near this. It was bad enough Trevor would be there, but Trevor didn't have a wife and kids counting on him. Trevor's mom lived with his sister and her husband. In many ways, Trev was the lone wolf Marco had once been.

When he didn't respond, Marco's voice dropped. "Tell me you're going to be okay."

Jonas lifted his chin, put a hand on Marco's shoulder, and squeezed. "I'm going to be okay, Marco. Don't worry about me."

"I love you. I'll always worry about you," Marco said gruffly. Jonas's throat bobbed, emotions filling him. "When do you leave?"

"Day after tomorrow."

"We weren't ready to lose you so soon," Marco said. "Cassidy and the kids are going to be a wreck."

Jonas hated the thought of leaving them for months. The kids would be totally different beings by the time the tour was done, and he would have missed it all.

"You could come to the concert in Albany. You and Cassidy haven't had a night out in a while. We could see each other one more time before I'm in the thick of things."

Marco stared at him a long time, trying to read the secrets he wasn't used to keeping from his brother anymore. Not since Austin.

"I'll ask Cassidy," he said and then headed for the door before turning to face him. "If she doesn't apologize and admit she was wrong, she doesn't deserve you back."

Jonas looked up, startled. "What?"

Marco's lips twitched. "You don't think I recognize that mopey, lovesick look on your face? I hate that she hurt you, but everyone deserves a second chance. Just make sure she earns it."

And then he was gone, leaving Jonas to thoughts he didn't want.

When his phone chimed two seconds later with a tone he hadn't heard in nineteen months, his heart leaped, and his stomach clenched.

PAISLEY: Thank you again for today. I couldn't have done it without you.

She could have, and he was tempted to say she'd done everything without him for months, but he decided being a dick wouldn't help either of them.

JONAS: I'm glad I could be there for you.

It was all he'd ever wanted to do. Be there for her. Help her through it and maybe have her with him if and when his life fell apart again.

PAISLEY: I was trying to think of a place to go for lunch tomorrow, and then I realized there's nowhere I'd rather eat while in Grand Orchard than Cassidy's. So, same time, same place?

His hands shook as he typed his answer.

JONAS: I'll be there.

God, he was a fucking idiot.

♫ ♫ ♫

When he walked into The Golden Heart Café the next day at lunchtime, Paisley was already there. She was dressed more like her old self, in ripped black jeans and an oversized T-shirt, but one side of it was hanging off her shoulder, showing a tantalizing amount of skin that made his dick twitch and his stomach tighten.

She gave him a small smile when she saw him, and it lit up his insides further.

When he got to the table, Willow arrived, took their order, and winked at him as she left, just like she'd done the day before—a repeated moment that brought back as many good memories as pained ones. A silence settled between him and Paisley he wasn't sure how to break.

"How are your parents?" he asked finally.

Paisley turned solemn, and the half smile that had been on her face the entire time disappeared, making him want to kick himself. "Good as can be expected. Their business keeps them busy, but Mom panics if I don't text or call enough. It's the only thing I'm sorry about in coming back."

"I'm surprised they let you," he said quietly.

"I'm an adult, Jonas. I make my own decisions," she said, lifting her chin defiantly. He couldn't help notice the difference again from two years ago. Once she'd doubted every single thought she'd had and now she was a strangely confident woman.

He'd missed it. He'd missed her first steps outside her shell, flexing her wings and becoming who she was supposed to be, and he hated it. But he was also glad she'd emerged and not retreated back into her invisible self.

While they ate, they talked about nothing and everything—the bandmembers and what they'd been doing before she'd pulled them back together, about his classes and how he felt like he'd let Brady down by no longer sitting at the mixing console with him.

It felt the same as the talks they'd had before and not.

It made his heart hurt and also jump for joy.

He wasn't sure if he could take her back and risk being abandoned all over again.

He wasn't sure she wanted him back.

When they left the café, she paused at the sidewalk like she had yesterday. Her bodyguard stepped forward again, hovering off to her side, but the air of disdain he wore was different than the other bodyguards, as if he had a right to the emotion, and it made Jonas wonder again about the man's relationship with Paisley.

Paisley looked from Zane to Jonas. "Do you want to take a walk?"

He didn't. He needed to get the hell away from Paisley and the spell she cast around him every time she was near. He felt every ounce of resolve he'd had not to be swept into her universe again drifting away as desire and hope tried to fill in the wounded gashes she'd left behind.

As if she knew he was hesitating, she reached over and twined their pinkies together. He almost jerked back even though he himself had tangled them the same way at the farmhouse the day before. That had been different. That had been comfort at a time of grieving. This felt like the old them sliding back together.

Then, he remembered what she really wanted was to pretend they were together in order to draw the asshole from the shadows. *Fuck*. If anyone was an idiot, he was, for letting himself believe, for even half a second, that her touch and her smile meant there was hope.

"Let's go," he finally said.

He tightened his fingers around hers and drew her down the sidewalk in the direction of his apartment. At least there, they wouldn't be in the line of sight of the stalker. There, he could ask her what her relationship was with Zane and see if there was something more to this than just her taunting her sister's killer.

Marco's voice mocked him, *If she doesn't apologize and admit she was wrong, she doesn't deserve you back.*

The tree-lined street to his apartment was quiet, the epitome of quaint, small-town living where neighbors all knew each other. People who'd watched Cassidy grow up and knew Brady before he was famous. Some of them waved to Jonas as they walked, and not one single thing felt out of place, and yet, he had to remember there was someone out there coming for them.

At the steps to his apartment, he hesitated. If they went into his place, there would be no shield between them. No bandmates. No Brady and the studio crew. No bodyguards or customers at the café.

She let go of his hand and journeyed up the steps ahead of him.

"Do you still have instruments spread out all over the place?" she asked, waiting for him by the door.

He shook his head. "No. I've given most of them to the high school. I just kept the drums and the guitar."

He unlocked the door and waved her in before following her inside. Much like the very first time she'd been there, he tried to see what it would look like through her eyes. If she'd notice all the changes. Cassidy had helped him decorate it in the last year. The cheap, bachelor furniture that had once been Brady's before it was Marco's was all gone. In its place was a cushy, light-brown leather couch and distressed oak tables over a colorful woven rug he'd picked up from one of the indigenous booths at the music festival Brady and his family ran. The place felt rustic and warm where it had once felt temporary. There were pictures on the wall of Jonas and his family along with pictures of him and Brady at the studio. White sheers covered the windows so the light streamed in but softened the space, making it feel almost dreamy.

It was how it felt to have Paisley there. Like something he'd once wished upon a star but never thought would happen again. A dream coming true. A dream he was worried he couldn't afford.

"Wow," Paisley let out a breath. "It doesn't even look like the same place."

He chuckled. "No, I guess it doesn't."

He looked down out at Zane waiting at the foot of the stairs. "He need anything?"

Paisley ducked her head out and asked,"You good, Zane?"

Zane nodded, but his jaw was tight.

Jonas shut the door before going into the tiny kitchen. He grabbed two water bottles and handed one to Paisley who'd sat on the couch with her bag at her feet. When he joined her, he left as much space as he could between them, but it still felt too close.

"How long has Zane been with you?" Jonas asked.

"Since right after the funeral. Why?" Paisley asked.

"He just seems...vested in you."

"What's that supposed to mean?" The graceful arch of her brows furrowed together.

Jonas debated for all of two seconds before just telling the truth. "It seems like he's more than your bodyguard."

Her mouth dropped open. "Are you...jealous? Of my bodyguard?"

Fuck. Was he? Maybe. But it wasn't just Zane. It was anyone she'd had in her life after she'd left him behind. She looked toward the door as if she could see Zane at the bottom of the steps, her eyes narrowing even more.

"Zane's the one who trained me in self-defense. How to kill. He gave me something I didn't have, confidence in my strength, but then..."

She trailed off, and Jonas felt like an asshole because she'd felt strong, and then, yesterday, he'd done everything he could to make her feel weak.

"If it makes you feel any better, my foot is bruised, and my ribs are sore."

She gave him a small smile that made him long to kiss it, to feel her breath and hear the catch in her throat when he touched her. Those sounds and sensations haunted him in his dreams in a way his time with Ashley never had.

Her eyes grew serious again. "I never meant to hurt you."

He wasn't sure if she was talking about yesterday or months ago. It wasn't the apology he needed, deserved, but he also didn't care at the moment. It just felt right to have her on the opposite end of his couch. Even if it was just to pretend for a little while that they'd found their way back to each other so her sister's killer would emerge once more.

His gut churned at the idea that this might all still be because of him.

"If this is happening because of me..." Jonas said, setting the water bottle down and rubbing his chin where his stubble had reappeared. It grew back faster than he could shave it off these days. "The only people I've really pissed off are Artie and Mel."

Paisley pulled her knees up to her chest, and it caused the T-shirt to slip farther off her shoulder, taunting him.

"Have you heard from your mom at all?" she asked. He was surprised she asked, knowing it was a sore spot in his life, but maybe she just needed to move away from her pained past to something in his.

"Last I heard, she'd gotten another sentence for some infraction. She's happiest in prison it seems," he responded. Before, it had the power to wound him deeply—the fact that his own mother had no desire to get out, see him, and make sure he was okay. But now, he'd sort of accepted it. The therapist had said her staying didn't have anything to do with him, that it was about her. She said it didn't mean he wasn't lovable. While he was slowly trying to accept it, it was hard to realize when Maliyah was the only woman he'd loved who hadn't left him.

"I'm sorry," Paisley said.

"Honestly, my life is better because she's not in it. Who knows what would've happened to me if I'd stayed in Austin with her. The people she brought into her life..." Jonas shrugged. He could have ended up like Artie, dealing drugs and living a life of crime. He'd have been unfulfilled, searching for something, because there was a piece of his soul that craved the music he'd found now.

"You're breathtaking." Paisley said it so quietly he wasn't sure she'd said it at all.

"Excuse me?"

Her cheeks flared as if she hadn't realized she'd said the words aloud.

"You're so strong and open and caring, even when you have every right to be closed off. To be some dickwad, like Asher Riggs. Instead, even when it's been battered and bruised, you still wear your heart on your sleeve. How do you do it?" she asked.

Her words slammed into him, trying again to fill in the crevices of hurt and aching loss that lived deep inside him. Gaps she'd left along with his mother and Mel. But it also opened the sealed box he'd stuffed his emotions for her into, tearing it apart and making him want, all over again, the one person he couldn't have.

CHAPTER THIRTY-TWO

Paisley

ILLUSIONS OF BLISS
Performed by Sarah McLachlan

The light beaming from Jonas was almost blinding. His soul had always called to her, drawing Paisley to not only the loss but the strength she saw streaming from him. But now, the glow seemed larger, brighter, fuller. He'd changed from a tortured teen into a resilient man, one who saw his faults and flaws but wasn't holding himself back because of them.

Before she could stop herself, Paisley had unwrapped her arms from her knees, risen, and slid onto his lap. His hands caught her as she wobbled but didn't move away once she was stable. His eyes flicked down to her lips so close to his they were almost touching. The energy shifting in the minimal space between them was palpable. God, she'd missed this so much. Him. The feeling of being home. The feeling that, somehow, by just standing at her side, he made her a better human being. They were stronger and fiercer together.

She hated herself all over again for letting him go. Letting them go.

His eyes grew wide and then closed, as if looking at her was too much. His hands on her waist tightened, fingers digging into the flimsy tee and embedding into her skin.

She bent her head slightly, placing her mouth against his. A mere touch. Soft lips pressing against even softer ones. It was hardly sexual. Hardly anything. But her body ignited, and a soft, raspy moan escaped her, causing her lips to part.

"Fuck." It was a tortured groan that escaped him.

Then, his tongue was in her mouth, and he was devouring her. Licking, sucking, gliding over her. Demanding a response she easily gave. Drinking him in. Drinking the strength of him.

He drew her closer until her chest was tight against his, molding the seams of them into one. Her hands went to his hair, and she thrilled at the silky feel of it twining through her fingers just as she had years ago. She tugged at the strands, and he growled, as if the pressure turned him on even more.

Whenever they were joined like this, they'd always felt like two unstoppable forces colliding into one. Atoms joining. It was beautiful and heady. His hands slid under her shirt, and the feel of his touch on her bare skin sent goosebumps trailing over her and need crawling through her stomach and chest. She moved so she was completely straddling him, joining their jean-clad cores in a way that built pressure and had her moving in order to find relief.

He shifted, muscles rippling as he easily flipped her just like he had in the hallway at the studio. She was on her back on the couch with his body pressed into her in one smooth move. The weight of him was heavy and welcome. His lips coasted down her cheek, over to the corner of her jaw, and then down her neck, wet and hungry. Beautiful.

She moaned again, arms circling his waist, pushing at his T-shirt, raising it so that she too could explore his skin. She felt alive. Seen. Whole. Like she always had with him. Why had she denied them both the comfort they could have brought each other over Landry's loss?

Guilt.

She was the reason Landry was dead.

It should have been her.

But Paisley wasn't dead. She was here. And she needed this. She needed to feel like an actual human being and not a robot in a bubble. Not just one piece of a band that the world knew as The Painted Daisies. Not a person with two missing chunks of her soul.

He pulled her shirt down farther, tugging aside the cup of her bra and taking a breast inside his sweet mouth. Licking and nipping while his hand twisted the other gently through her shirt, commanding her. Leading her body. The power and passion she'd experienced in the hallway came back. He was all strength and control. She loved it. Wanted it. Wanted him. Wanted to know what it would be like to have him inside her. She craved all of him.

The hard, thick length of him pushed into her belly. Her hand popped the button on his jeans, sliding inside, gripping him.

He groaned, but her touch had brought his hands and his mouth to a sudden stop. His forehead came to rest on her chest above the breast he'd been consuming. His breath drifted over her wet nipple, and she gasped, her legs encircling him, trying to bring him even closer.

Instead, it pushed him away. He pulled back, sitting again on the opposite side of the couch. It left her feeling bereft...alone... shivering for more reasons than just the cold air that hit her naked skin. He stared at her with eyes heated and hungry. She could tell he wanted it as much as she did, but his words said the opposite.

"No, Paisley," he said in a raspy whisper.

"Why?" she asked, pain twisting in her gut at his rejection. She deserved it. She'd pushed him away one too many times.

"I'm not making love to you on a couch, with your bodyguard at the foot of my stairs and your friends waiting for you. I'm not going to rush any moment I have with you. I can't. You deserve better. *I* deserve better."

God, he was right. She took whatever she could from him every time she was with him. She left him branded, scarred, and broken without thinking about what he wanted, what he deserved. Maybe there was something inherently wrong with her.

"I'm sorry," she breathed out, adjusting her clothes. "You're right. I'm...so selfish. I just..."—she looked up at him as the words broke out of her like a cry—"missed you."

"Why did you do it?" he asked, pain bleeding from his words. "Why did you send me away?" There was the tortured teen she'd once seen. He'd hidden it away until he couldn't help but show it, just like she hid the old Paisley behind a version of Landry.

"Guilt. Like the notes said. I didn't deserve to be happy...not if I...not if we...were the reason she was dead to begin with." She closed her eyes. "Being with you... It always made me feel a thousand different things, and all I wanted was the emotionless bubble I'd found until I could figure out how to heal. You wouldn't let me have that...you wouldn't let me feel nothing."

He inhaled sharply at her raw honesty.

"I can't do it again, Paisley. I won't. Either you let me in, let me be there completely and absolutely without ever pushing me away, or we stay two people who work together."

"You're right. You deserve to have someone who is completely and utterly yours," Paisley said as her heart pounded and her core ached. "I just... What if he succeeds? What if I die? I just wanted—just needed—to know what it felt like at least one time. To be embedded into each other...to be really and truly whole."

Her words were out and fading away as his eyes widened. His breathing seemed erratic, almost a pant.

"Fuck," he said. His favorite word, full of different meanings. This time, it was full of anguish. "I can't take you—have you that way—for just one night, Paisley. It would break me."

She took a shaky breath and stood. Could she give him more? Move forward with him instead of shoving him away like she had everyone else? Deep inside her, the girl he'd first met, the one who'd texted him for two years on tour, wanted her to reach out and grab everything he offered. That girl wanted Jonas at her side, in her life, forever. Since Landry's death, she'd lived behind a screen, only coming out to play jagged notes on her piano before diving back behind it where no one could really see her. She couldn't do that with Jonas. Like she'd told him, he wouldn't let her. He drew her out into the light.

But if she accepted his terms and then something happened to her because of the stalker, she was worried it would turn him into the person he fought every day not to be. Angry and broken. But maybe...maybe when this was all over, they could have a chance at a new beginning—one they could make wholly theirs.

She moved so she was next to him again.

"You're right. We should wait. But when this is over, Jonas, when the man responsible for all of this is behind bars or dead and out of our lives for good, then... Then, I want everything you offered. I want us to find a way back to what we were and to never let go."

She searched his eyes for an answer, and she suddenly realized it didn't matter what happened with the stalker. If Jonas rejected her right now, as she deserved, she'd never find her soul again. His turning her away would take the last piece of her heart that remained after Landry's death—the one she protected as if it was the last diamond on earth.

Jonas's hands settled on her waist, drawing her closer, until his ear rested on her chest, and she recalled his words from two years ago. He'd said he was listening to the rhythm so he could match it. A harmony. The song that was exclusively theirs.

"I'm not Superman, Paisley. I won't be able to take another hit."

His words were cracked and loaded with emotions, and they knotted her insides until they were sharp and painful, because she'd been the one to take the last shot.

"Thank you," she breathed out. "Thank you for giving me another chance."

He looked up. "Everyone makes mistakes. It's how we learn. Maliyah and Marco have pounded that into my brain."

He was so beautiful it hurt. She didn't know what to say. She was just grateful he wasn't throwing her out the door.

Paisley's phone buzzed.

FEE: Tell me I'm not going to have to send a hitman after a certain blond music producer.

PAISLEY: Not even close to being funny.

FEE: Seriously, where are you?

PAISLEY: I'm coming back to the hotel now.

Paisley put her hand on his face, thumb circling his cheekbone. "I have to go. Fee and the others are looking for me," she said. "But I promise. I promise I'm going to do everything I can to not hurt you ever again."

She shivered from the enormity of what she was doing. The enormity of having another person's well-being in her hands. She wondered if this was what Landry had felt, always having to protect her.

Paisley twined her hand with his. His fingers flexed, tightening, and his eyes turned bright and watery. A wave of panic hit her because she didn't know what the hell she was doing or how to keep the promise she'd just made him. All she knew was she couldn't fuck it up again. And when the old voices came back, taunting her with her stupidity, she fought against it because this was her last chance with Jonas, and she was desperate to do it right.

She slowly let him go, grabbed her bag, and walked to the door. Jonas joined her.

Zane's face was impassive as they emerged from the apartment, but there was still an aura of disapproval about him that had lingered since yesterday. When she'd asked to work out together the night before, he'd said he had things to do for Reinard, but really, she knew it was because of Jonas. He'd never once seen her with anyone else, and even if he had, it wasn't his place to judge her. It was only his job to protect her.

"I had the car brought around," Zane informed her, head tilting toward the SUV waiting for her on the curb.

He led them toward the street. She'd just turned to say goodbye when Zane shoved them against the side of the O'Neils' house. "Stay here!" he demanded and took off at a dead run. The driver of the SUV jumped out as well and fell in behind Zane as they gave chase.

Jonas pushed Paisley behind him. With her back to the wall and Jonas's tall body in front of her, she couldn't see anything, but she could hear the pounding of Jonas's heart. It was a rapid staccato that echoed hers.

"Maybe we should head back inside," Jonas bit out, shoulders tense, as if he was waiting for a hit.

Stupid. Stupid. Stupid. You should have let him be. The chant ran through her, adding to her shaky breath and limbs.

They both stood there for a moment, hesitant. She'd just peeked around his arm when the driver reappeared around the front of the house. He was barely out of breath, but he was frowning.

"Who was it?" Jonas demanded.

"Didn't get a good look at his face, but it was a guy with a beanie, tattoos, and reddish-brown hair. Fucking disappeared when he hit Main Street."

Zane returned with a gray beanie and a thin, black hoodie in his hands. The two bodyguards shared a look. "Maybe we'll get lucky and get a DNA hit. Let's bag it," Zane said, and he went to the back of the SUV to get one of several kits their bodyguards carried everywhere these days.

Jonas's body was still tight as he turned to look down into Paisley's face.

"I don't want you to be alone."

Paisley looked at the two bodyguards. "I won't be. And when I get back to the hotel, the others will be there."

"Stay with one of them tonight? Don't stay by yourself. Please." Jonas's voice was deep with concern.

Paisley had no one to blame for this but herself. She'd taunted the stalker on purpose, but that didn't mean she was going to bring her friends into this. She wouldn't put them in danger too.

"Paisley," Jonas growled as if he could read her mind.

"It's not their fault, Jonas. This... It's all on me."

"And me! If you won't stay with one of them, then either stay here or let me come back to the hotel with you," he insisted.

Her eyes grew wide, glance slipping to his mouth.

His hand came up and ran a thumb along her lips. "Not for that. I'll sleep on the couch."

"I have bodyguards, Jonas."

"I know, but..." Jonas shot a look at Zane again, who was in deep discussion with the other guard and talking into his mic to the other members of the detail. "It isn't the same."

She relented. "We're leaving first thing in the morning, so just come stay at the hotel."

Relief settled over his face, and it did something to her insides, warring desire and fear that she'd hurt him again or that he'd get hurt by just being around her. "I'll pack a bag, say goodbye to my family, and meet you there."

She nodded and stepped toward the SUV with him at her side. He opened the door for her before Zane or the driver could get there.

"I'll see you in a few minutes," he said as if he was reassuring them both.

She slid her hand over the stubble on his cheek one more time.

The door shut, and then they were driving away. She glanced out the back window and saw him standing in the drive, stance wide, arms crossed, looking both ways down the street. Then, he turned and headed for his brother's house with determination in his stride.

God, she'd missed him. Missed feeling like she could do anything if he was at her side. That, together, they could take on the world. But she was also afraid that, in leaning back into him, she would cause something worse...something more permanent to happen to him or her or the people they loved. Her fear for the band grew.

She should tell them...but they were barely getting their feet on solid ground again. They didn't need to know the earthquake was coming. Did they?

CHAPTER THIRTY-THREE

Jonas

STILL LOVING YOU
Performed by Scorpions

When Jonas entered the back of his brother's house, laughter was in the air. Jonas found Chevelle and Skylar in the living room. They had a tee set up with a ball sitting on top of it, and the baby had a bat in her hand.

"What are you doing?" Jonas hurried forward in time to grab the bat just before she swung.

"I'm teaching Skylar how to hit," Chevelle said with a smile.

"You can't play ball inside the house, Chev. You know that," Jonas told his nephew.

Chevelle looked crestfallen because Jonas never scolded him. Jonas was the fun uncle. The one who gave them ice cream for dinner when Marco and Cassidy were out on a date night.

"What do you think would have happened if she'd hit it?" Jonas took the ball off the tee and held it so Chevelle could see the direction it would have gone—to the stained-glass window on the front door.

"Aw, she's not strong enough for it to go that far. And Dad says mistakes aren't permanent. It's how we learn."

Jonas's heart tugged because it was what he'd just told Paisley. He wanted to believe it from the bottom of his soul because if he lost her again, there would be nothing left of him but a permanent shell—worse than the one that had been there for the last nineteen months.

Cassidy came from the back of the house and stopped as she saw the tee sitting in the middle of her living room. "What's going on here?"

She looked at the ball and bat in Jonas's hand and frowned.

"Preventing catastrophes," Jonas said with a smile. He handed the ball to Chevelle. "Why don't you take it out back?"

Chevelle nodded and pulled Skylar and the tee with him toward the back door.

Cassidy followed them. She left the back door open and shut the screen so she could hear the kids in the yard as she started pulling things out of the refrigerator for dinner.

"You eating with us tonight?" she asked.

"No. Actually, I'm heading over to the hotel to stay the night with the band. We're leaving for Albany first thing. I just wanted to say goodbye to you and the kids before I left."

"Marco said you were leaving early. What happened?" Cassidy asked, peeling the skin off an onion.

"Asher-fucking-Riggs happened."

"The kids aren't ready for you to be gone. I'm not ready. We won't see you for months. What are we going to do without you?"

It tugged at some of the broken pieces in Jonas's heart, sliding them together again. He was loved and wanted here. He was whole. Even if things didn't work out with Paisley, he had people who would forever be a part of his life, people who cared about him. Not everyone had abandoned him. There were actually more who'd stuck than who'd left. He had to remember that.

"I'm going to miss you too, Cass," he said, sliding an arm around her shoulder and giving her a sideways hug. "You'll have to film Chevelle's games for me, and we can video chat so I can see the kids." They stood there for a moment in silence. He swallowed and said, "Did Marco ask you about coming to the concert? We'd get to see each other one more time."

She nodded, turning her full, concerned gaze on him.

"Are you really okay with all of this? Being with the band? With Paisley?" she asked.

Jonas let her go and leaned on the counter next to her. "Would you think I was an idiot if I said I was giving her another chance?"

Cassidy inhaled sharply. "Wow."

He looked down at the floor, hand tapping on his thigh. "She was trying to heal in the only way she knew how. I feel like she deserves her own second chance, you know?"

Cassidy hugged him like he'd just hugged her. "You have one of the biggest hearts of anyone I know, Jonas. You're right. She does deserve a second chance, but I'm just wondering what changed."

He wasn't sure he could put it into words. Paisley hadn't really apologized, but she'd shown him she was sorry. She'd shown him that she wanted him, not just physically—although the passion running between them was big enough to be its own creation—but as her partner. The person who made her whole. And somewhere, deep in his soul, he knew they belonged together.

He turned and picked up the onion and knife Cassidy had left on the counter and started dicing for her—a job he'd taken on many times in the last few years in this kitchen. As much as Cassidy loved cooking, she hated chopping onions.

"We have a connection, Paisley and I," he said. "What I felt for Mel was just hero worship. What I felt for Ashley was just..." He faded off.

"Lust?" Cassidy teased. Two years ago, he probably would have flushed at just her saying that word, but he was a grown-ass man. Lust wasn't anything to be embarrassed about. Sex and desire were part of the human experience. Beautiful in their own way.

"Yeah, I guess," he responded. "It was definitely just physical. She never owned a piece of my soul. I never owned a piece of hers. We were just..."

"Friends with benefits?" Cassidy offered up, and this time, he laughed with a shrug.

"Yeah, I guess that fits." He didn't say anything else as his hands moved fast over the cutting board just like Maliyah and Cassidy had both shown him.

"And it's different with Paisley?" she pushed.

"Not even comparable. We just...fit."

She nodded with a small smile. "Okay, but if she hurts you again, I'm boycotting all things Daisies, and I'm going to start a social media smear campaign."

Jonas laughed because the idea of the ever-upbeat and optimistic Cassidy doing anything so negative was almost ridiculous.

"Don't think I can't," Cassidy said. "Or that I won't. She doesn't get to hurt my brother twice."

The word brother filled his heart, taking the air from his lungs for a moment.

He finished the onion, washed his hands, and then hugged her one more time. "Okay, I'm going to go pack and head out. I'll say goodbye to Chevelle and Skylar in the yard."

He kissed the side of her head.

"Wait. What about Marco?" she asked.

"I'll stop by the office on my way to the hotel." But he wasn't sure he would. He'd probably just send Marco a text because if he was in Marco's presence again, he knew he'd be spilling his guts about everything. Last night had been hard enough.

He spent a couple of minutes in the backyard, squeezing his niece and nephew as his heart tightened again at the thought of not seeing them for months. Then, he headed back up the stairs to his apartment.

It wasn't even an hour later that he was walking out the door, having showered, changed, and packed. He pulled an oversized suitcase onto the landing and went to lock the door. His hand and heart both froze as he saw the note stuck just above the handle.

It was scribbled in handwritten red ink with no picture, and it read: *If you get back together with her, you're both as dead as her sister.*

Cold fingers of dread ran up his spine.

He looked around and saw no one, just the lights inside the O'Neils' and his brother's house. Thankfully, the kids weren't in the yard anymore, but his stomach churned, thinking that they might have been out there when the stalker had come up the steps. Had they seen anything? If he questioned them, he'd have to tell Marco and Cassidy what was really going on, and he'd promised he wouldn't. Not yet.

He stuffed the note into his pocket, headed down the stairs, and strode off toward downtown with his suitcase rolling behind him. When he got to Marco and Trevor's office above Sweet Lips, Trevor was alone. He'd missed Marco somewhere along the way.

He handed the note to Trevor.

"Where was this?" Trevor asked, jaw tightening as his eyes narrowed on the words.

"Taped to my door just now," Jonas responded and then caught Trevor up on the man Zane had chased down the street.

"Did you see the guy?" Trevor asked.

Jonas shook his head. "No. Only Zane saw him."

Trevor's jaw ticked.

"I'm going to stay with Paisley at the hotel tonight," Jonas said. "I don't want her to be alone, and she still refuses to tell her friends."

"Marco's hurt that I'm joining Reinard. I'd like to tell him about this," Trevor said.

Jonas's stomach churned. "Give us a few more days, Trev. I don't want him to feel like he has to come running after me. You'll be there. Her detail will be there."

Trevor was silent for a moment before nodding in agreement.

Jonas looked down at the note Trevor had now bagged. "This is because of me, Trev. The only person I know who I've pissed off this bad is that weasel Artie. Do you know where he's at?"

"Last I checked, the warrant was still out for his breaking parole two years ago." Trev's voice died away. "But I'll check again. I'll also reach out to Mel's family to make sure he hasn't made contact."

Jonas's chest ached from the range of emotions he'd experienced over the last few days—competing emotions that were painful and strong. "It would be easier if he just came for me, but that's not what he wants, is it? He wants me to feel as shitty as he does by taking away the person I care about most."

Trevor shot him a look. "Care? As in present tense? That didn't look like caring at the studio yesterday, Jonas. That looked like some pissed-off shit."

Guilt hit Jonas hard, and he felt like an asshole all over again, especially after she'd said how Zane had made her feel strong. But he knew he'd do the same thing all over again if he had to. "She was telling me she was going to lead a fucking stalker to her door without telling anyone. I was just proving a point."

"By trying to frighten her."

Jonas ran a hand over his hair. "She scared the hell out of me, Trev. I just reacted. It wasn't right, but it worked."

"Talk to your shrink lately?" he asked, and that, more than anything, hit home.

His jaw tightened. "This was different."

Trevor stared at him for a long time. "I don't want you to get hurt, Jonas, but I won't let you manhandle anyone either."

Jonas headed for the door, done with the entire conversation. "Just find the piece of shit, and we won't have to worry about it."

Then, he slammed the door behind him and headed toward the hotel with his heart heavy and his mind whirling.

CHAPTER THIRTY-FOUR

Paisley

LOVE GIVES LOVE TAKES
Performed by The Corrs

For some reason, the entire band had congregated in Paisley's hotel room. There was food littered on the round table in the corner, and Fiadh had shot glasses with lemon vodka lined up on the TV console. Leya was dancing on the bed as Adele crooned in the background, and Nikki and Adria were hanging off opposite sides of the couch. Paisley had tried to get rid of all of them multiple times, knowing that Jonas was going to show up at any second, but her friends had adamantly refused to leave.

"We have one night to let loose before the hounds come sniffing back around," Fiadh said. "One night. We deserve this."

"We can't be hungover tomorrow," Paisley told her. "Asher will kill us if we show up to rehearsal in less than tip-top condition."

Fiadh frowned at Asher's name. "We're not drunk," she insisted. "We're tipsy. Letting off some steam."

"Remember when Landry took us to that strip club in Vegas to blow off steam before the last tour?" Nikki said with a soft smile.

"No. I wasn't there. I wasn't allowed," Paisley groused, but Landry's name hadn't hurt quite as badly this time when it was spoken. It still dragged down the center of her, but it wasn't enough to cause her to buckle.

Leya twirled on the mattress, finally losing her balance and collapsing on the bed. "Remember when that one guy accidentally-on-purpose lost his thong? That was the first time I'd ever seen a guy's junk before."

Everyone stared open-mouthed at Leya. "Wait. What?" Adria said, pulling herself from the couch to land on the bed at Leya's side.

Paisley sat down in a chair at the table. She'd thought she was the only member of the band who hadn't been with someone before. None of them really had time for a serious relationship between tours and appearances, but Paisley had thought there'd been someone in all of their lives at different times. Adria, Landry, and Fee made no secret of the people they hooked up with, even taking people home from concerts like typical rock stars. And while neither Leya nor Nikki had taken anyone home—that she'd known about—Paisley hadn't thought it meant there'd never been anyone.

"You have a brother, Leya. You never, ever saw his penis?" Adria said.

Leya shuddered and made a face. "Yuck! No!" Then, she sat up and looked down into Adria's face. "Wait, does that mean you've seen your brother's?"

"The nanny used to bathe us together when we were little," Adria said as if it was the most normal thing in the world.

Maybe it was. Paisley didn't have a brother. She'd only had Landry, and there were so many years between them, she couldn't remember a time when they'd actually been in the tub together, even as kids.

The only thing Paisley knew about a guy's body parts was what she'd seen in biology class, on the internet, from Landry's descriptions, and from touching Jonas. She flushed thinking about it, thinking about how much she'd wanted him to slide into her today and finish whatever it was they'd started years ago.

Fee's eyes narrowed in on Paisley. "Little Bit, you're awfully quiet over there. Have you seen someone's junk? Like a six-foot-something, blond-haired, green-eyed someone's?"

Paisley shot a look at the door, wondering again how to get them out of the room before he showed up, but also not wanting to because the band hadn't been like this in a long time. Just sitting together, talking, sharing, and opening up—real friends.

Leya looked at her with a smile. "Kim Ji-an! What base did you and Jonas, the sex god, get to?"

Paisley cringed at the use of her full Korean name. No one used it except her parents.

"Sex god? Puhlease," Nikki snorted right as Adria said, "Base? Really, Leya? What are we, twelve?"

"He's totally a young Thor," Leya insisted.

"Ladies. Please. Our Paisley is not going down that troubled path again," Fee insisted.

This caused Paisley to turn even redder, which made Fiadh's eyes narrow.

"Oh. My. God. Please say that's not where you were this afternoon."

Paisley's chin came up. "What happened with Jonas was my fault, Fee. I'm the one who cut him off. All he wanted to do was be there for me while I grieved. I just didn't know how to let him. Not when..."

She stopped talking, afraid that everything would come pouring out—not only how she'd wanted to live in an emotionless bubble but about her training with Zane and baiting the stalker.

All the smiles, laughter, and teasing left the room, and Paisley hated it. They'd had such a light moment. A moment they needed. She swallowed hard, put on her best Landry smile, and said lightly, "I have high hopes of seeing his junk in the near future."

Perfectly timed, there was a knock on the door.

"*Hey ram*, did you just conjure him into reality?" Leya said.

"Ms. Kim, you have a visitor," Zane's voice carried through the door.

Paisley's smile turned real as she whispered, "Zane doesn't approve of sex-god Jonas."

The entire band burst into giggles, like they were twelve instead of women in their mid-twenties.

Adria got up, dragged Leya from the bed, and grabbed Nikki's hand as she went by the couch. "Let's scram, Daisies. Our Little Bit has a hot date."

Paisley didn't think her blush would ever disappear.

They opened the door to find Zane poised to knock again, and behind him, Jonas towered, dwarfing her bodyguard.

"He's got a suitcase. What do you think the sex god has in the suitcase?" Leya giggled softly in a pretend whisper to Adria.

Adria rolled her eyes. "We need to have a serious discussion, Leya. One I thought you already had with your mom, your grandmother, or...someone. How did you get this far in life without us knowing you knew so little?"

Fiadh grabbed the bottle of lemon vodka, but instead of leaving, she came toward Paisley and said in a hushed voice,

"Landry's not here to say this, so I will. No means no, whenever it's said and however many clothes you have on. If he cares about you, he'll wear protection. And if he hurts you again, I'll slaughter him with my bare hands."

Paisley reached out and hugged Fee to her. They held on tight, the two of them feeling Landry's loss the most. Paisley spoke quietly into her hair, "Thank you. But he's just here as a friend. And remember, the Kim sisters hurt him far more than he ever hurt me."

Fee squeezed her back even harder before she let go. As she passed Jonas, she waved a finger and said, "I may not be as big as you, but I fight dirty. Plus, I have a dozen security members at my beck and call. Don't make me use them."

Jonas pulled his suitcase into the room, and Fee shut the door behind him after shooting another look in Paisley's direction. They could hear Fiadh talking on the other side of the door to Zane but couldn't make out what she was saying before she also disappeared. Even though the music Leya had been playing through the wireless speaker was still going, the room felt quiet with the band gone.

Jonas left his suitcase up against a wall, stuffed his hands into his pockets, and looked around the room at the shot glasses and the mostly empty food cartons.

"I interrupted a party," he said.

Paisley realized he was nervous. Nervous to be alone with her in a hotel room. She couldn't blame him. She'd all but attacked him at his apartment, and he'd said he didn't want to go there with her yet, but being alone together here would definitely put temptation in front of them both.

Paisley started cleaning up while Jonas watched.

"They haven't let their hair down like that since...in a long time," Paisley said.

"I could have come back later. I didn't..." he breathed out, looking up at the ceiling. "Now, they think we're..."

"Getting down? Doing the deed? Making love?" Paisley teased.

Jonas huffed and then chuckled. It was a deep sound that rippled through the air and sent a shiver over Paisley's skin. She tried to ignore it by concentrating on the reason he was there. "It's better they think that than them knowing the real reason you're here."

He didn't respond, but she could feel the strain between them. She threw the last of the containers away and turned to face him with regret in her voice. "I really screwed up. I led him right to us."

Jonas crossed the room in two long strides and pulled her into his chest. "This is actually my fault, Paisley. There was a note on my door when I left my apartment just now. I think this really is Artie. I think he's the one who did all of it."

Jonas's words were tortured.

Paisley hugged him as waves of emotion flew through her. Anger and remorse. The one question that had haunted her for all these months on replay: *If she hadn't been with Jonas, would Landry still be alive?* She could have walked away from him. Landry had wanted her to, but she'd ignored her sister's wishes. She'd been naïve enough to think she could have Jonas and Landry and the band.

Maybe no one was allowed to have it all in this life. Maybe you had to choose between love and success and family. But then, the image of Brady carrying his daughter down the stairs at the studio flashed before her. He had it all.

She pushed herself away from Jonas reluctantly. "I'm going to go get ready for bed."

He swallowed hard and nodded, watching her as she dug through her luggage for a pair of pajamas.

After washing her face and changing in the bathroom, she stared at her reflection. She looked younger than almost twenty-one, especially makeup-less. She touched the star by her eye. For so many years, she'd barely glanced at herself in the mirror because she'd hated the mark, hated that it made her even more different than the sea of White faces at her private school where the Hollywood elite had sent their children. Every time she'd been teased, it had been Landry who'd rescued her. She'd let her sister fight her battles for her for years.

Working out with Zane had been about more than just the stalker. It had been her way of trying to find some of the inner strength Landry had always had, and it had helped some. But nothing ever made her feel as confident and sure as she did when she was with Jonas. With him, it was as if she could see herself through his eyes, someone who was strong and brave and knew what the hell they were doing.

Maybe relying on him made her as weak as relying on Landry had. Maybe it was like Landry had said to Ronan in the video all those months ago—that she was using them all to hide behind. Or maybe it was just proof that everyone needed someone in their life who could show them the best parts of themself so they had the strength to face their flaws. So they wouldn't be alone when life tossed a grenade in their direction.

When she came out of the bathroom, all the lights were off except for a lamp on the bedside table. Jonas had put on a pair of sweats but had no shirt on as he lay on the couch. His sculpted chest was enough to cause her feet to stall as she took in every powerful line. Caught as she was in the beauty of him, it took longer than it should have to realize how ridiculous he looked on the sofa. His feet were dangling over one arm, and his head was hanging well off the other.

She forced herself to move forward until she'd stopped in front of him. His eyes traveled from her bare feet, up her thin cotton sleep shorts, hesitating on the strip of skin showing at her waist, and then continued to the pale-pink camisole and her breasts that were hardening under his gaze. His throat bobbed, and then his eyes finally landed on hers. Her body flooded with heat at the desire she found in the dark depths.

"You'll never sleep on that couch," Paisley said, her voice quiet like it used to be before she'd tried to be Landry. "I have a king-sized bed. There's plenty of room for both of us without even touching."

"I don't think that's a good idea," he said, his voice deep and raspy.

It lit her body up, tingling all the way down to her core. He was probably right, but she wasn't going to let him stay there.

"Fine, you take the bed, and I'll take the couch. It's perfect for tiny people like me."

He shook his head, and her eyes narrowed, hands landing on her hips.

"Don't be such a gentleman, Jonas. Either you stay on the bed with me, or I sleep on the couch. Your choice."

CHAPTER THIRTY-FIVE

Jonas

BRINK OF DESTRUCTION
Performed by Sarah McLachlan

Paisley was dressed in pretty much nothing. Her thin, white pajama bottoms allowed him to see the brightly flowered pattern on her underwear, and her pink camisole only accented the way her breasts were hard and straining against the fabric.

It matched the hardness straining against the sweatpants he'd put on. He'd foolishly thought being in some clothes would be better than sleeping in his underwear. But their nearly bare bodies were almost more tantalizing than completely naked ones would have been. It had the hint of what was to come that lingered in the air.

With her hands on her hips and her narrowed eyes, Paisley looked like a fairy trying to scold a giant. His lips twitched as he tried not to laugh.

"What?" Paisley demanded.

"Just... You're sort of bossy now."

Her mouth fell open, and it took every ounce of willpower he had not to slide his arm around her and thrust his tongue inside it.

She turned on the ball of her foot, stomped over to the bed, and pulled back the covers with a huff. "Fine, sleep there. When you wake up with a cramped neck, don't blame me."

She turned off the lamp, and moonlight filled the room instead. The curtains were open, but they were on the top floor, facing the orchards, so it was unlikely anyone could actually see into the room.

He adjusted on the couch and realized his back was already cramping up. He'd be useless if he tried to sleep there. Still, he debated for a long time the wisdom of going to the bed. He wanted to. He ached to be next to her, even if he never touched her.

He finally let out a long sigh, grabbed the pillow he'd been using, and went to the bed. She was on her side, turned away from him, but when he lay down, she flipped over, her gaze meeting his. The moonlight shimmered over her face, casting part of it in shadow, but her eyes were still glittering.

He wanted to slide his fingers along the skin he remembered feeling like the ivory keys she played. Smooth and cool. But he wouldn't. They'd agreed to wait, and it was the right thing to do. If he let even one finger touch her, he'd lose the small grasp he had on his control. He wouldn't stop until she'd called his name in a breathless whisper.

"Do you really think it's Artie?" she asked.

All thoughts of kisses and orgasms flew from his head.

"Yes," he said somberly.

She frowned. "The original police reports... They thought the notes and what happened to Landry were separate events."

Jonas thought back to that awful time and Marco's words

that the killer had been someone trained to do so, while the stalker letters had felt wild, uncontrolled, and hateful.

"I think growing up in a gang, seeing people murdered, can give you a similar kind of experience," he finally responded.

"I'm not sure just seeing it would be enough. Even with Zane's training, I couldn't shake you yesterday," she said, and Jonas felt like an ass all over again for withering her confidence. Once upon a time, he'd been pissed when Landry had done the same thing.

"I think if Landry had known what you do now, she might have had a chance to fight off her attacker," Jonas said. "Being trained can only be a good thing. Marco has taught me some things, so I wasn't exactly clueless yesterday."

They stared at each other for a long time.

"Do you want to know something that's even more fucked up?" she asked.

He didn't respond, and she just continued.

"It turned me on. Your strength. The way you could just... control me."

His dick went from semi-hard to full-on.

"That's because of the way we feel about each other, Paisley. In your heart, you knew I wouldn't hurt you."

She stared. "Maybe."

"I've never played games with sex," he said, swallowing hard. "There are lots of people who enjoy it."

God, he ached to show her just how good he could make her feel, control or no control.

"You've had sex..." She swallowed, closed her eyes, and then opened them again. "Of course you have. Just look at you. Leya was right. You're a sex god."

A slow chuckle escaped him, and she smiled softly in return.

"So...you haven't?" he asked.

Her smile faded. "No. There's only ever been you."

He hated the asinine, animalistic side of him that liked that she'd never been with anyone else. Millions of people had her face hanging on their wall, dreaming about her, but he wanted to be the only one who actually got to touch her.

If they kept talking about sex and control and being turned on, the tiny bit of willpower he had left was going to disappear, and he'd prove to her that he knew what he was doing, limited experience or not. Games or not.

"Go to sleep, Little Bit," he said.

"Now who's being bossy?" she teased.

"We'll take turns," he said, the deep thrill of that thought making him even harder. Her breath came out in a sexy little pant that did nothing to improve his situation.

"Promise?" she asked.

"Fuck, Paisley. Stop talking. Stop talking or I won't be a gentleman," he groaned.

She smiled, a shy but seductive smile that about killed him.

"I missed this. Missed feeling like I was truly seen...wanted," she said quietly.

"You're all I've ever wanted."

"Except for whomever else you've slept with."

He shook his head and couldn't stop himself from reaching out to tuck her hair back away from her face. The zap of electricity hitting his fingers only increased the pain in his lower region.

"Even when I was with Ashley, all I really wanted was you."

Her eyes closed, as if his words pained her, but she didn't say anything else.

As he watched, her breathing evened out, and her hands loosened on the sheets as sleep took over. He was still awake, hours later, when the moonlight slid across the sky, fading farther into the west. His body was craving release and rest in equal measure, but he was afraid if he closed his eyes, she'd disappear. That lying beside her would all have been a dream. Eventually, the exhaustion from days of high emotion pulled him under, and sleep found him.

♫ ♫ ♫

It felt like his eyes had just shut when her phone alarm jangled, waking them both. He jolted, realizing that, somehow, they'd shifted while asleep. Her back was tucked up against his front. His arm was slung across her waist, and their feet were tangled together. Never in his entire life had he woken to such a feeling of peace. Of belonging. Of everything being right in the world—even when nothing was. When, really, everything was going to hell all over again.

Paisley turned in his arms so she was facing him, a sleepy smile appearing on her face, eyes blinking open. God. She was fucking beautiful. Stunning. The hard-on he wasn't sure had ever gone away the night before was back in full strength.

Her eyes drifted down his chest, toward the twitching in his pants, and then back up to his face. She leaned in, touching her soft lips to his, a whisper of a kiss like she'd started with the day before. But it sent painful swirls of need and desire rushing through him. Even after sleep, she still tasted like heaven. Like sweetness and vulnerability and power all mixed together.

Her hands sank into his hair, fingernails scratching his scalp, and they both let out a raspy moan at the same time while her alarm music continued to fill the air behind them.

Then, his phone went off as well—Trevor's text tone—and they both laughed.

"Good morning," she said, her smile turning wider.

She rolled out of his embrace, and he let her go but hated it.

She stopped the alarm, and he reached for his phone to read Trevor's text.

TREVOR: He definitely was in Grand Orchard.

Jonas sat up, hope blooming.

JONAS: You found him?

TREVOR: No. Found his rental abandoned out by an old shack at the back of the Romeros' farm.

JONAS: Are you staking it out? To see if he comes back?

TREVOR: He's not coming back.

JONAS: How can you be sure?

Trevor sent a picture. It was another note, and this one read, *I'll see you in Albany.*

Fuck. Fuck. Fuck.

Jonas hit the call button. "What's the plan?"

Paisley was at the closet and looked over at him in surprise.

"We're going to send the band's bus ahead, but we're going to lose the SUVs and switch to unmarked vans and sedans. Cars he's not used to seeing them in."

"The band's going to want to know what's going on," Jonas said.

Paisley came over and sat at the edge of the bed next to him.

"She's going to have to tell them, Jonas. Either she does or Reinard and his team do. It's up to her," Trevor responded.

I swallowed hard.

"I'll let her know."

"I'll see you in about an hour," Trevor said and then hung up.

"What?" Paisley asked, eyes wide.

He told her what Trevor had said, and her hand journeyed first to her star and then down to the anxiety ring with its little beads.

"Before...it felt like a dream. A nightmare. But I still felt like there was a shield between me and him and what had happened. Now, it's like I threw a brick through the glass, and it's come down around me. I'm such an idiot." She shook her head.

Jonas wrapped an arm around her shoulder and dragged her up close.

"He would have come no matter what you did, Paisley. He doesn't want me to be happy."

"Did you get any threats when you were with Ashley?" she asked.

Jonas frowned. He hadn't. But then, he and Ashley had never been photographed on the street with hands and bodies twined. He'd never posted on any social media about being in a relationship with her. They'd been study partners with benefits. Other than Marco and Cassidy, there weren't many people who'd even known they'd had anything more than friendship. Not even Willow had suspected, and she was one of Ashley's best friends. He said as much to Paisley, but instead of making her feel better, it only made her more agitated.

She pulled away from him, grabbed her clothes, and headed for the bathroom. "I have to tell the others. I don't want them to hear it from anyone else. Can you let Trevor know so none of the detail spills the beans first?"

She was rambling, breathless, but she didn't wait for an answer. The bathroom door clicked shut behind her, and he shot off a text to Trevor, letting him know that Paisley wanted to tell her friends first.

His fingers lingered over Marco's name in his contacts, debating once again about telling his brother. Cassidy's soft smile and Chevelle's laugh hit him. Marco had Cassidy and the kids to worry about now. Jonas was a grown man who could take care of this with Trevor at his back. They'd tell Marco after. Marco would be pissed, but if it was over, there'd be nothing left for him to worry about.

At least, that was what Jonas hoped.

CHAPTER THIRTY-SIX

Paisley

LOUDER
Performed by Lea Michele

The entire time Paisley was getting ready, she was kicking herself. For starting this. For not telling the others. For allowing Jonas and Trevor to convince her to bring some of the security team into the loop. But underneath it all, there was a perverse sense of anticipation. It might finally be coming to a close. She might finally be able to look her sister's killer in the face and demand answers.

She'd never hated someone she'd never met before. She'd never really hated anyone, not even the kids who'd bullied her in school. But she hated Artie. She hated that he'd hit a girl he supposedly loved. She hated that he'd ruined Jonas's friendship with someone he cared about, and she most certainly hated he'd been idiot enough to mistake Landry for her. He'd cared so little about her life that he'd not even bothered to turn Landry around and look her in the eyes.

Her anger had her applying her makeup heavier than she'd meant to—deep slashes of cat-eye liner and dark, smoky shadow. It was a look Landry had favored, and it suited Paisley as well, even if it wasn't her norm. She pulled on a pair of torn jeans and a lacy tank before stepping into a pair of spike-heeled ankle boots. Her outfit was like her tattoo, some tangled mix of the old Paisley and Landry.

When she came out of the bathroom, Jonas was pacing. He'd thrown on a T-shirt, but he was still in his sweats. He eyed her from head to toe, heat in his eyes but also worry.

"Don't talk to them without me, please. I just need to jump in the shower really quick," he said. Her stomach flopped as she realized how selfish she'd been hogging the bathroom. She hadn't had to share in a very long time. Growing up, she and Landry had always had their own. On the road, when they'd first started touring as opening acts for other bands, they'd sometimes shared two or three to a hotel room, but on their last tour, they'd each had their own space again.

"I'm sorry I took so long," she said.

"Don't be. I'm the one in your room, but please give me five minutes so I can go with you," he said.

He grabbed a few things and headed for the bathroom.

It was Paisley's turn to pace the room. She was worried that if Jonas was with her, the band would take it out on him. But she also didn't want to hurt him by not waiting for him like he'd asked. He wanted to be there for her in ways she hadn't let him before, and she couldn't take that away from him now—not when there was the possibility she might get him back in her life.

As a compromise, she sent out a group text, asking everyone to meet in her room in twenty minutes.

FEE: Should we have given you the birds-and-bees talk, Little Bit? Were you shocked?

ADRIA: Leave her alone. Paise didn't need advice from any of you.

NIKKI: It's too early to be going at each other already. Just make sure we have coffee, Little Bit. Lots of coffee.

PAISLEY: Did you all get drunk? I told you Asher will kill us if we aren't 100% today.

FEE: Do not speak that man's name this early, especially when I'm hungover. I might vomit again.

LEYA: We didn't get drunk, Paisley. There was still plenty of lemon vodka left when we went to bed.

FEE: There's nothing left now.

Paisley's worry grew. Even before Landry's death, Fiadh's life had been full of loss. Loss that twisted in a very different way because her family was still very much alive but off-limits to her. Happy, carefree Fee had always been a cover, but it was a cover that felt a bit unstable ever since Landry had died.

Paisley placed a call to room service, ordering coffee and pastries. She'd just hung up when Jonas came out of the bathroom. Every time she saw him, he seemed more attractive. She'd just seen him minutes before, and yet he still seemed somehow brighter, bigger...more.

He was in normal Jonas apparel of jeans and a T-shirt. This one was gray with the soft peachy Painted Daisies logo on the pocket that all the roadies wore. He had Chucks on his enormous feet, and his hair was slicked back, wet with droplets shimmering off the golden edges. The soft waves were already springing back to life, and she wanted to muss it up, to run her fingers through it and hear the breathy moan he'd done just minutes before, in the bed, before his phone had gone off.

She swallowed and looked away. "The band will be here in a few minutes. Just so you know, they think we...you know."

Jonas crossed the room and pulled her hand into his—the one she'd been unconsciously worrying her anxiety ring with. His index finger slid along the beads. "I want to make love to you, Paisley. I want to make love to you all day, all night, and into next week. But I won't do it while this is hanging over us. Like you said, we need to put this behind us to see if we have a chance at a future. We need to come to terms with the fact that I'm the reason Landry—" He couldn't even finish the words.

She pulled her hands from his and placed her palms on his cheeks, forcing their eyes to meet. "I think we both have to stop blaming ourselves for Artie. We've given him too much power, letting him terrorize us. I just want it to end. I want it to finally be over, so we can actually heal.

He nodded but didn't get a chance to respond as a knock came on the door.

"Ms. Kim, it's room service," the bodyguard on the other side of the door said.

Jonas went to the door, looked through the peephole, and then opened it.

The room-service cart rolled in, and the waiter took a moment to set up the coffee and pastries. Paisley signed the slip, and then he departed. Just as he was leaving, the others came ambling into the room. None of them looked hungover, not even Fee, although her eyes were shadowed. They all shot Jonas smirks and eye rolls as they walked by him. It would have been funny if Paisley hadn't called them there for more serious reasons.

"Thank God," Nikki said, heading straight for the coffee as she rubbed at her temples.

"Do you have a headache?" Paisley asked, worry filling her.

Nikki shook her head. "Not a migraine but a leftover-from-alcohol kind of headache. Which is why I know better than to drink."

Paisley waited for everyone to fill their cups and plates and find a seat.

"What's up?" Adria asked, glancing at Jonas again. He was in his defensive stance, looking like he was going to jump anyone who even glanced at her wrong.

"I haven't been completely honest with you," Paisley said, swallowing hard.

Fiadh put her cup down with a clatter, waiting for her to continue.

Paisley took a deep breath and ran a finger over her ring. "I did want us to come back to Grand Orchard to finish the album, set up the tour, and get Asher off our backs, but I...I also wanted to find Landry's killer."

Silence took over the room.

"What exactly does that mean?" Leya asked, her normally smiley face frowning. It reminded Paisley that it wasn't just Fee who'd changed. Leya used to be all smiles too. They'd been the fun ones. Landry had been the leader, Nikki the peacemaker, Adria the broody one, and Paisley had been the shy one. Now, they were all something else, some distorted version of their old selves.

Paisley took a deep breath. "I've been getting notes again. Since we came back. It's what I hoped would happen."

There was a series of gasps and startled versions of, "What the hell?" that went through her friends.

Fee's eyes went immediately to Jonas. "Did you know this?"

Paisley jumped to his defense. "He found a note I was hiding, but only two days ago, Fee. I—"

"How could you keep this from us?" Leya burst out. "Does security know? Does that arrogant Secret Service agent following me around know?"

Paisley swallowed hard. "No one knew until the day before yesterday."

"*Dios*," Adria said quietly.

It was Nikki's eyes that settled on Paisley's for the longest and figured out what Jonas had. "You were using yourself as bait."

"Oh, fecking hell no." Fee jumped up, coming toward her, and Jonas stepped up next to Paisley. He didn't say a word, just stood there. Fiadh eyed him but didn't close the remaining distance. She just shook her head in disgust as her curls danced about. "Landry would've killed you herself!"

"It was stupid...but...it worked, and now they have a good lead. The first lead in almost two years," Paisley's voice cracked, and suddenly her hand was engulfed in a large one—Jonas shoring her up.

Leya's eyes grew wide. "They have him?"

Paisley shook her head. "No, but they're ninety percent sure they know who it is. The problem is, he's left Grand Orchard. He left another note. He said he's waiting for us in Albany."

"Us?" Adria asked, glancing toward Jonas.

Paisley looked up into his face and saw his jaw was clenched tight. He already felt responsible for this, just like Paisley did. But she also believed what she'd told Jonas earlier. They had to stop giving Artie power over their lives. "It isn't his fault, Ads."

"It's that guy. From your past? The one who roughed up your friend?" Fiadh asked Jonas.

"Yes," Jonas finally spoke.

"And he killed Landry because he thought she was Paisley?" Leya's voice got small.

"How could anyone think Landry was Little Bit?" Fee rolled her eyes.

"From the back, at dusk, and if he hadn't really been around them to compare their heights..." Jonas shrugged.

"Something doesn't feel right," Nikki said. "It just... He killed her guard too. Neatly. Quietly. That doesn't seem like some obsessed, jealous rage."

"Regardless of what we think or how it does or doesn't add up, he's here, threatening Jonas and me. He's waiting for us in Albany, so security has been increased. We're not going on the bus today. We're dividing up and taking vans and sedans. Different cars than we've been using," Paisley told them. "But...if you don't want to do this...if you want to go home, I'll call Asher and tell him we're canceling the tour."

Fiadh inhaled sharply. "No way am I giving that asshole Riggs the satisfaction of us quitting. It's what he wants. He wants us to break our contract so he can have our money and finally wash his hands of us. No fecking way."

Paisley moved away from Jonas, dropping his hand and instantly feeling the loss in every ounce of her, but she needed to comfort her friend. She tucked her arm through Fiadh's. "You can't decide for everyone, Fee."

Fiadh scowled but bit her lip and said nothing.

The others were silent for a long time.

Adria was the first to speak. She met Paisley's eyes, chin raising as she said, "My family—like yours—has already been through a lot. Tati...what happened to my sister... I'm not really keen on putting them through more, but the Rojas family has never given in to bullies, criminals, or killers before. My dad would be the first to tell me not to walk away, so I'm in."

Paisley felt Fiadh's tension ease ever so slightly.

"I'm assuming the Secret Service knows? Which means my dad has already been notified. I'm actually surprised I haven't heard from Mom. The United States doesn't give in to terrorist threats, right? Like Adria said, our family isn't going to cave now. I won't either," Leya said, but her hand shook as she spun the cup in her hand.

They all looked to Nikki. She'd done more than just replace Landry on guitar by giving her bass parts to Finn in the shadows. She'd also taken over all Landry's lyrics in addition to her own because her voice was the closest to Landry's gritty depths. If they lost Nikki, it would be difficult to recover. They might be able to eventually, but not soon enough to stop Asher from suing them.

Nikki rubbed her temples. "I'm still not sure I can believe this is the man who killed her. But if there's a chance that we can find out, then I'm in."

Paisley's body broke out in goosebumps. For the first time since she'd brought them all back together, it felt like they were actually a team again. A unit. One goal in mind. End the asshole who'd taken the person who'd brought them together.

CHAPTER THIRTY-SEVEN

Jonas

RELEASE
Performed by Imagine Dragons

Jonas and The Painted Daisies traveled to Albany in thoughtful silence, and when they got there, they spent three days preparing for the concert. The band rehearsed at The Palace while he and Zia hustled behind the scenes, trying to pull together a show that wasn't supposed to happen for days yet.

In addition to the increased staff that came with the tour kicking off, Reinard, the FBI, and the Secret Service all sent more people until there was a dense sea of men and women surrounding the Daisies. They spread the band out across several hotels in the area, hoping to make it harder for the stalker to know where everyone was. Any time they left the hotel or the theater, they played a shell game with all the cars heading in different directions. It felt like they were living in an espionage movie.

For three days, they heard nothing. There was no note, no sightings, just a silence that left everyone on edge. All the agencies were flexing their muscles, trying to find Artie, and it was almost asinine that they were coming up empty.

The day before the concert, Jonas was rooted to a spot offstage, watching as Paisley crooned into a microphone, when Zia found him. He didn't say anything to her as they stood listening to the band. Paisley's voice filled the theater and landed directly in his heart, every word, every syllable, every note resonating deep in his soul.

"If you don't ease up, everyone's going to think you're the stalker," Zia teased.

Jonas dragged his eyes from Paisley down to Zia. She wasn't much bigger than Paisley, but her hair was full and curly, adding height to her. She arched a thick brow at him, brown eyes twinkling.

Jonas gave her a wry shrug. "I can't seem to help it."

Zia laughed softly.

He smiled before turning serious. "I'll ease up once they've found him."

Zia pulled on his arm, spinning him three hundred sixty degrees and pointing with her finger at all the muscled men and women with guns and Tasers. Jonas's eyes landed and stayed on Ronan Hawk and his goddamn camera for a moment before Zia had successfully turned him back toward the stage.

"Do you see all this security?" she asked. "He isn't going to get to her."

The layers of protection should have made Jonas feel better, but for some reason, it made his skin crawl, like there was something they were all missing. A piece they hadn't put together.

That's where his brain was at as he and Paisley exited the theater later that afternoon—on the lack of progress and no word from Artie. Maybe he'd given up because the security had been too thick, but that idea didn't feel right either.

His gut and chest were equally tight as they made their way into the back alley. It was a large space, big enough for semi-trucks to pull in and drop off stage equipment, and it was empty except for a single black sedan waiting for them. The rest of the band had already headed back to their various hotels.

Jonas opened the back door of the car, and as Paisley went to slide in, there was a loud ping on the sedan's roof, like a heavy rock had been thrown. His heart rate spiked, eyes darting around, brows drawn in confusion. It wasn't until another clang joined the first that his brain caught up, and then pure panic filled him.

"Gun!" he shouted, his voice cracking with fear, and he acted on instinct, shoving Paisley inside the car and yelling, "Get on the floor!"

Paisley made a sound of protest, face as panicked as he felt, but when the roof was hit with another bullet, she ducked. Jonas dropped to his haunches, adrenaline pumping, hatred for Artie swimming in his veins, and tortured fear for Paisley's life almost paralyzing him.

He used the vehicle as a shield while Trevor and two other bodyguards raced toward them.

"Get her out of here," Trevor yelled into the mic, yanking on Jonas's arm and pulling him toward the cargo bay as Paisley's car spun out, kicking up dirt. Gunshots followed the sedan out of the alley.

Jonas's heart slammed in his chest, the terror inside him turning to fury as the car disappeared. A chant in his head began, growing slowly louder, telling him to find Artie. To end him. To end this. So, when Trevor tried to pull him inside the theater, he jerked away. Instead of running to safety, he sped toward the shots coming from a window on the top floor of the four-story building behind the theater.

Gunfire rained on the blacktop around his feet, and Jonas zigzagged as gravel debris spattered up his legs. Anger burned, fueling him. Trevor shouted at him, words he couldn't decipher because of the blood pounding in his head and rushing through his veins. The only call he heeded was his own silent chant.

Find him and end him.

The back door of the building was locked, but it was in an old wooden casement, and Jonas didn't even think twice about throwing his shoulder into it. Pain ratcheted through his arm, but he repeated the motion, and this time, the frame buckled and cracked just as Trevor's voice broke through the rage.

"Jonas! Fucking wait!"

But he didn't. The doorway led into an emergency stairwell, and Jonas bounded up it, taking the steps two or three at a time. His feet echoed on the cement, sending the sound upward as hate rampaged through him. Artie had cost him everything. So much fucking pain.

As he rounded the stairs on the fourth floor, he realized he couldn't hear the gunshots anymore, only Trevor's feet pounding on the stairs below him, calling after him, and dread settled in. Jonas would lose him if he wasn't quick enough.

He burst through the door at the top and raced down the hall. An old man came out of one of the offices, and Jonas flung him to the side. The man cried out, but Jonas didn't stop, focused solely on reaching Artie. He shoved open the first door on the right, closest to the theater, and a trio of women looked up with huge eyes from where they hid behind their desks.

He swirled around and took off toward the next office. He smashed open the glass door so hard it cracked, the sound sharp and brittle in the darkened room. It was silent, but there was a tension in the air Jonas could feel.

"I'm here, asshole. Come and get me!" Jonas growled into the quiet.

He turned, feeling along the wall in the dark for the light switch. Pain exploded through his head as he was hit from behind with a hard object. He sagged toward the wall, palms outstretched, catching himself, just as a second blow struck him. He landed on his knees, a tortured roar escaping him. He couldn't fucking let him win. His eyes swam, and he fought the black threatening to sweep him under. He swiped a hand out at the feet of his assailant. He'd barely gripped an ankle when a crowbar slammed down onto his bicep, sending ripples of agony through him. The metal clanged as it hit the ground, and his attacker turned, fleeing into the adjoining room.

Trevor burst in with his gun drawn. He glanced down at Jonas before continuing through the doorway into the next room. Jonas struggled to his knees, his arm screaming as he tried to use it to push himself up. He'd barely gotten to his feet and taken a shaky step toward the door Trevor had gone through when he returned, holstering his weapon.

Jonas staggered around him, but Trevor caught him in a death grip. "He's already gone, Jonas. He went down the fire escape. We have men following him."

Fuck!

Loathing and despair surged through Jonas, but through the haze of emotions came the physical pain. His head was ringing, and when he put his hand to the back of it, he came away with blood. White dots flickered in his vision.

"What the hell were you thinking, Jonas?" Trevor growled. "No weapon. No training. You'd end up dead, and then what the fuck would I tell Marco? He'd never speak to me again. He's barely speaking to me now, thinking I've betrayed Garner and him by going to work for Reinard."

Jonas moved past him, needing to see for himself that Artie

wasn't there. Two windows were open, letting in a cool breeze, a storm brewing and darkening the sky. One of the windows led out to the fire escape, and the other looked down into the theater parking lot.

"How the fuck is he able to sneak past everyone, Trev? This place should have been locked down."

"They cleared the building this morning, Jonas. It's not like they're sitting on their hands and just waiting for him to kill someone."

"Paisley. Not someone. He wants to fucking kill Paisley." The agony ripped through his chest five times worse than the pain in his head.

Trevor's throat bobbed. "I know."

They glared at each other for a moment before Trevor asked, "Did you see him? Was it actually Artie?"

Jonas groaned internally. No. He hadn't seen the guy's face. He shook his head, and his eyes landed on a paper on the floor by the window. He picked it up, and the skin on the back of his neck prickled. The picture was of Paisley from the day before, singing onstage inside the theater. He knew it was from the day before because she'd worn a skintight skirt that had clung to her hips all day and tortured him. They'd barely gotten inside the door of her hotel suite before he'd pushed her against the wall and kissed her until they were both breathless.

Artie had fucking been there. He'd taken a photograph from inside the fucking theater. On the note, Paisley's face was scratched out, and the words read, *If you leave her, you can save her*.

Jonas's hands clenched, fisting the note.

Goddamn it.

The horrendous truth raced through him. It wasn't a new thought. It was one he'd had over and over again since the day he'd first met Paisley Kim and argued the skills of ABBA with her. The truth was, he couldn't have her. He couldn't stay with her. Not if he wanted to keep her safe. Landry had been right all along. They didn't belong. Not because he was some screwed-up kid with anger issues and no potential, but because Paisley would never be safe at his side.

Trevor took the paper from him, worried eyes scanning Jonas's face. "You're bleeding, Jo-Jo. Let's get you looked at."

When they went back into the first room, men were flooding it. Men who would fingerprint and scan every corner, but who Jonas had no faith in because they still hadn't caught one weasel of a human being—a gang kid with no training—while the men in the room had thousands of hours of it. The fury he'd felt when he'd realized it was bullets shooting at Paisley filled him again.

He wanted to slam all of them into the wall, just like he'd wanted to put a fist in the faces of the men who'd shown up too late the night Landry had died. Trevor was at his side, and maybe he could feel the anger coming off Jonas in waves, because he put a hand on Jonas's shoulder and said in a soothing voice, "Breathe. Let's go get you checked out and then get you back to the hotel. Paisley has got to be scared and worried about you."

It was a low blow because Trevor knew Jonas couldn't stand the thought of Paisley frightened and alone. But it got him out of the room without smashing walls or people.

Once they were in the hallway, he tossed off Trevor's hand and stalked toward the stairs. He'd only gotten down two flights when his eyes started to swim again. Trevor was right there at his side the entire time. He paused while Jonas got ahold of himself and then spoke into his mic, asking for an EMT to meet them at the hotel.

There was a flood of cop cars and the detail's vehicles in the parking lot when they emerged out the back of the building. Fucking Ronan Hawk was on the cargo bay of the theater, filming it all.

Jonas crossed the lot and used one hand to lift himself onto the bay, bringing himself up next to the man. They were almost the same height, and Ronan might have been lanky, but he had muscle behind his Hollywood player looks. It wouldn't be an easy fight, but Jonas was confident he could take him.

"Stop filming," Jonas demanded.

Ronan's eyes narrowed in on him. "Not going to happen. I've waited two years to finish this. They deserve to have their story told."

"Not their grief and loss. That's private. They don't need you showing it to the world."

"Don't they?" Ronan asked. "I hate to break it to you, but that's exactly what they need."

Jonas stepped forward, grabbing Ronan's shirt, his fist tightening as he wrestled to control the anger and hate and despair threatening to overwhelm him. He wanted to hit the man, just like he'd wanted to hit Artie and the useless security team. He wanted to send everyone and anyone who didn't have Paisley's best interest at heart spinning out into the dark recesses of space.

But he wasn't the same man who'd swung at the photographer two years ago or who'd slammed his way through a sea of bodyguards who hadn't been there for Landry. He'd changed, hadn't he? The hate pounding through him made him doubt it. Maybe he'd never change.

"It would be a mistake to hit me," Ronan growled, eyes flashing.

A mistake. God, he didn't want to keep making the same

ones. He didn't want to be his mom who never learned, never saw anything but herself and what she wanted.

Ronan and Jonas glared at each other for a long moment, and then Jonas dropped his hands, turned on his heel, and stepped off the cargo bay to where Trevor was waiting to take him to Paisley. To the one person who he never wanted to let down again.

CHAPTER THIRTY-EIGHT

Paisley

LIVE BEFORE I DIE
Performed by The Corrs

Even though she was safe, tucked into her suite at the hotel, Paisley was still shaking from head to toe. Her body couldn't stop shivering. They'd been shot at. She'd been shot at. And Jonas… God, she'd left him there. She paced the room, twisting the beads on her ring, heart pounding viciously as she waited.

She texted Jonas. She called Jonas.

Nothing.

She couldn't breathe. Ice tugged through her veins, and she felt like she was going to pass out, her vision blurring and the sights and sounds going dim in a way they hadn't in a long time. She forced herself to the door, opening it and drawing the eyes of the two men standing there.

"I…I need to know. Have you heard? Is Jonas okay? Did they catch the stalker?"

The men exchanged looks.

"Trevor and Jonas are on their way to you now."

Relief washed over her. Jonas was okay. She sagged against the wall, and one of the guards frowned. "Are you okay, Ms. Kim?"

She inhaled slowly and sharply. "Yes." She stepped back into the suite and then spun around again, belatedly thinking of Zane. Guilt flew through her as she hoped he was okay as well. "And Zane? Do you know where he is?"

"With the others, combing the scene."

Thank God, she thought, returning to the suite and resuming her tread back and forth across the room. The more she paced, the more her fear and worry turned to anger. How dare Jonas shove her in a car and leave himself out in the open! He could have been killed. What would Paisley do if she lost him on top of losing Landry? God, she loved him too much to lose him now.

Her feet stalled. Her heart stopped.

She loved him.

Of course she did. She may not have put those words with the emotions, but it had always been there. She loved him deeply, passionately, and without end.

By the time the suite door opened, she'd gone through the gamut of emotions and landed back on anger at the thought of him doing something so stupid and reckless—even if it was as reckless as she'd been, trying to lure the stalker out on her own.

When Jonas entered, they stared at each other for what felt like a decade. Jonas scoured her from head to toe, as if to make sure she really was okay. Then, she was in his embrace, hugging him tightly. Breathing him in. Relief and love filling her.

"Thank God, you're okay," Jonas said into her hair. He kissed the top of her head and squeezed her tighter but with only one arm.

She pulled back and noticed for the first time that his other hand was behind his head, holding an icepack that had blood on it. The sight made her breath leave her body again. She'd never been fond of blood, but after finding Landry...seeing blood churned her stomach even more, brought back haunted visions and terrifying dreams.

"You're hurt! What happened?" she asked, shaking off the nausea and trying to turn him so she could see how bad it was, but he had his feet planted firmly on the ground, holding her tightly.

"Artie hit me with a crowbar. I'm fine," Jonas grunted.

"Artie! You confronted him? Did you catch him?" The thought of Jonas fighting with Artie had her stomach lurching and her knees giving out, but Jonas caught her, tightening his grip even more. He wouldn't let her fall. He never had. He'd always tried to catch her, even when she'd forced him away.

His eyes were full of anguished failure when he looked down at her. "He got away."

God, she really might throw up. "We need to get you to the hospital!"

Jonas shook his head. "An EMT looked me over downstairs. He says I might have a slight concussion and a hell of a headache, but I'm okay."

Jonas dragged her toward the chair in the living area of the suite. He sat down, and she sat in his lap, turning his chin so she could assess the damage for herself. Blood had caked onto his dark-blond hair, but his thick strands hid the majority of the bandage. Her breath hitched, tears bubbling up that she forced back.

"I'm okay, Paise, honest," he said.

They searched each other's eyes for the truth as a range of emotions flew through them. The one that remained behind was relief. They were both okay—for now. But how long could they go on like this? With Artie sneaking in around their defenses?

"Please tell me you didn't go after him on your own," she begged. The idea of Jonas facing Artie by himself was too much for her heart.

When he looked down, dread filled her, making her breath catch. Her voice was shaky as she said, "You didn't want me to put myself out there as bait, and yet, you going after him is pretty much the same thing."

Jonas's eyes closed and then opened. "He isn't trying to kill me, Paisley. He wants me to suffer, but not like that. He wouldn't have any more fun if I was dead."

"Fun!" Paisley shook. "Jonas, do you hear how sick that is? If he had to, he would kill you."

His long fingers ran along her cheek before settling on her collarbone. His jaw was clenched tightly, and he was clearly battling his emotions. When he finally spoke, it stabbed at her heart.

"I think I should leave the tour. Go back to Grand Orchard."

She shook her head, tears filling her eyes. "What? No!"

He dragged a hand through his hair, wincing as his fingers hit his wound. "I can't stay. I can't stay knowing I'm the reason he's hunting you. I won't do it. I shouldn't even have come to Albany. I don't know what the fuck I was thinking."

His eyes were tortured.

"Don't you dare leave me," she said, soul tearing at just the thought of not having him at her side. They had to make it work this time. They had to because she was sure he was the only person who would ever make her feel this way, and if he took away the piece of her soul that had finally returned, she'd never get it back.

Jonas inhaled sharply but didn't respond. Instead, he rested his ear against her chest, listening to wild rhythm of her heartbeat.

"I need you, Jonas. I need you here. I can't... I won't be able to make it through what's coming without you."

She turned on his lap so she was straddling him, and then she began devouring him, slowly but with a fury fueled from not only the emotions of the day but the ones pent up for years. She kissed her way down his neck, over to the other side of his jaw, and then back up to his mouth, and when he moaned, she slipped her tongue inside, tasting him, finding the soft inner recesses and exploring the silky heat.

His hands dug into the skin at her waist. The pressure of his fingers turned the well of loss and love and anxiety into a steady stream of lust. She shivered, goosebumps littering her skin as every vein and molecule seemed to awaken at the same moment, screaming for his touch.

She slid her hands under his T-shirt, yanking at it, breaking their kiss long enough to pull it over his head, and then settling her palms back down on the smooth contours underneath, reveling in the flex of his muscles as she glided down them first with her fingers and then with her tongue. The path of wet kisses was a quick series of eighth notes announcing the start of a new song, and when he groaned, raspy and breathless, she could hear the first full lines bursting like a sunrise onto a new day.

When she reached inside his underwear to slowly stroke him, he gasped, "Fuck, Paisley. You have to stop."

She shook her head, not only because her body was clamoring for relief but because she needed to hear how the song continued. How the soft lines became a resounding chorus. She pulled back long enough to yank her T-shirt over her head and undo her bra. Jonas's eyes grew hooded as he took her in, like they did every time he saw her in this partially naked state. Her body burned everywhere his gaze settled, but it wasn't enough. She needed his touch on all the aching pieces of her, so she lifted his hands from her waist and put them on her breasts.

"I need you, Jonas, and I think you need me. I don't want to wait any longer. If something had happened to you today..." Her voice cracked. "If I'd never been able to experience this again... this heady, uncontrollable desire I feel every time we touch...it would break me. Remember how you said you weren't Superman? That you couldn't survive me leaving you again? It's the same. I won't be able to survive it either. We belong together."

She squeezed his hands, molding them to her, and his breathing stuttered.

"Make love to me, Jonas," she whispered, a soft beg she knew she'd never recover from if he denied her. "Make me forget everything else but you and me. Prove to me that what we have, what we feel, is worth all of this."

She set her mouth on his softly, shaking with need and hope and longing. She knew the exact moment he gave in because he took control. His kiss turned almost punishing in its intensity as he nipped and sucked and bit, hands exploring and sending delicious swirls through her needy body.

He broke their kiss, and she whimpered, but then he was lifting her, carrying her easily through the suite to the bedroom, and kicking the door shut behind them. He set her down on the bed and took a step back, watching the way her chest heaved and her eyes cried out for his touch.

He unzipped his jeans and slid out of them before joining her on the bed. He put a hand to her chest, pushing her backward gently before flicking a finger along the waistband of her yoga pants, a question returning to his eyes. There was only one answer. An answer her body had been crying out for years.

"Please. Don't stop," she pleaded.

He slowly pulled at the fabric, drawing it down and

peppering kisses along her skin, adding notes with every stroke. But he stilled when he found her core bare. His eyes flashed back to hers as he hissed, "You're not wearing any fucking underwear."

She couldn't help the small laugh that escaped her. "No panty lines."

His forehead landed on her thigh, inches away from the part of her that was literally crying out for him with such enormous need she thought she might shatter before he even had a chance to touch her.

"Never again, Paisley. If I know you're like this...fuck," he growled. Then, his tongue found its way home, and she cried out at the very first flick.

She trembled as he consumed her, tortured her, tantalized her with fingers and mouth until she did break apart, body bucking, quivering, exploding as she chanted his name. He had a cocky, sure smile on his face as he placed kisses up her stomach, over her chest, and back to her mouth. She wrapped a leg around his thigh, drawing him closer.

The hard length of him coasted across her belly, and the release she'd just reached burned back into a new craving.

"I need you inside me, Jonas. I have to have you," she gasped, her hands traveling along his soft skin that was such a contrast to the strength coiling underneath. "Make me completely yours...let me make you completely mine."

Jonas's mouth was harsh and demanding as it landed on hers, as if he hated and loved her words all at the same time. And then he was gone, standing up and moving away, and she wanted to cry. She wanted to beg and plead for him to come back.

His beautiful eyes were dark-emerald pools, half-mast with lust as he reached down for his jeans and his wallet, pulling out a condom. She sighed with relief, her body clenching in anticipation as she watched him tear open the packet with his teeth and slowly roll the condom on. It was the most sensual thing she'd ever seen. Him, getting ready for her. Protecting her. Loving her.

And then he was back, hovering above her, more questions in his eyes that she answered by drawing him closer, spreading her thighs, and allowing him to settle between them. The heavy weight of him on top of her was the headiest of pleasures and the sweetest of comforts.

He pushed into her, eyes watching hers as he filled her. It hurt for a moment, and she bit her bottom lip. He paused, gaze searching as he tenderly kissed the spot on her lip she'd bitten and waited for her to adjust to him. He resumed the slow sweeps of mouth and tongue that made her moan and buck her hips into his, proving she was ready for more. Ready for all of him.

They began moving, finding a rhythm that built to new heights as the song they were creating burst louder in her head. Their bodies were slick, sliding against each other while hands and tongues danced. A blaze of light and sounds and color filled the space around her until she was on the edge of splintering again. Until she felt every single ounce of the love she had for him pouring from her veins into his.

CHAPTER THIRTY-NINE

Jonas

RUNAWAY
Performed by The Corrs

Being inside Paisley was a life-changing experience. Once upon a time, just being next to her had felt that way. And now, being joined to her, moving in her slick heat, listening to her whimpers and moans...it was like nothing he'd ever felt before in his life. It was more than peace, more than love, more than belonging. It was like the very first atoms in the universe colliding together. Creation happening right there and then.

He felt her quiver, felt her clench tightly around him. He was determined to feel her come around him before he let go. To know that he'd brought her to the brink and taken her over along with him one more time.

When her entire body vibrated and she cried out his name like it was the chorus of a new song, he was gone. He plunged over the edge with her, reveling in the beautiful, torturous heaven that was Paisley and him together.

Their breathing came in heavy pants as their bodies slowly came to a stop. He turned to his side, drawing her up against his chest, but not yet willing to pull out of her. Not yet willing to make them two instead of one.

Her face was buried in him, arms wrapped around his waist, and he suddenly realized his chest was wet. She was crying. Panic filled him, and he drew back enough to look down at her.

"Paisley. I'm sorry! Are you okay?" Worry leaked into every syllable.

She looked up at him, enchanting eyes, dark and shimmery, but there was a smile on her face that eased his concern.

"It was just so beautiful, Jonas. So...beautiful. Did you hear it? Did you hear the song we made?" she asked, her voice soft and full. It brought tears to his eyes. Tears he refused to shed. He wouldn't be the fucking guy who cried in bed.

His arms tightened around her. "I may not have heard it, sweetheart, but I felt it. Every last beat."

She reached up to kiss him, a soft touch that felt like a promise. A promise he wanted to keep but wasn't sure how. He kissed her forehead and then reluctantly pulled away from her.

"I'll be right back," he said. He disposed of the condom, cleaned up, and then started to dampen a facecloth to bring back to her when she appeared in the doorway. He stood there, staring like an idiot at her naked, gorgeous body.

"Bath or shower?" she asked, the soft tone of the old Paisley showing, a moment of hesitancy that he didn't want her to feel. "You have blood in your hair, and I have..." she trailed off, pink hitting her cheeks.

He eased over to her, pulled her naked body up against his, kissing her and then murmuring his answer against her lips. "Shower then bath. It'll ease your soreness."

They showered slowly, hands exploring but never going

quite all the way again. Then, he filled the tub with water and the bath salts the hotel had provided, holding her hand to help her in before sitting behind her and pulling her to his chest. They lay in the warm water, talking about music like they had once upon a time, about the notes she heard in her head as they made love, and it made Jonas shiver and stare at her in stunned awe. A new layer of Paisley he'd uncovered.

When the water turned cold, they moved back to the bed, still naked, and lay tangled together, limbs twined. Words eventually faded away as hands and lips took over. He didn't lose himself inside her again, but they still found pleasure in each other. Pleasure and comfort that allowed the terror and fear of the day to just disappear and let sleep find them.

♫ ♫ ♫

After being woken up by a throbbing head and a painfully hard dick, Jonas kissed Paisley goodbye while she was still mostly asleep. The band would be arriving soon to spend the day getting ready for the concert, and he wasn't sure he could handle their questions or their teasing.

He'd hardly seen his own room since arriving, sleeping next to Paisley each night, watching over her with a fierce protectiveness he wasn't sure anyone else on the detail felt—except for maybe fucking Zane. And yet, even he hadn't found Artie.

Just like every morning when Jonas left her suite, Zane was waiting outside, glowering. Everything about the man irritated Jonas. Not only had he taught Paisley how to fight without seeing what she was really going to do with that knowledge, but it felt like he was judging everything she did...or at least everything she did with Jonas.

"Where were you yesterday?" Jonas demanded.

Zane's eyes narrowed. "Excuse me?"

"When she was getting shot at. Where the hell were you?"

"I don't answer to you," Zane grunted. "But it was Good Friday. I was at church. Maybe you should try praying for your sins sometime."

"Praying to your god almost got her killed," Jonas growled, stepping into the man's space, and the bodyguard just straightened his shoulders and shoved out his chest.

"You're the one putting her at risk," Zane said. "If you weren't here, there would never have been shots fired in her direction."

It hit Jonas right in the gut, tearing a bullet-like hole into him. Zane was right. It was what Jonas had said to Paisley himself before she'd begged him not to leave, begged him to stay and make love to her.

He turned on his heel and walked away, furious at himself not only for losing his temper with Zane but also for not being able to get in the car and drive back to Grand Orchard. He'd never survive if he couldn't see her each day with his own eyes. He'd be a wreck. A human being in the shape of a knotted rope that couldn't be unwound.

He'd showered and was sitting on his unused bed, debating calling Marco, when she sent him a text. She was heading to the theater with the other Daisies.

PAISLEY: I miss you already. How is that possible? I can't wait till our day brings us back together again.

And she ended the text with an abundance of heart emojis.

It was the stupid heart emojis that did him in.

The love they symbolized. God. He loved her. He fucking loved Paisley Kim. Grammy-award-winning singer, songwriter, and leader of The Painted Daisies. His stomach clenched. It wasn't the first time he'd thought himself in love. It wasn't even the first time he'd thought himself in love with Paisley, but it was the first time he felt the truth of it in every piece of his soul and knew without a doubt that she felt it back even without either of them saying it.

Landry had been wrong. Not only did they deserve each other, they needed each other. Fuck Artie. Fuck Zane. Fuck anyone who thought he and Paisley shouldn't be together. They'd felt the entire universe when they'd made love last night. Paisley had heard fucking music!

He wanted to tell her. He had the *I love you* typed out before he stopped himself with shaking hands. He couldn't tell her in text the first time. He had to say the words when he was looking in her eyes and could watch the soft smile take over her face and hear her quiet reply.

So instead, he forced his brain to focus on the job he was in Albany to do. He went to the theater and helped Zia as they pulled all the last-minute threads together for the concert. As the day waned and security showed up and dismantled the video equipment in the sound booth that they thought might have been hacked in order for Artie to get the picture of Paisley, the doubts hit him all over again.

Because he loved her more than anyone or anything on this planet, he had to do everything he could to keep her safe. Right now, the only way to do that was to leave the tour. Separate them. Just until they found Artie. Just until they could put an end to this for real. He hated it. He wasn't sure he'd survive it, but he couldn't be selfish enough to stay. That thought spiraled, burrowing deep inside as the day progressed.

When he finally saw her, it was from a distance, across the changing room where she was sitting with the other Daisies as a team of hair and makeup people worked on them. She saw him in the mirror, and a smile lit her face. It landed in his chest, loosening and tying the knots all at the same time. When he didn't smile back right away, her lips fell. He didn't need her worrying about him or them or anything but the concert at the moment. It was going to be challenging enough for her and her friends to perform without Landry for the first time. So, he forced his lips into a grin and winked at her before retreating to the stage with Zia.

Backstage was full of nervous energy. Even if there hadn't been the shooting the day before, it was the first stop on a long tour, and everyone was anxious about if and how it would come together the way they'd planned. If at all possible, the security had become even denser. But Jonas had no faith in them. Artie had slipped past them repeatedly, as if he were a ghost, a figment of Jonas's past who blew through with the breeze.

There was no opening act today. Asher hadn't been able to arrange for their opener to get to Albany in time, so as the crowd started to fill the theater, the steady hum was all for the Daisies. The air felt expectant, the type of energy he'd felt every time he'd waited for Paisley to return to him.

He didn't realize she'd joined him until she hooked her pinky with his and squeezed. "Hey," she said in the soft, breathy tone that had been Paisley when he first met her.

His pulse quickened as he took her in, looking every inch the beautiful rock star she was. Her hair had been curled, long waves that accentuated her cheeks in the half-up-half-down style she favored, and her eyes were layered with liner and mascara that drew attention to their glimmering depths. Her full lips were a bright pink that matched the Sweet Memory daisy the world associated with her. While she looked stunning, all he could think was how much more he liked her bare, sharing her body and soul with him and only him. His heart stuttered, and he bent to kiss her softly, trying not to smudge her lipstick.

When he lifted his head, she had a wide smile on her face that reached her eyes. Then, she turned to look out at the darkened stage, listening to the loud clamor of the audience filing into the theater. Her smile faded, finger finding her ring, and he wanted to kick himself for not remembering her anxiety sooner. For not forcing himself into the dressing room so he could hold her hand and try to stem the tide. He pulled their joined hands up to his lips and kissed her palm.

It brought her eyes back to him instead of the stage.

"You're going to be incredible," he said, meaning it.

The soft smile returned to her face, any worry she felt leaving it.

"Honestly? It doesn't even matter. Because the truth is, whether we're incredible or we suck eggs, when we're done, I get to step off the stage and into your arms."

Jonas's throat clogged, the love he felt wanting to spill out of him again.

He took a deep breath and would have said the words if he hadn't been cut off by Fiadh as she and the other Daisies joined them.

"Little Bit, you need a group hug?" Fiadh asked, worry in her voice.

Paisley smiled. "I *want* a group hug, but I don't *need* it."

They all stared at her, shock on their faces followed by joy as they realized she was serious. That for the first time, she wasn't having a panic attack at the thought of going onstage. The five women hugged each other tightly, and it was Adria's eyes who found Jonas's over Paisley's head.

Thank you, she mouthed silently. Pride filled him, knowing that he'd been able to give Paisley even one shred of peace. He only hoped that, somehow, she'd still have it if he had to leave until they found Artie and brought their nightmare to an end.

The stomping and screams got louder as the house lights dropped and dry ice filled the space with mist. When the band finally stepped onstage, the audience went ballistic. It took a full two minutes for them to calm down enough for the band to be heard. The same high-strung emotions running through the women onstage were felt in the crowd, and it only grew as the performance progressed, each song ramping up the wild frenzy.

As the second-to-last song of the night came to an end, and Paisley's and Nikki's voices faded away, the noise in the audience was deafening. They'd skipped the song that would have had Landry as the primary vocal. He'd known they weren't going to sing it as soon as Paisley had slid over to Nikki, and they'd gone back to the drums, talking to Adria off mic. He ached to hold Paisley, to find out what had been going through her head when she'd decided not to play it.

It was hard to read this version of her, alive in a different way than she'd been last night, writhing under him. Regardless of the anxiety she'd battled in the past, she'd always become a powerhouse onstage, but tonight, there was something even more dynamic about her, as if she was daring the world to find them wanting.

It wasn't until she hit the first three notes on her keyboard, cueing the final song—"The Legacy"—that he saw her hesitate. She played the notes and then stopped with her hands frozen above the keys. She took a deep breath, looked around at her bandmates, glanced toward the side of the stage where she couldn't see him but knew he was waiting for her, and then out at the audience again. Silence had taken over the theater as the crowd waited with bated breath. Paisley played the same three notes once more, and he saw her hand shake. She glanced back out to the audience as her fingers came to a stop for a second time.

"I'm having a little trouble with this final song," she said into the mic. "It's something a little extra special. It's for the person..." her voice cracked. "The fiercest, bravest, smartest person I knew. I hope you like 'The Legacy.'"

Her voice got stronger as she finished her little speech. Then, she hit the notes again, and this time, she didn't stop. The video came on behind her. The flashes of Landry as a little girl, then as a teen. The images showed her dancing onstage, singing, and laughing with her arms wrapped around Fee and the other Daisies. Her smile was enormous, and her eyes seemed to send secret messages to those watching. Landry's voice was a ghost-like tremor dubbed softly through the song, fading away. The crowd was sniffling, cheering, sobbing.

When Paisley got to the line about leaving a mark that would never be forgotten, her voice faltered again, the tears and emotions audible, and one after another, her friends' voices joined hers when they weren't supposed to step in until the chorus. They came together. They held each other up. They showed the world the beauty of friendship and love.

Jonas's eyes filled with tears. They were all so damn fierce, but Paisley was the brightest and best of them. Landry had known it, and he could almost feel her there beside him, watching her little sister step out of the shadows to become everything she was supposed to be.

When the last note faded away and the video went dark, the audience sat in stunned silence for a long moment before erupting into applause and stomping feet and screams that topped anything Jonas had ever heard, even when he'd watched the most famous bands play at the Apple Jam Music Fest. Even louder than when Brady-fucking-O'Neil took the stage.

Paisley took a few steps away from her keyboard, looked out

into the audience, and said, "Thank you. Thank you for coming. Thank you for loving Landry as much as we do. Thank you for showing up when we needed to know we could do this without her. We love you all."

As she spoke, Fiadh set down her instrument and came over to put her arm around Paisley's shoulder. One by one, the other bandmembers did the same, leaving behind their instruments, huddling together, and hugging each other tightly. Holding on.

The crowd was still going wild, demanding more, but Jonas knew they were done. Not only because the show wouldn't have an encore act, but because none of the Daisies would be able to sing after this. Even from the side, he could see the tears traveling down their faces. Slowly, they unwound, held hands, and bowed to the crowd. Fee's voice thanked the audience again, and then, still joined, they walked offstage.

It was fucking the most majestic thing Jonas had ever seen. Strength on display for the world. He wiped at the tears on his face as they came nearer. He wasn't sure there was a dry eye in the place. The roadies were all swiping at their eyes. Zia was sniffling and trying to hide it by filling his and everyone else's headset with directions for the crew to start packing up.

When Paisley got close enough, she dropped Fee's hand and ran to him, colliding with his chest. He held her tight, hiding his face in her hair. She was sweaty, radiating heat, and he didn't give a damn about any of it. He only cared that she was there with him. Her hands fisted into his T-shirt as her body convulsed with sobs.

He raised his eyes to look at the others. They were all struggling to pull themselves together.

"*Dios*," Adria said, fingers dragging under her eyes. "I'm not sure I can do that dozens of times."

"It'll get easier," Zia said softly. "Tonight was the worst because it was the first time. As much as I hate to agree with

Asher, it might have been a good idea to get this one out of the way before the rest of the tour."

No one responded. Instead, the Daisies headed back toward the dressing room after shooting Jonas a warning look. *Don't leave her*, they said silently. He wouldn't. Not now. But he did have to. For a little while. Just until Artie was behind bars.

Paisley finally got ahold of herself enough to pull back from him. Zia handed him a box of tissues and then scuttled off, yelling at a roadie who was packing Fee's harp. Paisley looked up at Jonas with red-rimmed eyes. He pulled a tissue from the box and wiped gently at the makeup. Her sad gaze remained on his as he tenderly cleaned her up.

"Thank you," she said softly.

His heart clenched.

"You're the most incredible human being I know," he said. "You were... I don't even have words, Paisley. You are a beautiful, stunning, force of nature. I'm in awe of you. I'm in love with you." The words finally slipped out.

Her eyes grew wide, and then a smile tilted her lips up for the first time since coming off the stage. "You love me?"

He nodded. "Screwed-up timing to say it here." He waved around to the bustling backstage and all the people moving around them.

His stomach flopped again, thinking about what he had to say next, how it was going to upset her. But it was the only way he knew how to protect her.

"It's why I have to leave," he said quietly.

Waves of emotions crossed her face, but anger was the last to appear. "You can't tell me you love me and then say you're leaving. That's ridiculous."

"Tell me something. If you'd known you could save Landry by walking away from me that night, would you have?" He didn't wait for an answer. "You know you would have, and I wouldn't have blamed you. So how can you ask me to stay?"

Sadness battled with the anger in her expression.

"It's different, Jonas. If you leave...we may never catch..."

Her words ripped at him as they faded away. Not only had she not said she loved him back, but now she was basically asking him to stay just so they could catch Landry's killer. While he knew it wasn't the only reason she wanted him there—he knew she truly cared about him—he wondered if her feelings went as deep as his did. She'd walked away from him before, closed him out with relative ease, while he was struggling to tear himself away even when it was to protect her.

He looked over Paisley's shoulder and saw Marco and Cassidy coming toward them, hands joined. He'd forgotten he'd told them to come. Forgotten he'd asked Zia to make sure they had tickets left at the box office.

His brother's eyes darted back and forth between him and Paisley. Marco was good at his job because he knew exactly how to read people and situations, and Jonas knew he could see the tension between Jonas and Paisley.

Cassidy was dressed up in a bright-blue dress that bared her shoulders and clung to her torso before flowing softly out and down to just above her knees. Marco was more formal than normal in jeans and a button-down.

"What an incredible show," Cassidy said, reaching over to hug Paisley.

Paisley shot Jonas one last look before turning to Cassidy with a soft smile. He didn't have it in him to smile at the moment. Marco's knowing eyes watched Jonas carefully.

Cassidy let go of Paisley and turned to wrap Jonas in a hug as well.

"It went better than I expected," Paisley said, her voice quiet. "We skipped a song, but the crowd didn't know." Jonas's heart clenched because she sounded more like the old Paisley than the fierce woman she'd become, and he knew their argument was the reason more than any of the other emotions she'd experienced that night. He was an ass.

Marco reached over, hugged Jonas, and let go before asking quietly, "You good?"

Jonas pushed his brother away, ran a hand through his hair, and then said in a voice that wavered, "No, I'm not good."

When his eyes landed back on Paisley, she frowned.

"Don't," she begged.

"He's going to hear it anyway. You think Trevor is going to continue to keep it from him after yesterday?"

Marco's face grew grim. "What's going on?" he asked.

Paisley glared at Jonas, arms crossing over her tiny frame.

"The notes started again," Jonas said.

"And this is the first I'm hearing about it?" Marco asked, and Jonas could hear the hurt in his tone but also the worry. "What do they say?"

"I-won't-ever-let-you-be-happy kind of shit," Jonas said. "Same as before. But he's escalated. She was shot at last night."

Marco's face turned grim, and Cassidy's eyes grew wide. "Oh my God."

"Damn it, Jonas. Where's Trevor?" Marco's eyes scanned the chaos backstage.

"Getting the vehicles ready," Jonas said.

"Do they have any leads?" Marco asked.

"It's definitely Artie. He said if I leave... That I need to leave her to keep her safe," Jonas's voice cracked, and he hated it because it made him feel like the little kid Marco had first met instead of the man he'd become.

"How are you doing?" Cassidy's eyes were directed at Paisley.

"I'm fine. Actually, I'm glad. I want this to be over. But Jonas thinks he should walk away even when this could be our chance...our chance to finally get the asshole..." Paisley's eyes filled with another round of tears, and it wound every nerve in his body even tighter. He didn't want to be the reason she cried. She'd already cried enough for an entire lifetime.

He reached for her, pulling her to him. At first, she stiffened in his embrace before wrapping her arms around his waist and resting her cheek on his chest. He was torn in half. Torn with the need to stay and the need to go. He didn't know which one would win.

CHAPTER FORTY

Paisley

NOT AFRAID ANYMORE
Performed by Halsey

Paisley was exhausted. In the last twenty-four hours, it felt like she'd experienced every possible human emotion. For a brief moment, she'd felt at peace. She'd gone onstage knowing Jonas was waiting for her, watching her, loving her. And now... God, he wanted to leave—after everything they'd been through.

She didn't know what she'd said to Cassidy and Marco before Zane came to get her. Just like she had no idea what she'd said to the crew congratulating her while she made her way to the car. She only knew she wouldn't be able to keep up her front for much longer.

When she got back to the hotel—by herself because she'd left before Jonas joined her in the car—Zane walked her to her suite. As she put her hand on the doorknob, his quiet voice halted her.

"He doesn't respect you."

She turned to see a cold disdain on his face.

"What?" she asked.

"If he respected you, he wouldn't stay."

Her heart hammered, feeling the pain of Jonas's words at the theater. The need he felt to leave. "You don't know anything about him. What he wants or what he's going to do."

Zane's eyes narrowed. "Maybe not. But I wouldn't be a good friend if I didn't tell you the truth."

Years of people judging her, telling her she was stupid, made the wrong decision, bloomed inside her. "Is that what we are? Friends? I could have sworn you were my bodyguard."

Then, she turned and walked into the suite. She'd been a bitch. She'd been Landry, and it didn't feel good at all. It felt wrong, but she was too tired to try and fix it.

Her steps faltered when she found all the Daisies in her suite. They'd changed into more relaxed outfits with less makeup and softer hair that made them look more like college students than rock stars. Tommy was with them, lounged on a sofa with a glass of dark liquid in his hand that made her want to rip it out of his grasp and pour it down a drain.

Flowers filled the room, champagne bubbled from a tiny fountain, and a mound of food was laid out in a buffet along the dining room table. It took her a beat to realize what was going on, and then she groaned internally, remembering the after-parties from their last tour. She'd forgotten about them, just like she'd forgotten that sometimes Tommy or Nick had important people show up—press or sponsors. She wasn't sure how she'd keep herself going for much longer.

Leya traveled on ballerina-like feet over to her. "You're here! Finally. Go shower and change, then we're going to celebrate."

"Leya...I don't..." She swallowed hard.

A lot of times on the last tour, she'd been able to skip the after-parties. Landry had always read how worn out she was from the performance and had sent her off to her room while her sister handled the small gathering. This time, there was no Landry. The only thing left of her was the legacy she'd left them and her words in a letter telling Paisley she was the real leader.

Paisley tightened her jaw. "I'll be right back."

She headed into her bedroom, locked the door, and then slipped into the shower. She washed away the heavy makeup and hairspray. Washed away the sweat and sadness of performing without Landry. Washed away the sweet bitterness of Jonas's words. "I love you. I have to leave." On repeat.

She didn't even bother drying her hair. She just tucked it up in a messy bun, dressed in soft leggings and a tunic top, and headed out into the living area with bare feet.

In addition to the Daisies and Tommy, Asher and Ronan had shown up. There were a couple of other people she didn't know, but when she scanned the room for Jonas, he wasn't there. Her heart faltered. He wouldn't leave without saying goodbye, would he?

She shook her head. He'd been talking with Cassidy and Marco when she'd left The Palace. Earlier in the week, they'd talked about going to dinner with his family, but going out in public right now with the stalker wasn't wise. She wouldn't have been able to go because of the after-party, anyway.

The only good thing about the party was the food. Her stomach grumbled at the thought. Performing made her almost as hungry as she was exhausted. She found her way to the buffet, fixed a plate, grabbed a water, and headed toward the couch. It wasn't any of her friends who joined her. Instead, it was Ronan.

Normally, he had a tiny video camera stuck in his hands, but tonight, it was as absent as his beanie. His exposed hair glowed a warm chestnut. Reds and golds weaved into it that shimmered in the soft lighting of the suite.

"You were really great tonight," he said. "More than great… It was stunning. The entire show."

Ronan was a flirt, but just like the missing hat and camera, there didn't seem to be any innuendo in his words tonight, only a sincere compliment.

"Thanks," Paisley said.

"She would have been fucking elated. I can almost see her, standing on the coffee table, demanding everyone confirm just how epic the show was." A small smile appeared on his lips that was joined by a faraway look in his eyes, and for the first time, Paisley wondered if there had been something more than business going on between Landry and Ronan.

He was right though. Landry would have been shimmying and shaking on the coffee table, toasting them all with champagne and telling everyone and anyone how talented Paisley's words were. It hit Paisley's already overtaxed and overwrought body with another round of emotions.

God, she missed her. Missed her with an ache that would never go away.

When she didn't respond, Ronan continued, "She was right after all. She built you a mountain, and now you're standing on top shouting at the world, demanding to be seen. Not even a speck of a shadow left behind."

The lump in Paisley's throat grew, her appetite disappearing, and she set her plate down as tears flew down her cheeks.

Suddenly, Ronan was pulled over the back of the couch and tossed toward the wall.

It took everyone by surprise. Ronan's face was shocked, Paisley's heart was pounding, and the room went silent. Paisley turned to see Jonas, his face a deep grove of anger, fists clenched at his side.

"What did you say to her, asshole? Why is she crying?" Jonas demanded.

Paisley stood on the couch, reaching for Jonas who stood behind it. "No. Stop. You got it all wrong, Jonas. He wasn't being mean."

"Trying to finish what you started yesterday? Do I need to get a restraining order to keep you from hitting me?" Ronan growled.

Paisley's eyes turned wide. "You hit him?"

Jonas's body was shaking as he tried to control his rage. Flashbacks to the day he'd pummeled the photographer for saying disgusting words filled her.

"I didn't hit him! But he was filming the shooting, Paisley. Like it was nothing out of the ordinary. Just another day in the life of The Painted Daisies," Jonas said, voice rippling with anger.

Asher stepped between the men, stared at Jonas, and then said in a quiet voice that demanded his order be followed, "You need to leave."

Jonas's eyes closed as he continued to fight for control, fists clenched so tight Paisley knew there would be marks in his palms from his nails. She touched his shoulder gently. "Let's go to the other room."

"Are you sure that's a good idea?" Asher asked, a frown taking over his face as he took in Jonas's tightly held body.

"Jonas would never hurt me," she insisted.

Jonas's eyes popped open, settling in on her, and she saw the regret there, knew that he was battling more than just his anger. He was battling his past. His childhood. The losses in his life.

She slid over the top of the couch, wrapped her fingers in his, and pulled him toward the bedroom. Fee stepped toward her, worry in her eyes, but Paisley just shook her head. She knew what she was doing.

In the bedroom, she closed and locked the door behind them. Jonas turned to her, head down, body trembling. "I'm sorry."

She circled his waist with her arms. "Don't be. You were defending me, Jonas. Like you defended me to the photographer. Like you defended Mel. Don't ever apologize for caring enough to protect someone you love."

His tense stance eased slightly, but his arms were still at his sides instead of on her.

"Ronan was actually being kind," she continued, trying to talk him down. "He reminded me about some really nice things Landry had said...about me...for the documentary. It's why I was crying. I just...miss her."

Jonas's arms finally went around her, squeezing tight, as he buried his face in her hair.

"I'm so screwed up sometimes still, Paisley," Jonas's tortured voice traveled through her. His pounding heart hammered in her ear that was pressed against his chest. "I react first. I'm working on it, but it will probably always be part of me. I'd never hurt you...but—"

"No, but. You wouldn't hurt me. End of story."

"I was so angry yesterday. If Artie hadn't gotten the best of me...if I'd been able to lay my hands on him...I'm not sure what I would have done," he said, the quiet admission ripping out of him and the thought that he could have been even more violent eating him alive.

"Jonas," she said his name, waiting for him to look at her before she continued. "You're a defender, not a killer. You may have smashed him around a bit, but there's no way you would have ended his life."

He searched her face. "How can you know that?"

"Because I know you. Just like you know me. Just like you knew exactly why I pushed you away and why I didn't tell anyone about the new notes from the stalker. There's no way we can hide from each other because we're really one soul in two bodies."

He let out a small groan, and then he was devouring her, kissing her as if they'd never kissed before or as if it was the last time they would. Powerful and fierce, lips and teeth and tongue demanding she respond, and she did, easily letting him seek refuge in her embrace. Her body came alive at the touch. Heat filled her, twirls of desire circling low in her belly, and then she was consuming him back, claiming him just as he was claiming her.

Clothes disappeared, and their bodies collided again. The party taking place on the other side of the wall was forgotten as they touched and tantalized and tortured each other. Slow and fast. Hard and soft. Paths of fingers followed by tongues. The glorious build to the summit that had them crashing over it in wave after wave. Deep emotion embedded into each kiss...each touch...each move. Until all that was left was the two of them, floating in a universe of their own making where the rhythms and sounds of the song they'd started singing to each other four years ago was finally coming to its crescendo. When the chorus was done, there'd be nothing left of the singular people they'd started this life as. There'd only be the "them" that they'd become.

CHAPTER FORTY-ONE

Jonas

WITHOUT YOU
Performed by Mötley Crüe

The hotel suite had been quiet on the other side of the bedroom door for at least an hour. Paisley was snuggled into his chest, passed out. She'd already been exhausted, both physically and emotionally, before they'd made love. He felt like an ass, yet again, for losing himself in her but was also grateful he'd been able to do so. Making love to her had taken every ounce of anger he'd felt toward Ronan and Artie and the thought of leaving her and washed it away. The sweet, heated sex of the day before was nothing compared to the all-consuming, soul-encompassing lovemaking they'd experienced tonight.

He flung an arm over his eyes as memories of his anger in the suite with Ronan filled him and regret curled back in. He wasn't sure he'd ever escape his violent nature, but being with Paisley calmed him even more than pounding the bag in Marco's gym. It was like she dripped Valium into his veins with her touch—hell, with just a look.

A buzzing came from his phone in the pocket of the jeans he'd dropped to the ground. He hoped it didn't wake Paisley, but he was reluctant to untangle them enough to answer it. They were set to leave for Boston on Monday, but today, she should rest. She needed it, and he needed the day to decide what to do. Quit or stay. Protect her by walking away or remain with her and continue to make her a target.

His stomach flipped nastily.

He slowly eased out of her embrace, and she was sleeping so soundly she didn't even register he'd left. It was what he'd wanted, but somehow, it also tore at him a little—that she didn't notice when he was gone. Stupid. Scars of his childhood eating at him.

He grabbed the phone and had to do a double-take.

TREVOR: The FBI has Artie in custody.

His heart leaped. He almost woke Paisley to tell her it was over when Trevor's next text stopped him.

TREVOR: He's in California. If you want to watch the interview, you need to come to the command center in Reinard's suite.

Jonas frowned. Artie could have easily gotten to California from New York since the shooting, but it didn't make any sense. Why would he leave when he'd promised to continue to rain hell down on them?

Jonas threw on his clothes, darted one last longing look toward Paisley, and then left the room as quietly as possible. The two bodyguards outside Paisley's door hardly glanced at him, and he registered with relief that neither of them was

Zane as he headed down a floor to the suite Reinard had secured.

When he entered the room, there was a small group collected around a set of computer screens that included Holden Kent—Leya's Secret Service detail—a smattering of FBI agents, Trevor, and some of Reinard's folks. Trevor tilted his chin up in acknowledgment of Jonas as he stepped in beside him.

Normally, the computers showed the views from the cameras in the hotel, including the extra ones they'd assembled outside Paisley's suite, the balcony, and the hallway off of it. This morning, the screens were filled with an FBI interrogation room where Artie sat across from two agents—a man and a woman both in suits.

Jonas hadn't seen Artie since they'd almost killed each other in Austin four years ago, but he seemed to have aged ten times as much as Jonas had. Artie had always had a look in his eyes that talked of knowledge beyond his years, a toughness that screamed from his veins. But now there was a raggedness to him that spoke of life on the streets. He was still muscled and tattooed and wore a tank top that showed off both, but the tank was filthy, as was the bandana he wore holding back his greasy, brown hair. He'd once had a nose ring, but now there was just a jagged red mark, as if it had been ripped from his nose at some point.

Looks never told the whole story, but he didn't have the air of someone who had the money for rental cars, hideouts, tech equipment to tap into video feeds, or the high-powered rifle that had shot at them two days ago.

Jonas shot Trevor a confused look. Trevor's jaw flexed, teeth grinding.

"Let's start again at the beginning," the male agent said.

Artie groaned, pounded a fist on the table, and barked, "I've told you everything."

The woman slid a clear bag with a paper in it over the table toward him. "You admit you've been sending Carmella Lassinger threatening letters."

Jonas's heart sped up, fear for his one-time friend still pounding through him even though she'd abandoned him and never looked back.

"They aren't fucking threatening. They're fucking love notes. Mel is all I've ever wanted. I can't fucking breathe without her..."

The female agent picked up the note and read, "If you don't take me back, we'll both end in fiery flames."

Artie glared, leaning back in his chair and crossing his arms over his chest.

The agent slid another bagged paper over the table. "This. This is the letter you left for Paisley Kim two years ago. This one is definitely not a love note."

"So what? It's a fucking note. That asshole she's with cost me Mel. I got two years for breaking into her house to try and find her. Two years, and then I get out only to find him cozying up to some fucking rock star as if he's going to get love and money. No fucking way. He doesn't get to have what he stole from me."

"What happened that night, Arthur? That night at Swan River Pond? You thought it was Paisley Kim, right? Did you even realize it wasn't her after you'd slit Landry's throat? Did you not know until you heard it on the news?" the male agent demanded, rising, walking around to Artie's side of the table, and leaning into Arthur's face.

Artie's eyes narrowed. "I didn't fucking kill that bitch. I left the goddamn notes, sure. But I didn't kill anyone. Soon as I heard what had gone down, I got the hell out of that shithole of a town. Wasn't going to have anyone pointing a finger in my direction and sending me back to prison for something I didn't do."

"We don't believe you, Arthur, especially with the new notes you've been sending. Pissed all over again that Jonas is going to be happy, going to get everything you don't have. The woman. The money. The fame."

Artie's eyes went wide. "What the fuck? They're back together?"

He growled and ripped the new note from the female agent's hand.

"That asshole. Un-fucking-believable. I can't even get close to Mel, and he's all cozied up to his bitch again?" Artie crumpled the paper in his fist.

Jonas looked at Trevor as a new fear flew through him. "He didn't know. It wasn't him?" Jonas whispered as his heart picked up pace, pounding so hard it felt like it might leap from his chest.

"Could be a ruse. Don't panic, Jonas. Just let the agents finish," Trevor said, but Jonas could tell Trevor didn't believe it either. Artie wasn't their guy. Not now.

"Where'd you get the AX50 rifle, Artie? The one you used two days ago to shoot at Paisley Kim outside The Palace in Albany?" the female agent asked.

"Don't call me that," Artie demanded. "I don't own a rifle. Ain't my style. If I'm going to end you, I'm going to do it up close and personal." Artie put his fingers like a gun right under his own chin. "I'm going to look you in the eye when I pull the trigger."

"You didn't look Landry Kim in the eye. You slaughtered her from behind with a knife. You repeated that same action with her bodyguard. Two people you were cowardly enough to kill without looking them in the face while you did it." The male agent continued to invade Artie's space, talking in his ear.

Artie tried to shove his chair to the side, but it was chained down.

"I told you. I had nothing to do with that. I'd heard the film crew was going to be showing up at seven, so I left the note and got the hell out. The first car was just arriving as I took off. Got a speeding ticket as I fucking raced away."

"The film crew? You saw the film crew show up? If you did, you were on the premises when Landry Kim died. No ticket is going to clear you of her death, *Artie*," the male agent said, emphasizing the name Artie had asked not to be called.

Artie shook his head. "No, it wasn't that Hawk guy who showed up. This was a military dude. Shaved head, tattoos up his neck, dressed in black. He parked in the orchard too. I was making my way back to the piece-of-shit truck I had stashed there when I saw him drive through the trees."

"The Painted Daisies had a whole host of bodyguards on site. Many with military backgrounds."

Artie shrugged. "All I know is that I got the hell out before the fucking cameras were there."

"You didn't get a ticket in your name that night. We would have found it by now," the woman said, pounding away on a laptop at her side.

Artie snorted. "You think I was using my own fucking name and I.D.? How dumb do you think I am?"

"What name were you using?"

He fidgeted in his chair.

"You're our number one suspect right now, Artie. Two murders, attempted murder, stalking, harassment. You'll die in prison," the male agent said.

Artie slammed his fist into the table again. "I'm not going down for fucking murder. I told you, I left the goddamn note and then got the hell out of there."

"So, tell us the name you were using," she pushed.

"Jack Lassinger!" he shouted back at her.

"Mel's dad?" Jonas breathed out in surprise just as the female agent said the same thing with a frown.

"I stole his I.D. back when Mel and I were first dating. I had a friend who could create almost identical fakes."

"No way a cop thought you were a forty-plus-year-old man."

"We created an entire profile that was supposed to be his son. I've been using it all along to find out about the Lassingers by pretending I was related to them," Artie growled. Then, he glared at the two agents. "I wouldn't give you that information and cut my chances of finding her again. No fucking way. But I'm not going down for killing that Daisy chick. I didn't slice up anyone."

Jonas felt like he was going to throw up because if it wasn't Artie, they were back to square one. They had no clue who was after Paisley.

Artie picked up the crumpled note. "I didn't send this one. I didn't even know Jonas-fucking-Riccoli was back with her. I haven't been anywhere near New York in two years. You said they got shot at again? Two days ago? I spent the entire day in the pool room at the Spider's Nest right here in L.A. Plenty of people saw me there."

Jonas couldn't watch anymore. He had to get back to Paisley. He had to tell her the good and bad news. This wasn't Artie. This was someone else. The notes from before...someone was just using them to cover their trail. He frowned. It didn't make any sense that whoever it was now was still telling Jonas to back off. To leave her.

Trevor was on his heels as he stormed out of the room and started down the hall.

"Jonas, wait."

Jonas spun around, catching his eyes with worried ones. "I don't get it, Trevor? If it was Artie before but not now, who the hell have I pissed off?"

Trevor eyeballed him. "They'll check out the ticket and his alibi for the shooting. It could still be him."

"You don't believe it any more than I do," Jonas said, heart hammering.

Trevor didn't respond for a long time. Then he said, "This might not be about you now, Jonas. Or rather, not you specifically."

"What do you mean?" Jonas asked.

"Maybe the guy just doesn't want Paisley with anyone. Maybe they knew about the notes from before and are using it as a cover."

"It was never made public what the notes said, Trev. Just that they were getting them."

Trevor nodded.

Dread filled Jonas. "You think it's someone they know."

Trevor stepped backward. "I'm going to go discuss it with the team."

"I'm going to go find Paisley," Jonas responded.

They stared at each other for a long moment and then flipped around, going in opposite directions with worry and fear coasting through them both.

CHAPTER FORTY-TWO

Paisley

INVINCIBLE
Performed by Pat Benatar

Her alarm went off, and Paisley groaned, reaching for Jonas. It was a little overwhelming how quickly she'd gotten used to waking up with him next to her. When her fingers found nothing but cold linens, she sat up, blinking her eyes and searching the room. "Jonas?"

Panic filled her as it had last night before he'd shown up at the hotel. Fear that he would leave, which was ridiculous because she knew, deep down in her heart, he'd never leave without telling her. Not after having their bodies twined together and *I love you* slipping from his lips.

She pulled on a robe and opened the bedroom door. The living area of the suite was clean and sparkling without a single trace of the party from the night before. She hadn't heard housekeeping come and go, but then again, she hadn't even heard the party after she'd gone into the room with Jonas and gotten lost in him.

Her phone alarm went off again, the sound harsh in the silence of the suite. She went back into the bedroom and shut it off. While every single cell in her being wanted to go find Jonas, she only had half an hour to get ready for her one-on-one interview with Ronan, and it would be better to do the interview without Jonas if he and Ronan were just going to provoke each other.

Exhaustion was still hanging on her as she showered and straightened the mess that was her hair from going to bed with it wet. She put on the bare minimum of makeup she needed to cover the dark circles under her eyes and threw on jeans and a blouse she'd never worn before. It had a gauzy, see-through white outer layer with tiny blue daisies spread out over it that, from a distance, would almost look like polka-dots. Beneath it was a pale-blue tank. When she'd bought it, she'd thought it was something Landry would have purchased, but now, she realized it was too soft for Landry, who'd always favored harsh lines and bright colors. But it also wasn't something the old Paisley would have ever worn either.

The truth settled in. She wasn't Landry, and she wasn't the old Paisley. She was someone new, holding on to pieces of all of them.

In her past, she'd let Landry, her parents, the band, and their management all make decisions they thought were best for her. She'd acquiesced without a fight. Jonas thought walking away, leaving her, was best for her too, but she wasn't going to just sit by and let that happen. She needed him here, and she knew, in her heart, he needed to be with her. She would keep him at her side if it was the last thing she did, just like she would keep the band together somehow. Landry had known she could do this long before Paisley had the faith to see it herself. But she was right where she belonged now, with the Daisies and with Jonas. Both of them filled her soul.

She looked in the mirror and stared. Instead of her eyes going first to her star birthmark like they usually did, they went to her lips. They seemed redder than normal. Sensitive still from all the kissing she and Jonas had done in the last two days. Her face flushed, thinking about the soft whimpers she'd let out the night before as Jonas had commanded her body. She'd completely let go, and he'd led her into the delightful abyss that was them together.

For the first time in what felt like years, and may have been forever, Paisley smiled at her reflection. She was Paisley Kim. Loved by one man. Leader of a famous rock band. Two years ago, she would have lost her nonexistent breakfast at the idea of meeting with Ronan and talking about herself. Now, she was anxious in a different way. Now, she couldn't wait to show him, and the world, that she wasn't a shadowy reflection of her sister.

She slid into a pair of low-heeled ankle boots, grabbed her keycard and her phone, and headed for the door of the suite. Outside, two men stood. Neither of them was Zane, and the guilt from their conversation the night before filled her again. She needed to apologize.

"I'm going down to Ronan Hawk's room for my interview. Are you supposed to come with me while I'm in the hotel?" she asked.

"Jim will stay here. I'll go," one of the men said.

She headed for the elevator, and the bodyguard had her stand off to the side until it opened and he cleared it. They traveled down three floors to Ronan's room. Paisley was surprised he wasn't in a suite at the top, because Ronan certainly had enough money and fame for one. He'd been Hollywood royalty from a family of stars even before he'd won an award at the Avalyn Film Festival for a film he'd made after Landry's death. Paisley wasn't sure why Ronan felt the need to finish their tiny documentary now. But then, she remembered his comments from the night before. He'd cared for Landry in some way. Maybe, like the band making "The Legacy," finishing the documentary was Ronan's way of honoring her memory.

It softened her heart a little toward him, making her see him as more than the player she'd always thought he was.

She knocked on his hotel door, and Ronan's voice yelled out, "It's unlocked. Come in."

It sounded weird. Forced and garbled. But when the bodyguard opened the door, the room was empty. The light in the bathroom was on, and the door was shut.

"I'll be right out," Ronan said, the strange tone still in his voice, and it knocked at Paisley's confidence, unease settling through her.

The bodyguard cleared the room and then looked down at Paisley.

"You good?" he asked.

She hesitated before nodding. He'd be right outside the door. It wasn't like he couldn't come bounding back in if something went wrong.

"Lock the door behind me," he said.

She did and then turned back to the room, moving toward the table by the window where Ronan had his laptop and a bunch of papers spread out.

When Ronan didn't appear after a minute or so, her stomach started to twist more, wondering if he wasn't feeling well. How awkward would it be to have someone waiting for you while you were sick just on the other side of the wall. Her sympathy grew, dashing away her unease, and she went to the bathroom door, wondering if she should knock and check on him.

"Hey...if this isn't a good time, I can come back," she said, finger finding the beads on her ring for the first time all day.

Muffled noises came from inside, and the skin on the back of her neck prickled.

"Ronan? Are you okay?"

A large crash, as if something had fallen into the tub, had her reaching for the handle while fighting a sudden urge to flee. She swallowed, not exactly wanting to see Ronan half-dressed or sitting on the toilet, but also not willing to let him bleed out if he'd hurt himself. She turned the handle, slowly opening the door as she called out his name again.

As her eyes landed on the scene in the mirror, she froze with the door partially open. Ronan had duct tape over his mouth, and he was slumped in the tub with his hands and feet bound with zip ties. Blood trickled from his forehead, sending a trail over his closed eyes. She lost her breath, fear imprisoning her and locking her feet into place.

Before she could force herself to move, the handle jerked out of her grasp. The door swung inward as she stumbled into the bathroom. A startled cry escaped her just as a huge hand settled over her mouth, and her gaze met Zane's. Confusion mingled with the fear as her blood pounded in her ears, and her chest squeezed tight.

What the hell was going on? Why would Zane detain Ronan? A wave of nausea churned through her. Was Ronan the stalker?

She pulled on Zane's hand that was clenched tightly against her mouth, a million questions running through her brain. Zane's dress shirt was askew, tie crooked, and hair wild from the struggle he'd obviously had with Ronan. But it was his eyes that had the blood draining from her face and her pulse hammering.

They were wild with fury.

She tried to talk, tugging harder on his wrist, but the pressure on her mouth grew fierce until her lips felt like they were embedded into her teeth.

"Shut up," he hissed. "I need to see if the idiot at the door is going to react to your cry. You shouldn't have done that."

Silence followed as they both waited, Paisley with a feeble hope that the man outside would come bounding in. Hope that this was just some frightening test Zane was putting the other bodyguards through. Because there was no way she'd trusted this man with her life...her body...her world, and he was turning on her.

A sob got caught in her chest. Had she made another stupid decision?

When the door of the suite remained shut, Zane pushed her back until she was jammed up against the sink. His eyes strolled over her, from the top of her head down to her toes and back.

"How can I have been so wrong about you?" His face contorted with disgust and anger, and Paisley's stomach fell further, the urge to throw up twisting and burning inside her as the truth hit her. Zane was not the good guy.

"I thought you were an angel. I saw how you cared for your parents and the band, and I thought I'd finally found someone who deserved to be protected. Loved. Adored."

She tried to talk again, but he pushed so hard against her mouth that it forced her lips open, and his palm hit her teeth. Her spine curved backward over the counter, pain spiraling through her.

"My sister was like you, sliding into bed with whoever would have her, spreading her legs for all the boys in school until I couldn't walk the halls without hearing one of them bragging about having had her. Just like Ronan last night, bragging about you coming to see him and how he couldn't wait to finish what he started—so he could get his *hands* on you."

Paisley's eye grew wide, darting to the unconscious body in the tub. If Ronan had said that, she doubted he'd meant it in a sexual way. Because even when he'd flirted, he'd never made any moves on her. Landry and Adria had always been his targets.

"I guess he doesn't care that you've already ruined yourself with Jonas." Zane spat out Jonas's name like he was the lowest of the low.

Paisley felt tears hit her eyes, not only from fear but his words. Words had always wounded her. Bullies telling her she wasn't good enough. That she was stupid. Ugly. A witch with that mark. And now...now she could add whore because that was what he'd implied. She was tired of being judged. Considered less. What she had with Jonas was beautiful. Something that lifted them both up. Made them better. She wouldn't let him destroy that with his vile words.

She pushed with both hands against his chest, trying to move him away, but he slammed his body into hers completely, shoving a gun she hadn't realized he held into her cheek. She gagged as terror built, and tears coursed down her cheeks.

"My sister died because she was fucking a guy at a party. They didn't run when the first shots were fired. But her killer did my father—the world—a favor because there was one less harlot for him to save. Like God cleansing the world of Sodom and Gomorrah."

The coldness of his voice as he spoke about his sister made her body quiver. All this time, she'd thought he'd been overwhelmed with the same kind of loss as she'd had, but instead, he was full of a gross satisfaction.

She scratched at his hands and arms, bucking against him, trying to create leverage and space between them, but he just shoved her back into the counter, his body a wall she couldn't move as the pain at the base of her back grew to a howl from the edge of the counter. Zane pulled the gun from her cheek and directed it toward the tub and the unmoving Ronan.

"Would you even care if I killed him? Because if you don't stop struggling, I will," he said.

She froze.

"Good girl," he said. His eyes traveled down to her breasts that were heaving under the see-through top. His hand on her mouth and the adrenaline pounding through her was making it hard to breathe. The room swam, her vision blurring.

"What am I going to do with you, Paisley?" he asked, his voice an infuriated growl. "Do I take you with me? Can I turn you back around? Or are you already too tarnished to be cleansed?"

She let her hands drop to her sides, finding the edge of the counter, hoping she could use it for leverage. The movement caused her chest to push into his, and she wanted to recoil, but instead, she forced herself to stay where she was as she gripped the cool surface like a lifeline, waiting for the right moment.

His eyes dilated, looking down to where their bodies touched. "I want you. How is it possible that even knowing what you've done, I still want you? We would have been married before I took you the way God intends. But now...damn it... maybe I need to teach you a lesson."

His hand with the gun returned to her, trailing the muzzle down her cheek like a finger. Like a perverse, tender embrace. "I'm going to take my hand off your mouth, but if you scream, I'll shoot you both. I'll make it look like he did it, and that I was too late to save you. Nod if you understand."

Paisley did, and her eyes tracked his hand as it slowly let up from her mouth and moved to tangle in her hair. She ran her tongue on the inside of her lips, tasting blood.

"Temptress," he growled, watching the movement of her mouth.

Paisley froze again.

"Did you...did you kill my sister?" Her voice cracked, horror and pain ripping through her.

The gun on her cheek stilled as his eyes narrowed. "I didn't even know your sister. I hadn't even paid attention to The Painted Daisies until I saw your face on the news. You were devastated but holding it together so beautifully. And I thought, 'Here's someone finally worthy of my protection.'"

Waves of acid burned through her stomach and throat as she fought to remember what she needed to do, how she could use her lower body strength to fight back. But he would know. He would know every single move because he'd taught them to her. A tortured sob got stuck in her chest as her eyes rested on the gun.

A noise in the hallway caught their attention. Someone talking to the bodyguard.

Zane's face turned in that direction, head tilted, and Paisley used the flash of distraction to her benefit. She pushed up and away, creating a space for her to pull her knees up, using her feet to push him away.

He whipped back around and shoved her against the counter again, but, raised as she was, it sent her butt skidding backward on the marble until she crashed into the mirror. He grabbed her ankles in his one free hand as she tried to kick him.

"Knock it off," he hissed.

A loud siren-like sound went off from the bathtub. It jerked their eyes in that direction. Ronan was awake. His hands were behind him, still tied but fiddling with something—his phone—the SOS alert blaring through the room. It would send the emergency call if he didn't stop it in the next thirty seconds.

Zane let go of her, stepping toward the tub.

Pounding came from the door followed by shouts.

Relief and new waves of fear skittered through her as Jonas's deep voice called her name. She leaped off the counter, screaming, "Jonas!" She only reached the bathroom doorway as Zane abandoned Ronan in order to grab her. His hand claimed her wrist, squeezing until she gasped. She ducked, trying to spin under his arm to twist his elbow backward like she'd been taught, but he knew every move she was going to make and recaptured her easily with a strong arm locked around her waist, forcing her back into his chest. She kicked out at him, shins, kneecap, trying to get higher to his groin, but he ignored every move she made, lifting her off her feet and dragging her from the bathroom into the main room. He moved them backward, toward the window and the balcony.

The battering on the door grew more furious, Jonas's voice screaming her name.

"Stop fighting!" Zane growled in her ear, but she didn't listen.

She continued to twist and turn with every ounce of strength she had. She dragged a heel down his shin and screamed Jonas's name again.

Zane's gun came up, pointing first at her and then toward the entrance.

"I didn't want to kill anyone," Zane spat. "You're making me do this."

The beep of the keycard unlocking the door sounded like a bell in a starting gate. Blind terror swam through her because she knew it would be Jonas coming through the door first.

"Jonas, he has a gu—" Zane slammed the gun into her head, and she crumpled to the floor, lights flickering as her vision swam.

The door crashed open so hard it broke the wall behind it with a loud crack. Paisley saw Zane's finger squeeze, and her body and mind screamed, but when the shot came, it wasn't from Zane's gun. It came from the balcony behind them. Zane staggered, his expression one of shock followed by pain.

In that brief moment, Jonas charged, taking Zane to the ground and causing the gun in his hand to slide across the floor. Jonas swung his fist into Zane's face once, twice, and again. Paisley fought her spinning world to reach for the weapon with shaky fingers. Zane was shielding his face with one arm, the other hanging useless, blood soaking through his white dress shirt from a wound by his collarbone as Jonas continued to hit him over and over.

The glass door on the balcony shattered, and Trevor pushed his way through it, grabbing Jonas's arm and trying to stop it mid-swing.

"Stop, Jo-Jo!"

But Jonas's rage was fueling him, and he easily pulled away from Trevor to slam his fist into Zane several more times. But then, suddenly, he stopped, trembling as he pulled himself away and stepped back, staring down at the blood covering his fists.

Tears poured down her face as Paisley watched the beautiful man she loved struggling to regain control. Her chest ached, and her stomach burned as Jonas's tortured words from the night before came back to her—his fear of killing Artie.

"Jonas," Paisley groaned, fighting her way to her hands and knees as the world spun wildly around her.

Jonas's eyes flew to hers as she tried to crawl to him, still holding the gun she'd collected from the ground. He fell to his knees at her side and dragged her to him as Trevor reached for the gun, snagging it from Paisley's fingers and directing it toward the unmoving Zane.

She and Jonas clung to each other as wave after wave of emotions crashed over her. Fear. Relief. Disgust. Sorrow.

People poured into the room. Some in suits. Some wearing the black gear of their security company.

She closed her eyes, sobbing into Jonas's neck, and he squeezed tighter, a tortured sound from deep inside his chest escaping him. "I'm so sorry I wasn't here... I'm so sorry, sweetheart... Are you hurt?"

He pulled away slightly, scanning her for injuries. She shook her head, wincing as pain flew through it.

"Shit, you are!" He dragged his hands over her arms and legs, scanning every inch of her as she shivered. "Where does it hurt, Paisley? What did he do?"

He eyed all her clothes, still in place, but she couldn't respond, terrifying thoughts of what Zane could have done—what he might have done—taking her voice and increasing the sobs that wracked her. Her vision blurred again, and Jonas pulled her back into his chest. Safe. Warm. Home.

"I got you, sweetheart. You're okay. I got you," he mumbled as if reassuring them both.

Ronan was led into the room by two of Reinard's men, blood dripping down his face that was full of the same fury Jonas had shown. He saw Zane on the ground and flung off the arms of his helpers to stalk over to Zane and glare down at the unmoving man.

"I'm going to make you wish you were dead," Ronan growled. "You'll be begging to leave this world."

Trevor pushed Ronan back. "He can't even hear you, Ronan. And he's going to jail. For a long time. Assault. Attempted murder. Murder. That's the end of this story. You get me?"

Ronan and Trevor stood toe to toe, assessing each other. Paisley's shaking grew worse, uncontrollable tremors taking over her body. Zane hadn't killed Landry. Zane hadn't even known Landry. The notes from before were still unsolved. Landry's murderer was still out there. She was trying to say the words, trying to get them out, but they came out as mangled gibberish.

"Shh. It's okay. I promise. It's all okay," Jonas continued to soothe.

But it wasn't. Nothing was okay. They'd caught Zane. They'd stopped him, but nothing was resolved. Not for her. Not for the band. She couldn't breathe. The world spun more, the lights returned, and the world turned dark as she lost consciousness.

CHAPTER FORTY-THREE

Jonas

MORE THAN WORDS
Performed by Extreme

Every part of Jonas was hurting—fists, heart, head—as he rocked Paisley on the floor of Ronan's room. God, if they hadn't gotten there... All he could see in his mind was Paisley's body crumpled at the asshole's feet as he'd burst into the hotel room. He'd thought... He shook his head as tears filled his eyes, and he squeezed her tighter.

Suddenly, she went limp in his arms, and when he looked down, her eyes were closed. *Fuck.* "Trev..."

Jonas's panicked voice drew his friend's worried gaze. Jonas rose with her in his arms and laid her down on the bed.

"Paisley. Sweetheart. Open your eyes." Jonas fell on his knees by the bed, running a hand over her face.

Trevor handed off a groaning Zane to two men who loaded him onto a gurney the EMTs had dragged into the room and hurried over to Jonas. He lifted Paisley's wrist, checking her pulse. "She's fainted."

One of the EMTs joined them. "Let me in, sir."

Jonas reluctantly stepped back, fear flooding him.

The EMT was about to scan a light in her eyes when her lids began to flutter. She raised a hand, pushing at the man.

"Jonas?" she cried out.

"I'm here, Paisley."

The man stepped back, and Jonas was at her side again, dragging her fingers into his.

"Are you hurt anywhere?" the EMT repeated Jonas's question from before she'd passed out.

Paisley's hand went to her temple, wincing. "My head. He hit me with the gun."

Ronan was in a chair by the table where another EMT was checking him out, and he growled out a comment, "It must have been his M.O. Three of us have knots on our noggins because of him." His eyes met Jonas's.

The EMT felt Paisley's head. "It's going to hurt like hell for a few days. And both of you should be watched for concussions, but I think you'll be okay."

He cracked an icepack and handed it to her.

The EMTs went back to the gurney where a third member of their team was working on Zane. They had his wrist cuffed to the side rail and bandages shoved against his shoulder where Trevor had shot him.

"Can we get him out of here?" Trevor asked them, darting looks in Ronan, Jonas, and Paisley's direction. The men nodded and rolled the gurney away.

Ronan rose from his chair, watching with a glare as they wheeled Zane from the room, and then he turned to Paisley. They were both holding icepacks to their heads. It would have been funny if it wasn't so fucking serious.

"Those were some pretty damn good moves you put on him, Paisley," Ronan said, a bit of awe in his eyes. "Maybe if Lan had known them..." His voice faded away, and a misty look appeared in his eyes that he tried to hide by looking down.

Paisley sat up, listing sideways, and Jonas caught her, sitting on the bed next to her, wrapping his arms around her. "He didn't... He didn't kill Landry," she stumbled out the words.

Everyone in the room turned to look at her.

"How do you know that?" Trevor asked gently.

"He said...he didn't even know us until after...he saw me on the news at her funeral. He thought... He thought I deserved to be protected." Her voice was unsteady, fear and sorrow all mixed together.

A low bark emitted from Jonas's chest. "This wasn't protection."

Paisley trembled in his arms, and he wished he knew what to do to help her. But all he could do at the moment was hold her as relief flew through him. She was okay. She was alive. She was going to be scarred by this emotionally. It would add another awful memory to her life that had already been tainted, but he would make sure nothing but good came after this. He'd devote his entire life to it. No one was going to harm Paisley Kim again.

"He said...he was upset that you and I...he was ranting about sex before marriage...how I was no longer..."

Jonas got the gist of it. Even if they hadn't had sex until after the shooting at the theater, Zane hadn't known that. He'd seen Jonas coming and going from Paisley's room at all hours. Seen her kiss him. Fuck...

Trevor's jaw clenched, and it looked like how Jonas felt. Tight and pissed. It made him want to go down, find the gurney, and add a few more punches to the ones he'd already landed. His knuckles were busted open, aching, but Paisleys' sad voice hurt worse.

"The FBI is going to want to talk to both you and Ronan," Trevor said. "But, Jonas, why don't you take Paisley up to her suite. Get her away from this."

He looked around the room. The shattered glass. The blood on the floor. The place where she'd been held against her will.

He rose from the bed and lifted her into his arms.

"I can walk, Jonas," she said, but she wrapped her arms around his neck and didn't fight it as he strode from the room.

"I know. This is for me, sweetheart. I need you close."

They strode past a dozen men and into the elevator. She put a hand to his jaw, rubbing the stubble that he hadn't shaved because he'd barely gotten dressed before he'd gone down to see Artie's interview with the FBI. When he'd returned to find she'd gone to the interview with Ronan, it hadn't raised any alarms until Jim had said that Zane hadn't shown up for duty. His gut had churned with a strange premonition. Or maybe he'd just finally listened to it, because it had been screaming at him for days about the way the man had looked at Paisley. As if she was his. As if she was disappointing him.

He'd called Trevor, and they'd met at Ronan's. They'd barely talked to the guard before they'd heard the SOS going off inside. When a guest had come running out of the room next to Ronan's, Trevor had raced inside, shouting about the balconies and breaching the room from the outside.

Ripples of fear moved through him again as every emotion he'd felt standing outside that door returned. The absolute terror. The desperate need to get inside. To get to Paisley. He'd never been so afraid that it had almost paralyzed him.

"How...how did you know?" she asked.

"Later. We can talk about that later," he said.

The elevator opened, and he strode down the hall to where Jim still stood, anxious, hand to his ear, listening to the commotion over the headset. Relief filled his face upon seeing Paisley.

He inserted his keycard in the lock and opened the door for them.

Jonas went straight to the bedroom. He'd barely sunk down onto the bed, sitting with her in his arms, before she was kissing him in a fury of lips and teeth and tongue as emotions poured from her, fear and sorrow mingling together. He kissed her back with the same emotions, but also with love flowing through him. So much goddamn love he wasn't sure he knew how to contain it. How to box it in so it didn't consume them both.

She was the one to stop, dropping her forehead to his chest, fingers finding his. He tried not to wince as she grazed over the wounds on his knuckles from pounding Zane. She pushed back slightly, staring down at his hands that had beaten another human being. A piece of him had wanted to kill Zane, had wanted to swing until there was nothing left of the man, but he'd forced himself to stop. Not only for Paisley but for himself. He didn't want to be the angry man her friends feared. The one they all looked at as if he would one day break and hurt her. He'd had to prove to himself that he could regain control on his own. And he had.

"I'm sorry," she said. Her voice broke, and tears hit his knuckles. It about undid him that she was crying for him. His throat contracted, and his jaw tightened.

"Why? This isn't your fault," he croaked out.

"You've tried so hard to put it behind you. The rage. And somehow, I keep bringing it back into your world."

He put a finger under her chin, forcing her eyes to meet his. "Not you, Paisley. You bring joy and love. You make me feel like I'm actually the man I'm supposed to be. The anger...it got the upper hand for a moment today, but I took control. I found myself again."

Female voices burst into the suite, scattered and alarmed. The Daisies tumbled into the room with worry on their faces before their eyes landed on Paisley. He let her go, and as she stood, they swept her into a hug. He rose, starting to move away to give them a moment, but Fiadh's hand on his arm stopped him. She pulled him into the circle with them. He met her eyes above Paisley's head before slowly turning to look at each of them. Their expressions all reflected the same emotions. Relief and gratitude. "Thank you for saving Little Bit," Fee said.

He shook his head, a small smile appearing for the first time. "You need to start calling her Little Warrior instead of Little Bit because I guess she was already saving herself before we even got there."

Paisley snorted, but it brought a small chuckle from all of them. "Little Warrior. I think I love that," Adria said.

And they all stood there, hanging onto each other for what felt like a lifetime.

♫ ♫ ♫

Jonas ached to be alone with Paisley again, to release the emotions of the day through skin on skin until they found their way back to the serenity that was them together. But after the Daisies broke in, a series of agencies stopped by, all asking the same questions.

The good news was the stalker letters had been put to rest—Artie having confessed to the ones from two years ago, and Zane to the ones now. The man Zane had chased away from Jonas's place had simply been a paparazzi looking for a scoop. Landry's murder was still unsolved, but oddly enough, Artie had given them a new lead to follow—the man in the orchard. Trevor had gone back through the Garner Security notes from that day, and none of the team should have been in the portion of the orchard where Artie had been parked.

Just as the room finally cleared and Jonas pulled her up tight against his body, her phone rang. Her eyes widened, looking at it. "It's my mom. I was supposed to call her after the interview."

He kissed her softly and then stepped back. "Take it. I want to call Marco and Maliyah too."

She grabbed his hand as he went to move away and gently kissed his bandaged knuckles before moving toward the bedroom, raising her phone to her ear.

Dusk had settled in as he stepped out onto the balcony of the suite, hitting the call button on his phone.

"Hey, this is unexpected. How are you?" Marco said as he answered.

"Struggling," Jonas said. The word came out choked.

"What's wrong?" Marco was immediately on alert. Jonas stumbled out the story. Artie. Zane. The fact that the letters were solved but not Landry's murder.

"It makes sense with the original findings. They thought Landry and Ramona were killed by a professional," Marco said softly. "This isn't about you anymore, Jonas. That should be a relief."

Jonas pushed his bangs back. He needed to chop them off once and for all. Grow up. Leave behind the shaggy look of his childhood. Maybe he would. But then, memories of how Paisley ran her fingers through it and tugged at it when he was devouring her, made his insides light up. Maybe he'd leave it just the way it was.

"What's going on in that thick skull of yours?" Marco asked, the worry clear.

"I don't want my past to continue to dictate my future. Just like I don't want my anger to control my present. I love her. She deserves better than that," Jonas said. "But what if—"

"Stop," Marco commanded. "First, there is no one on this planet who could be better for her than you, Jonas. You have the biggest fucking heart of anyone I've ever met. You left your past behind you years ago. Look at what you've accomplished by getting your degree, co-producing albums, running the tour. You may not be a fucking rock star, but you're an inspiration, a model of what people can do if they let go of what's holding them back. Second, maybe you deserve better than her. Maybe you deserve better than being dragged around and playing second fiddle to a band and a fan base that won't ever let her go."

"Better stop before you say something about her I won't be able to stand," Jonas growled, and the tension in his stomach eased when Marco chuckled.

"You really do love her."

"With every single fiber of my being," Jonas said.

"Does she love you just as much?" Marco asked.

Paisley hadn't said the words. He'd felt it, but she hadn't said it.

"Yes," Jonas said.

"You hesitated."

"It's complicated."

Marco was quiet. "I know we often tell ourselves that. Cassidy and I...there were moments before we finally gave in to the truth, Jonas, where we said the same thing—that things were too complicated. But the truth is, giving in to love is really rather simple. Go tell her how you feel, put your heart out there, hold nothing back, and if she does the same, then she's earned a spot at your side. But if she can't do that, then no matter what you do, it won't work."

It wrenched a knife through Jonas's heart. The kid who'd never been enough for his mother. The thousand and one notes he'd mailed to the jail without ever getting one response. Mel's abandonment. The silence from Paisley for two years. He was a man from a screwed-up past, but Marco and Maliyah were both right. That didn't mean he didn't deserve love and happiness. He believed with every breath he took that Paisley was the one for him, but before he got completely lost in her, he needed to be sure.

CHAPTER FORTY-FOUR

Paisley

THE WORDS
Performed by Christina Perri

Mom was sobbing so hard she had to hand the phone to Dad. Dad was angry and cold, but underneath it, Paisley could hear the relief and the love. Paisley's heart twisted painfully inside her chest. It was as if her body ached from the inside out, joining the pounding in her head, and the cuts on her lips, and the bruise forming on her lower back.

While everyone was thankful there'd be no more ugly notes, no one was voicing just how devastated they were to be no closer to solving Landry's murder. Her sister deserved justice. The killer should pay for what he did to Landry and the bodyguard who'd served her selflessly.

"Your mother needs you home," her dad said quietly.

Guilt joined the regret and heartache in her chest, twisting and turning.

"This is my way of honoring her..." She caught the sob before it fully broke.

He was silent for so long she thought he'd hung up before he said gruffly, "Honor, Ji-An, is important, but not as important as staying alive. We will see you soon."

He hung up, and her stomach churned because of the pain she was causing them.

She could hear Jonas's deep voice out on the balcony, talking to his loved ones. She looked down at her hands, surprised to see how normal they looked. She had none of the blood that had been on Ronan and Jonas and Zane, but she could still feel Zane's touch, and it made her skin crawl.

She shed her clothes and stepped into the shower, resting her forehead on the cool tile. Her vision swam, the blood from today merging with the memories of the wound on her sister's neck, and before she realized it, she was crying again. Sobs of loss and relief and exhaustion.

Suddenly, Jonas was there, arms wrapped around hers, naked body tucked up against hers as the water poured over them. "I got you, sweetheart," he said, just like he had in Ronan's room. Just as he had after Landry had died. Just as he had when she'd sent him away on a swing set in her backyard.

She buried her head in his chest, ignoring the ache and just holding on.

Eventually, he turned the water off, toweled them both off, tucked them into the fluffy hotel robes, and led her to the bed. He wrapped them together, her back to his front, feet tangled, fingers twined. His chin nuzzled on her shoulder near her ear where the warm heat of his breath coasted over her, and her skin broke out in shivers.

"I love you," Jonas said quietly. "If you'll let me, I'll be at your side from now until my heart stops beating."

Paisley recognized it for what it was. Not a marriage proposal. Something better. A pledge. A promise to be there forever.

She turned in his arms so she could look into those bright-green eyes and see the beautiful boy who'd become a stunning man.

"Do you know when I first fell in love with you?" she asked.

His eyes widened, a slow smile appearing. "You love me?"

She rolled her eyes. "You know I do."

And then, she realized she hadn't told him. She'd felt every single ounce of it, had expressed it through hands and fingers and lyrics, but she'd never given him the actual words, and it filled her with another round of remorse. She didn't want him to ever doubt it...doubt her.

She took his face in her hands. "Jonas Riccoli, I love you more than all the lyrics in the world combined."

She kissed his lips softly, the heat of it curling through her, hand sliding into his hair, tangling there. He grasped her hips, pulling her closer, and the kiss deepened, turning from sweet and sorrowful to hungry and feverish. They lost themselves for what felt like minutes...hours...days in each other, mouths and fingers competing to show who loved who more.

She finally pulled back slightly, a small smile forming. "I think I loved you from the moment you told me Jim Morrison was overrated."

He scoffed, but his lips twitched. "You told me I didn't know what I was talking about."

"And you let me prove it to you. No one... No one had ever let me do that before. My opinions had never mattered."

He traced her eyebrows with a finger and then her lips. "Landry believed in you."

He said it softly, trying not to hurt her at the mention of her sister, and while it did hurt, it wasn't quite as much as it had been in the beginning. She'd never, ever be able to heal that wound completely, but it wouldn't absolutely break her anymore either.

"She did," Paisley agreed. "More than I knew. I'd listened for so long to the negative things everyone was telling me that when she suggested changes to my music, I thought it was just more of my mistakes being pointed out. But now I can see she was just trying to make her mark in the world too. Trying to be seen. She thought I was better than her, but really, we were the best together."

Jonas didn't say anything. His hand slid along her back, palms wide, pressing her to him, holding her there.

"When you came into my life..." Paisley continued, closing her eyes against the tears because she was tired of crying. "When you and I started making music together, it hurt her deeply. She felt useless. I know that feeling, and I hate that I made her feel the same way for even one second. I wish I'd been able to tell her that, for every song you and I made, there would be another one for her and me. The love I feel for you didn't displace hers. There was room for you both. For all of us."

Jonas kissed her forehead. "She would have gotten there, Paisley. We all would have gotten there."

Paisley ran her fingers along his chest slowly and then followed the trail with her lips. "I need to forget everything but the music we make together. I need to lose myself in it. Will you make love to me?"

And he hesitated, as if afraid that everything they'd been through during the day would be too much, but then he gave in as she continued to kiss and caress him. They played each other's bodies. A slow, simple allegro that built and built and built until it came crashing into the finale, sealing them together forever.

♫ ♫ ♫

She wasn't sure what woke her. At first, her pulse raced, thinking there'd been a noise in the suite, but as she cocked her head to listen, there was nothing. Nothing but the rhythm of Jonas's heartbeat under her fingertips. His warmth surrounded her, comforted her, made her feel as if she was right where she belonged.

Then, she heard it again.

It sounded like her name. It sounded like Landry.

Like that night by Swan River Pond.

Goosebumps broke out over her skin.

She slowly untangled herself from Jonas, slipping into one of the robes they'd discarded on the floor, and let her feet lead her just like they had that dreadful night. This time, they led her through the suite and out onto the balcony.

The sun was just starting to turn the sky from black to a mellow gray, a hint of orange and pink outlining distant clouds. There was a fountain on the balcony, and the soft gurgling of it was soothing. It reminded Paisley of being at the pond, the serenity she'd once felt there before it had turned into a nightmare. She turned her head toward the sound, and her breath caught, surprise filling her.

A swan was floating in the fountain.

At first, she thought it was fake—a statue or a mirage—but as she watched, mesmerized, it ducked its head under its feathers before untucking and glancing in her direction.

The bird's eyes met hers, black beads in the barely visible light.

It trumpeted...the noise she must have heard, sounding nothing like her name...and yet, she could hear the pattern of the syllables in its rhythm.

The majestic bird rose out of the water, spread its wings, and took off into the sky. Behind her, from the other side of the balcony wall, a few more birds suddenly took flight, voices echoing through the early morning sky as they fell in behind the leader.

Paisley watched them until they faded into the heavens.

"Thanks, Lan," Paisley whispered out.

The door behind her opened, and Jonas stepped out in sweatpants and nothing else, his glorious chest on display. He smiled at her, a lazy smile full of love and promises. Her heart sped up for another reason. For the simple joy of having him look at her that way.

He eased in behind her, pulling her into his embrace, placing a kiss on her cheek.

"What are you doing out here?" he asked, voice deep and gruff.

"Listening to the music of the morning," she said quietly. He nodded, understanding without judging, getting that her soul needed this.

The world slowly came awake around them. Doors slamming, car horns blaring, a motorcycle revving, people on the balcony below them talking. The gray sky burst into a brilliant series of pastel colors and then turned vivid neon before slowly settling into blue. And all the while, they just stood there, listening and watching.

It was a sweet memory layering itself on top of all her painful ones. Pretty soon, the beautiful ones would outnumber the bitter and dark. The black would still be there. It would still be uncovered sometimes. But it would only take a simple movement to shift the good back over the bad. Like the sky brightening and sending the shadows away.

Paisley stepped away, hooking her pinky with his, and said, "If we hurry, we can add our own notes to the day."

She drew him back into the bedroom where they tossed aside their clothes and joined their own rhythm to the ones the morning had brought. Every touch, every gasp, every kiss leading them to a perfect crescendo once more.

EPILOGUE

Jonas

LIFE IS BEAUTIFUL
Performed by The Afters

TWENTY-NINE MONTHS AFTER

The Daisies were three-quarters of the way through the tour, and the sold-out stadium in L.A. was alive with more screams, pounding feet, and clapping hands than at almost any concert they'd had to date. Maybe because they were back where it had all started for them, in the clubs around Los Angeles.

Jonas was backstage with the Kims, watching as the band performed.

Paisley had been nervous because her parents rarely came to their concerts, even before Landry had died, and since then, they'd seen the band as nothing but a memory of what they'd lost. They hated that Paisley was on tour, even while they understood it—or at least, they understood the monetary reasons.

Jonas wasn't sure they'd ever really understand how the music called to her. How it was embedded in her veins and written on her soul. They were hoping that, after the tour was done, The Painted Daisies would be done as well.

Jonas wasn't sure what was going to happen when they finished the last stop. Each of the Daisies had been through life-altering experiences in the last few months—danger pounding at their door and love finding its way in. But whatever happened to the band, Jonas knew Paisley would never give up writing, singing, and performing. Music was who she was.

Annie Kim was already near tears just watching Paisley and listening to the songs both their daughters had created. Jonas wondered how she'd handle the last song and the video that went with it.

He stepped forward and put a gentle hand on Annie's arm. "This last song... I don't know if you want to watch." He said it softly, full of compassion, but both her parents' shoulders went back, pride and strength on display. Jonas wondered if they realized how much their daughters had inherited from them, because the move was one he'd seen both Landry and Paisley do.

"Thank you, but we are fine," Kim Ji-ho—or Ji, as Paisley's dad had asked Jonas to call him—said.

And then the notes hit. The notes and the video.

Every single time the band played it, one or two or all of them broke down.

Tonight, maybe because she knew her parents were behind the scenes, it was Paisley's voice that cracked first, her band-mates picking up the slack, joining her on lyrics that weren't theirs. The stadium was filled with bubbles as Landry blew them as a little girl on the screen, fireworks ricocheting through the stadium, a light show that echoed the dance of Landry's feet and the twirl of her body through a field of flowers. Her face on the screen grew closer and closer until it centered on her eyes and the knowing lift of her brow.

Between the images and Landry's voice echoing through the stadium, Annie broke, putting a hand to her mouth and squeezing her eyes shut. Ji pulled his wife into an embrace, holding on to her in an unexpected show of emotions. The only feeling Jonas had ever seen Paisley's father express before was anger—an emotion Jonas was all too familiar with but was lucky to find easing out of his life the longer he was with Paisley, the longer her love pushed aside the scars of his past.

When the band's voice and instruments finally went silent, the audience was sobbing and stamping and screaming just as every audience had every time before. Just like the crew still wiped their eyes at the end of every show, and the band left the stage with tears trailing down their cheeks. It was never the full-on sobs of that first time, but the Daisies couldn't perform "The Legacy" and not cry.

Annie's body was wracked with sobs, and even Ji looked like his eyes were watering.

By the time Paisley came offstage, her parents were a mess.

She took one look at them and ran straight into their arms. Jonas tried not to hate it. It was the first time she hadn't run into his arms since the concert in Albany that had started it all.

As the three of them held on to each other, the band joined them, hugging the Kim family in a tight circle of squished arms and legs. "Get your butt over here," Adria said, looking straight at Jonas and holding out an arm. He joined them, everyone holding on to each other, savoring their memories of Landry.

Ji finally coughed and extracted himself and Annie from the Daisies.

"I'm going to go change, and then I'll be back," Paisley said with a watery smile to her parents. She lifted onto her tiptoes, kissed Jonas's cheek, and whispered, "Thank you for staying with them."

When she left, Annie looked at him as she wiped her eyes on a tissue. "It was...unexpected."

Jonas nodded, knowing it was as close to an apology he would likely get from her. He asked, "Shall we wait in the green room? That way, we'll be out of the way of the crew while they pack up."

He led them to the room at the back, and the Kims settled onto a couch together, hands still grasped tightly.

"Water? Something stronger?" he asked them.

"Water is fine," Annie said.

Jonas brought them each a bottle and then sat on a chair nearby, a sudden nervousness taking over him that he hadn't experienced in a long time. Maybe it was the way Ji assessed him, weighing him.

"Thank you," Ji finally said quietly, eyes meeting Jonas's.

"You're welcome."

"Not for the water," Ji cleared his throat. "After Landry died, Paisley was...lost. But now, she is more herself. I think this is because of you."

Jonas's cheeks flushed. He was pretty sure Ji would not appreciate the things he did with Paisley to ensure she never lost herself again, so that she never retreated behind a bubble of nothingness.

"I want to marry her," Jonas said. "I'm hoping we'll have your approval."

A small gasp from behind him made Jonas groan internally. He hadn't been intending to propose tonight, after a show, when Paisley was already full of emotions. And he definitely hadn't planned to do it with her parents, the crew, and all the other Daisies around.

He turned, meeting her eyes as she stood in the doorway.

She was in leggings and a flowy tunic top, ready for the after-party at the hotel. The top reminded him of the dress she'd worn on their first real date—soft blue with flowers spread across it. But it was her eyes that caught his, glimmering with love and humor because she knew this wasn't how he'd wanted this to go.

The rest of the band filtered in behind her.

He rose to his feet and met her halfway across the room.

"What did you say?" she asked. It was the shy, quiet Paisley who came out when she hardly ever reappeared anymore. Jonas's Paisley was confident and sure and hardly ever anxious onstage. She'd found her feet and her wings all at the same time.

"Sweetheart, nothing I said should be a surprise. You know I want to marry you."

"If that was your proposal, Jonas," Fee said, coming up behind them, "I'm going to have to kick your ass on Landry's behalf."

Jonas chuckled. "I'm not proposing right now, Fee. And even if I was, I'm sure mine would still come out ten times better than the grunt and growling demand of your man."

Fee's laugh filled the space. "Wait till I tell him you said that. And at least my proposal involved jewelry."

Thank God her husband wasn't there tonight. With all the traveling he did, you'd think he'd miss more than the handful of shows he had, but then he was as addicted to Fee as Jonas was to Paisley. They couldn't be apart for long without a craving, a deep insatiable urge, bringing them back together again.

"I'm starving. Can we please go back to the hotel so we can eat?" Nikki asked. A tanned arm went around her waist, a dark head bent to whisper in her ear, and then Nikki turned a splendid shade of pink. Jonas wanted to laugh because he had a pretty good idea what had been whispered in her ear.

Everyone filtered out to the SUVs and cars taking them back

to the hotel. But as Jonas walked with Paisley's hand in his, he realized her parents had never responded. Even though it wasn't their decision to make, and he knew Paisley would choose what was best for her, he also knew she'd want their blessing. Their lack of response tugged at all his old scars that he'd thought had finally healed.

♫ ♫ ♫

Hours later, as the after-party was wrapping up and people were slowly leaving, it was Annie who found Jonas. She hugged him, a display of affection that was as unlike Paisley's mom as the tears on display at the stadium.

"You should come to dinner tomorrow before you have to leave," Annie said. She patted his cheek but looked over to her husband. "Yes, Ji? They should both come to dinner?"

Ji grunted his answer with a curt nod, and Jonas's lips twitched. Perhaps that was the closest he would ever get to a seal of approval from Paisley's parents.

When everyone had finally left, the room was strangely silent, as if a storm had just passed through it. He turned to find Paisley at the grand piano placed strategically in the window of the presidential suite. The hotel was one of the most opulent they'd stayed at on the tour so far. The view out the window was a magnificent one, the landscape of the city laid out before them.

Paisley was typing in her phone, pausing every few seconds to play some notes on the keys. He watched in silent wonder for a few minutes. He was always amazed by the way she crafted her songs. How it flowed from her as if it was just part of the way she breathed.

He finally moved to sit down beside her, and she paused for a second to smile at him before returning to the music. He put one arm around her waist, drawing her up tighter, and the other found her thigh, rubbing almost unconsciously up and down.

Her breath caught, her body stilled, and then she looked up at him from under thick black lashes. "You're distracting me."

He grinned. "Sorry."

He stopped moving his hand but didn't remove it from her leg. He rested his chin on her shoulder, kissed her cheek, and then looked down at the words on the screen. Many weren't spelled right, but it never seemed to bother her anymore that he or anyone else saw the mistakes.

"What is this?" he asked as a couple of the words popped out at him.

"My acceptance song," she said, a full smile taking over her face, a twinkle in her eyes.

"Acceptance? As in marriage-proposal acceptance?" he asked with a little chuckle.

She nodded.

"I haven't asked," he said, feeling almost ridiculous now because they all knew it was going to happen, especially after what had been said earlier at the stadium.

She put her phone down, turned on the piano bench so that her calves were over his thighs and her chest was pressed into his.

"What are you waiting for?" she asked, suddenly serious.

He tangled one hand in her hair, tugging slightly, and the other danced slowly along the curve of her waist, drifting lower and lower. She let out a tiny gasp, her breath becoming uneven and her eyes darkening. He wanted to devour her. To taste every bit of the sweetness she offered every time he kissed her.

"You suddenly in a hurry to get married for some reason?" he asked. "Wait. You're not preg—"

"Don't be ridiculous." She slapped his chest.

He caught her wrist, bringing it to his mouth and kissing it before gliding his lips up her arm.

"And even if I was," she said, her voice growing thick, "that wouldn't mean we'd have to get married. This isn't the eighteen-hundreds, you know."

He nodded. Images of her with a round belly, carrying their child, filled him. He remembered what Cassidy had looked like pregnant, glowing and tired all at the same time, but she and Marco had been blissfully happy. He'd love to have that with Paisley. But they were only twenty-one. They had the rest of the tour ahead of them and decisions about the band to be made. They had time. Plenty of time.

As if she read his thoughts, Paisley put a hand to his cheek. "Landry's death... She didn't get to do all the things she'd said she was going to do. I just... I don't want to wait, thinking there will be a tomorrow. Because what if there isn't? I know we're young, and there'd be plenty of people out there betting we wouldn't make it, but I'd love to have a big wedding, dance the night away, and lose ourselves on a honeymoon for several months."

He looked at her, stunned. "Wait. There is so much about what you just said that is not what I expected. First, a big wedding? You want to be on display in front of a bunch of guests?"

She nodded. "It's a Landry thing. She wanted a big wedding. I want her to have it...through me."

"Okay...but the several months of a honeymoon?"

"Well, obviously, it'll have to be after this tour and before we record the next album."

"You're that sure everyone is going to say yes to continuing?"

Paisley shifted, pulling herself so she was straddling him, and her butt crashed into the piano keys, sending the sound reverberating through the room. He smiled, but his hands adjusted again. One at her waist, holding her steady, and one stroking her through the thin cotton of her leggings. Her breath hitched, but she kept her focus, not letting their bodies completely take over yet. Not finished making her point.

"The Painted Daisies are not going to be has-beens, Jonas. We're going to be making music until we're sixty years old and they have to drag us off the stage with oxygen tanks."

Jonas chuckled. "I think Maliyah would have a thing or two to say about you thinking sixty means oxygen tanks."

"Fine, we'll be a hundred when they take us off."

She slipped her hands under his T-shirt and yanked it over his head before setting her palms on his chest. The heat of her fingers spread through him. He was already struggling to concentrate on anything but the way their bodies were slowly rocking together.

"Ask me, Jonas." Her voice was a breathy demand, desire curling through her words as she ground down on him, igniting the fire that never fully disappeared.

"I'm not asking you here, half dressed, two seconds away from being inside you."

"Why not?"

"I want it to be another sweet memory. Not one full of sex and orgasms," Jonas groused.

"Every orgasm is a sweet memory, Jonas. Every single one."

He was done playing. He picked her up and carried her to the bedroom. He stood her on the bed and almost ripped the leggings from her body to find her bare underneath. He growled. "Paisley, what have I told you about this? Jesus. You're going to be the death of me."

She laughed as his head bent to her naked core. He spent the next hour punishing her, driving her wild with tongue and fingers before he embedded himself deep inside her.

After, he filled the tub with warm water, bath salts, and

bubbles. He helped her in before slipping in behind her and locking her body to his. It was a tradition they'd started as a way to unwind from the concerts, the parties, and their lovemaking.

Jonas reached over to the towel he'd folded very carefully on the side of the tub and pulled out a little black box. She squirmed in front of him, but he held her steady with one hand as he bent and whispered by her ear, "You are all the best parts of me, Paisley Ji-An. You are the music I will forever want to play. The notes that are embedded in my soul. And although I think I already know your answer, I'm still going to ask it. So, sweetheart, do you think you'd like to marry me?"

She didn't even open the box. She flipped so she was facing him in the tub, arms going around his neck. "I'd be honored to be the woman playing the songs at your side for the rest of our lives. So, yes, I'll marry you. I'll marry you. I'll marry you..." And she broke out into a few notes from the song she'd been writing earlier.

Then, she kissed him, and he kissed her back, and the rest of the world faded as they made music together once more.

♫ ♫ ♫

I hope you loved Paisley and Jonas's heart breaking, second-chance story as much as I loved writing it. Are you curious about the other Daisies? Do you want to know a bit more about what was happening in their lives the day Landry died? You can get exclusive scenes from each of their points of views, including Landry's, in the SWAN RIVER bonus material FREE with a newsletter sign-up:

https://www.twsspub.com/bonus/pdsm

Read the rest of the titles in the Painted Daisies series:
Book 2: *GREEN JEWEL*
Book 3: *CHERRY BRANDY*
Book 4: *BLUE MARGUERITE*
Book 5: *ROYAL HAZE*

MESSAGE FROM THE AUTHOR

Thank you for taking the time to read the first book in *The Painted Daisies* series inspired by Harry Stiles "Sweet Creature." I hope that the mix of music and story I built here will burn a memory into your soul you'll think about every time you hear one of the songs from now on.

Sweet Memory is the first book in a connected, standalone series. While each couple will have their own suspense plot line and their own happily ever after, you'll need to read the entire series to find out just what happened that day at Swan River Pond with Landry. The good news is that the rest of the series is coming to you this year, and you can order the next book, ***Green Jewel***, now.

If you like talking about music, books, and just what it takes to get us through this wild ride called life as much as I do, maybe you should join my Facebook readers' group, LJ's Music & Stories and join the conversations there today. Hopefully, the group can help ***YOU*** through your life in some small way.

Regardless if you join or not, I'd love for you to tell me what you thought of the book by reaching out to me personally. I'd be honored if you took the time to leave a review on BookBub,

Amazon, and/or Goodreads, but even more than that, I hope you enjoyed it enough to tell a friend about it.

If you still can't get enough (ha!), you could also sign up for my newsletter where you'll receive music-inspired scenes weekly and be entered into a giveaway each month for a chance at a signed paperback by yours truly. Plus, you'll be able to keep tabs on all my stories, including fun facts about The Painted Daisies and more.

Finally, I just wanted to say that my wish for you is a healthy and happy journey. May you live life resiliently, with hope and love leading the way!

ACKNOWLEDGMENTS

I'm so very grateful for every single person who has helped me on this book journey. If you're reading these words, you *ARE* one of those people. I wouldn't be an author if people like you didn't decide to read the stories I crafted, so THANK YOU!

In addition to my lovely readers, I'd be ridiculous not to thank these extra folks who've made this journey possible for me:

My husband, who means more to me than I can explain in one or a thousand sentences, and who has never, ever let me give up on this dream, doing everything he could to make it come true, and then CHEERING from the rooftops at my tiniest success. Here's to you being a "Kept Man" someday, my love.

Our child, Evyn, owner of Evans Editing, who remains my harshest and kindest critic. Thank you for helping me shape my stories, and reading this one a million and one times until I got it right.

The folks at That's What She Said Publishing who took a gamble on me, this wild idea I had for a series, and then were determined to see the best in all of it even when I chewed my lips to smithereens worrying that it would fail.

My sister, Kelly, who made sure I hit the publish button the very first time and reads my crappy first drafts and still loves my stories anyway.

My parents and my father-in-law who are my biggest fans and bring my books to the strangest places, telling everyone they know (and don't know) about my stories.

Kathy Hong Kobzeff who stepped in to sensitivity read this first book about a diverse female rock band, was gentle and forgiving with my mistakes, and more importantly, made sure I fixed them.

The talented Emily Wittig, who made the perfect covers for this heart-wrenching series.

Jenn at Jenn Lockwood Editing Services, who is always patient with my gazillion missing commas, my hatred of the semicolon, and scattered deadlines.

Karen Hrdlicka who ensures the final versions of my books are beautiful and reminds me the word "that" isn't always needed until she's blue in the face.

Aly Stiles for helping me see what I couldn't and not letting me give up on the first half of Jonas and Paisley's journey.

To the entire group of beautiful humans in LJ's Music & Stories who love and support me, I can't say enough how deeply grateful I am for each and every one of you.

To the host of bloggers who have shared my stories, become dear friends, and continue to make me feel like a rock star every day, thank you, thank you, thank you!

To a host of authors, including Stephanie Rose, Kathryn Nolan, Lucy Score, Erika Kelly, Hannah Blake, Annie Dyer, and AM Johnson, who have shown me that dear friends are more important than any paralyzing moment in this wild publishing world, MWAH!

To all my ARC readers who have become sweet friends, thanks for knowing just what to say to scare away my writer insecurities.

And I can't leave without a special thanks to Leisa C., Rachel R., and Lisa K. for being three of the biggest cheerleaders I could ever hope to have on this wild ride called life.

I love you all!

ABOUT THE AUTHOR

Award-winning author, LJ Evans, lives in the Northern California with her husband, child, and the terrors called cats. She's been writing, almost as a compulsion, since she was a little girl and will often pull the car over to write when a song lyric strikes her. A former first-grade teacher, she now spends her free time reading and writing, as well as binge-watching original shows like *Ted Lasso, Wednesday, Veronica Mars,* and *Stranger Things.*

If you ask her the one thing she won't do, it's pretty much anything that involves dirt—sports, gardening, or otherwise. But she loves to write about all of those things, and her first published heroine was pretty much involved with dirt on a daily basis, which is exactly why LJ loves fiction novels—the characters can be everything you're not and still make their way into your heart.

Her novels have won multiple awards including ***CHARMING AND THE CHERRY BLOSSOM,*** which was *Writer's Digest's* Self-Published E-book Romance of the Year in 2021. For more information about LJ, check out any of these sites:

For more information about LJ, check out any of these sites:
Website: www.ljevansbooks.com
Facebook Reader Group: LJ's Music & Stories
Goodreads: www.goodreads.com/author/show/16738629.
L_J_Evans

facebook.com/ljevansbooks
twitter.com/ljevansbooks
instagram.com/ljevansbooks
amazon.com/LJ-Evans/e/B071R365YK
bookbub.com/authors/lj-evans
tiktok.com/@ljevansbooks
pinterest.com/ljevansbooks

OTHER TITLES BY LJ EVANS

STANDALONES

The Last One You Loved

Charming and the Cherry Blossom

MY LIFE AS AN ALBUM SERIES

My Life as a Country Album — Cam's Story

My Life as a Pop Album — Mia & Derek

My Life as a Rock Album — Seth & PJ

My Life as a Mixtape — Lonnie & Wynn

My Life as a Holiday Album – 2nd Generation

My Life as an Album Series Box Set

THE ANCHOR NOVELS

Guarded Dreams — Eli & Ava

Forged by Sacrifice — Mac & Georgie

Avenged by Love — Truck & Jersey

Damaged Desires — Dani & Nash

Branded by a Song — Brady & Tristan

Tripped by Love – Cassidy & Marco

The Anchor Novels: The Military Bros Box Set

THE ANCHOR SUSPENSE NOVELS

Unmasked Dreams — Violet & Dawson

Crossed by the Stars — Jada & Dax

Disguised as Love — Cruz & Raisa

THE PAINTED DAISIES

Sweet Memory

Green Jewel

Cherry Brandy

Blue Marguerite

Royal Haze

CPSIA information can be obtained
at www.ICGtesting.com
Printed in the USA
JSHW080247280223
38293JS00001B/1